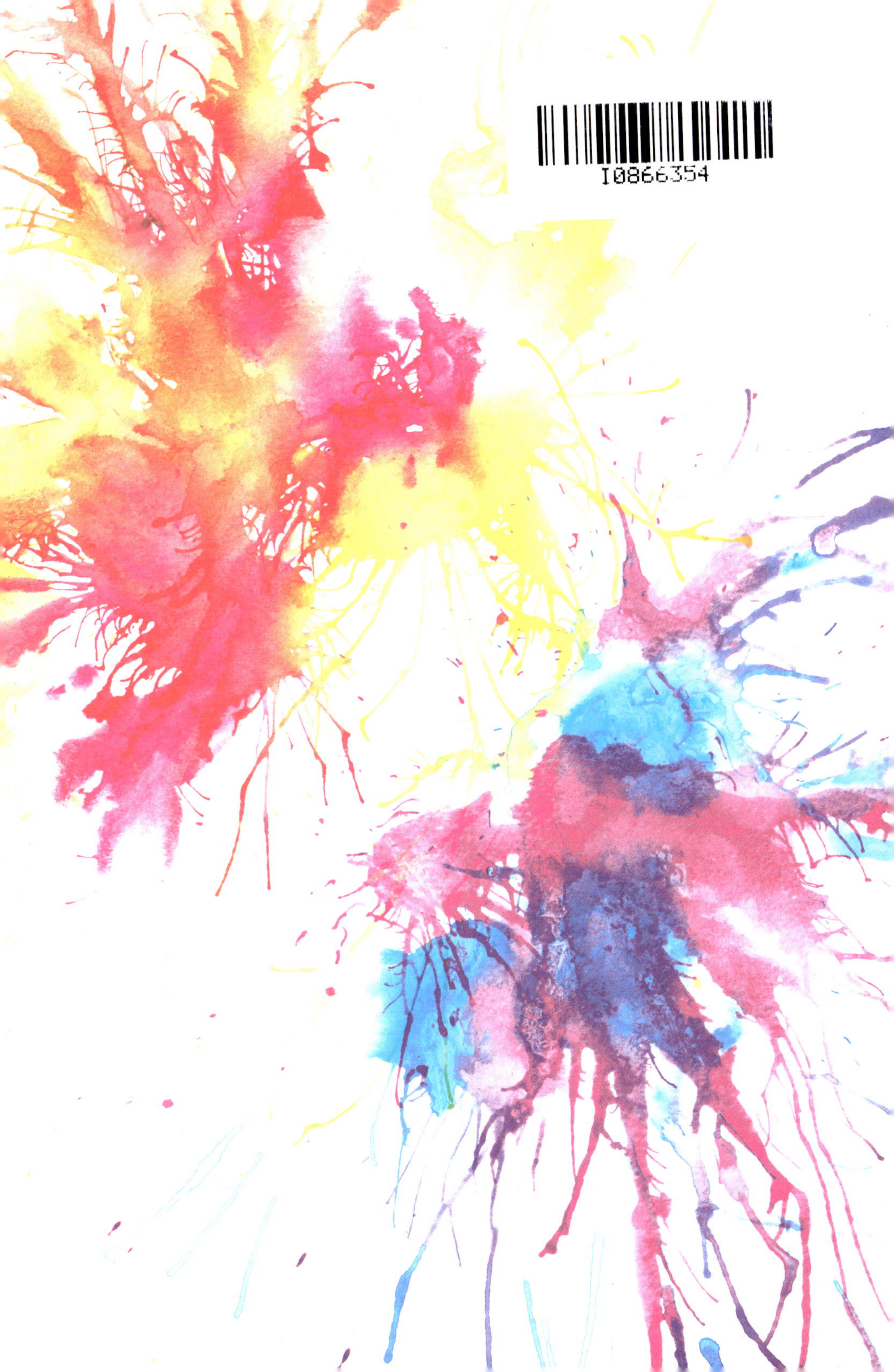

I0866354

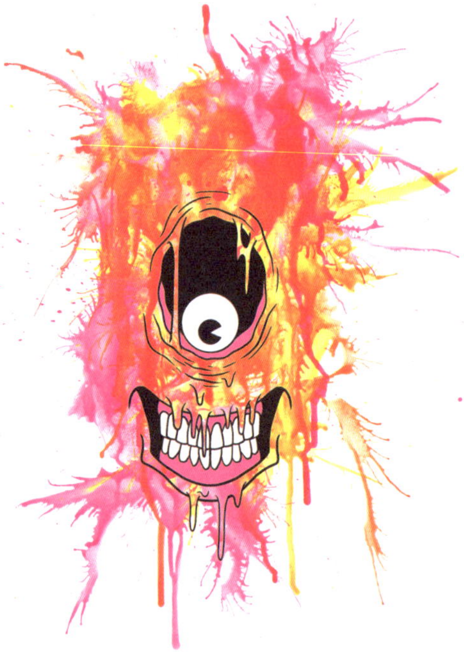

BRIGHTMARES

the Art of Alex Pardee

This book is for anyone who's not afraid to figure it out along the way.

Second Printing

All art, layout, design and any references to robotic leprechauns by ALEX PARDEE
@alexpardee
alexpardee.com

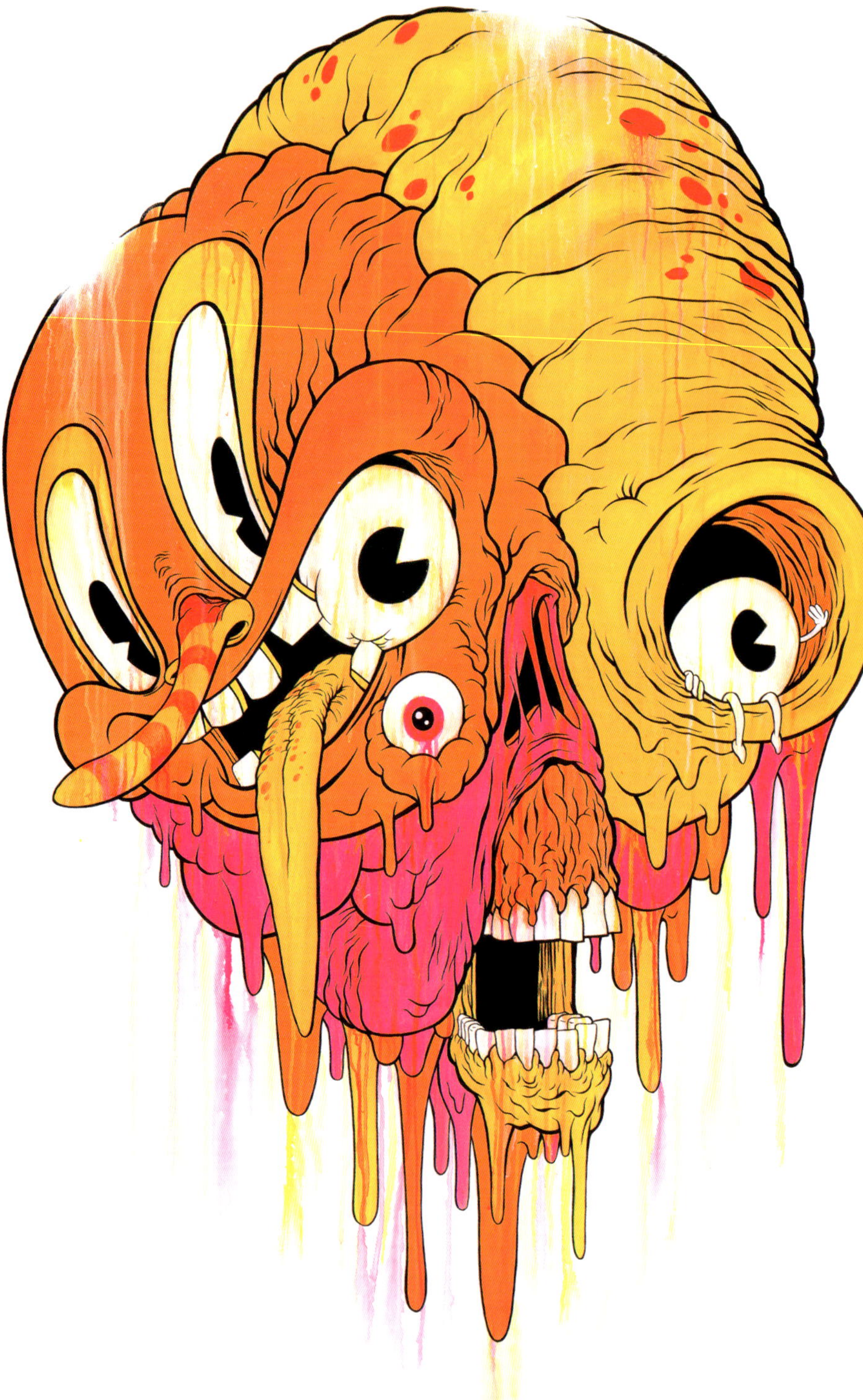

"Between day and night. Between happy and sad. Between light and dark. Between laughter and grief. Between silly and horrific. Between dreams and nightmares. This is where the Brightmares live."

—Alex Pardee

"Between two pillows."

—Del Griffith

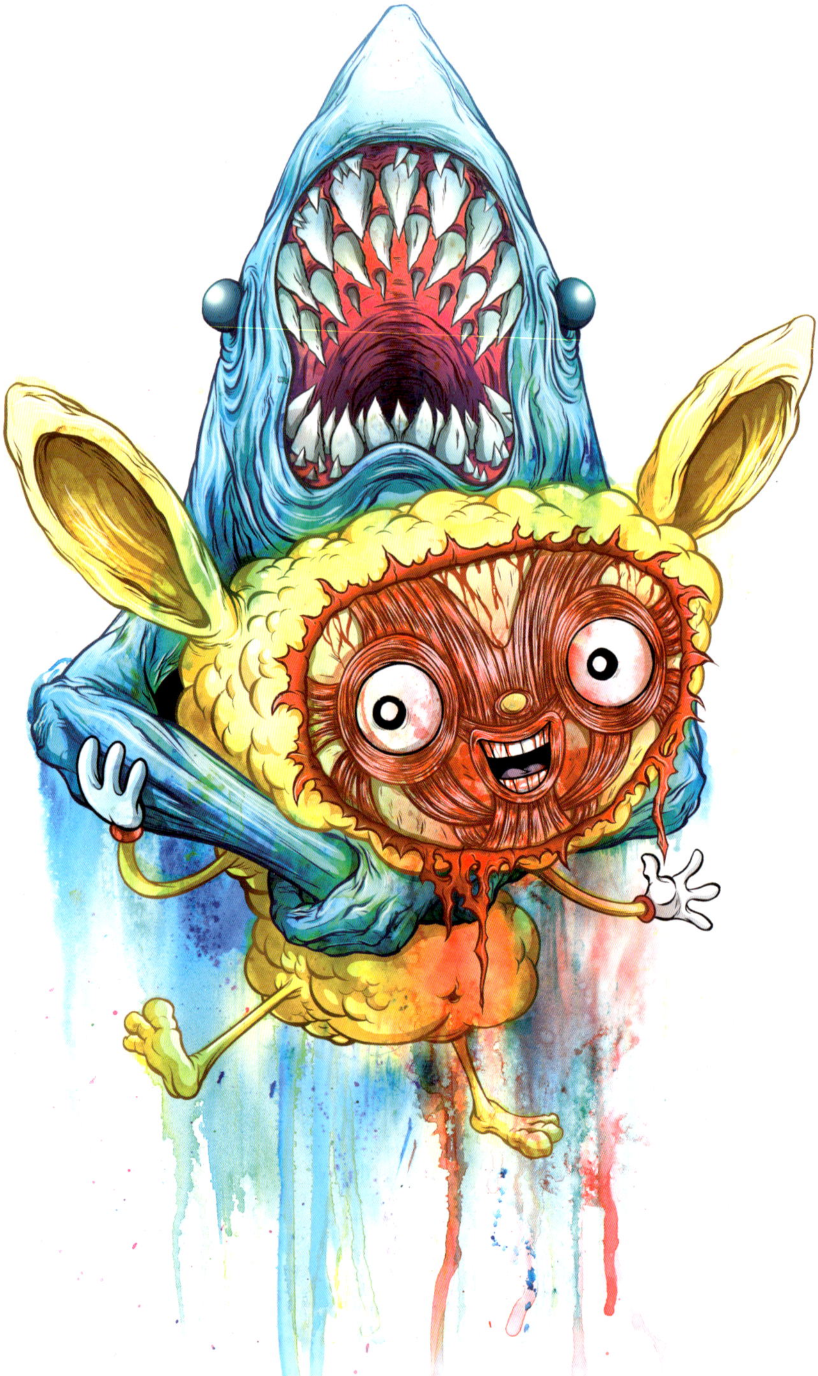

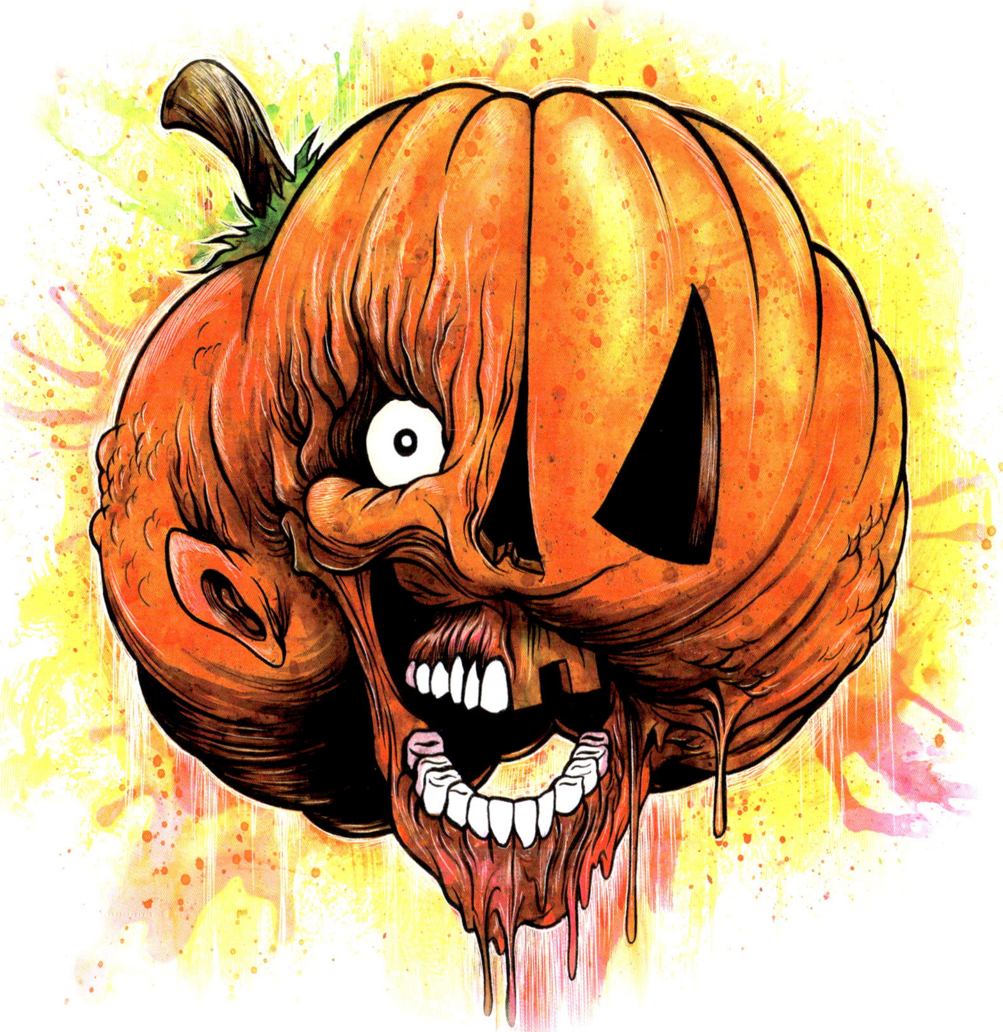

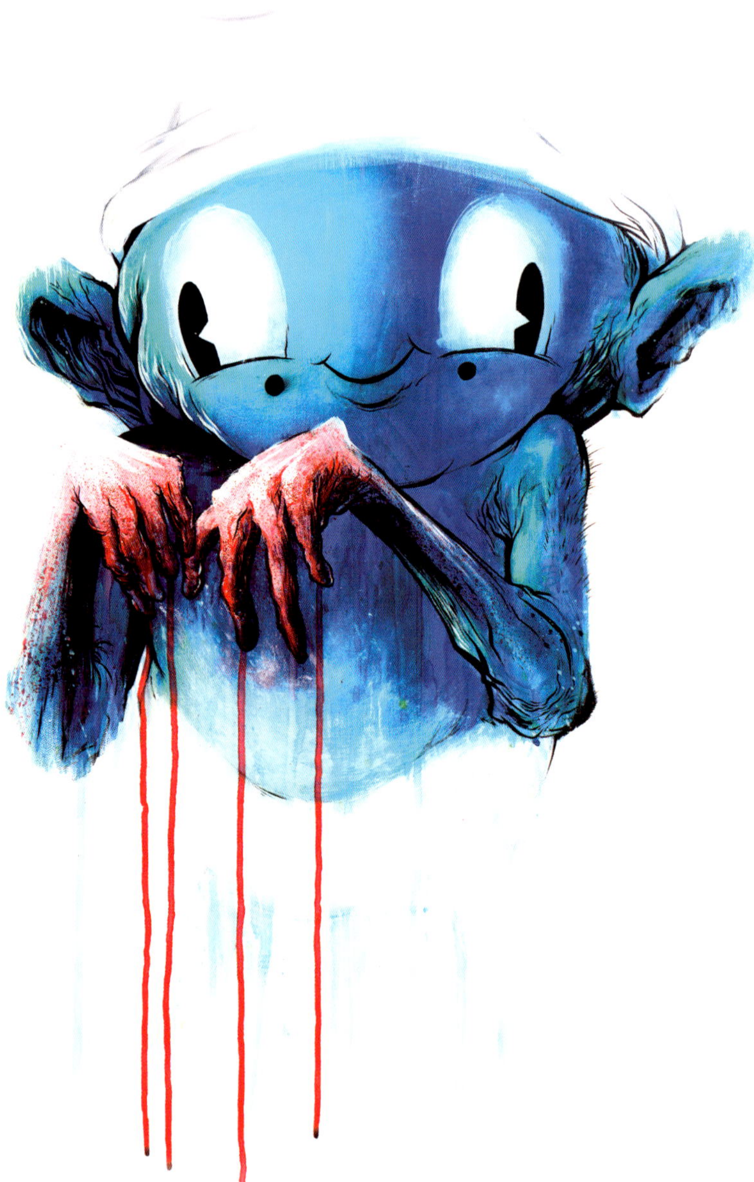

Guilty Smurf

One of the most MYSTERIOUS of all of the Smurfs, Guilty Smurf, kept to himself the entire time all of the other Smurfs were basking in the glory of the limelight from their Saturday Morning success. In fact, there wasn't a single MENTION of Guilty Smurf in all of Smurf-lore. That is, until after the... incident.

Envy had built up inside Guilty's soul as he sat in the darkest mushroom, silently pining for attention and fame that the other Smurfs were getting showered with. But he was too prideful to join the party after they were famous. So instead, he sat. And he stewed. And he HATED.

After 6 seasons of cartoons, he couldn't take the arrogance any longer. In one Smurfy afternoon, Guilty emerged from his mushroom and bare-handedly slaughtered all 24 of those famous tiny blue fame-whores. With blood drenching his cute blue hands, Guilty Smurf returned to the now-quiet village and slept happily forever.

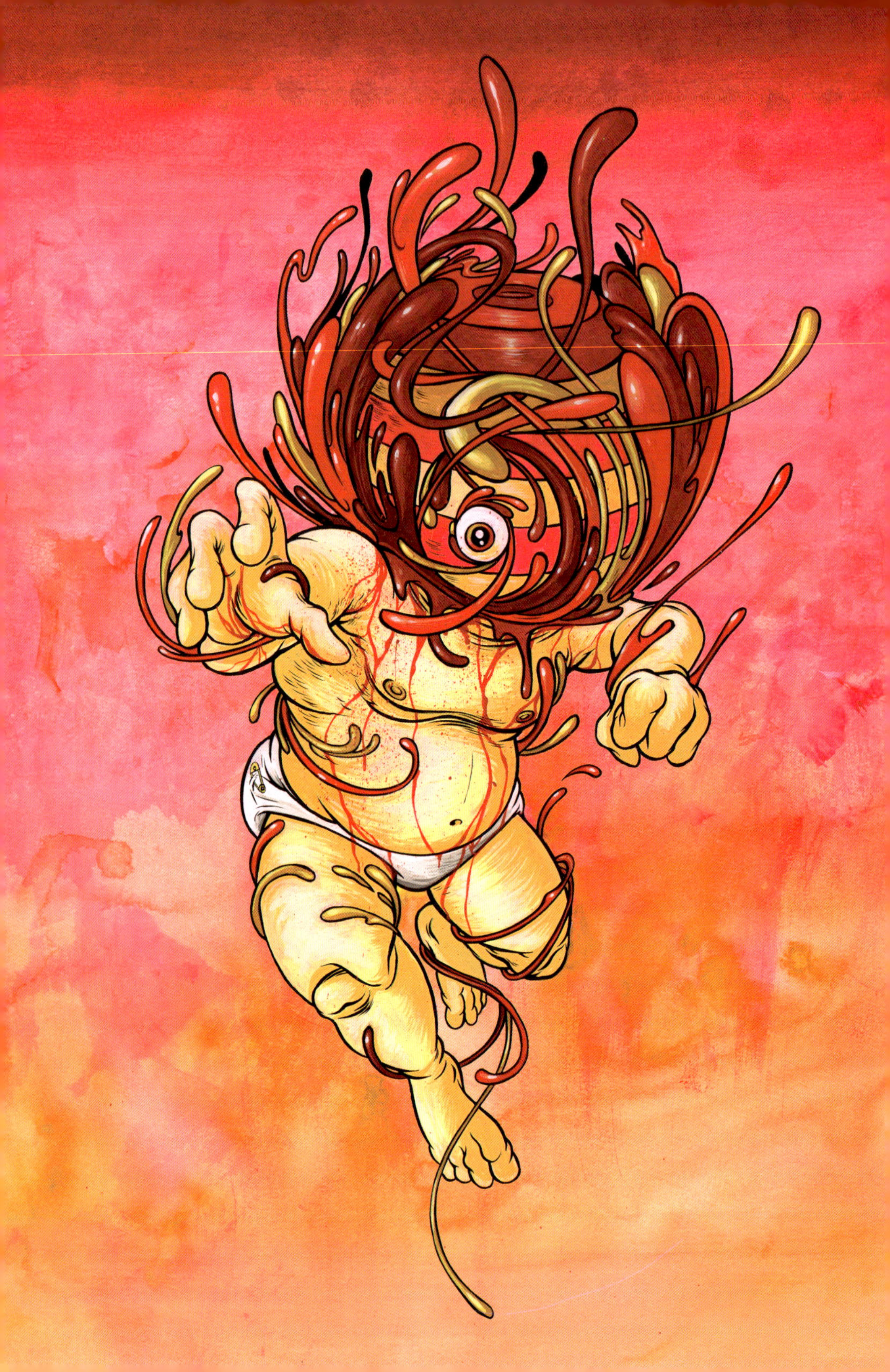

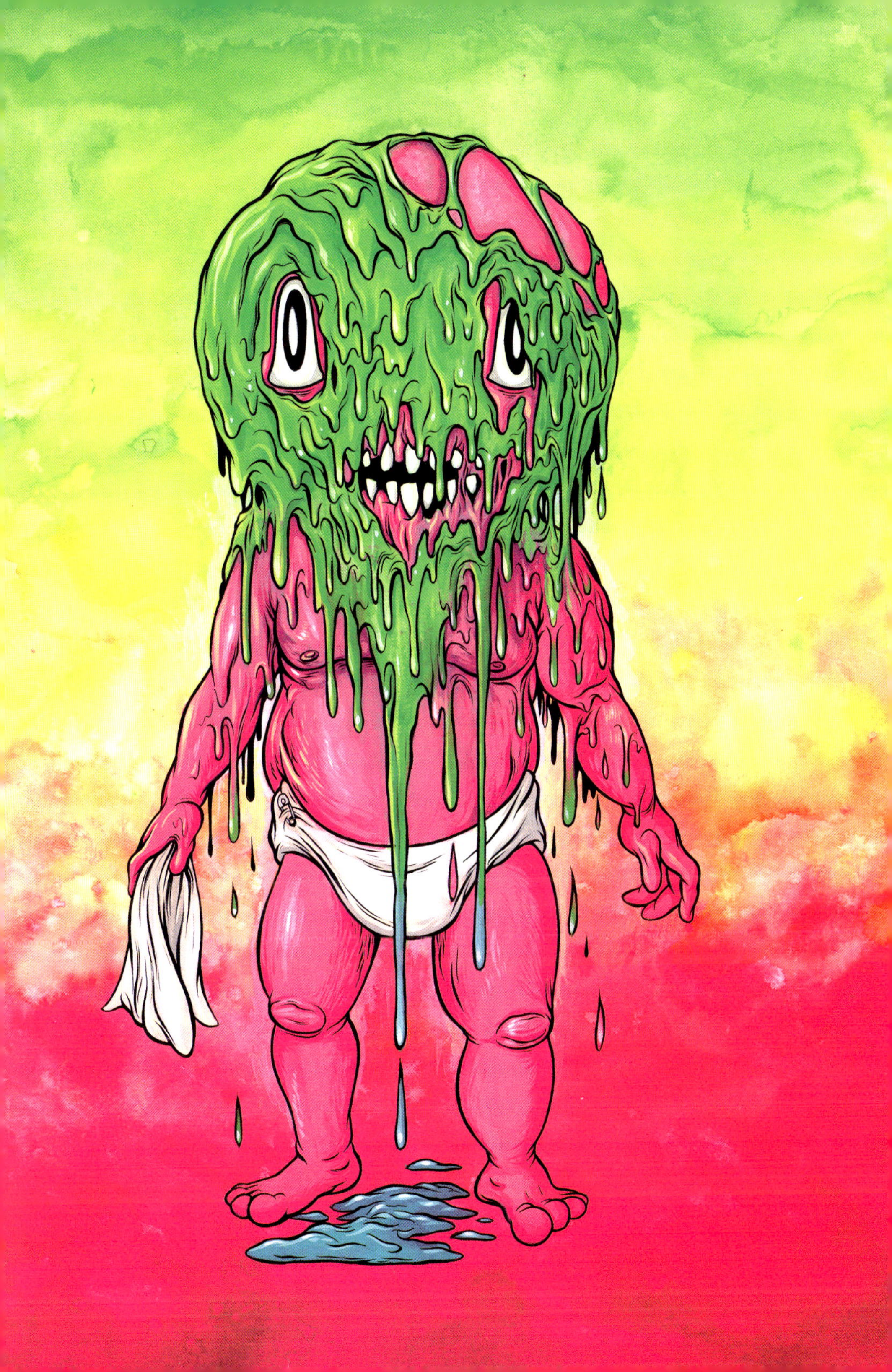

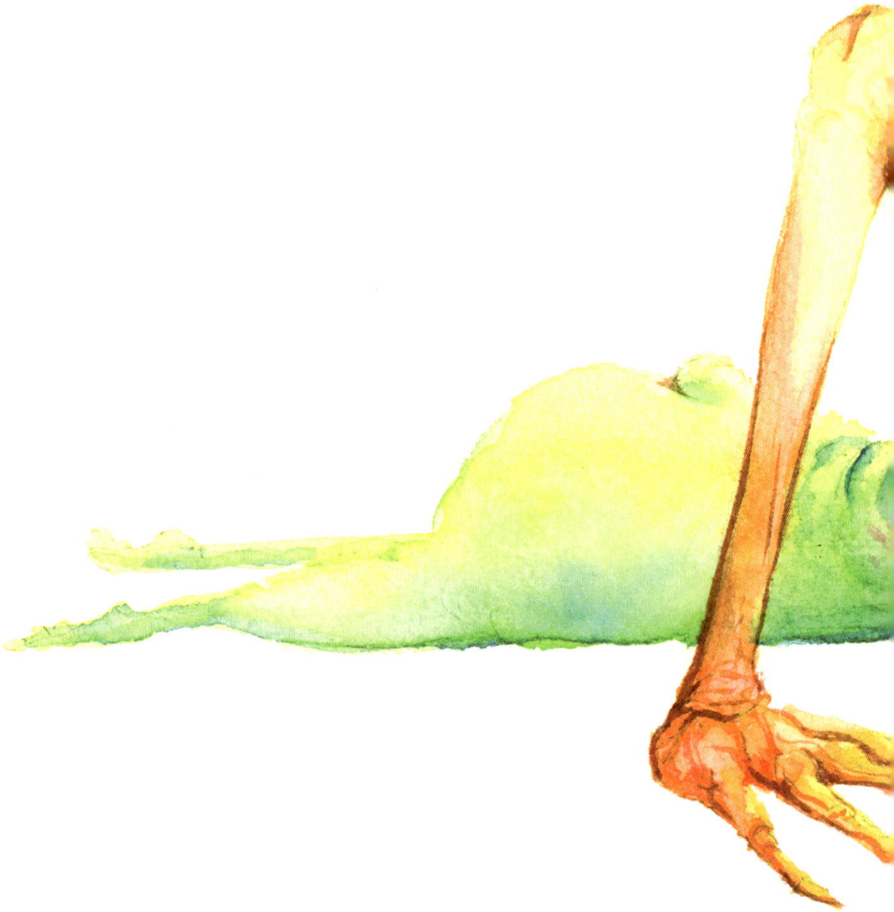

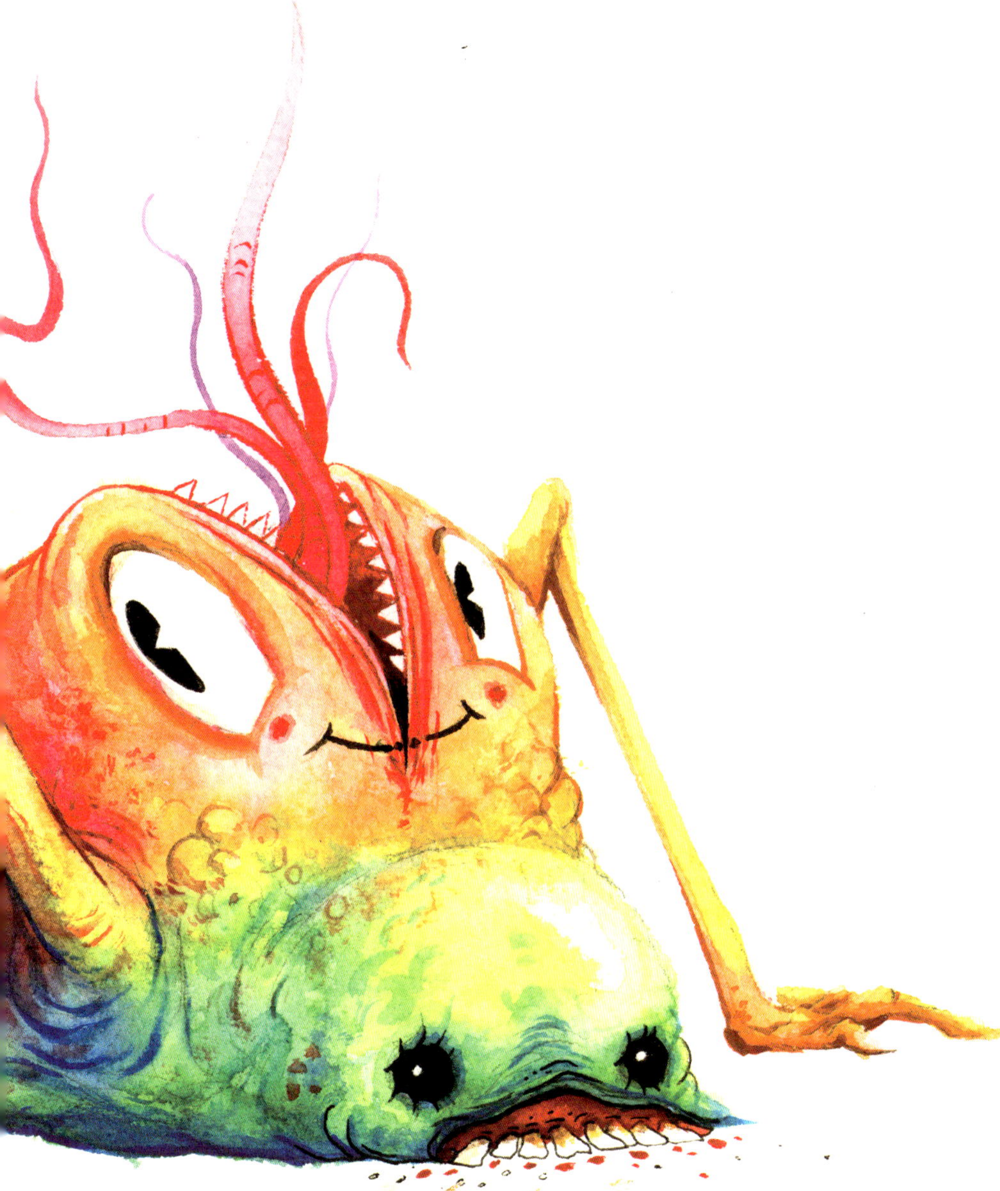

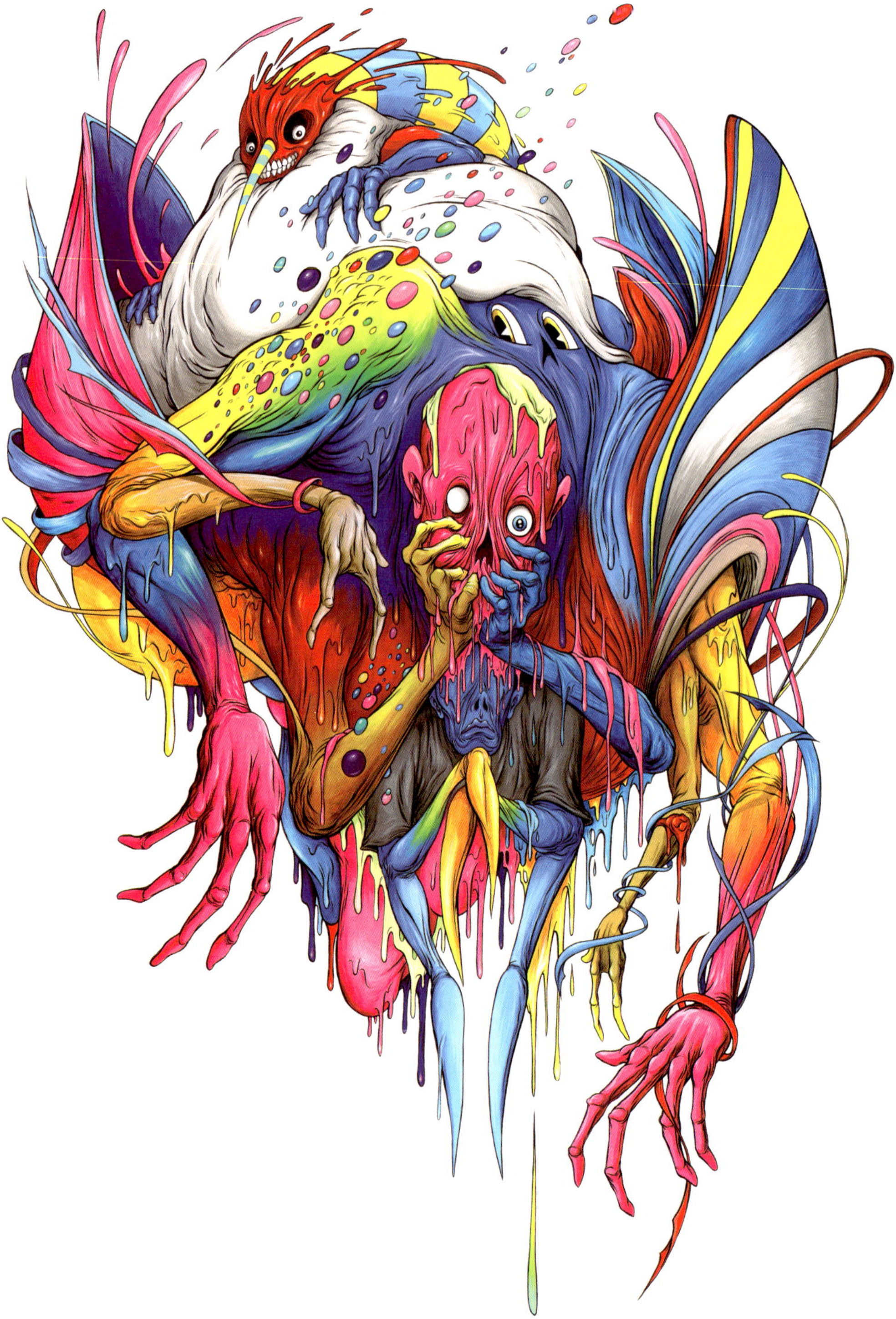

Defender

The sky was a single pantone shade away from being pitch black. The humidity made the night air feel as heavy as Joel's eyelids, which blanketed his bright blue lenses, shielding them from the silent flicker of a small TV that refused to turn itself off despite the infinite looping of a DVD menu showing a yellow dog and a boy with a sword. The only sounds edging their way into his bedroom were faint electronic snaps emitting from the bug-zapper hanging on a rope outside of Joel's window. In other words, this night was like every other night in Decatur... until Joel violently jerked up and gasped for an unobtainable breath. His teeth clenched and his eyes widened, accentuated by the glow of the TV shining solely on his frightened face. Joel attempted to pull his arms away from his side, perhaps instinctively to help him physically clear a passageway for some air to inhale, but he couldn't. His arms and torso felt magnetically adhered to his mattress. Within a heartbeat, he sucked in enough air to push it back out in order to squeal in pain as he felt something under his arms stretching. He was able to angle his neck and rotate his eyes far enough to see what the source of this pain was. His armpits had ripped open. Blood, skin, muscle and fluids that Joel hadn't been taught about yet were soaking into his bed sheets as his arms crawled away from his body and scampered on to the floor. At this point, Joel's squeals turned into uninhibited screams. In the milliseconds that his brain allowed him to think, all he did was wonder where his parents were as he watched his own arms transform into fleshy demonic serpents in front of his own wide eyes. What were his fingers changed into teeth, but the rest of his arms were barely recognizable as arms anymore. They were creatures, salivating and hovering over this paralyzed child wrapped in a bloodied Skylanders blanket. The monsters writhing in front of the TV forced the only light source to spatter new shadows all over the walls in Joel's room, increasing the number of horrifying shapes that were surrounding Joel from two to eight. Joel was going to "die by his own hand", he thought. Had he been any older, this revelation would have maybe garnered an ironic chuckle as he succumbed to death. But Joel was 8. He didn't understand irony. He hardly even understood reality. All he knew was that he was terrified. Moments later, Joel's detached arm-monsters warped their finger-teeth into a subtle grin and then lunged at his defenseless face. The exact moment that Joel felt the darkness of the creatures' breath, he woke up...again.

Daylight painted the room, drowning out the TV's once powerful glow. Dogs were barking in the distance outside. His arms were intact. Joel let out a confused sigh that quickly turned into an embarrassing one as he assessed that his Skylanders blanket was no longer soaked in blood, but instead in urine. Joel's brain attempted to tell his body that what had happened was a dream, but it was to no avail. Joel was changed. He started crying instantly. His body ached. He couldn't breathe, and he was afraid of his own arms. Unlike in the dream, his parents rushed in the moment they heard him start to cry to console him. But over the next few weeks, with the exception of some unfriendly growls, Joel fell mostly mute at school and found numerous ways to bind his own arms to his torso, causing enough commotion and concern to force his parents to keep him home and seek help.

As his parents jumped through the usual hoops of psychology and physiology in hopes of helping him, Joel neglected to tell them that he continued to dream about these creatures that were born from his own arms, and he continued to wake up in tears. After multiple prescriptions for everything from insomnia to ADHD to body dysmorphia to even Schizophrenia. But all of those treatments just sedated Joel, which meant he spent more time in his dream world, the world he was terrified to be a part of...

Eventually, Joel's father, Dennis, admitted to his wife, Dawn, that he may know of something that c
help. At this point, Dawn agreed, the two parents were open to trying anything.
Dennis confessed to a similar situation when he was a child in the late 1960s. Dennis, almost i
tears, did the best he could to re-tell the tale of a monster that he once dreamt about. When his st
was finished, he then shared with Dawn how HIS parents helped cure him.
"It was the sixties, you know", he said, "so every doctor around had an experimental drug of som
sort and my parents were getting desperate. They met an old, kind of odd guy who told them that
the other doctors were trying to repress these nightmares; trying to get me to pretend they were
there. But this doctor said that the only way to overcome these nightmares was to DEFEAT them
"What did that mean," Dawn asked, intrigued.
"It meant that he had something that would give me the power to FIGHT them," Dennis replied.
"HOW?"
"I'll never forget the day I met that him. Doctor Zerof. That was his name. In hindsight, it was like
was meeting Willy Wonka. He was an odd goofy man with a possibly made-up accent and a magi
pill. And what he told me as he held up a small blue pill that had the letters DFNDR embossed on
was that whenever I took one of these pills, I would be able to summon the 'good' dream monste
that roam around in dreamland. Dreamland, apparently, was a REAL place according to him. It w
where our souls vacationed to in order to escape the monotony of the Real World. And that thes
'good' monsters in Dreamland would help me fight the bad ones. Wow...saying it aloud now soun
just as absurd as I'm sure it did to my parents, but as a child, my eyes lit up. That's what I neede
My own monsters!"
"So what happened?" Dawn said.
"As a last ditch effort," Dennis continued, "my parents gave me the pills."
"And??"
"They worked..."
"Just like that? That's it??" Dawn sounded unsatisfied now.
"Not at first, they didn't. But eventually, yes. The pills helped me LEARN. They helped me HUNT
something to assist me in the fights. And eventually, I don't really know how to describe what the
helped me do. They helped me understand the dream world. The helped me control colors, and
shapes, and create these giant, horrifying, but 'good' monsters to fight the 'bad' ones."
"Were there any side effects?" Dawn said with a slight concern.
"Yes, there were... I was able to actually grow up and get married to a wonderful woman and hav
child with a good imagination," Dennis said as he snickered.
Dawn smiled coyly before she said "So... do you still know Doctor Zerof? Is he even still alive?"
"No, I never saw him after that day... but I still have a few of those pills. I still have some
DEFENDER."
"Do you think they still have any potency?"
"I have no idea."
"Well, then..." Dawn trailed off for a second before she continued, "what are we waiting for? Let
save our son."

To Be Continued...

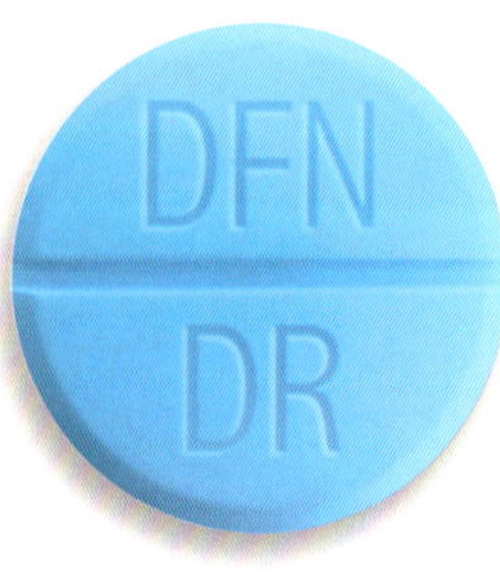

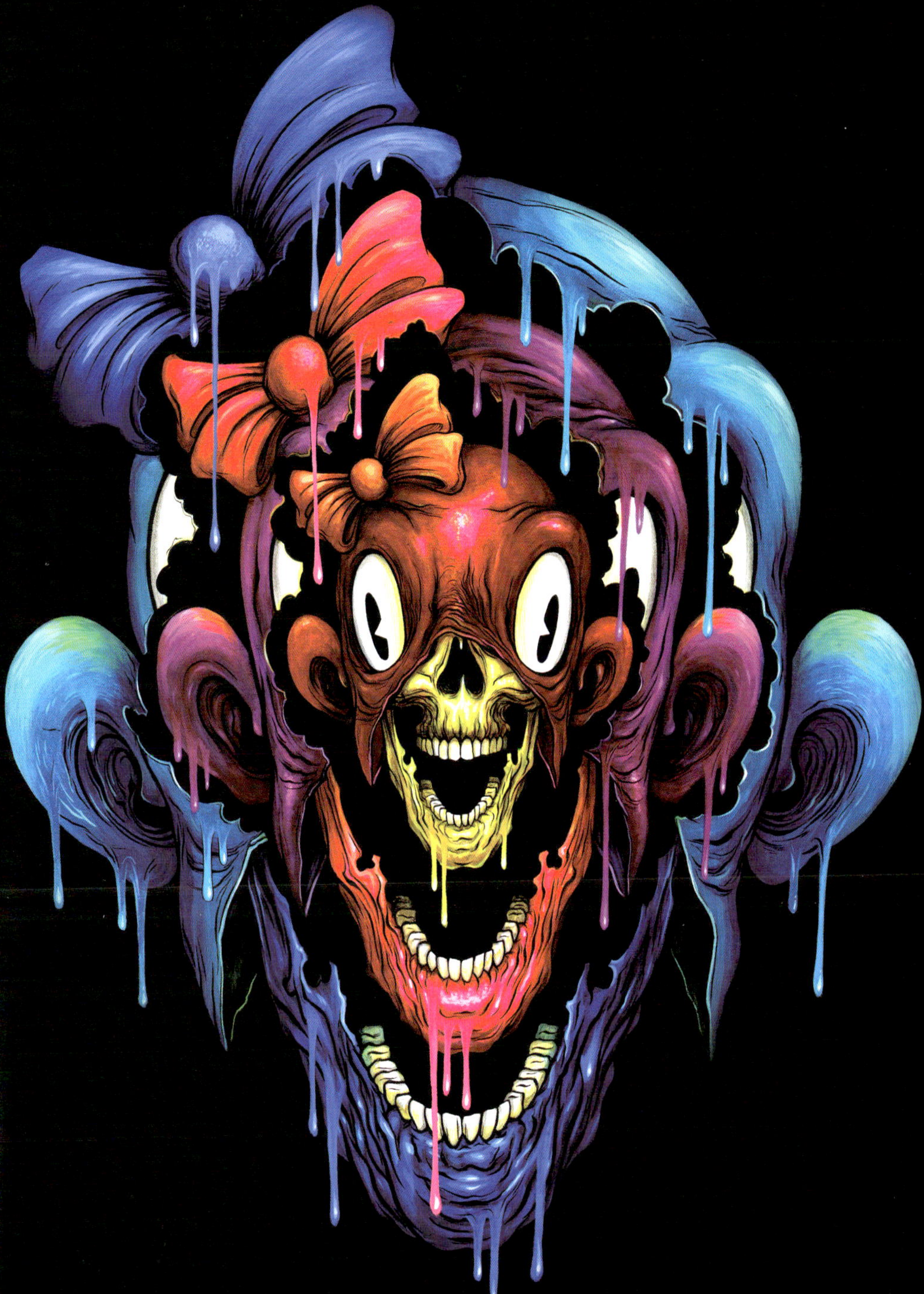

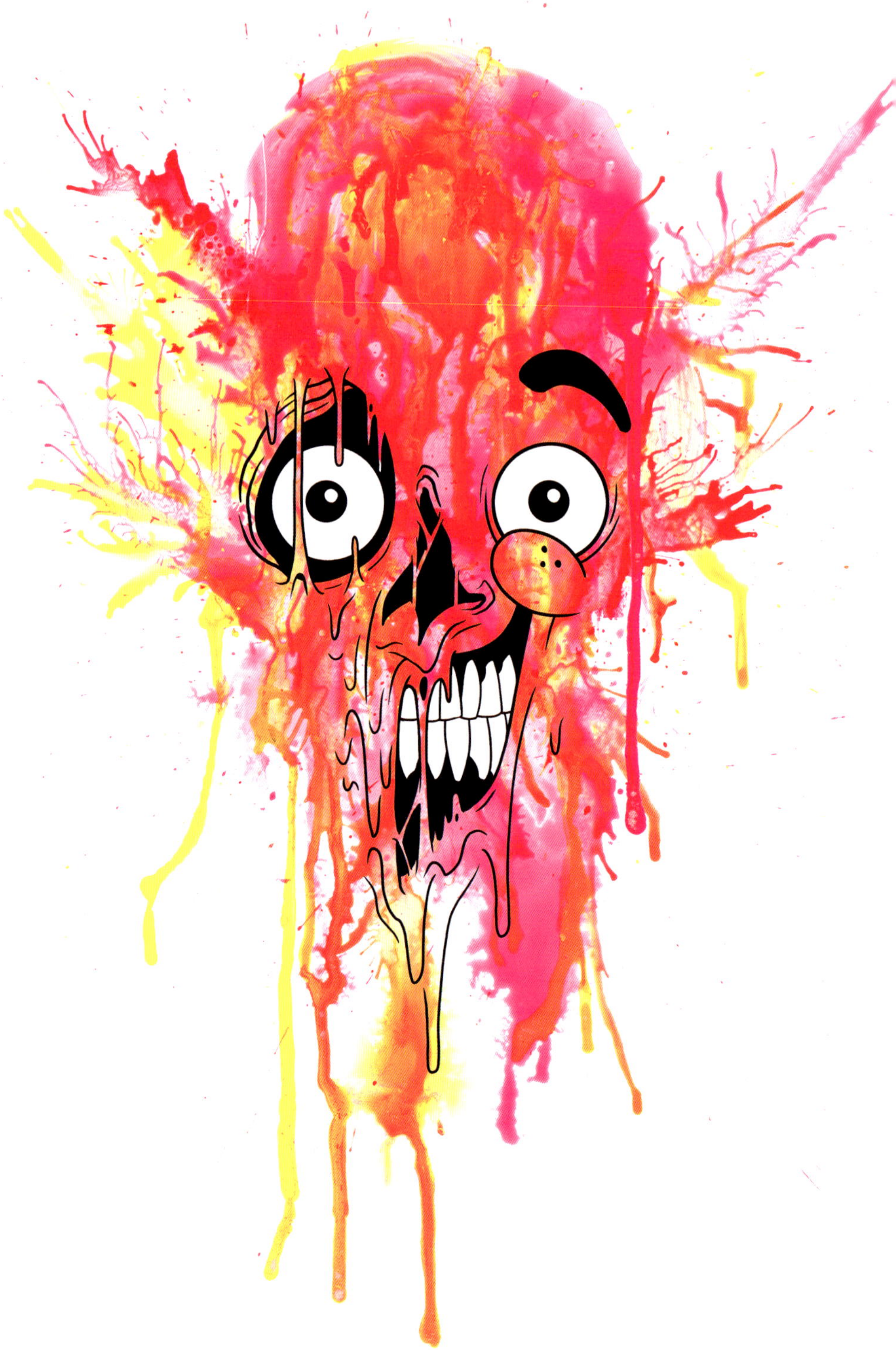

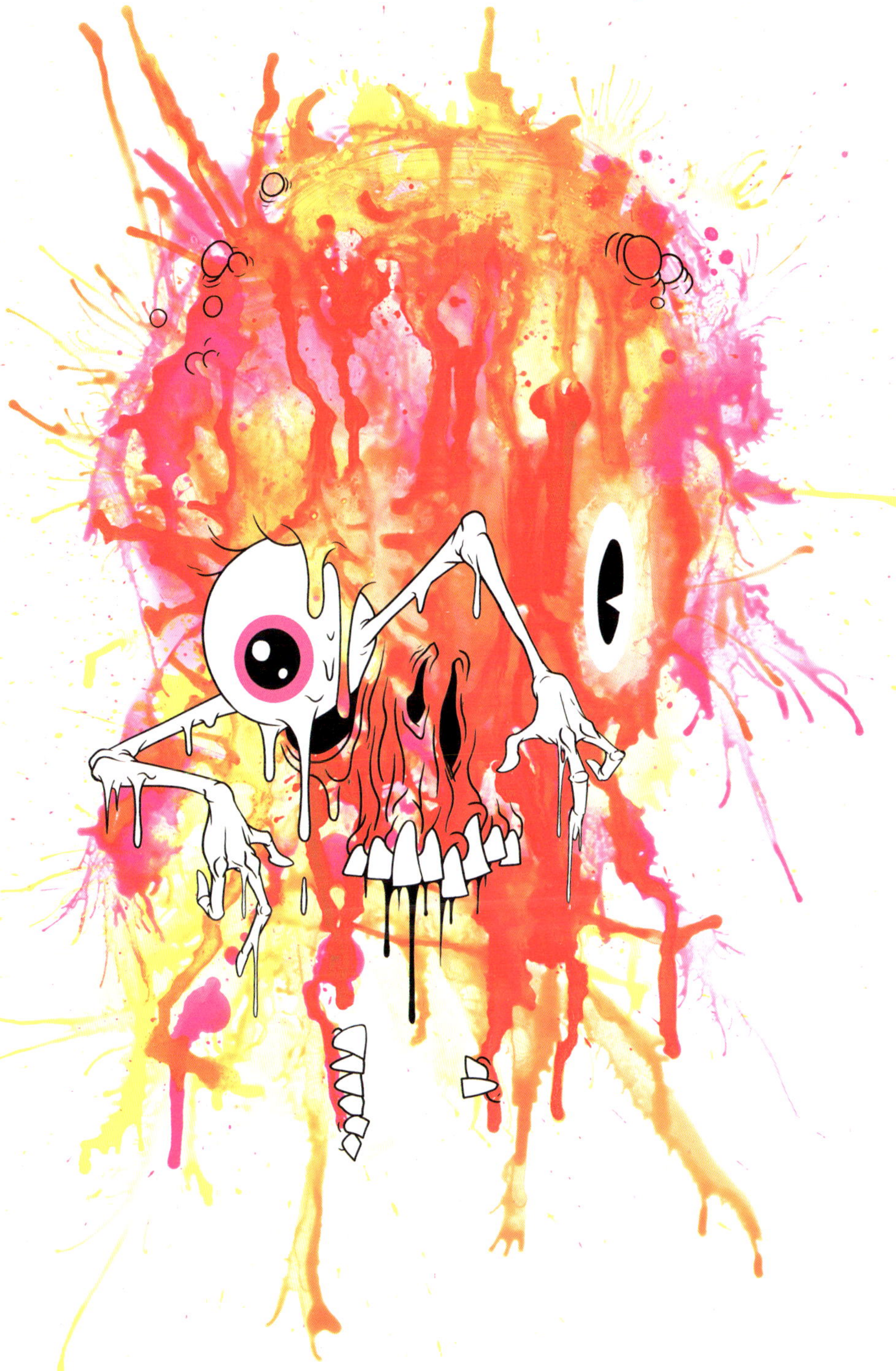

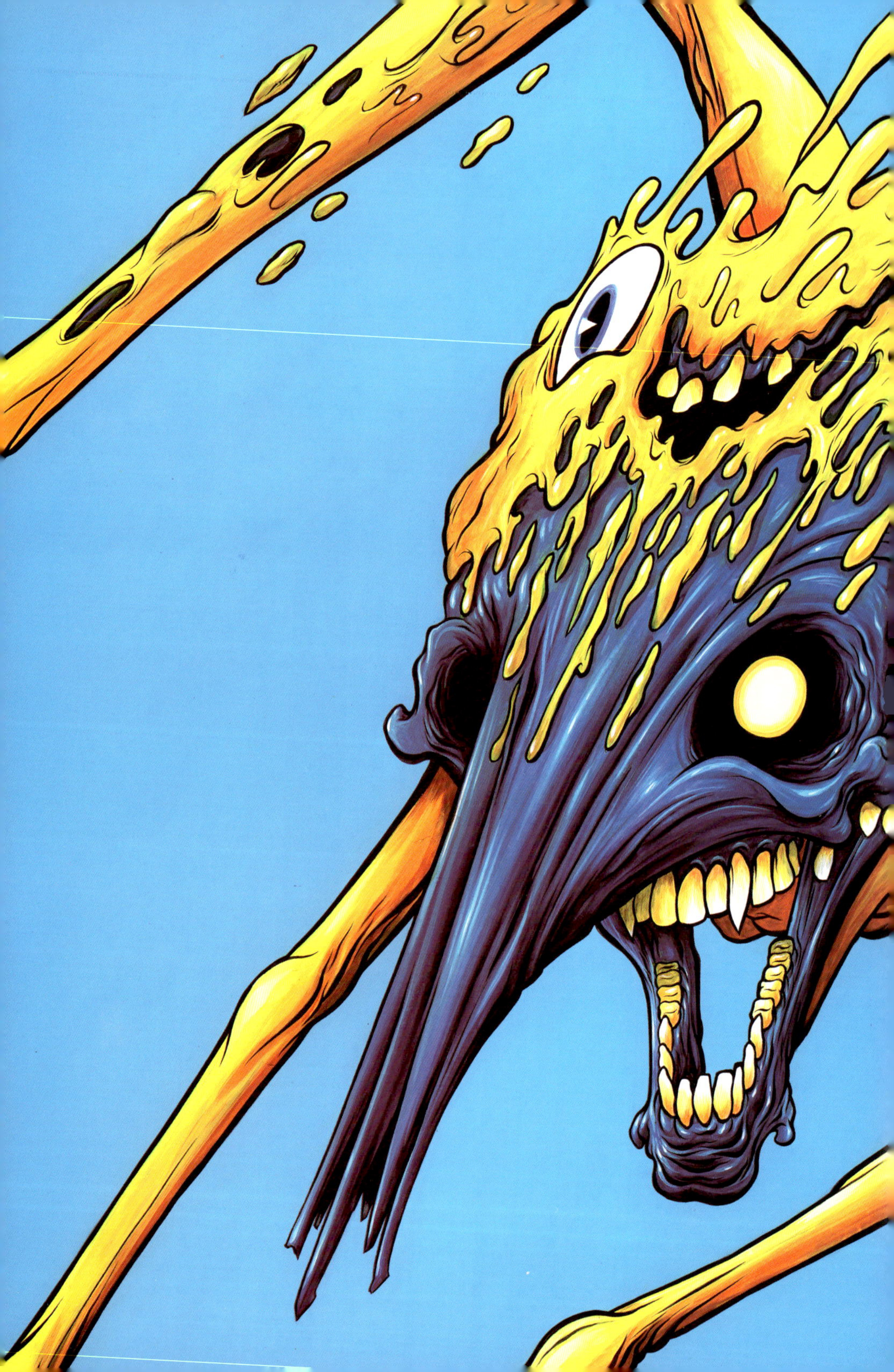

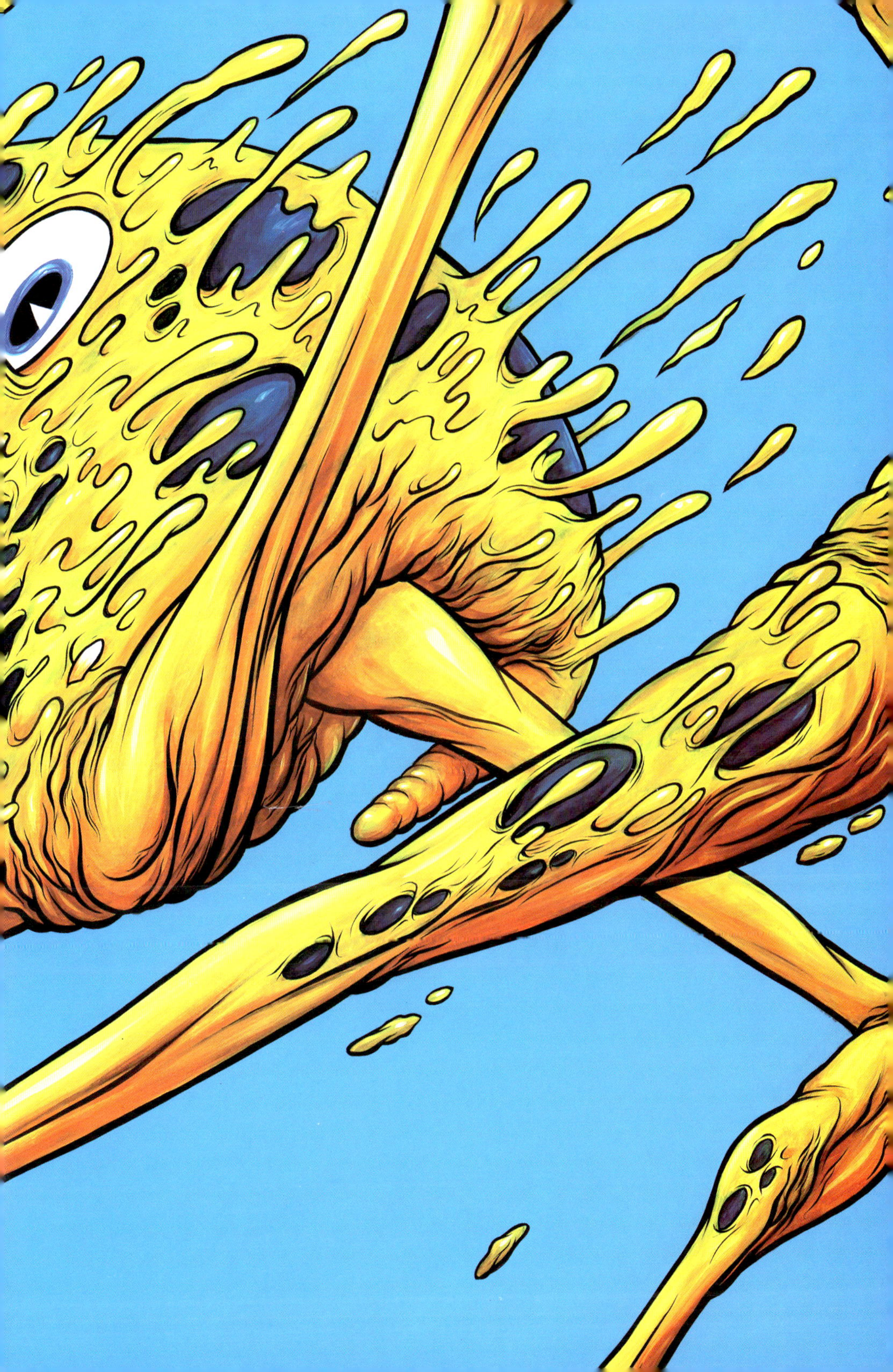

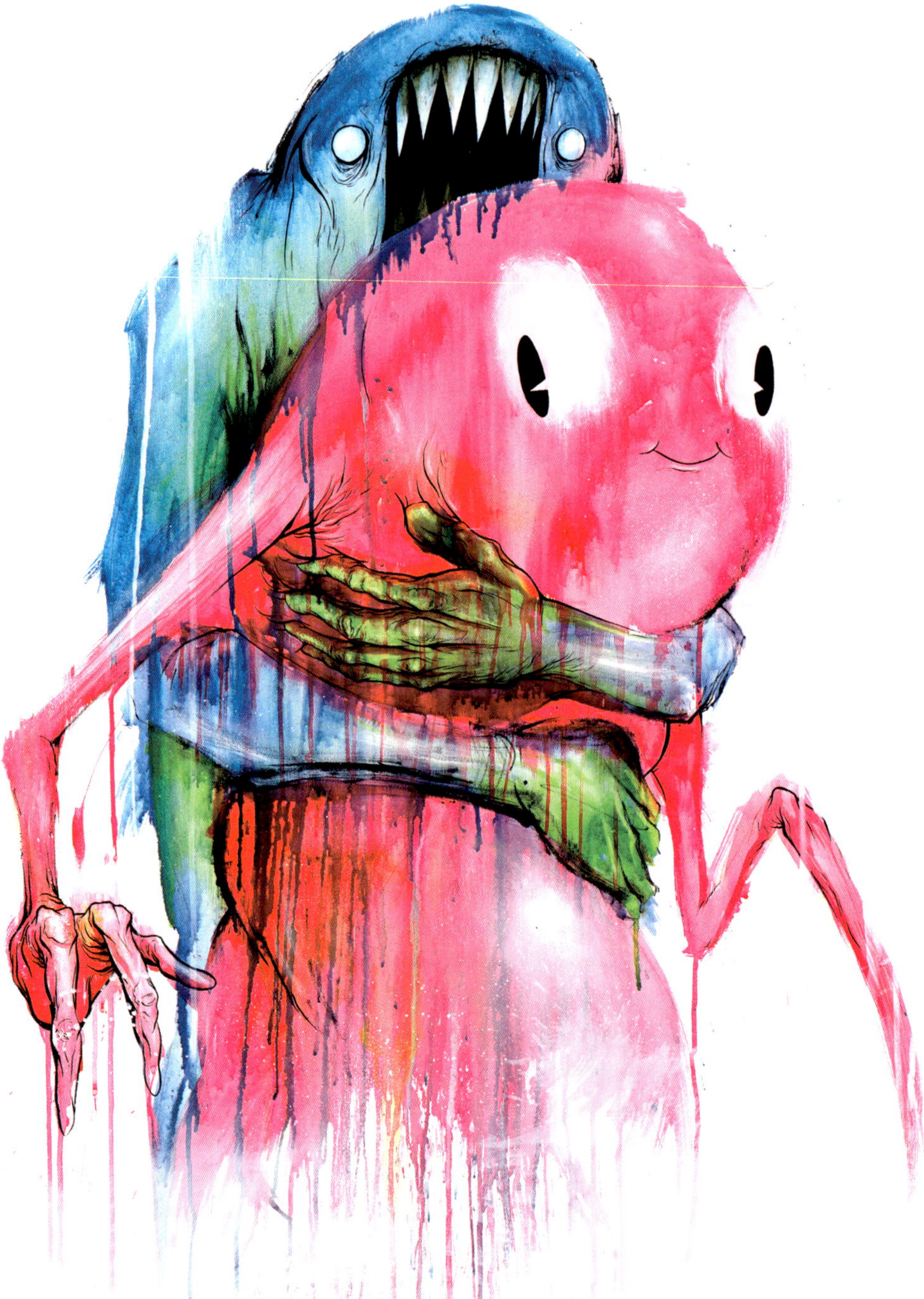

The Backpack

Two lonely treasure hunters, PACK & BACK, lived on opposite ends of the land of YUX, where they embarked separately on many quests in search of ancient artifacts scattered around the vibrant landscapes. However, both PACK & BACK also had their share of limitations by adventuring alone. PACK was obsessed with dirt and studying the different types of soil, deducting where buried treasures may lie, but lacked the strength and skill to dig. BACK, on the other hand, was strong and <u>LOVED</u> digging for treasure. He was obsessed with the dirt, too, but that's because he liked <u>EATING</u> it!

One day, PACK & BACK crossed paths while scouring the shores of a poisonous bog, and unexpectedly became immediate friends after sharing their mutual love for dirt. It was from that point on, that the new best friends shared their skills and abilities with each other, forming...THE BACKPACK, the greatest treasure hunters in the land of YUX.

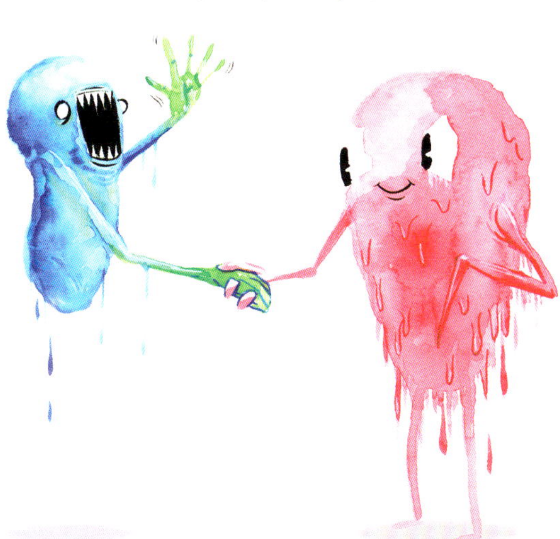

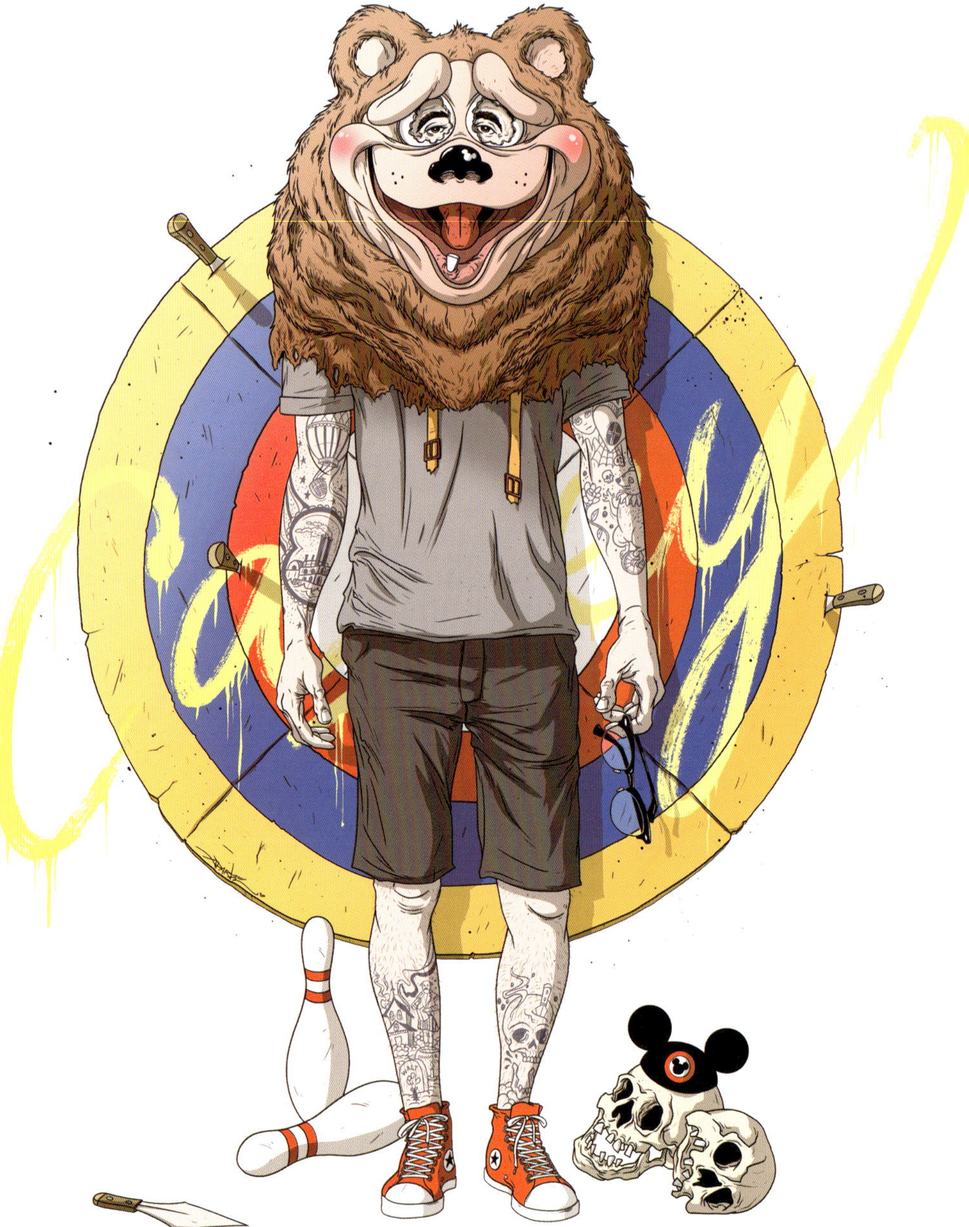

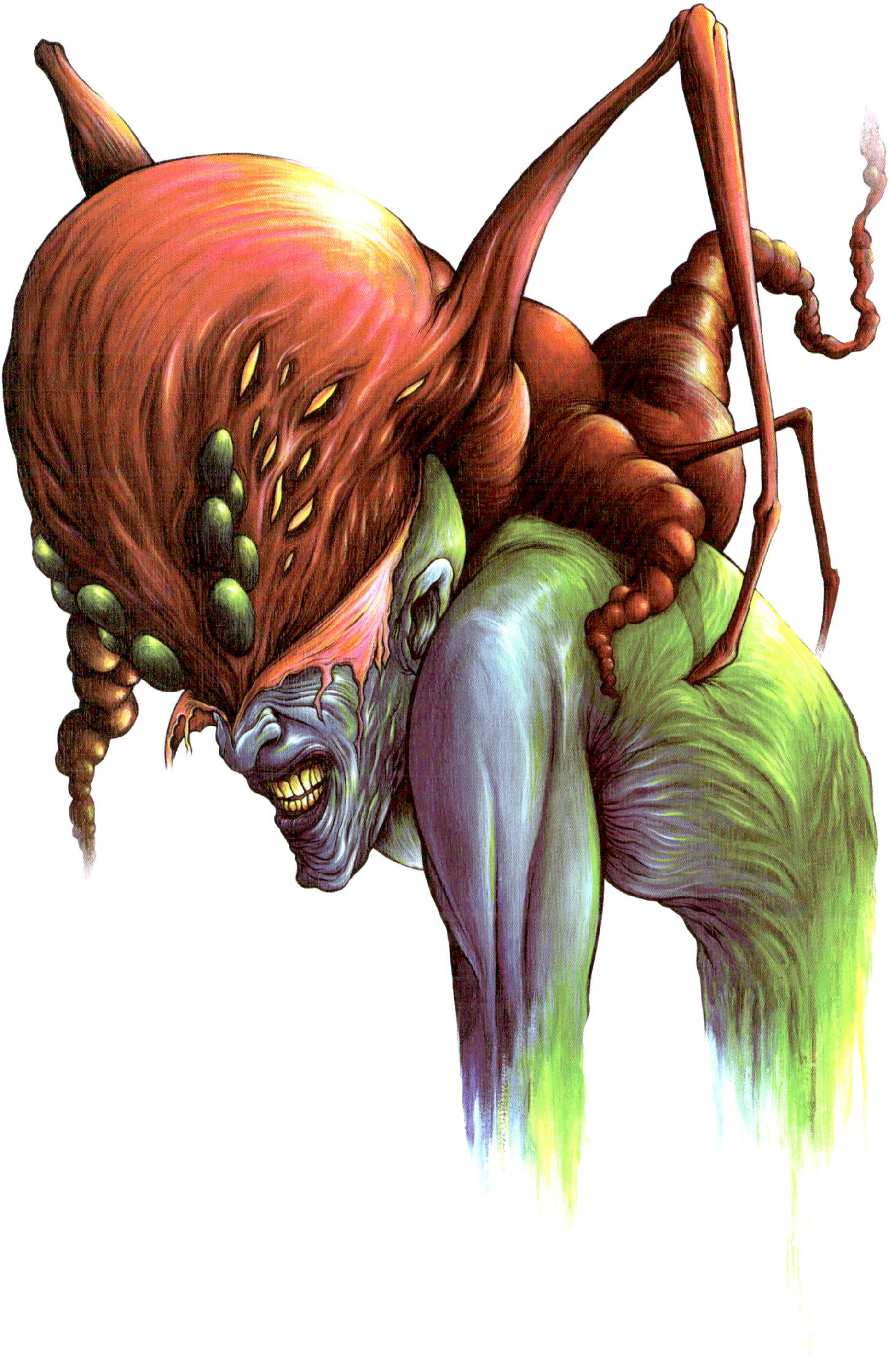

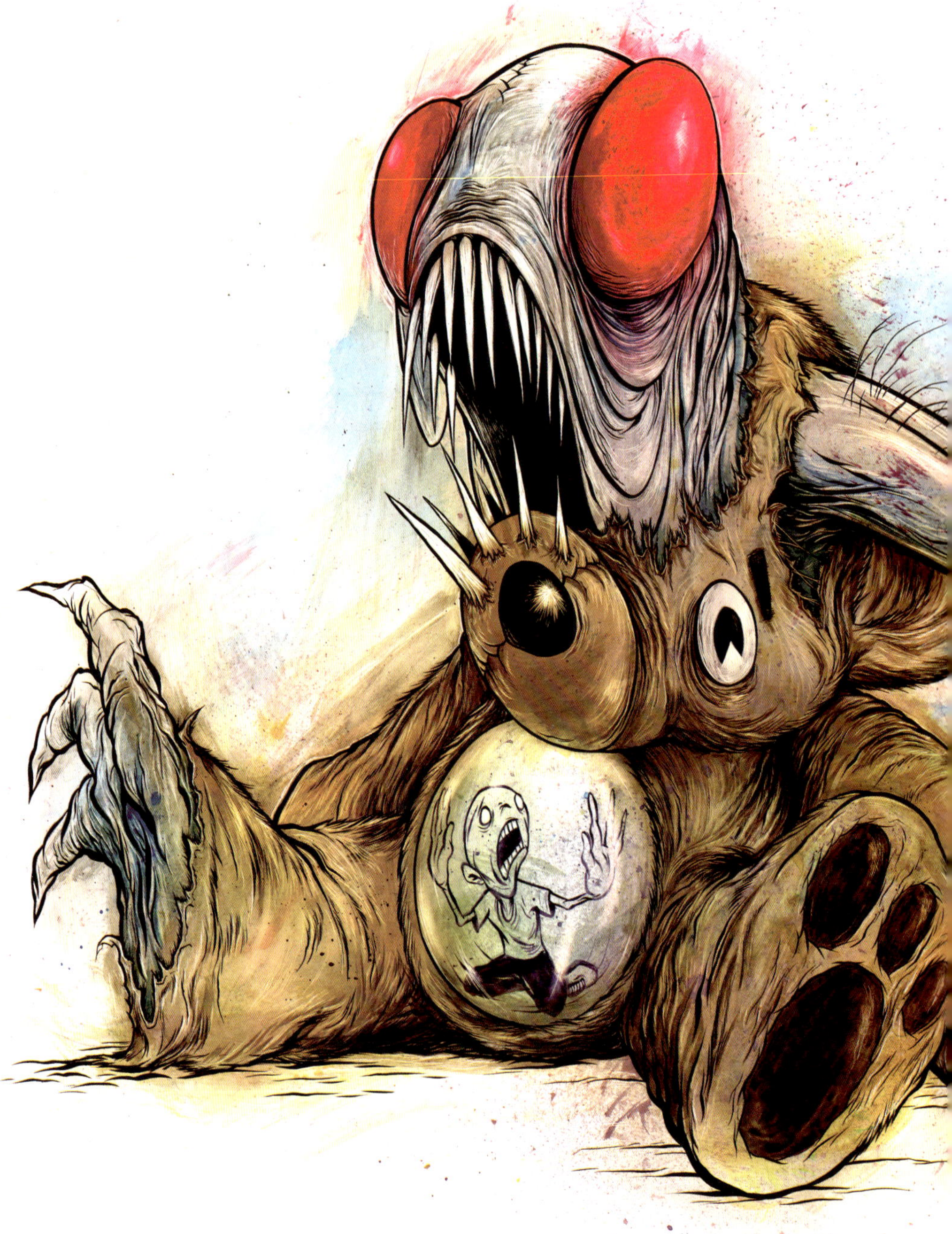

Teddy RooseFelt

As told by Darren Nash's father, Gerald:

"We didn't believe him. Little Darren had an overactive imagination. He cried wolf too many times. "Dad, the TV can see me! Dad, my cereal just jumped out of my bowl and ran away! Dad, my t-shirt stuck itself to me and is sucking my blood! Dad... blah blah." Of course none of that was true. We would humor him for years. I cut up his shirt and would tell him I could hear it scream. I would unplug the television and I made a little pretend "firewall" so that the TV couldn't see him. But it got overwhelming. Well, his grandmother made teddy bears and sold them to the local toy stores, and for his 6th birthday, she made Darren the largest teddy bear anyone had ever seen. She had everyone in our family help out with it, it was quite impressive. It took 6 adults just to get it up to his room. He loved that thing, named it Theodore RooseFelt, which I thought was a little too clever for a 6-year old. But soon enough, just like the TV, and the bed, and the toilet, he started making claims that something was inside of it. That while he slept, Theodore would inch closer to his bed, and even once, drool trickled from the stitching where the mouth was. Naturally, we were fed up. Nancy and I refused to humor him anymore.

On Thursday mornings, Nancy always made pancakes in the shape of rockets, and Darren loved those. He waited at the table every Thursday hours before Nancy would even crack an egg. But yesterday, he never showed up to the table. I went upstairs to his-room, and when I opened the door, I lost my breath and immediately felt drunk with confusion. Theodore, the giant teddy bear that took 6 GROWN MEN to position in his room, had been TORN to shreds, disemboweled of his cotton, and laid lifeless on the carpet. The room was in shambles, and Darren was nowhere to be found...

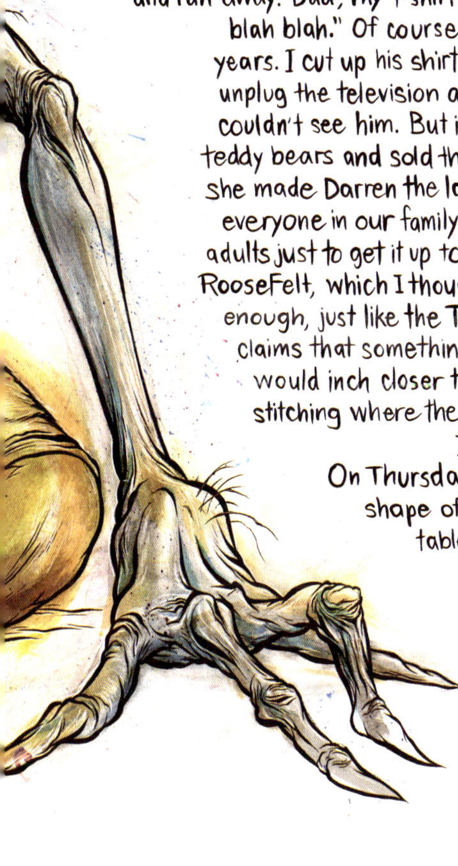

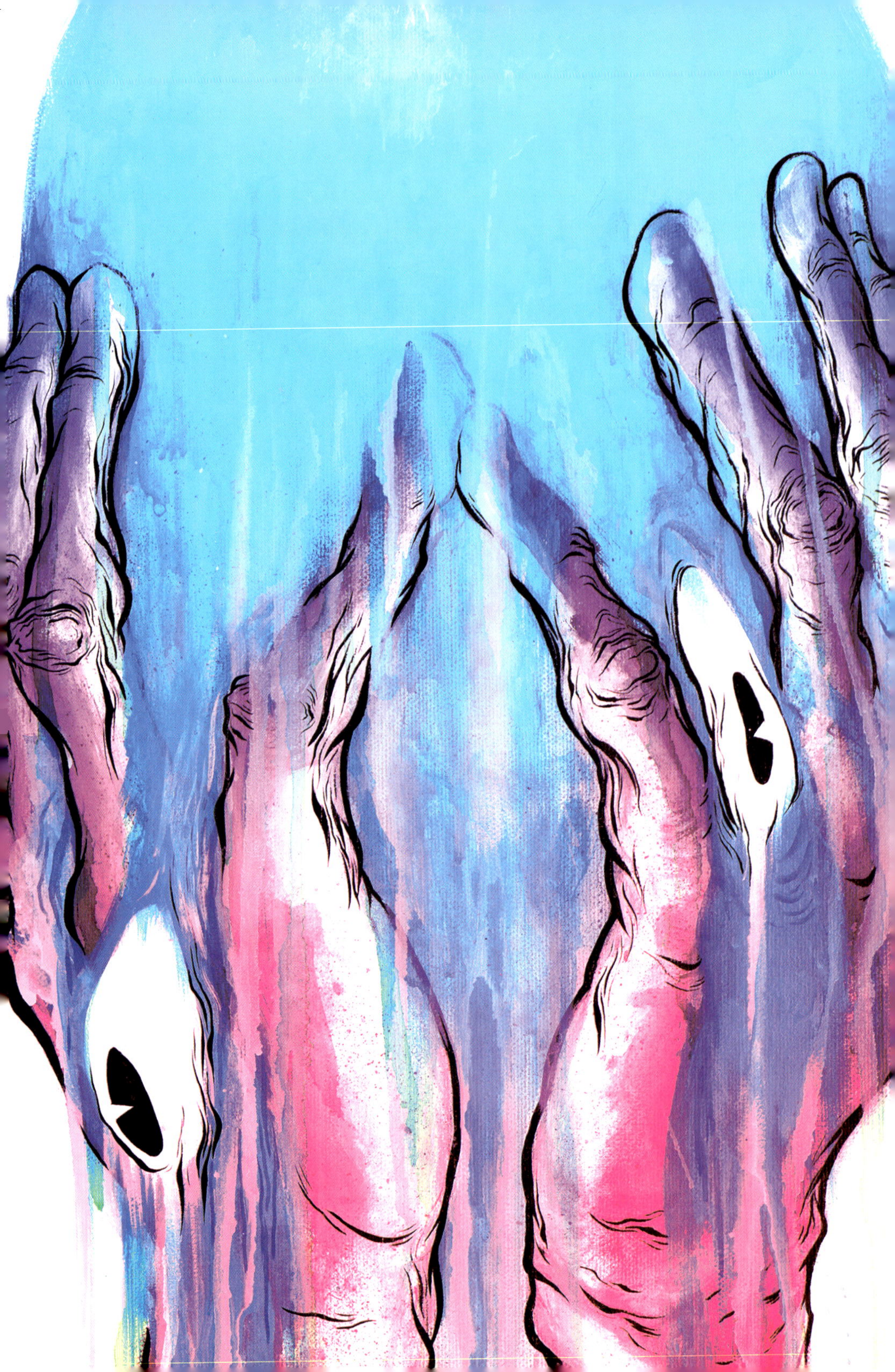

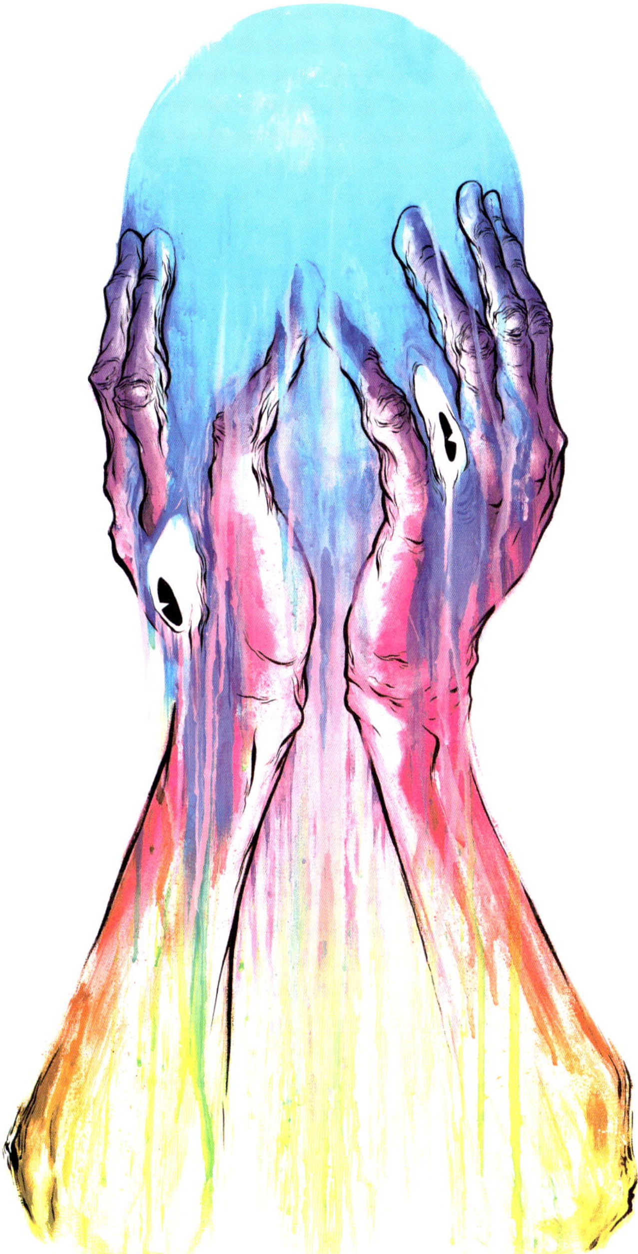

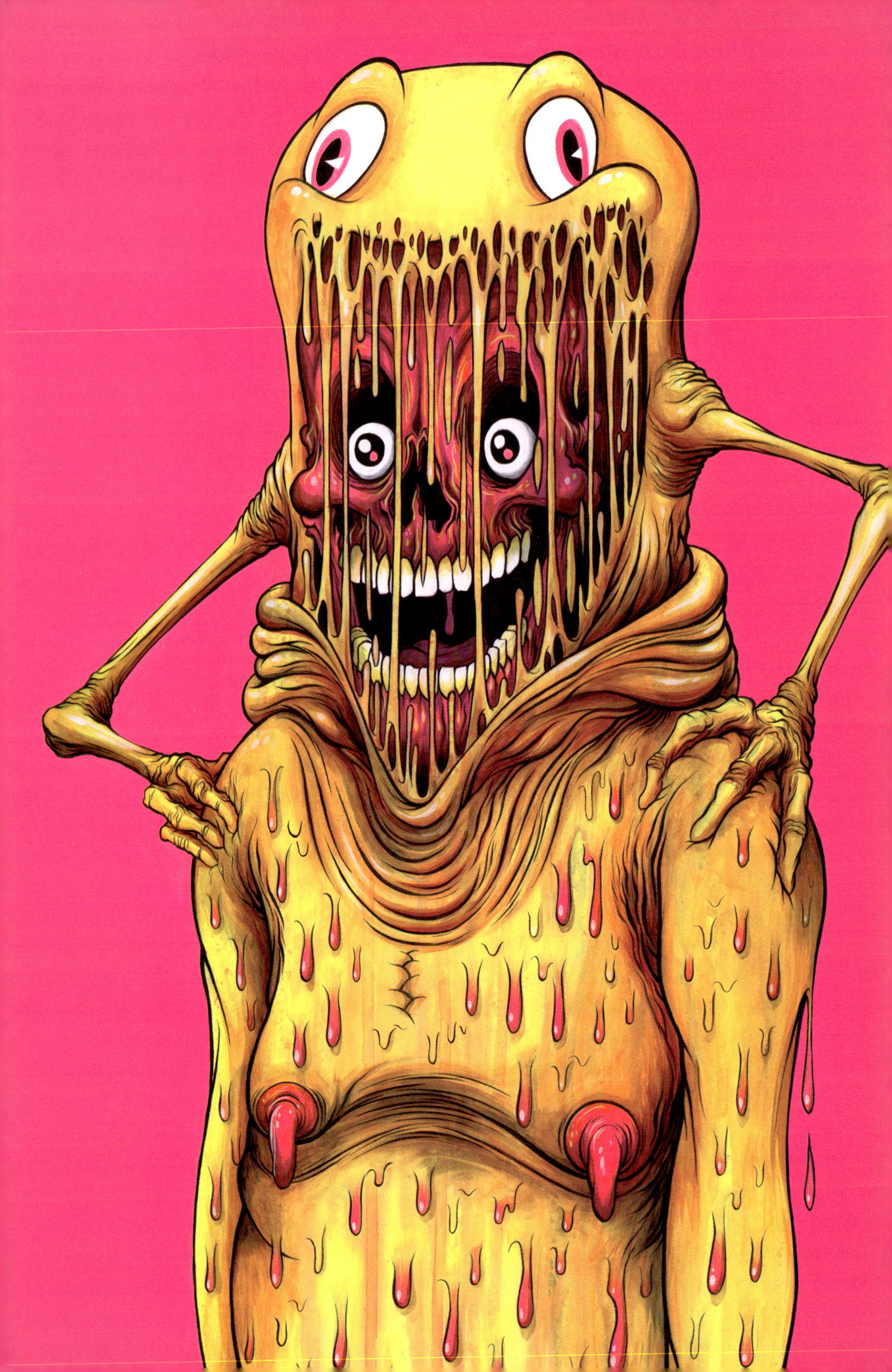

The Astronaut

Taken from the Diary of Christina Farmer:

-November 19th, 2017.

I was SO proud of Douglas. Well, I mean, I <u>AM</u> so proud of Douglas. I mean... I don't really know what I mean anymore. Despite the unintended burden I couldn't help feeling from having to raise Meredith practically on my own after the doctors discovered her tumors and amputated her feet, Douglas was living his dream. Not many of us can genuinely say that. But he was doing it. He was ACTUALLY becoming an astronaut. 2 years of classroom work. 3 years of tests. 10 months of survival training. And 21 years of telling me that someday he will blow me a kiss from 220,000 miles above our house. All for a 30-second spacewalk that... well... that might have... no. It's fine. Douglas is fine. He's just a little jaundiced from the trip and I'm just in disbelief that he's home safe. I better go make dinner for them.

-November 26th, 2017.

Douglas is <u>NOT</u> fine. He's sweating like a Chicago Bull. His skin has gotten yellower. Is that a word, "yellower"? Regardless, he is literally changing color in front of me. His skin is the color of a fucking Simpson, for Pete's sake. And it doesn't feel like <u>HIS</u> skin, if that makes sense. Ah, I know it doesn't. Nothing makes sense right now. He's so happy. He did it. Why can't I be happy too?

-November 28th, 2017.

Douglas' skin is sagging beyond belief. And he has growths forming out of his ears. He can barely hear me begging me for him to go back to the lab to visit their doctor. He keeps refusing. And... drooling...

But I can at least bring a doctor to him.

-November 29th, 2017.

I took Meredith to my mother's house to stay until Christmas after I found her crying next to Douglas' bed. There were marks on her neck. Not bruises... they were more like a pattern. It looked like a socket... I wish Douglas would admit something is wrong.

-December 1st, 2017.

Doctor Patton won't return my calls. He took <u>ONE</u> look at Douglas, mumbled something about having to "grab something out of the car" and never came back. Douglas' speech is completely unintelligible now.

-December 3rd, 2017.

Meredith bit my mother today. Why would she do that? What is going on? I'm so alone.

-December 10th, 2017.

Douglas won't let me leave. His nose is gone. There one day, gone the next. Just gone. His growths have fingers! He won't stop smiling. He stinks. I can't leave. I don't know where Meredith is. Everything is wrong. I don't know what's happening. I can't leave. I'm so ——

-February 5th, 2018

If you are reading this, I'm sorry. I'm sorry that I let Douglas go into space. I'm sorry for being supportive and allowing him to let me raise Meredith on my own. I'm sorry I wasn't stronger. I'm sorry I couldn't make him listen when I said he needed help. But most of all, I'm sorry that I let him escape. You are all in danger. But not me. No, not me... he won't ever hurt me... because I just found out that I'm pregnant again... and I can already feel my baby smiling.

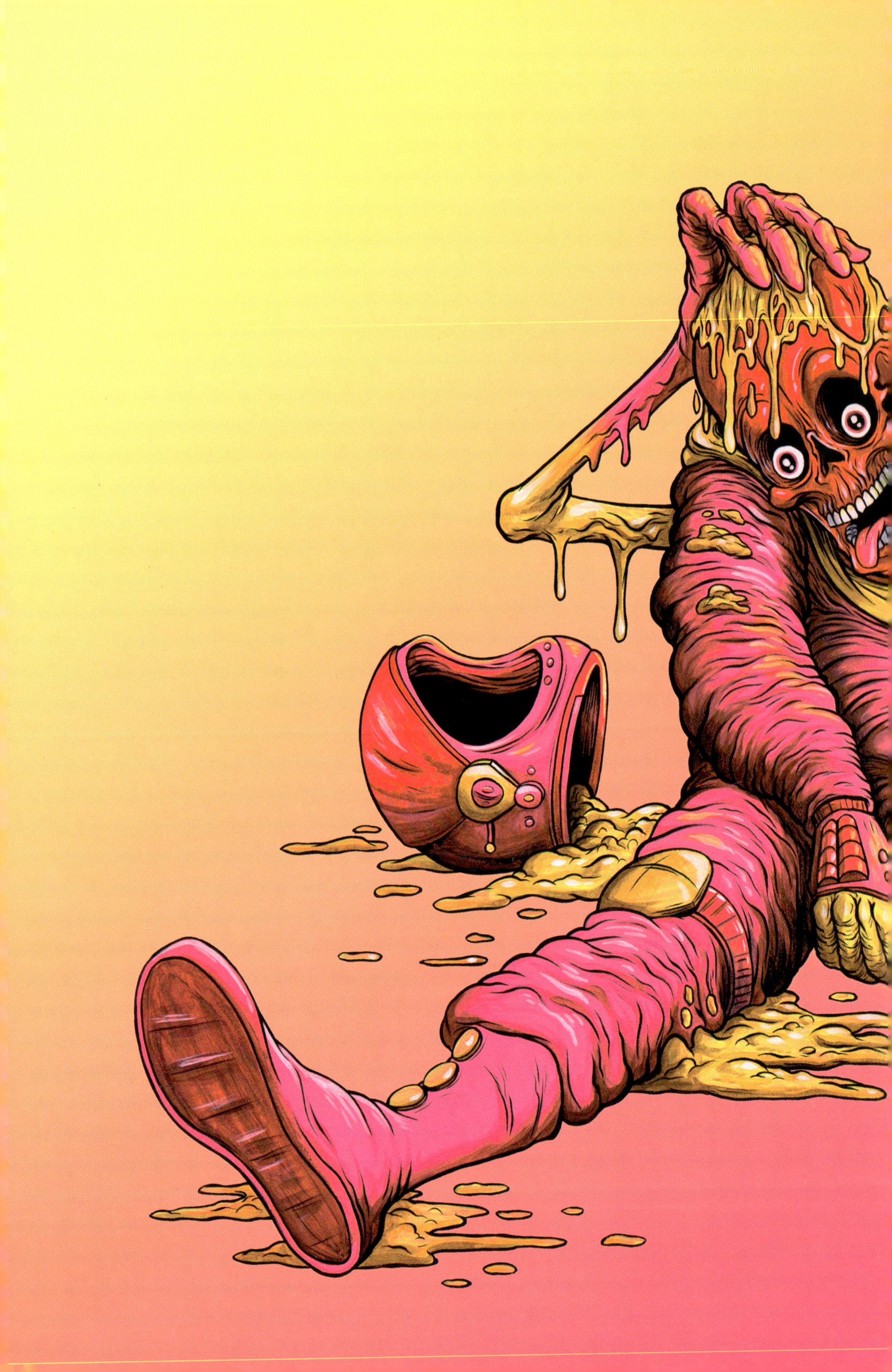

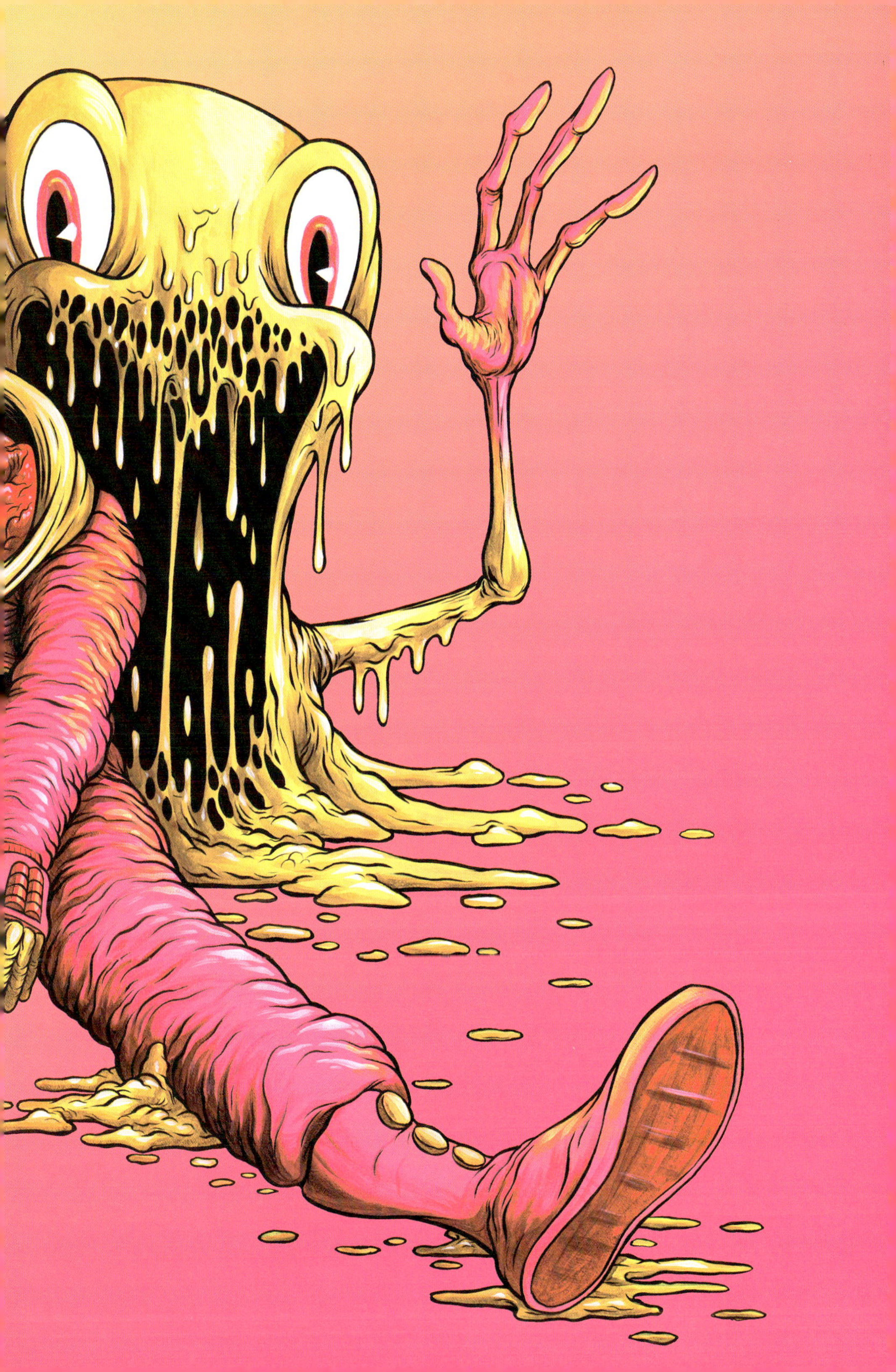

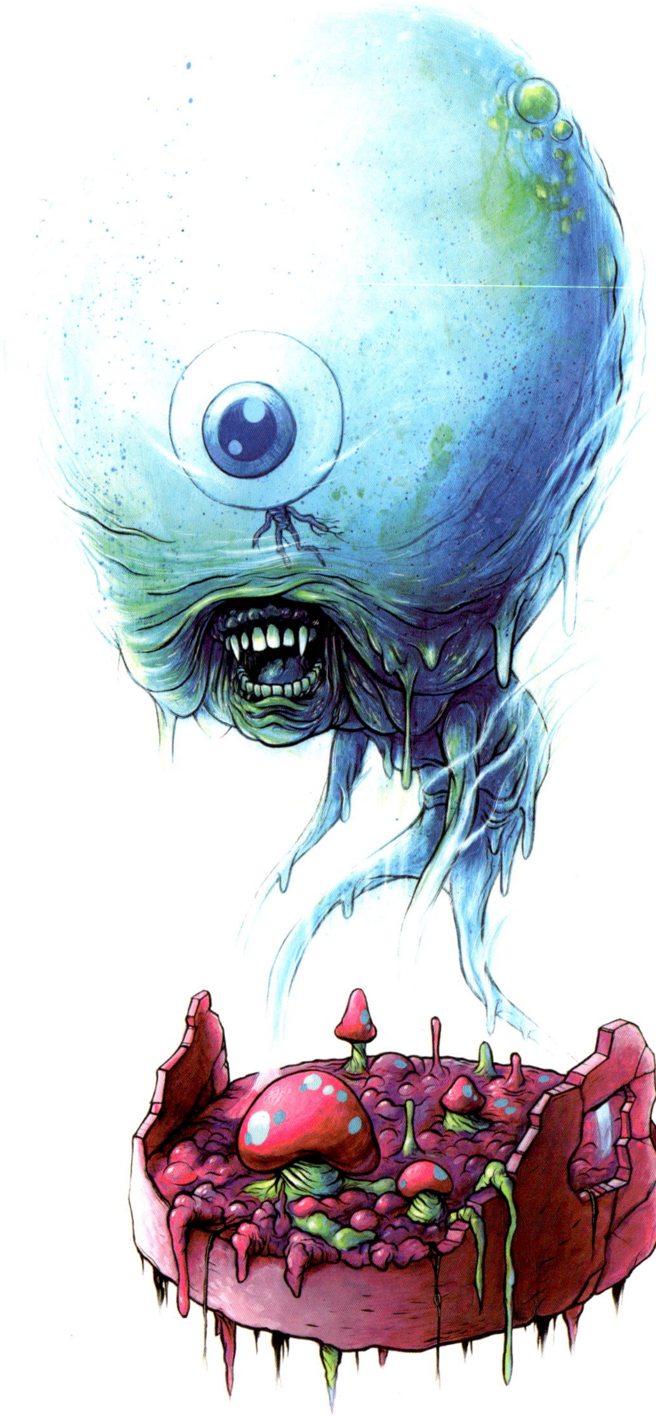

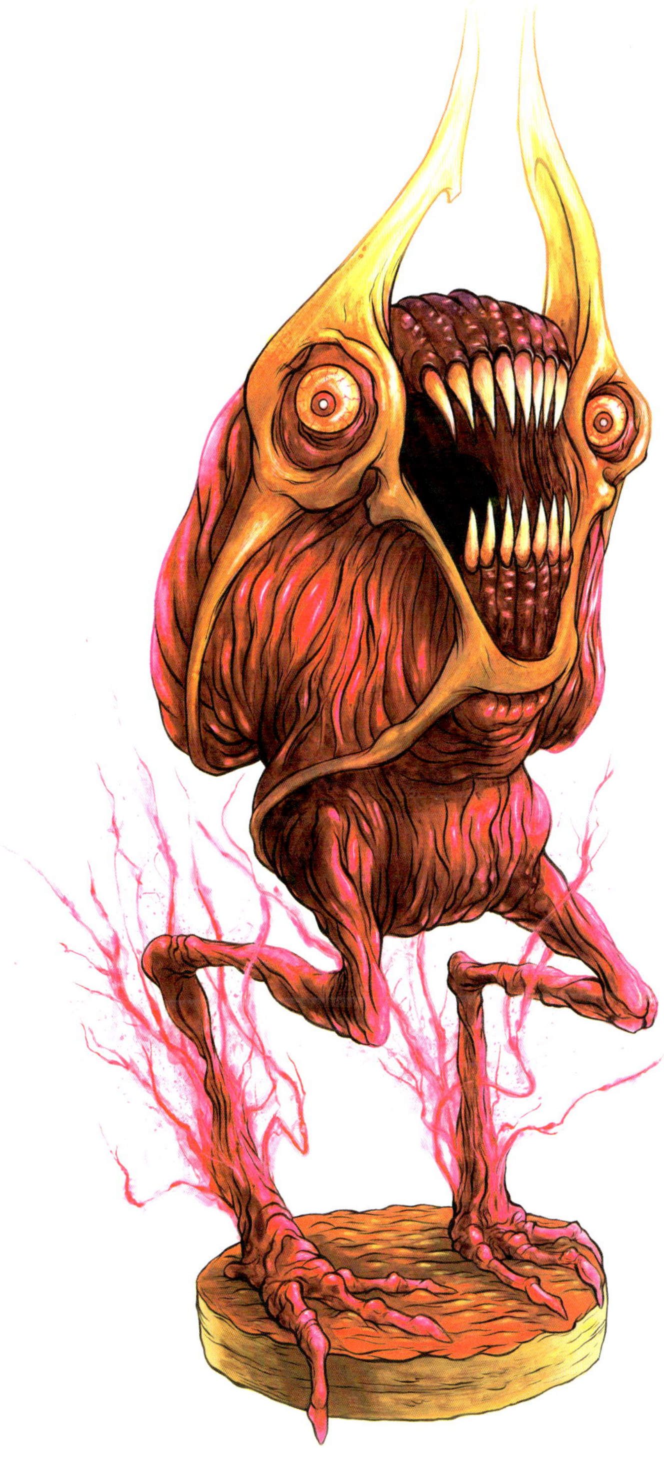

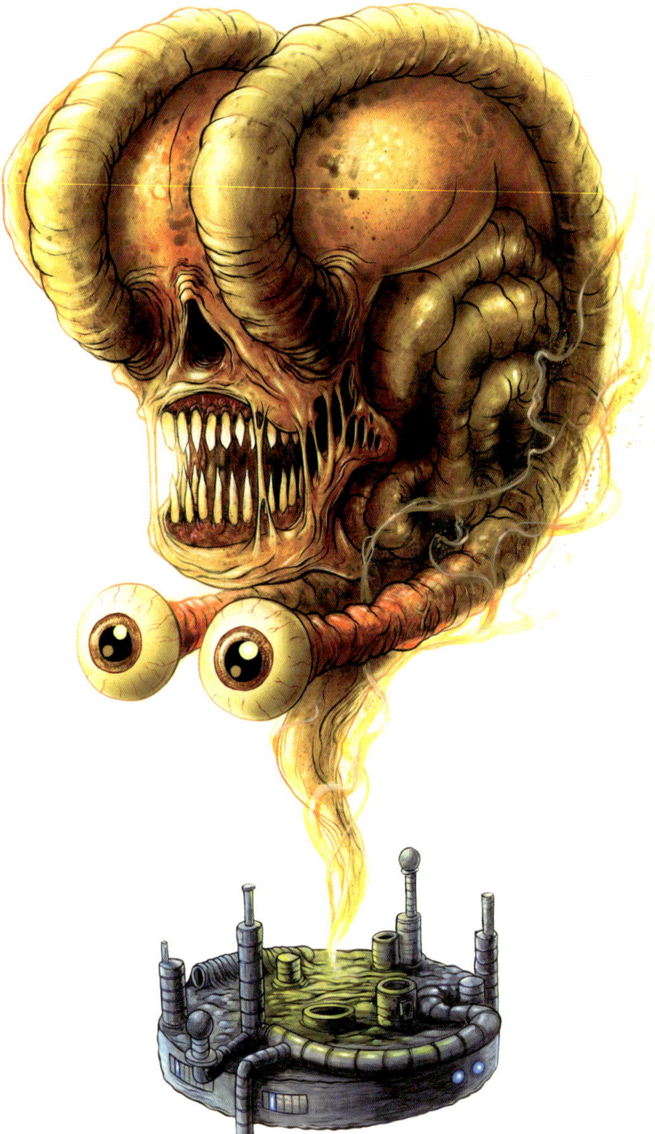

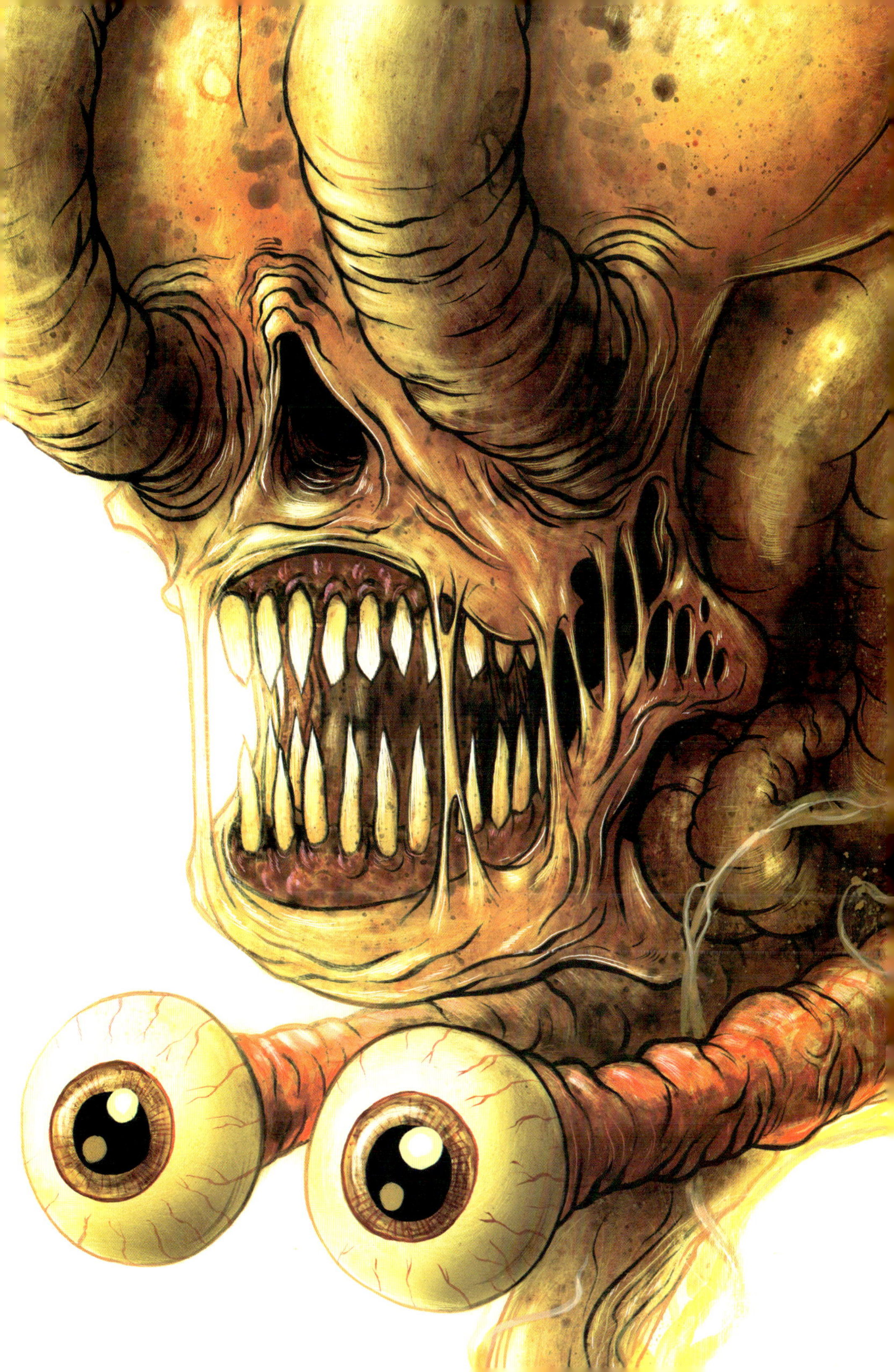

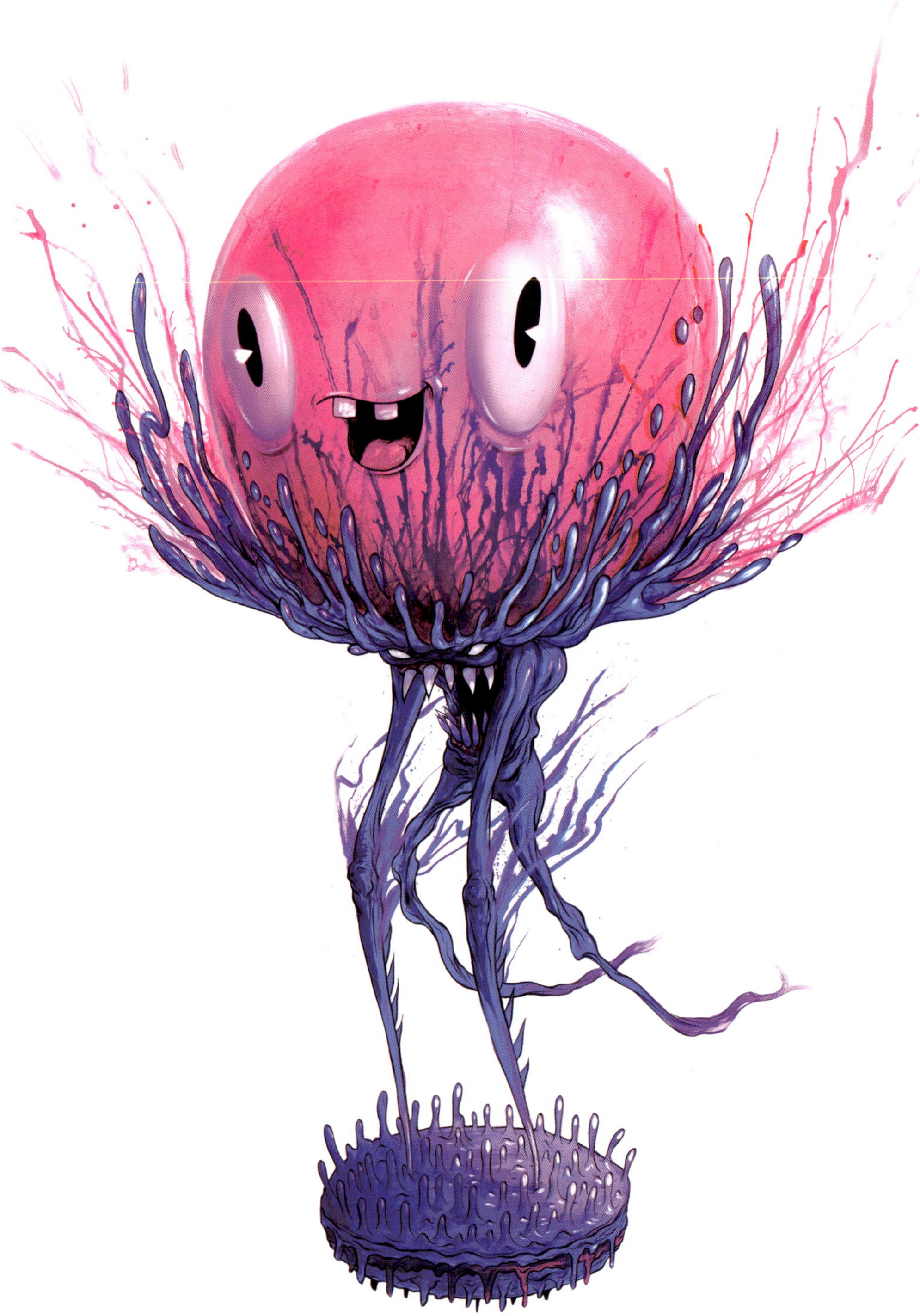

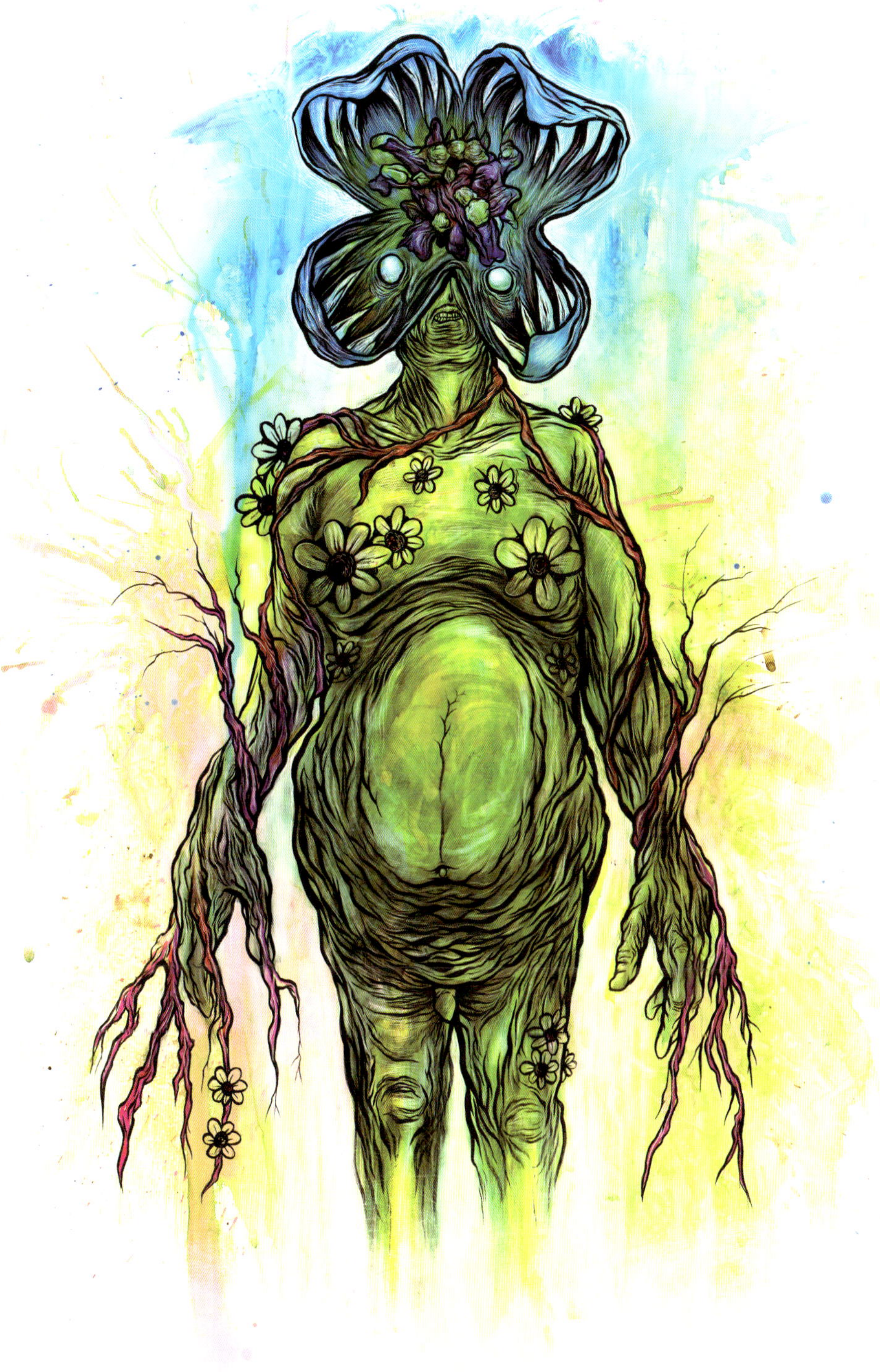

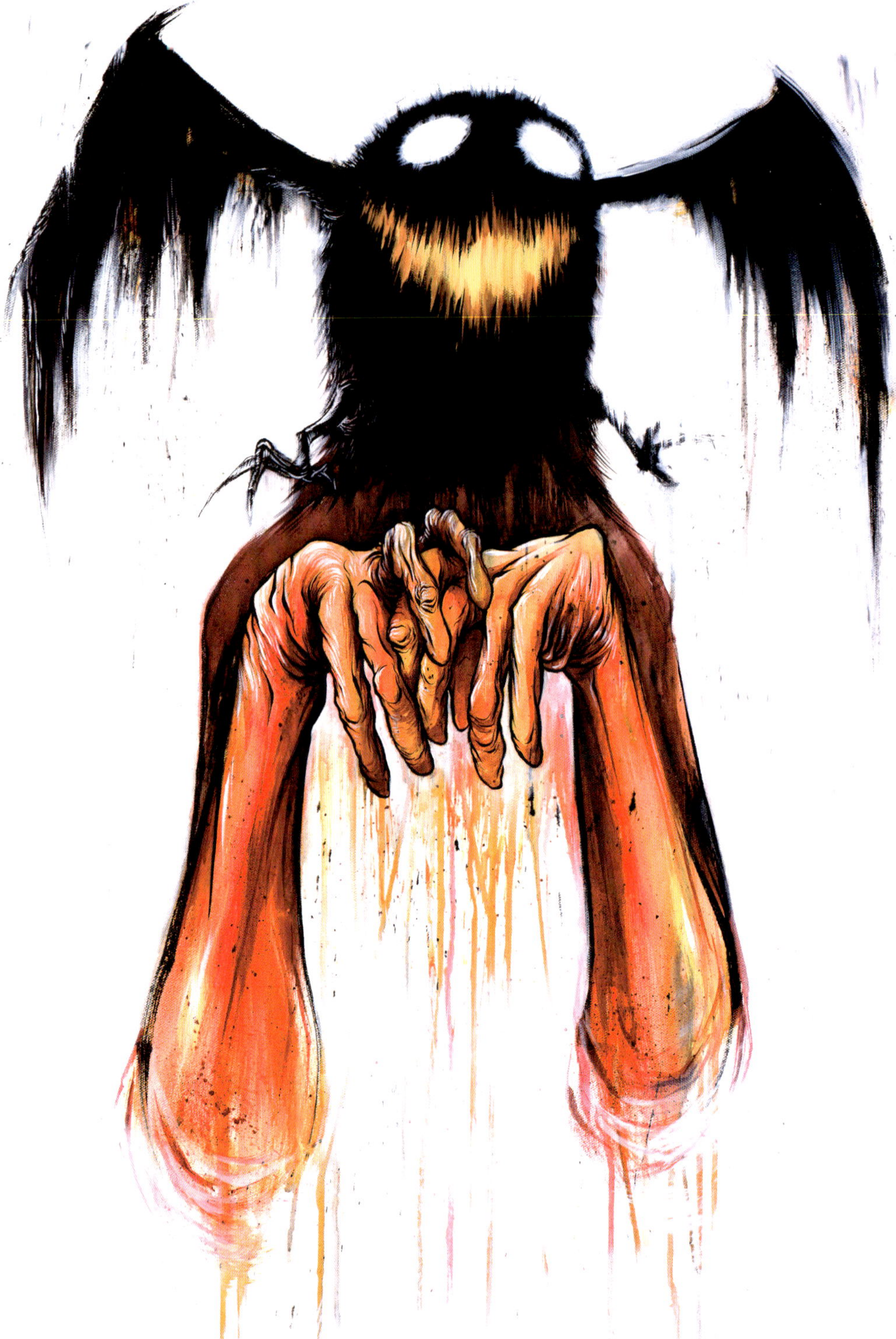

the Real Batman

Not many people know this, but BATMAN (yah, your favorite masked detective) was based off of an ancient mythical cult on whose lore basically told a story about a bat hunter who, in a fit of symbiotic revenge-rage, captured the bat that killed his wife and, since he couldn't live without his wife, he wanted to show the bat what it was like to depend on someone else for fe and love. So the hunter shoved the Bat onto his own head like mask and forced the bat to remain a part of him. Shortly after, the tables turned and the hunter's foolish attempt at revenge ackfired when he suffocated and died. The bat then took over the hunter's body and used his new found appendages and bilities to lead warriors to kill weak people because it was fun.

The End.

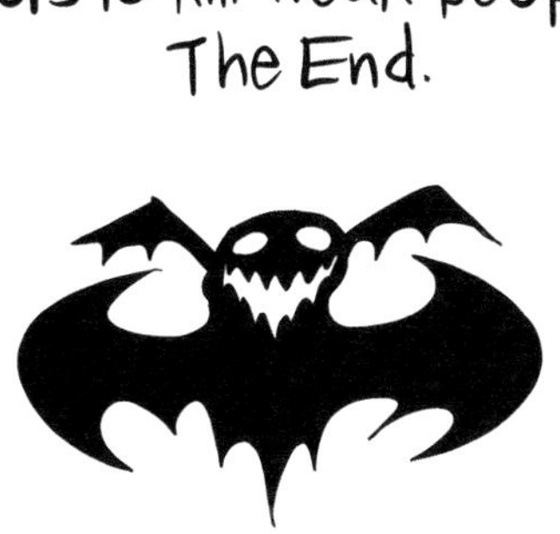

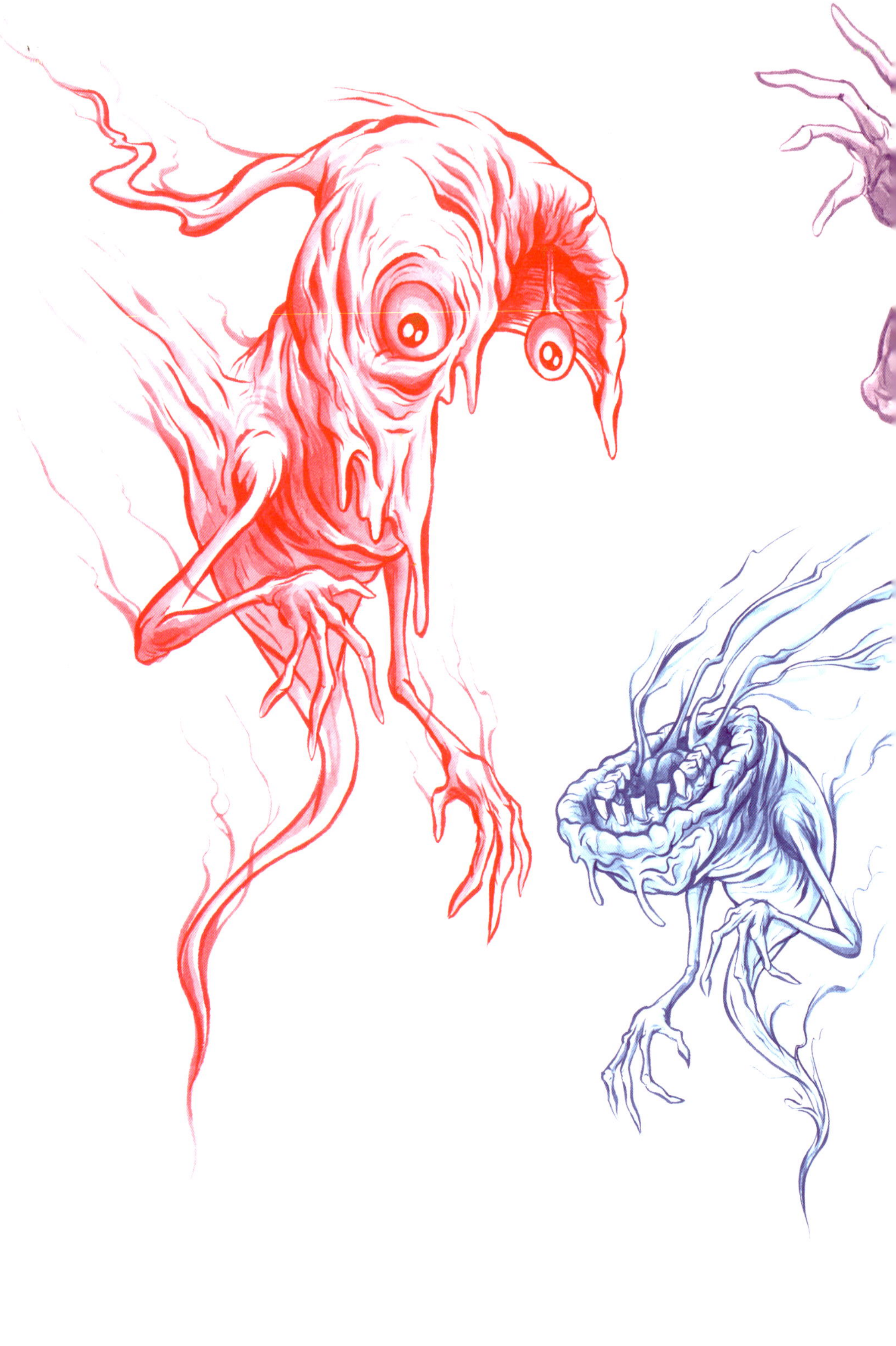

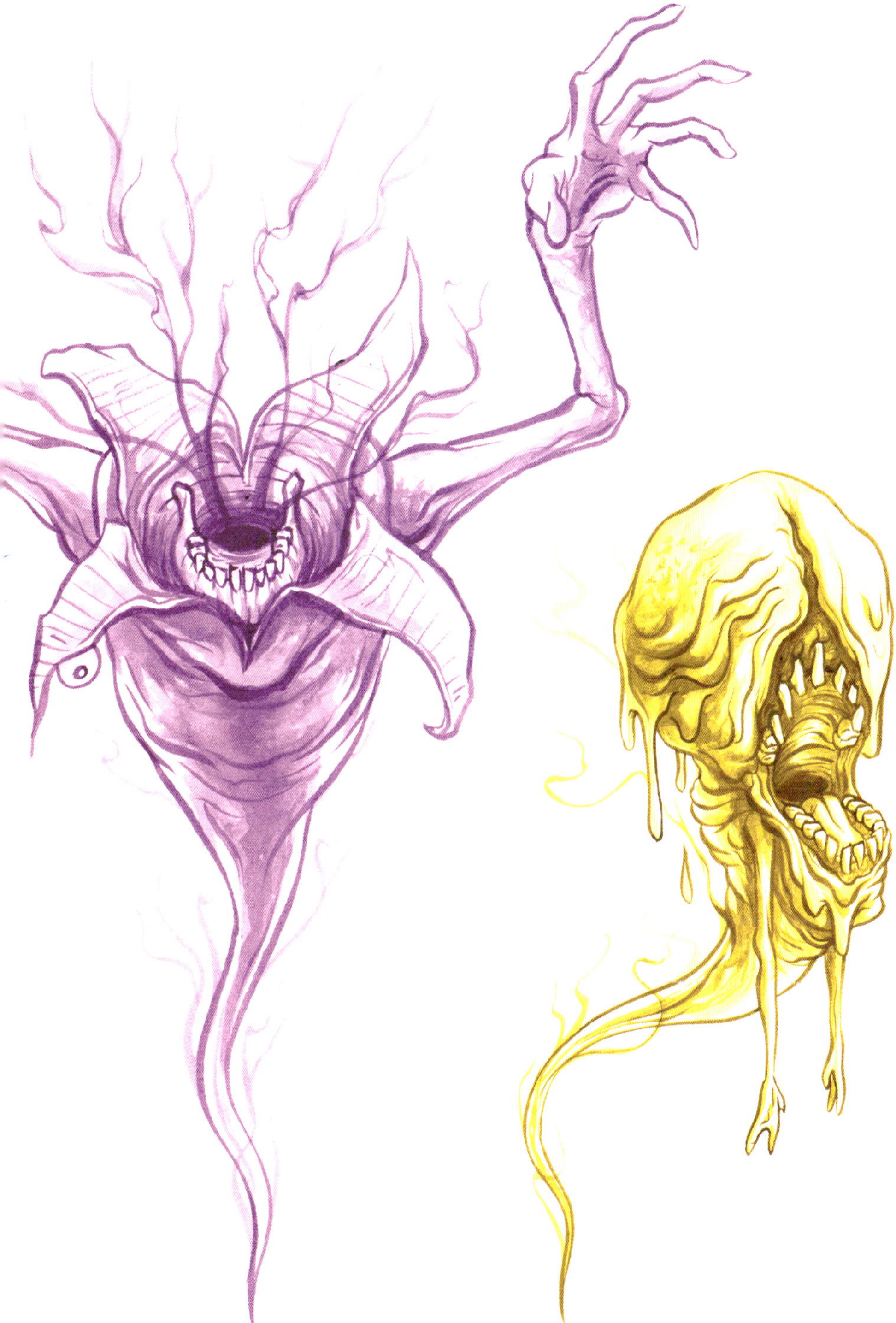

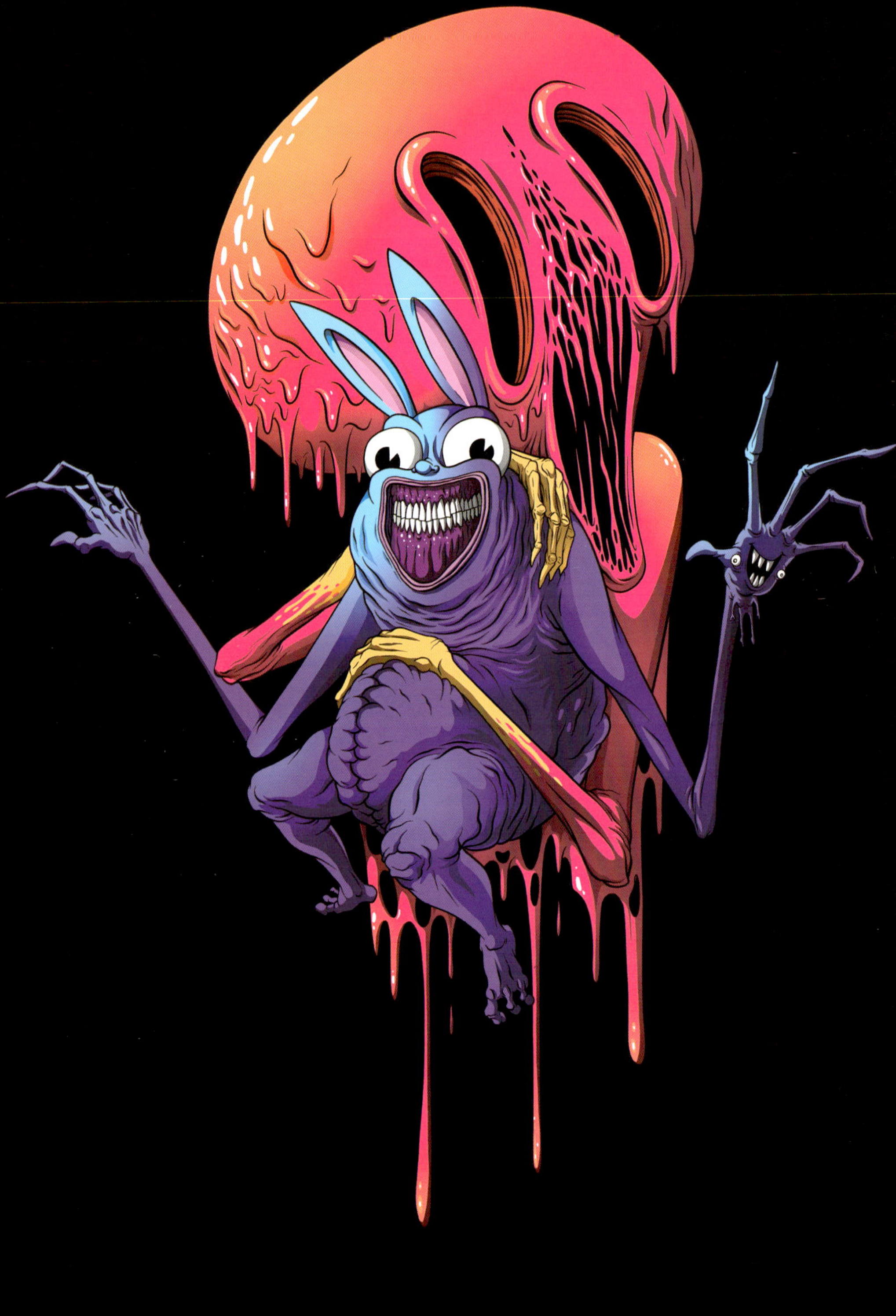

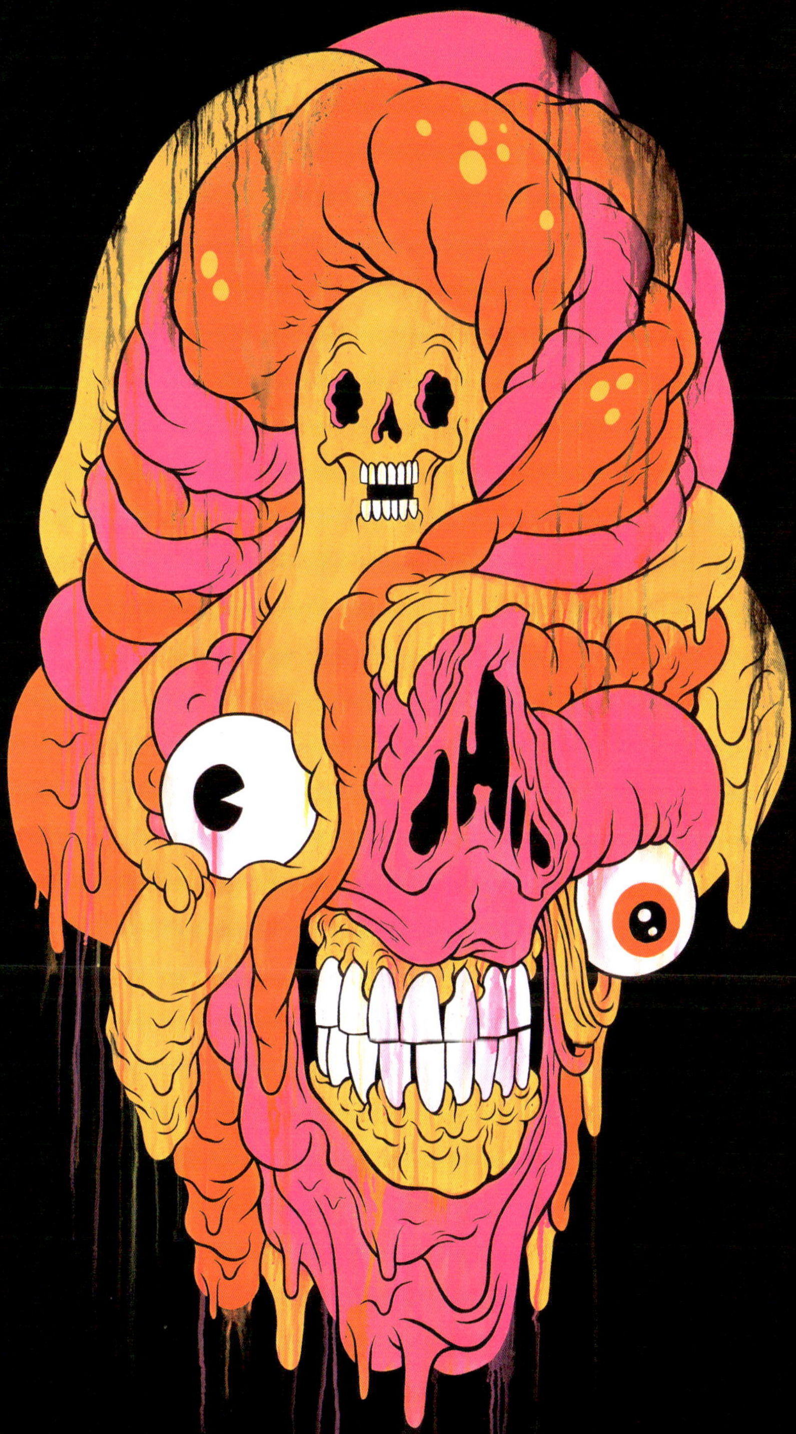

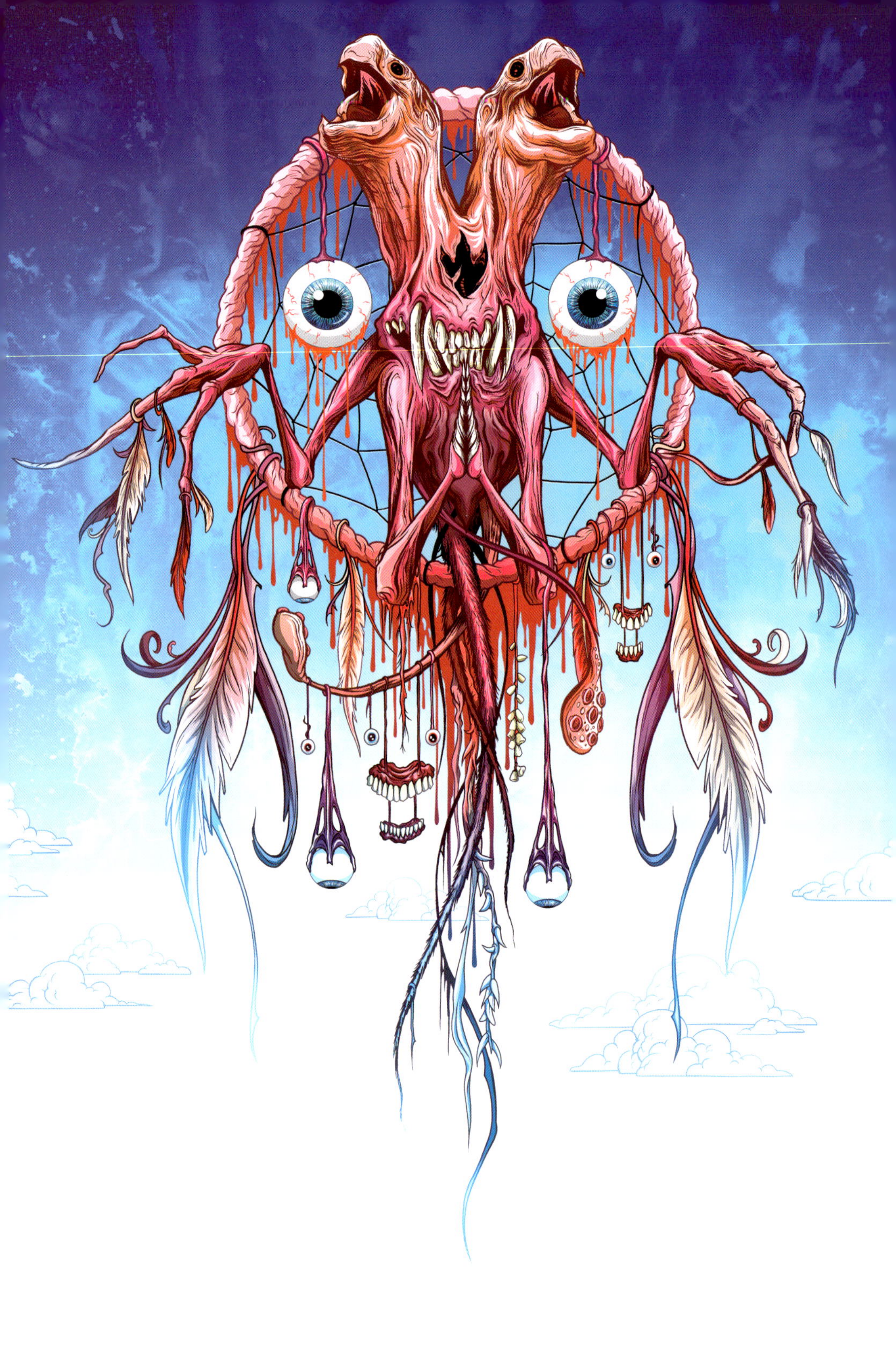

The Dream Gobbler

Whenever Uncle Randy returned from the 'Boriginies, he would tell me stories about the things he saw and heard. One time he saw a leopard as big as an elephant, and another time he learned that if you make the right clicking noise with your throat, you can control ants to do whatever you want.

But this last time, he said he barely made it home alive. When I asked him why, he told me that he was getting his dreams stolen from him, and that "a man who doesn't dream eventually doesn't breathe".

"How do you stop yourself from dreaming?" I asked.

"You can't... but the Dream Gobbler can."

"The Dream Gobbler", he said, "is a giant monster that lives in the clouds. And even though it's tried eating every kind of bird and tree and airplane that it comes across, nothing satisfies its hunger like the dreams of humans. And it uses those dreams to change the way it looks, so that no one can recognize it when they look in the sky. So if you wake up and you can't remember your dreams, perhaps it's because you got them taken away from you by a hungry Dream Gobbler. And after enough visits... I don't even wanna think about it."

Since Uncle Randy came home, I now make sure the windows are shut tight at night. Even though it's really hot usually...

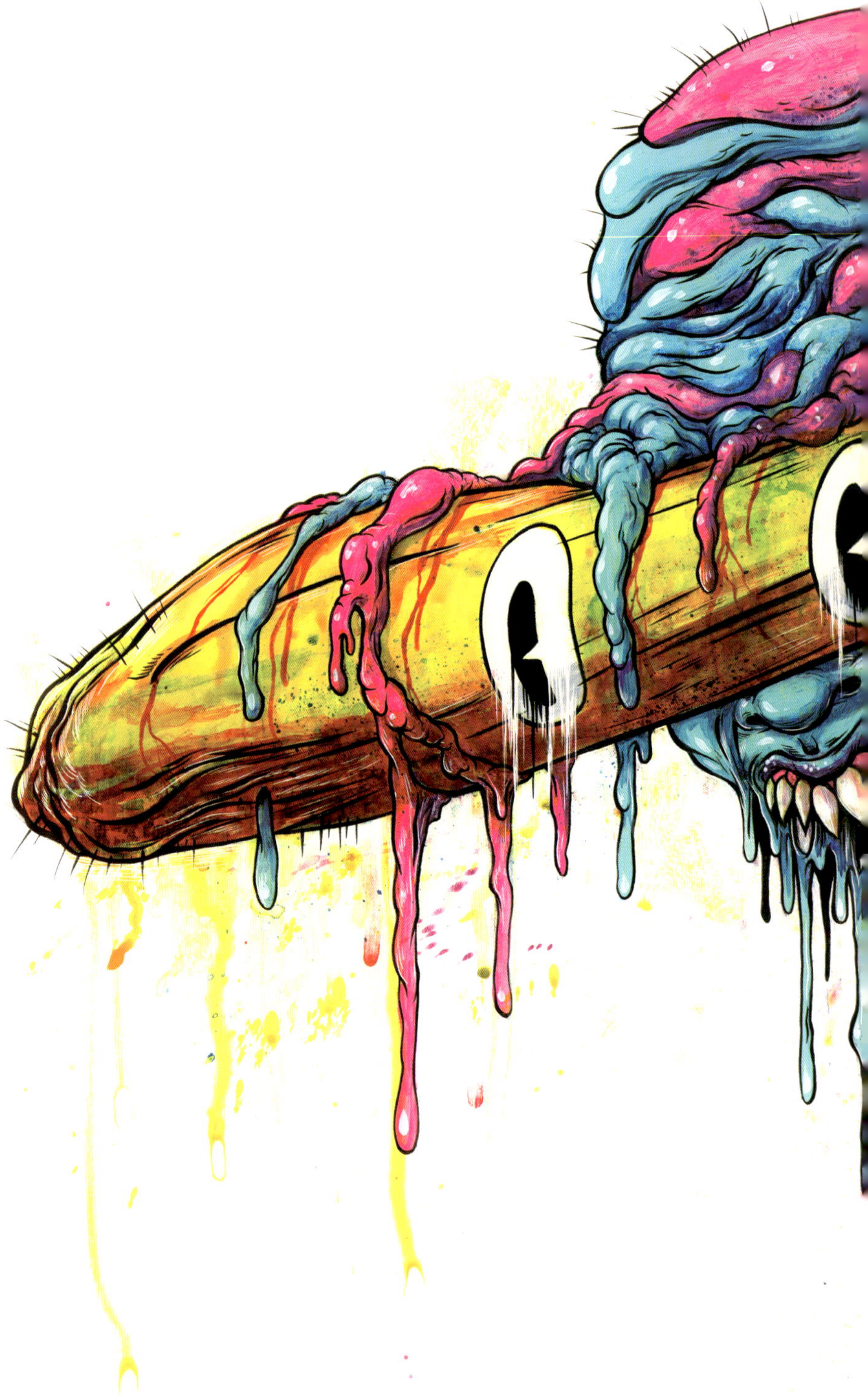

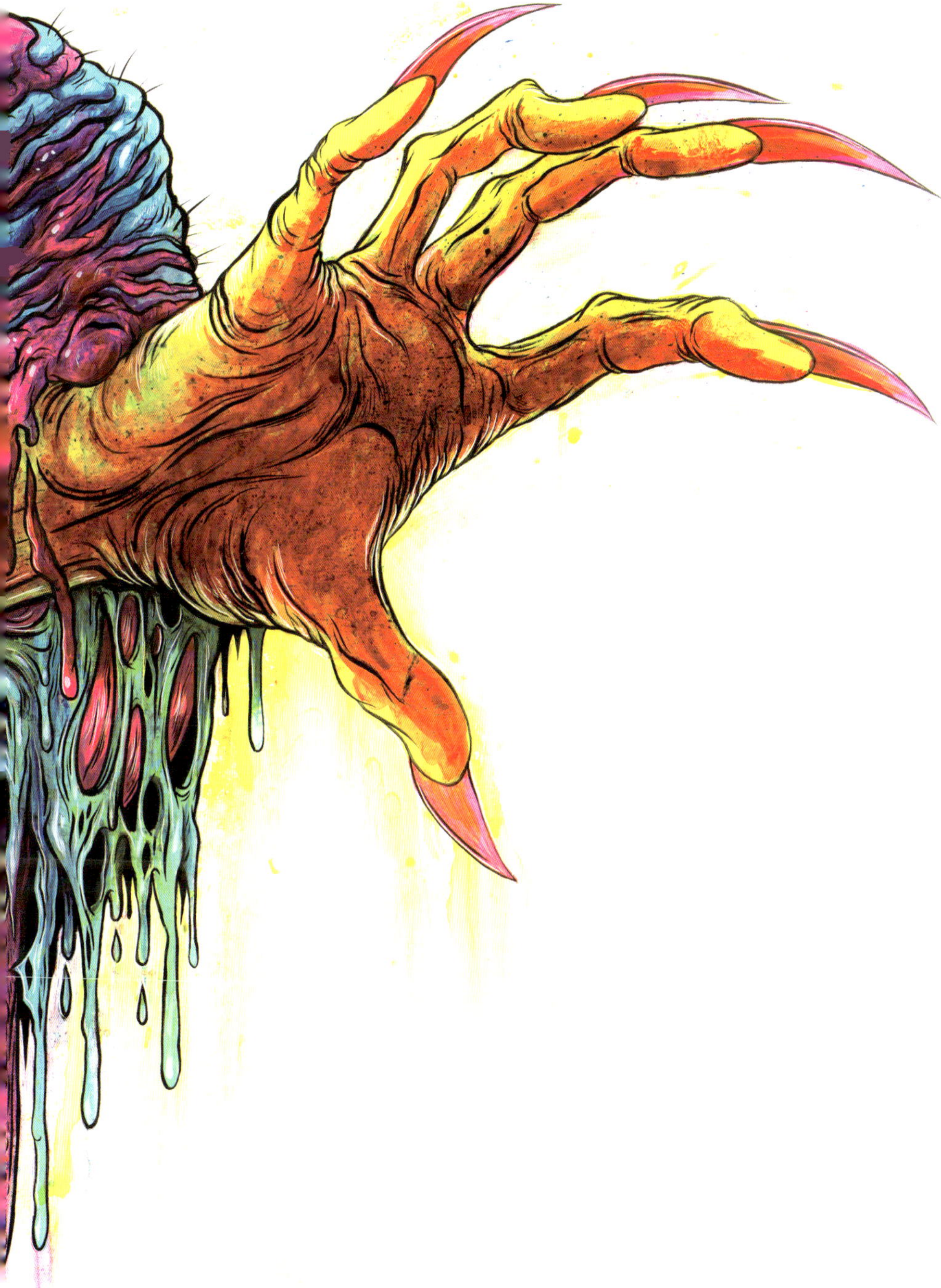

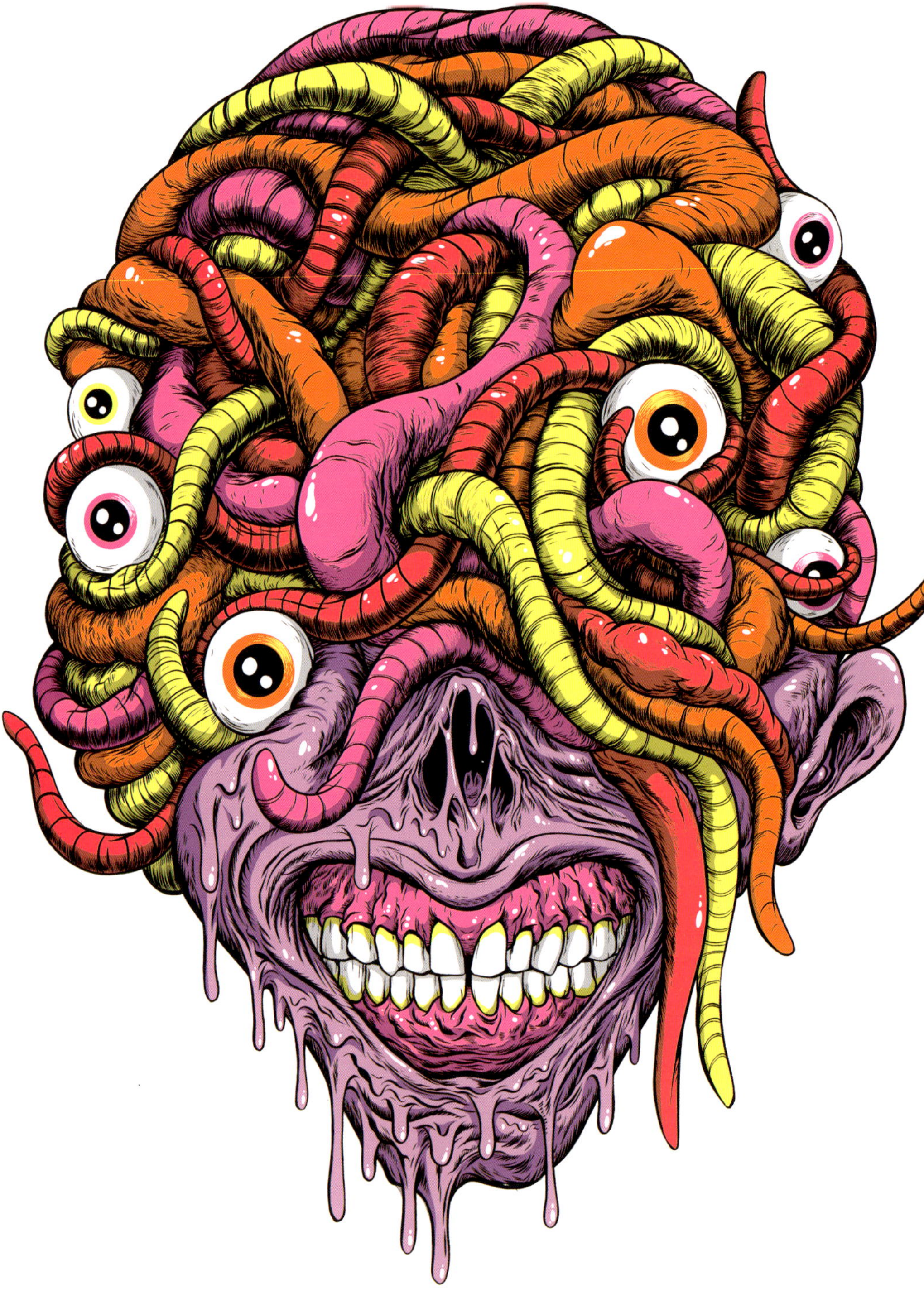

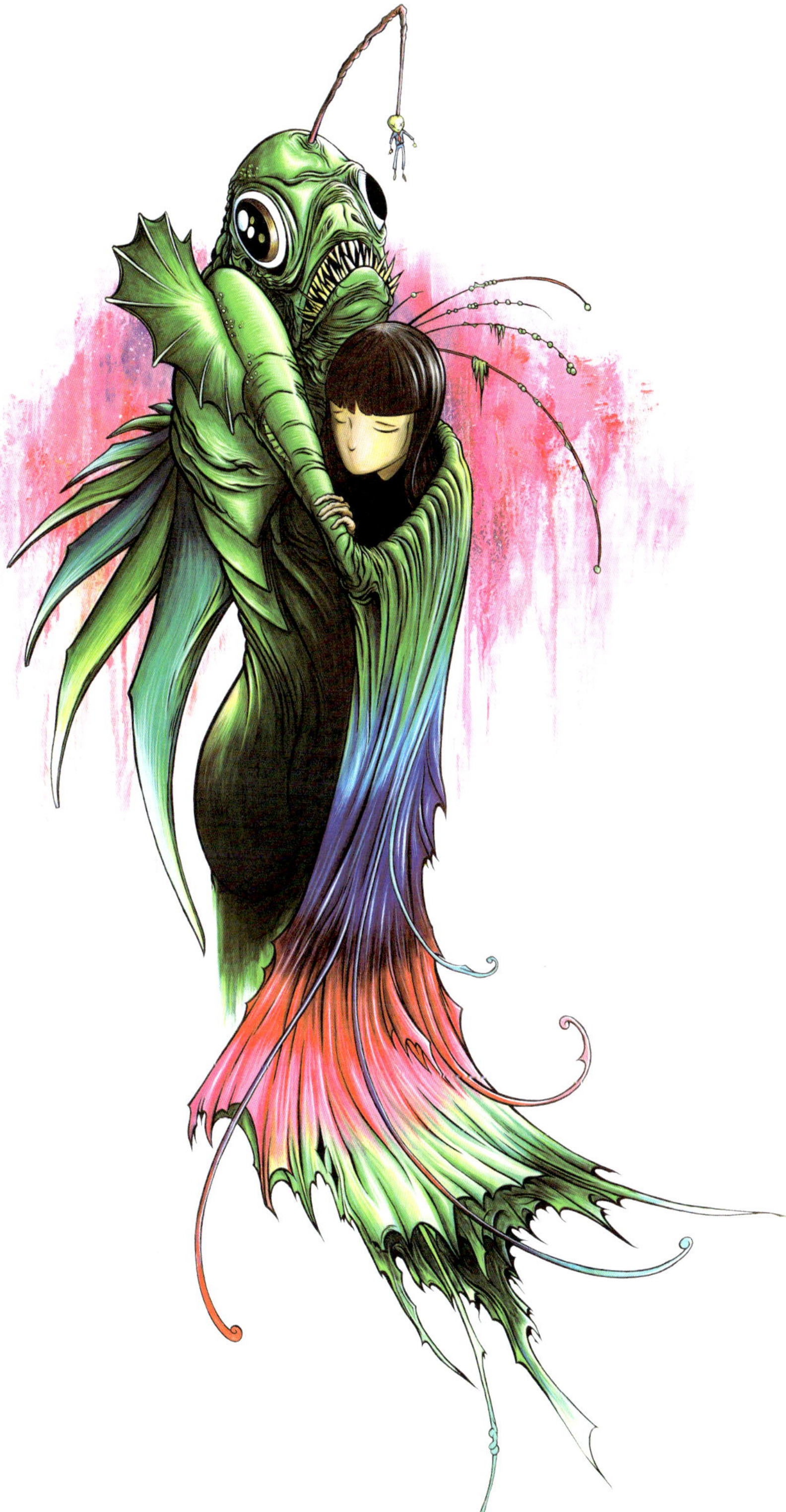

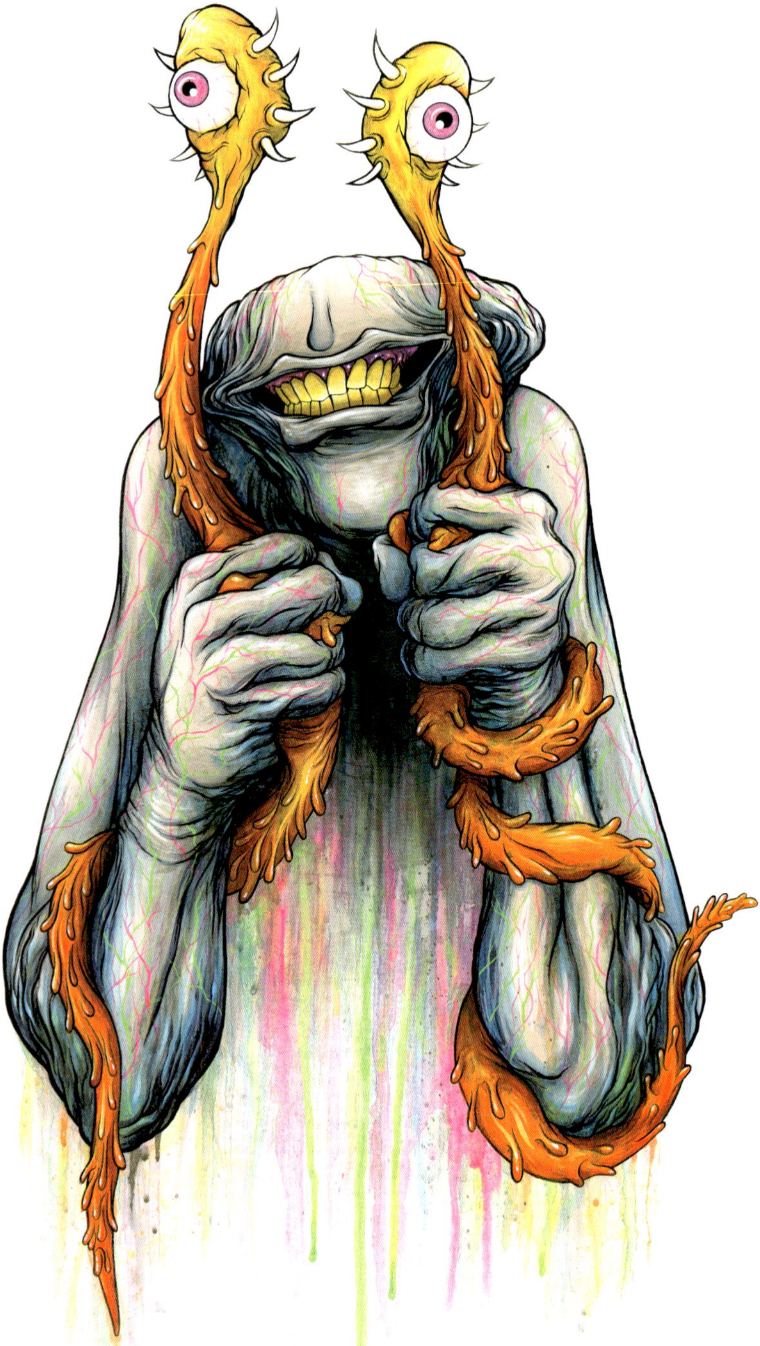

SnakeEyes

rank Carroll's biggest fear was dying alone in war like his father had in The Battle of the Bulge. In 1970, when he was 24 years old, Frank attempted to move from Detroit into Canada in order to dodge the Vietnam War draft and instead pursue his dreams of becoming a writer. Days before moving, Frank's girlfriend, Lorna, revealed that she was egnant and asked Frank to stay in America, accept enrollment in the Army, fight in the war and return home with a new career and a bright future. Frank was raised fatherless, and didn't want his own child to share that experience. If he moved to Canada, he would live, t he would have abandoned his child. If he enrolled in the Army, he could possibly die, but ne had the opportunity to fight and return home. Terrified but dedicated to his new future, and in love with Lorna, he agreed and accepted his enrollment in the Army.

9 weeks later, he arrived in Saigon as part of the 52nd Infantry and was dumped in the iddle of the jungle with his unit. Because of his initial hesitance to kill and obvious fear, he was extensively bullied by his fellow soldiers, often leading Frank to spend entire nights one, sleeping up in the trees, taking the job of lookout just to be separated from those who ullied him. At night, in the trees, though his attention never wavered from his lookout duty, would spend hours writing letters to his girlfriend and future child, sharing fantasies about eir bright futures. Eventually, Frank did make one friend in the jungle, a war journalist and omb-specialist named Peter who Frank had admired for his fearlessness with his camera nd his ability to defuse anything explosive, which had already saved their unit a few times. fter weeks stationed in the same small camp, Peter convinced Frank to separate from his unit and be Peter's lookout and protection while he goes and investigates a secret tribal age that was rumored to be a refuge for Vietnamese mystics and supposed witchdoctors. Peter told Frank that if he helped locate this secret village and keep them safe, they could th take credit for the groundbreaking article that Peter would write, helping Frank launch a career in journalism...

They left hours later in the cover of the night.
Frank led them through the jungle, hacking and slashing through trees, stealthily avoidin the Viet Cong, clearing the path of snakes and spiders, all while Peter shot photos and shared information that he had heard about this secret village they were trying to find, escalating his fantasies of sharing the Pulitzer Prize.

Exhausted, fevered, and starving, they found it. On the surface, this "secret" village resembled a leper colony, with many of the helpless villagers suffering from obvious deformities and ailments, too weak to even oppose Peter and Frank's intrusion. Peter suggested that they leave, fearful of catching an illness and disappointed that the rumor weren't true. But Frank noticed a subtle glow emitting from behind one of the trees and insisted they check it out before leaving. Behind the trees was a makeshift grass hut marked with a symbol that looked like 2 serpents. Inside it, they found the secrets they were looking for. Unlike anything they had ever witnessed, they stumbled in on a group c deformed, decadently robed elderly men and women, chanting amongst a bright green smoke and dancing around a skeleton. And the skeleton... was alive. Peter's camera already in hand he managed to snap about 6 shots before they were noticed, and when they were, each one of these infected mystical tribespeople turned and screeched, their eyes glowing and their teeth gnarling. As the mystics held their hands up toward Peter and Frank, the living skeleton turned its head and looked directly at them as they fled.

Darting out of the village as quickly and as carelessly as they could, Peter slammed his shin against a rogue branch and got his entire leg stuck, stopping him from moving forward. Closely behind them, the trees began to glow green, and the screeching from th mystics could be heard in the distance. Hastily, Frank hacked at the branch with his machete until Peter's leg was finally freed just as they saw the mystics enter into their eyesight. Hobbled, Peter put his arm around Frank as Frank dragged them both as quickly as he could. The mystics not far behind, Frank knew the only way to hide was up in the trees, as he had spent nights there escaping his daily bullying.
Mustering his adrenaline, Frank helped Peter up into a tree, and Frank followed, where they covered themselves in thick leaves and branches. There, they sat motionless as they watched the entire village of mystics and lepers pass beneath them. Hours passed as they sat in the trees. When they both felt they were finally safe, they descended from the tree and let out a large sigh of relief.

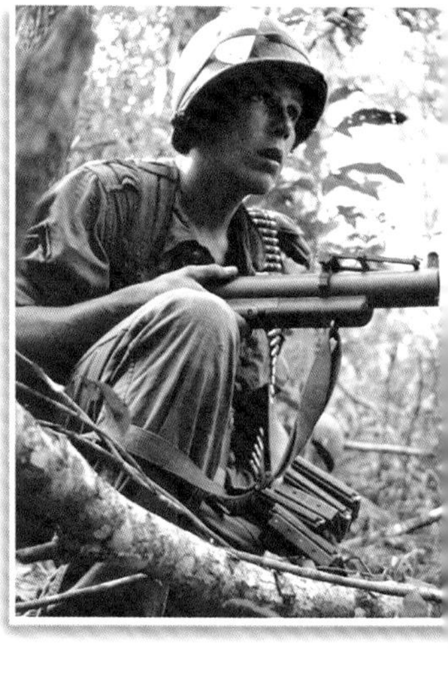

"We're going to be famous, Frank! These shots I got! What we saw!? Those... people?! I can't wait to write about it" Peter said, excitedly.
"Let's just get home," Frank replied...

2 steps into their journey, however, Frank's future fame instantly vanished. At the base of the ree they have been holding onto for dear life, Frank heard a click as his foot pressed into the mud, and he knew what had happened. He had stepped on a mine. Frank looked at the round. Peter looked at Frank. Frank looked up and back at Peter and asked, "Peter... can you help me? Can you do anything? Can you defuse this?"

Peter looked at Frank with a subtle hint of guilt for only seconds before he held up the camera and pointed to it as he said, "I can, Frank, but... I'm going to be famous."

And just like that, Peter hobbled away into the jungle as Frank stood there, watching Peter abandon him, knowing that at any moment, Frank would face his biggest fear. He would die alone in the jungle. Tears in his eyes, and a body filled with regret and anger, he pulled out a pen and a piece of paper and began writing a letter to Lorna and his baby. He got as far as "I love y-" when the mine exploded, disintegrating most of Frank's torso and the top half of his head. Frank laid in the middle of the jungle in Saigon, alone, and dead.

or days, Frank's body lay still in the jungle, his love letter faded and nearly evaporated from the moisture of the jungle, his body affected the same way. Withered, dampered, and torn apart, praying mantises and ants had already begun taking shelter in his torso. It was at this state that a cloaked figure appeared amongst the brush. Surrounding the figure was a familiar green smoky aura. Hunched over Frank's lifeless corpse, the stranger opened a bag, removed a dead pig from it, and crudely removed the pig's intestines and eyeballs, discarding the other remains. The intestines were cut into two long pieces and stretched out on the wet ground. The eyeballs were shoved into the ends of the guts, and the stranger began to chant.

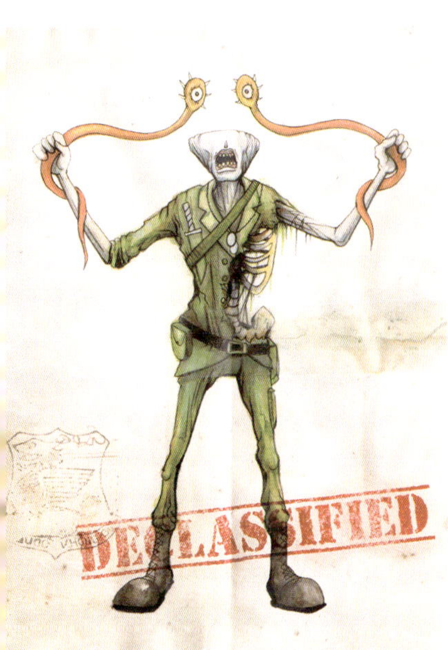

Smoke filled the forest, monkeys and other wildlife could be heard screeching in the distance, bright green lights emitted from the stranger's hands and reflected off of the condensation on the jungle leaves, resembling some kind of distorted third world disco.

More chanting. More rumbling. The pig intestines changed color, began to move, and then slithered their way around Frank's exposed dead arms, making their way to his hands. Simultaneously, Frank's muscles twitched, starting with his legs, and moving up to the half of his head that was still intact. His body began to stand, and soon it was fully upright. The stranger, still cloaked, stood back and watched as the intestinal serpents wrapped themselves around Frank's hands, moved their heads in place above Frank's severed nasal cavity, and seemed to mentally link with Frank's newly reanimated body. With the serpents' functioning eyes now floating above Frank's head, a brand new complete face was formed. At this moment, Frank's mouth peeled open and he let out a bellowing scream, which quickly changed into a subtle and confident smirk.

Frank was alive...

To Be Continued...

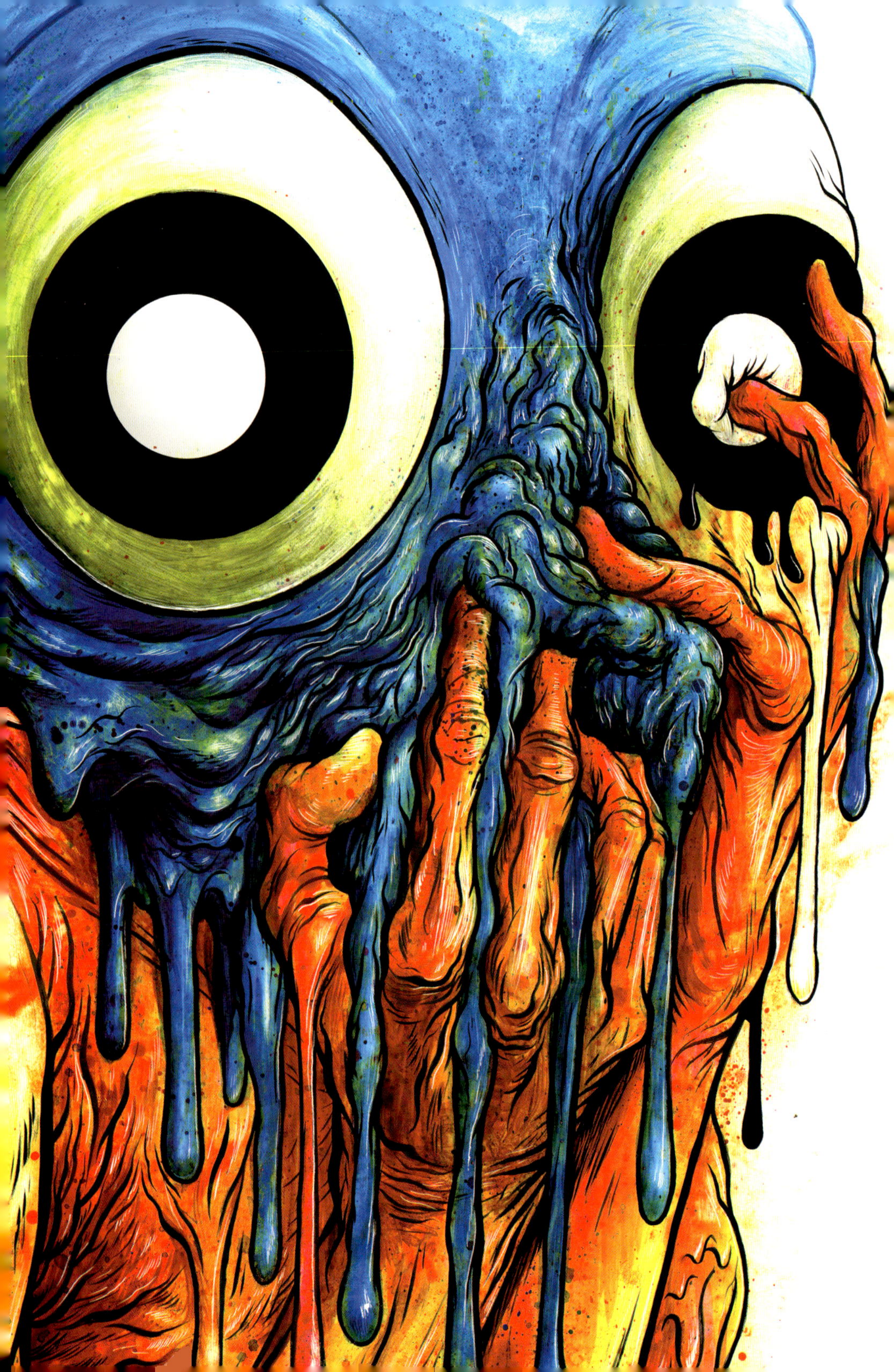

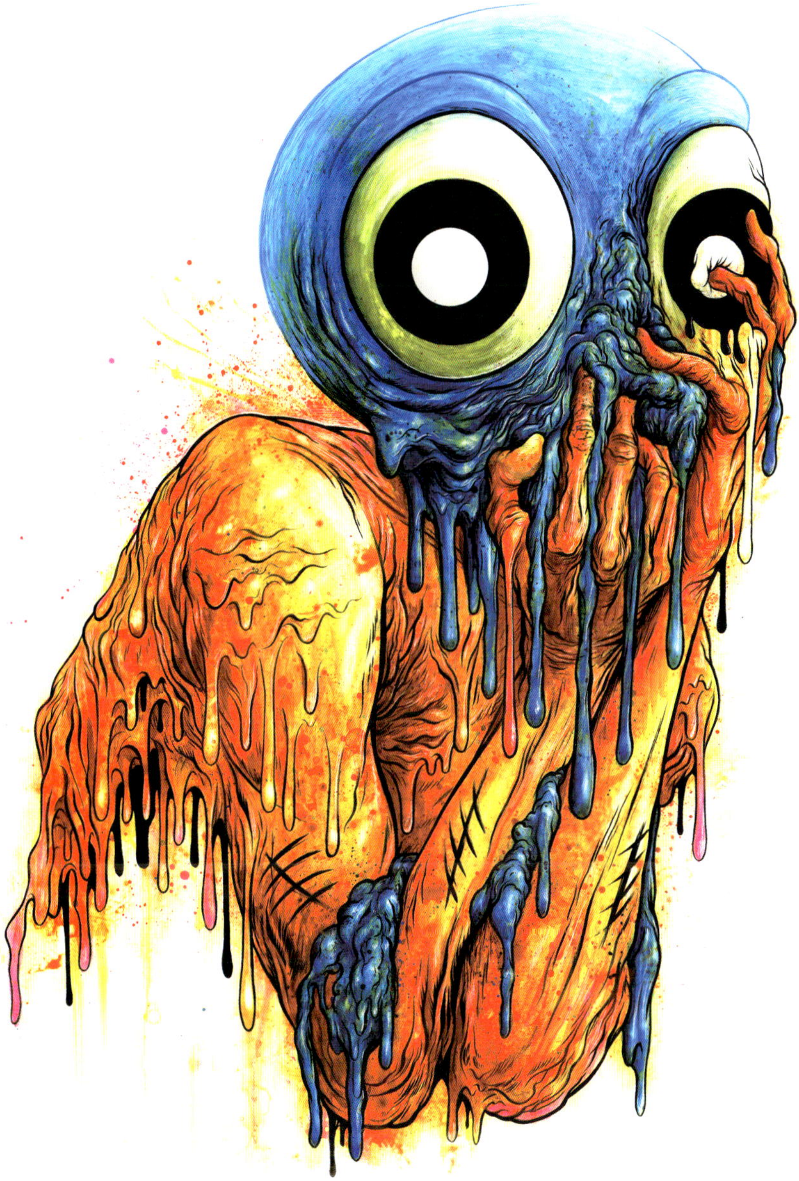

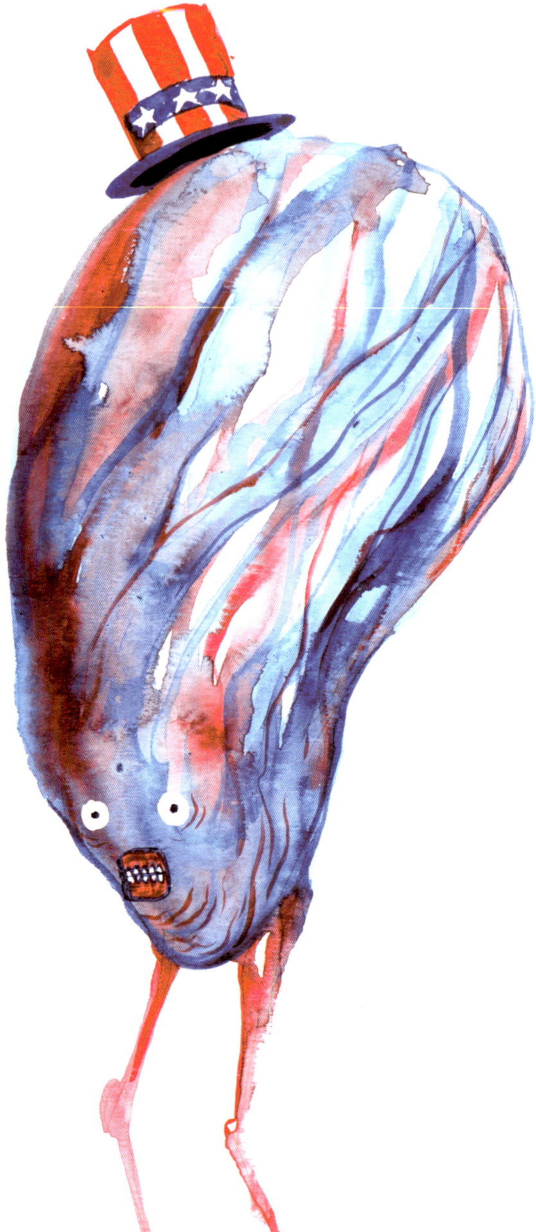

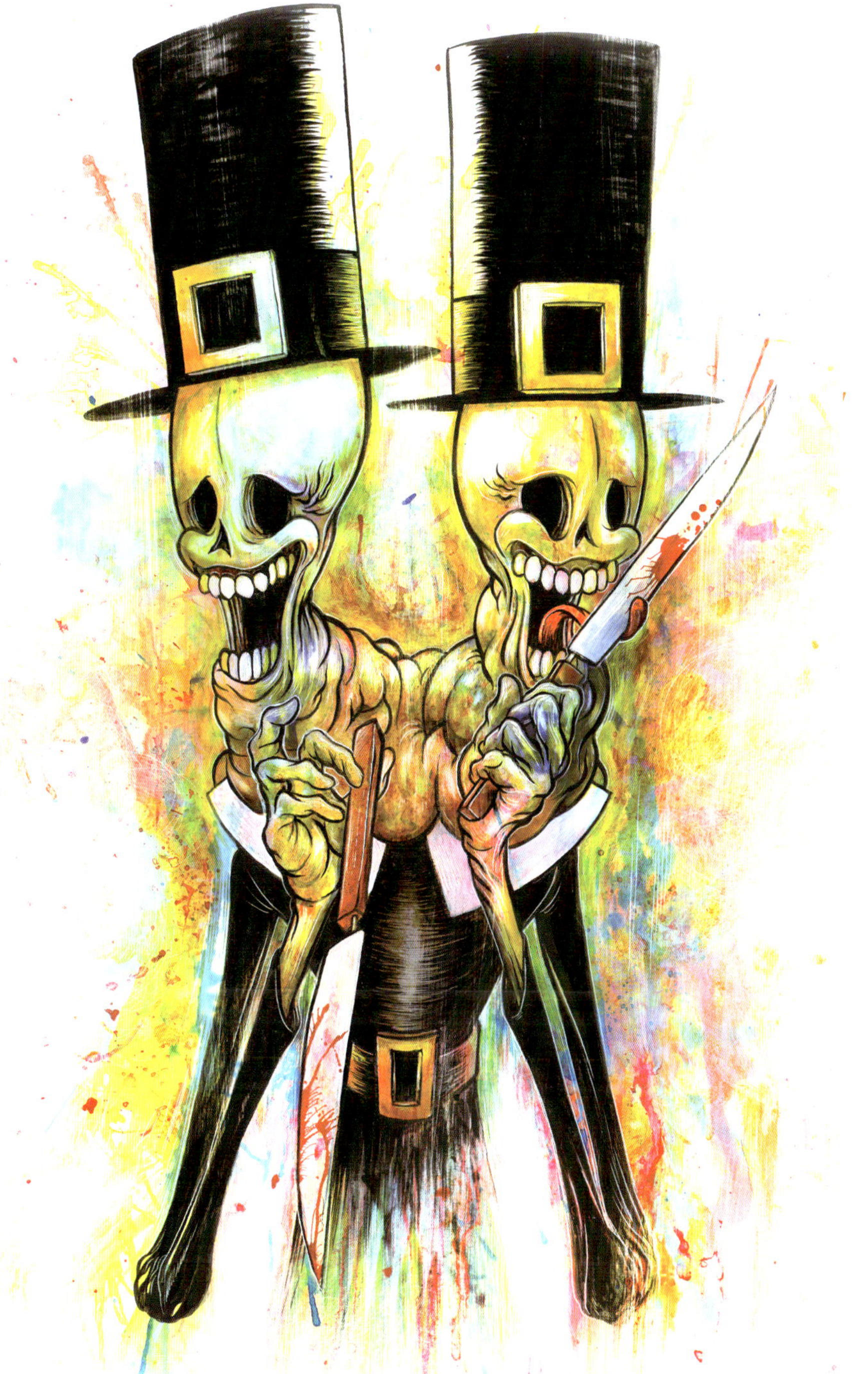

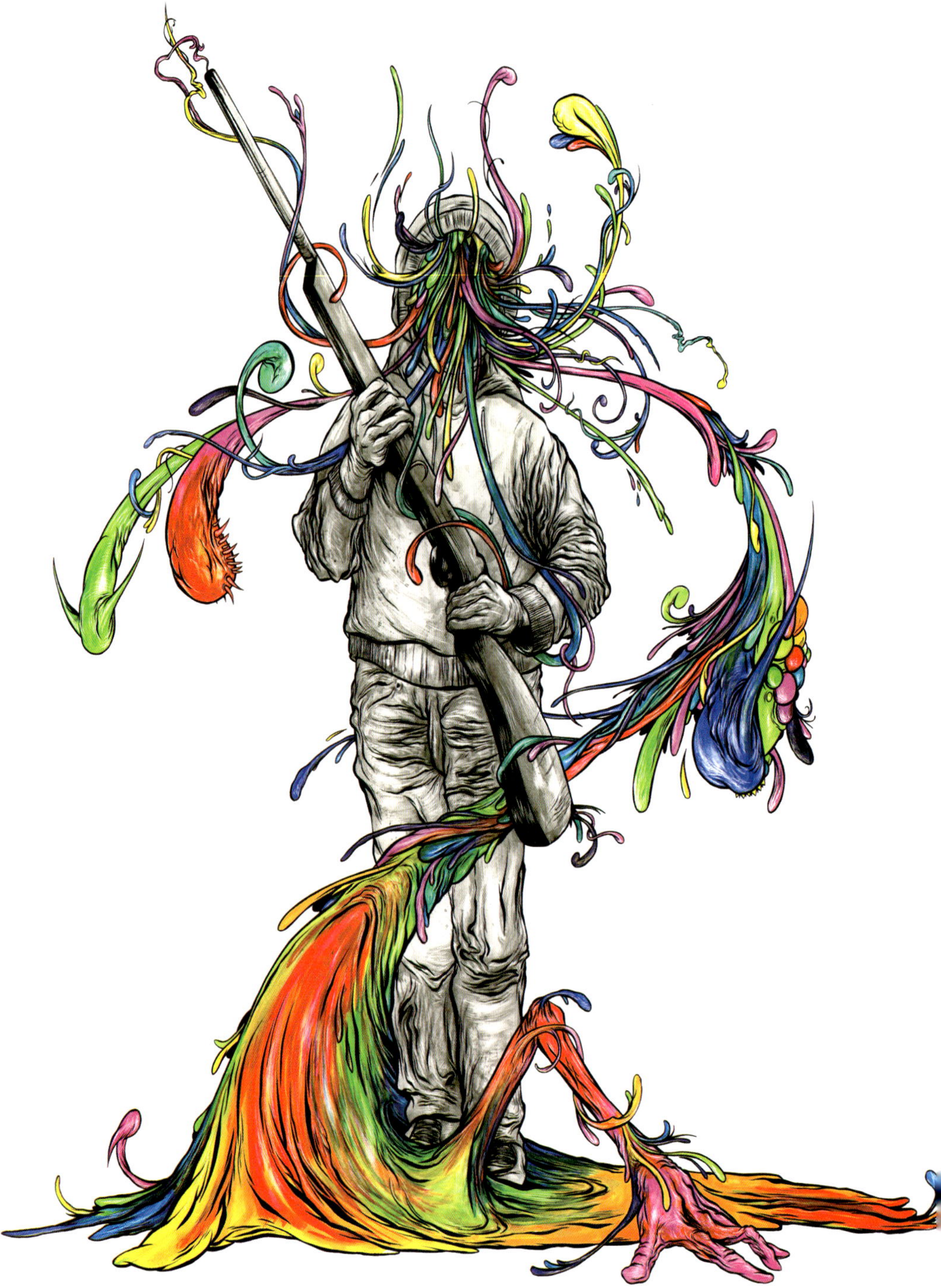

Father Killer

Found inside the journals of Gregg Patterson:

October 24, 1987

I never really wanted to write anything in this journal except stories about dragons and cyclopses and stuff before. But today is different...

After I was born, my mom produced an overabundance of white blood cells in her body because of a disease. So whenever she would try to eat, the blood cells would think that the food was an enemy, and they would attack the food by making her vomit it up. By the time I was 4, Mom weighed 79 pounds and all she could eat was rice, bananas and plums. Dad never believed she was sick. He used to say it was 'cause of guilt for her cheating on him before I was born. He said she felt bad 'cause she knew in her heart that he wasn't my real Dad. But Mom never cheated, and Dad was really my Dad. Either way, Dad's always hated me 'cause he thought I ain't his. So when Mom starved to death when I was 9, Dad started being extra mean to me. He made me mow the lawn every day, which wasn't that bad, except he made me bite down on a piece of wood to keep my muscles tight while I did it so that I would "get my man-strength". But all it did was cut my mouth with splinters. He hit me a lot. Mostly when I would talk about Mom, or when I would beg to sleep inside 'cause it was too cold in the shed. And he would make me shoot things, too. "G'head, you take this rifle and you point it at them bunnies and you pull that trigger to get some fuckin' hair on that little girl chest 'a yours!" So I did it. Bunnies, squirrels, even the occasional cat that hopped our fence just because it was OUR property, he said.

And it wasn't even for food. Dad was a vegetarian.

My childhood was disgusting.

But after 13 years, I finally rebelled.

Today was the day that I killed my father.

October 25, 1987

I slept through the night. And for the first time in my life, I remembered my dreams. I dreamt that my life is finally... going to be beautiful. I wonder what all that noise and those lights are outside of our house.

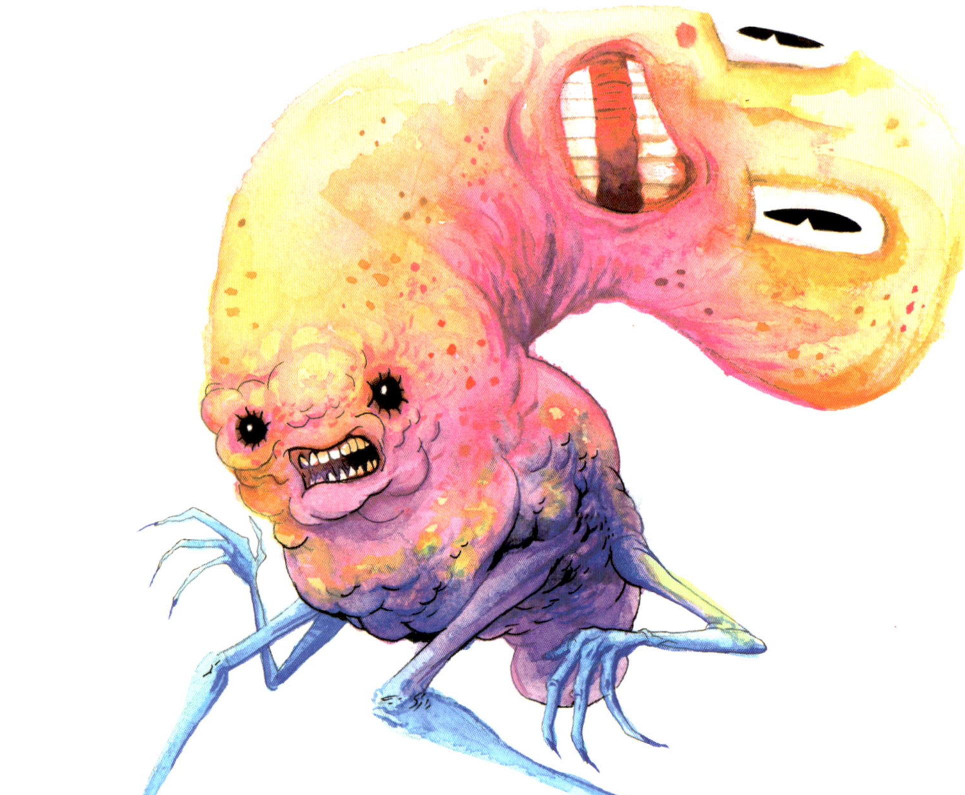

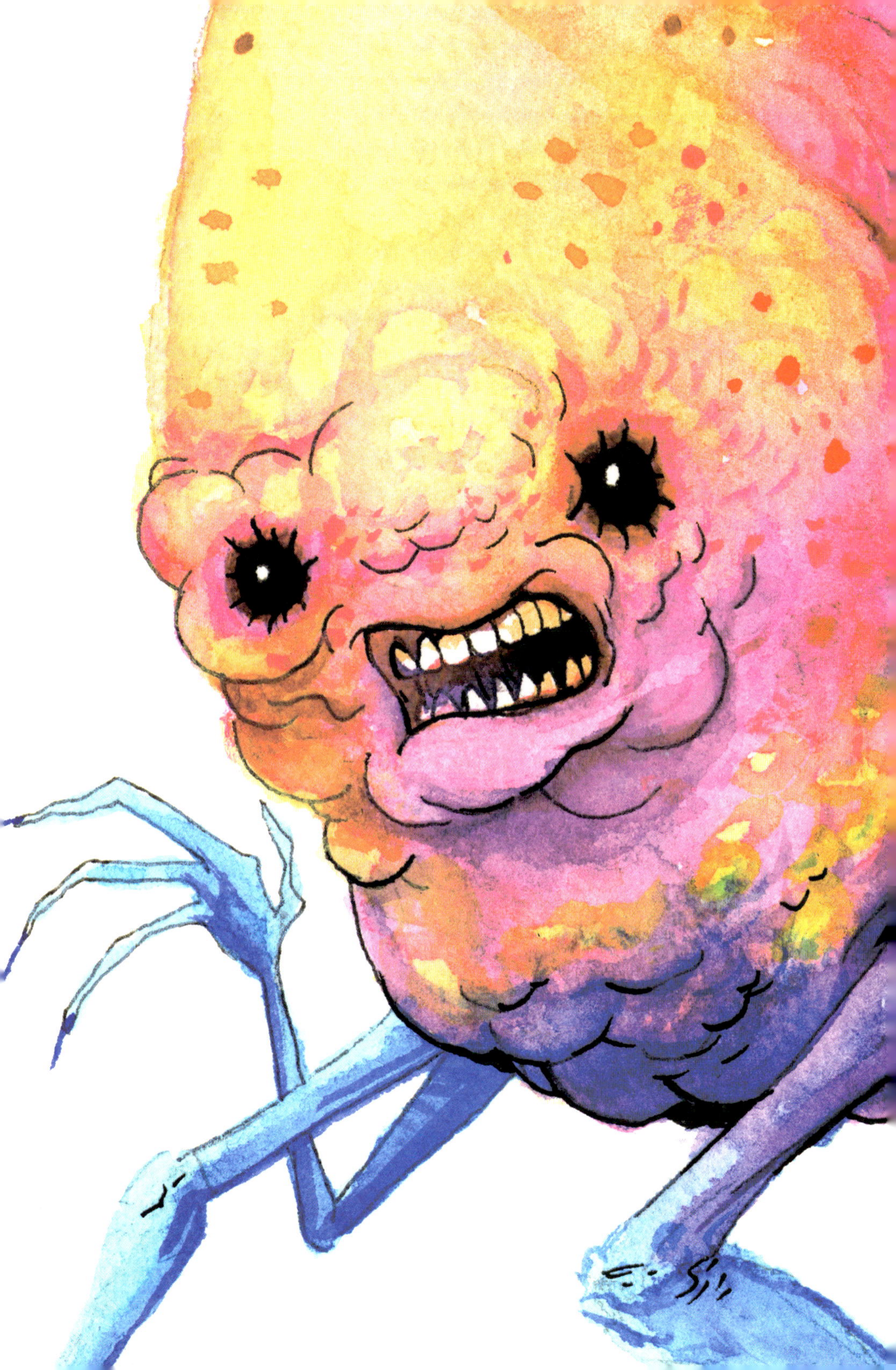

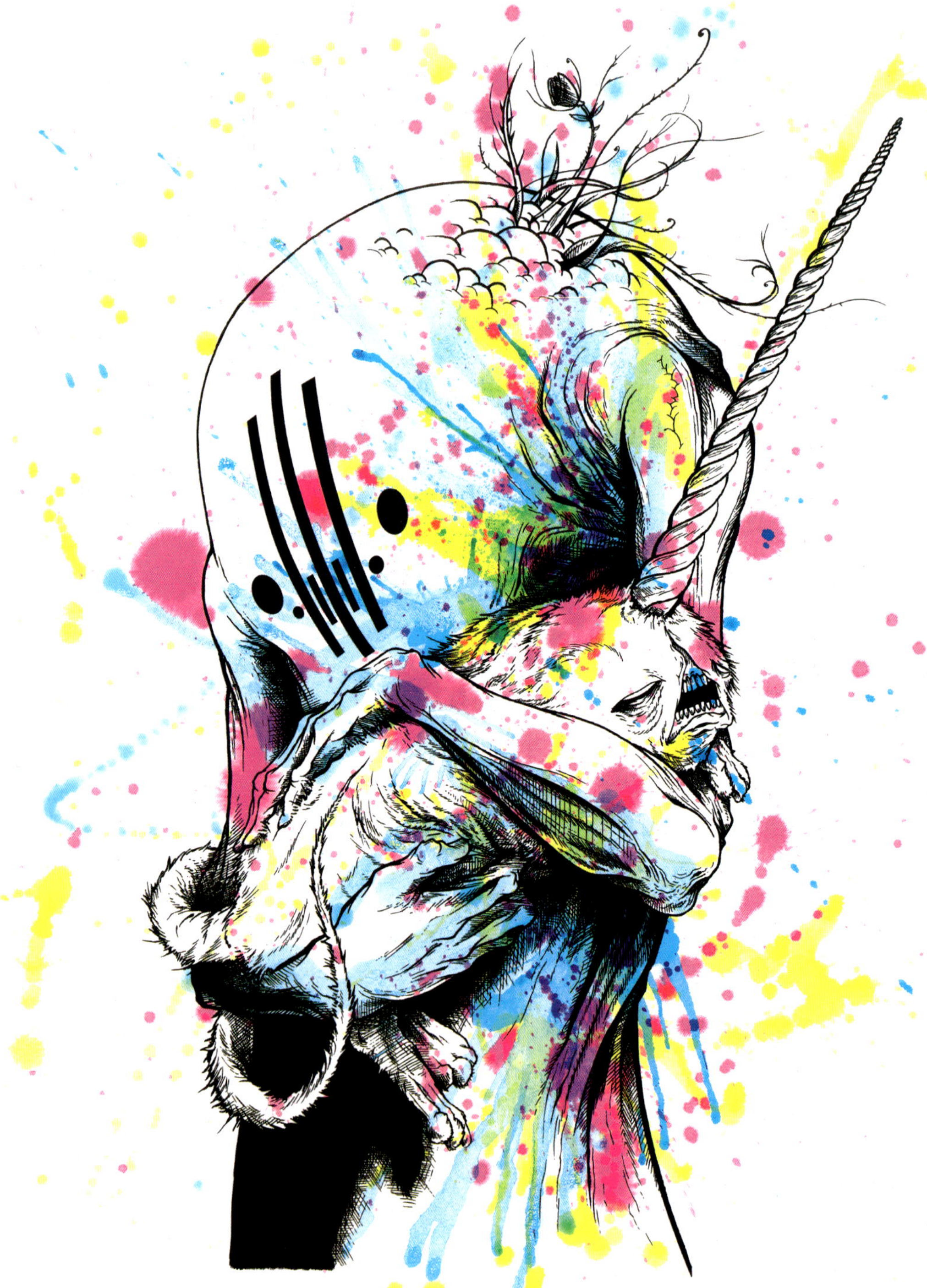

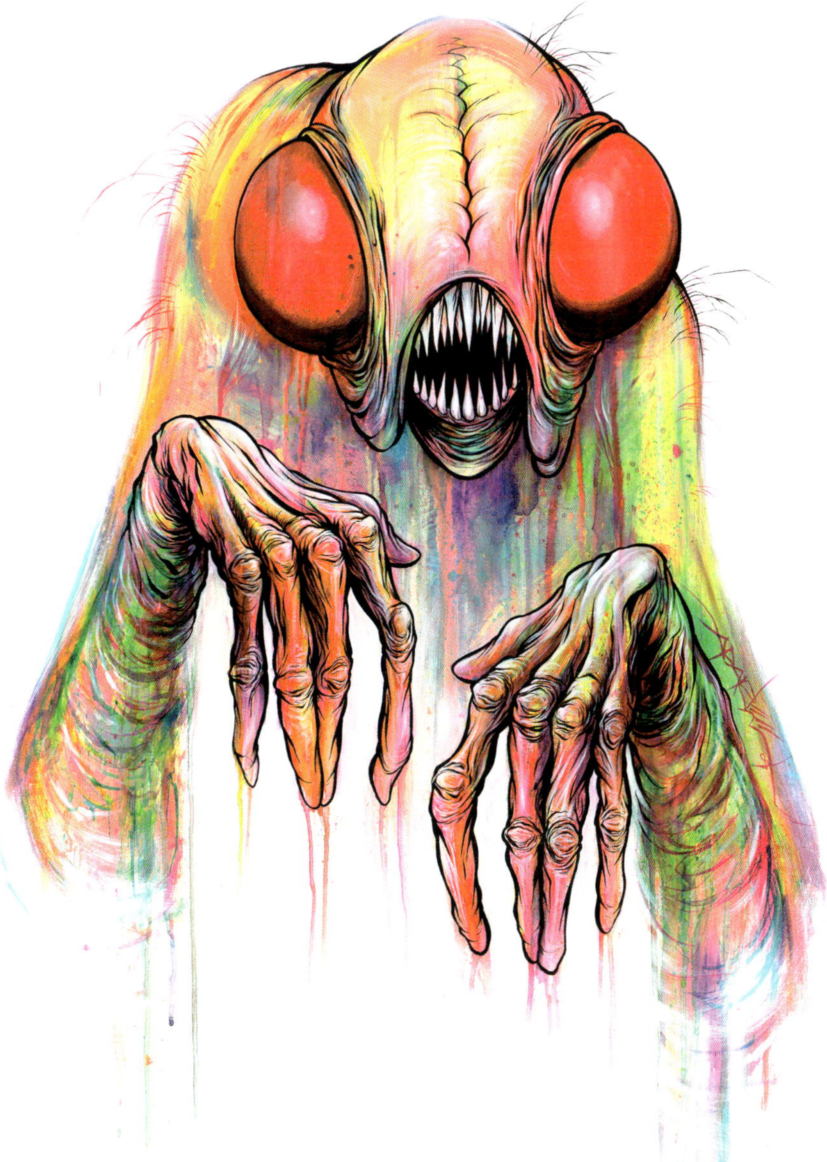

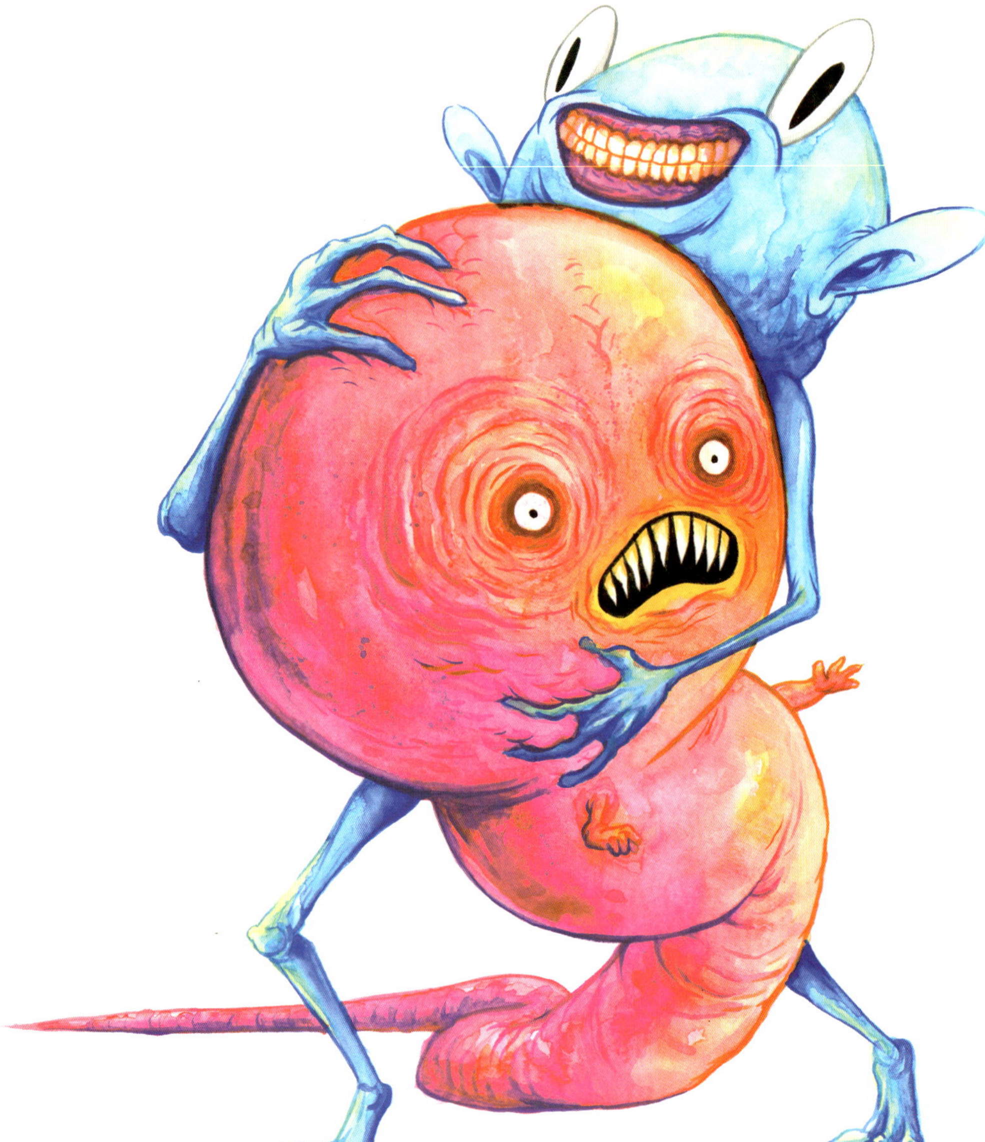

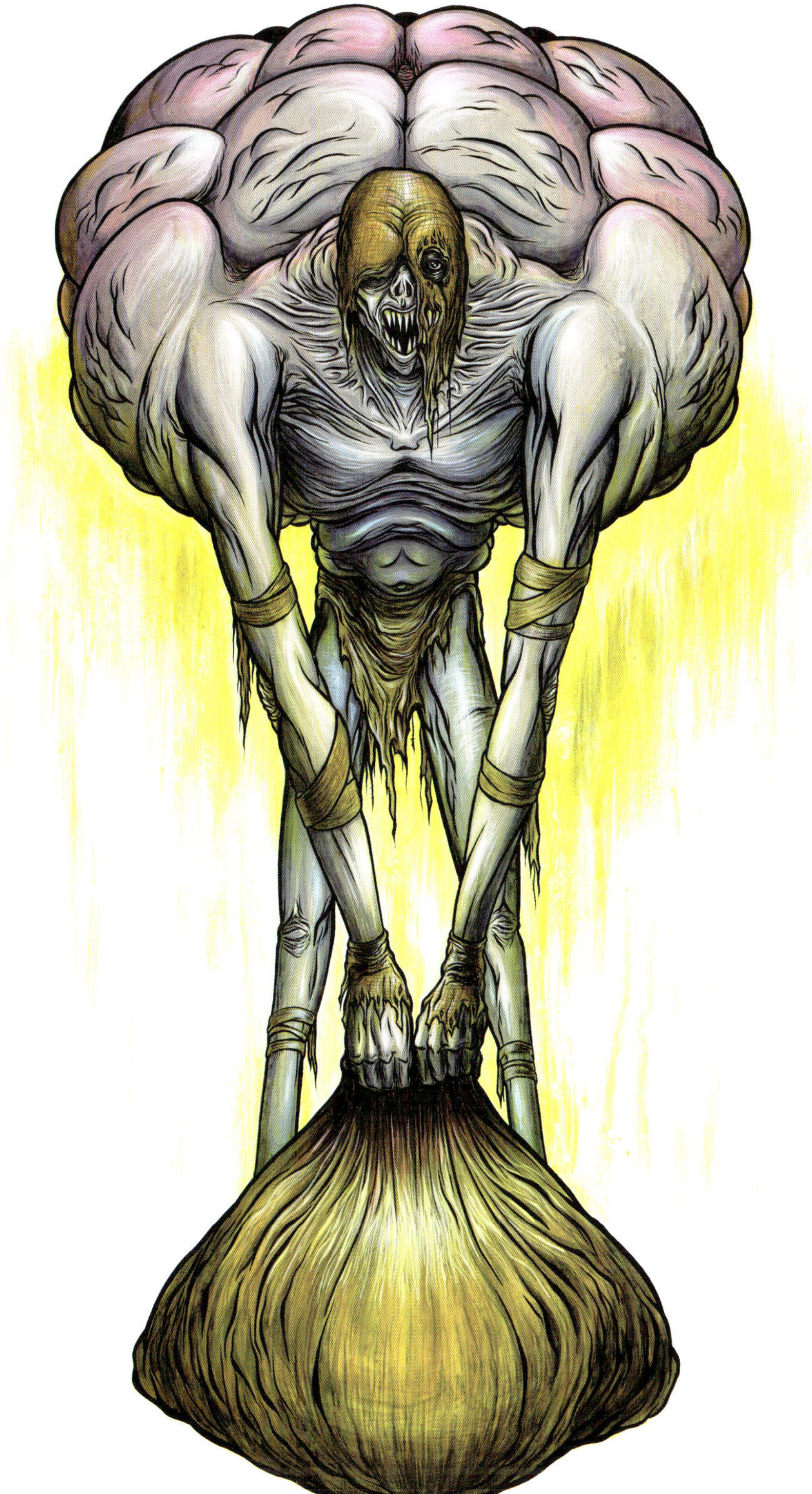

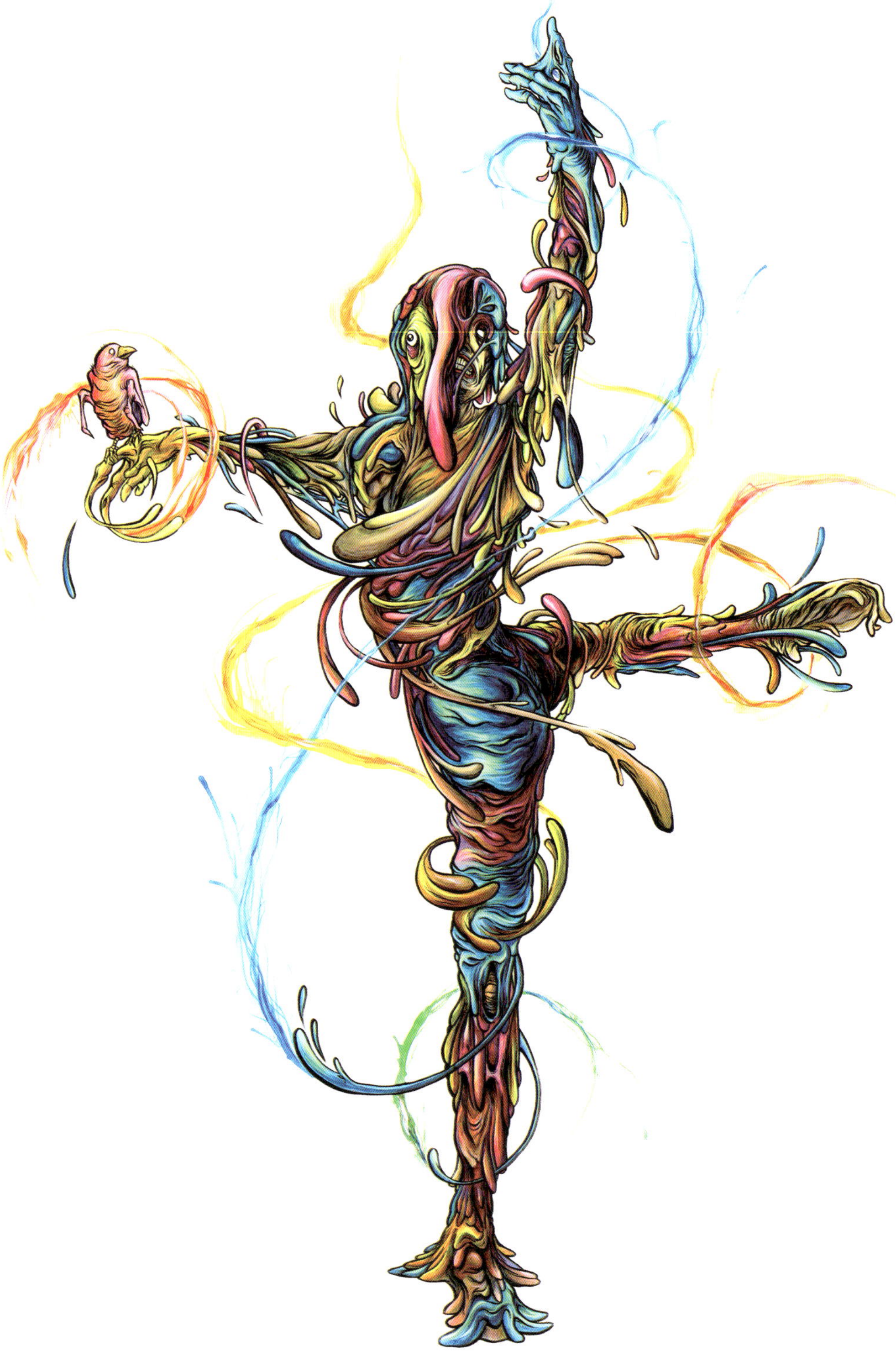

The SKIN THIEF

Joelle Moreau's skin was worth a fortune. The routines she had to endure in order to eep her skin pristine would seem alien to anyone outside of the fashion world in Paris, rance. But to Joelle, who was too famous to actually live in Paris and had to reside on ne outskirts in Barbizon, skin maintenance was just a normal routine, even if it did take to six hours each day. The rewards for her perfection grew exponentially after her first ajor magazine cover. Offer upon offer poured into her agency after her photos became e talk of Fashion Week— no thanks to the magazine photographer who had been filling for the regular photographer. He had duped her into being involved in a pathetic shoot vith a broken camera and had treated her terribly. It was simply Joelle herself who was nesmerizing. Her skin seemed to literally radiate on film. The caramelized sheen of her nblemished skin captivated the eyes of anyone who was lucky enough to view it. That, coupled with her dedication to caring for her skin and her career above all else, was what had made her a mint over the course of a few short years.

Needless to say, when Joelle developed a rash from an allergic reaction to a small mount of lavender in a new skin product that she had been asked to endorse, she did ot handle it lightly. She single-handedly prevented the product from ever seeing a retail store shelf, forcing the company into bankruptcy before it even had a chance. Meanwhile, starting on the day Joelle had first noticed the rash, she began having nightmares. But these nightmares were not her average disturbing visions. They were more vivid, realistic, and horrific than anything she had experienced prior. The first few nightmares she experienced contained imagery so terrifying to her, she could hardly ear to verbally recount them to others. She explained that in her dreams, anything that came into contact with her bare skin would stick to it, and when she moved, her skin would painfully peel off. Luckily, when Joelle's dreams became even more lucid, she developed the ability to consciously control her actions in her dreams. Therefore, she vas able to come up with a simple solution: she would not let anything touch her skin in her dreams.

lthough Joelle had managed somewhat to take control of her dreams, she was unable to control her rash, which was now spreading. It had started on the back of her hand, and despite treatment by two different dermatologists, it had eventually spread up the entire length of her arm. She had cancelled multiple photo shoots within a two-week period but she knew that a reputation for cancelling jobs is not something that a model ould afford to have at the peak of her career. The rash soon spread to her face and lips. n her eyes, she looked hideous. Joelle stayed inside of her bungalow in Barbizon and drank heavily to pass the time and while she waited for the rash to subside. When she ould fall asleep drunk, however, her central nervous system function would be impaired by the effects of the alcohol, making it impossible for her to control her dreams. As a resutt, her nightmares soon became much worse...

Her visions acquired a bizarre and terrifying addition to which she later referred to a the "Skin Thief." A gangly and awkward, colorful but sloppy lump of a man whose skin seemed to be constantly melting and reforming on his body, the Skin Thief would leave trails of watery flesh as he chased Joelle, screaming that he needed he skin for his enjoyment. Joelle wondered fearfully what kind of "enjoyment" he would derive from her skin, until she witnessed something appalling. Joelle, who had a small crush on her agent, Maxwell, would sometimes bring him into her dreams during her lucid states to comfort her. Later, when the Skin Thief haunted her nightmares, she would bring him in for protection. During one of many traumatic dreams involving the Skin Thief, Maxwell helped Joelle hide while he distracted the wet, disgusting beast. While peering out from inside a small abandoned café, Joell witnessed the Skin Thief suddenly pirouette and raise his arms up and down, flingir loosened and broken skin around like flesh-rain. The "dance" itself was far from threatening, but the effects of it were deadly. His performance summoned a barrag of featherless crows, which he had the ability to control. Realizing that Maxwell ha distracted him from Joelle, the Skin Thief sent the naked crows darting in his direction. Maxwell attempted to run, but failed to get far. As the Skin Thief's dance continued, the crows surrounded Maxwell, working together to peel all of his skin from his body with their beaks as he screamed in agony. The crows carried the ski through the air back to the Skin Thief and draped it over his melting body like a soggy, bloody blanket. Joelle, despite a vague understanding that it was only a nightmare, stood frozen in terror as she watched the Skin Thief rub Maxwell's skin against his body and writhe in demented ecstasy and the crows sang a song of gargling, blood-filled squawks.

This dream proved too much for Joelle's brain to process. The graphic and haunting image of the Skin Thief's rain dance, combined with her still-spreading rash, her alcoholism and her diminished sleep eventually drove her over the edge of sanity. Joelle decided that she would remove her own skin before allowing the Skin Thief "enjoy" it like he had enjoyed Maxwell's. So, in a fit of tears and madness, she took potato peeler from a drawer in her maid's quarters and began to peel off her own skin.

That night Maxwell stopped by Joelle's house to check on her, as he had been doir periodically since her tragedy had begun. He found Joelle, laying on the linoleum floor of the kitchen, alive, but unconscious from blood loss. There were piles and piles of blood-soaked skin shavings scattered around her body. She must have shaved off forty percent of her upper torso before passing out. Luckily, she was still alive, but the Skin Thief literally "pulled off" another heist. She would never be the same.

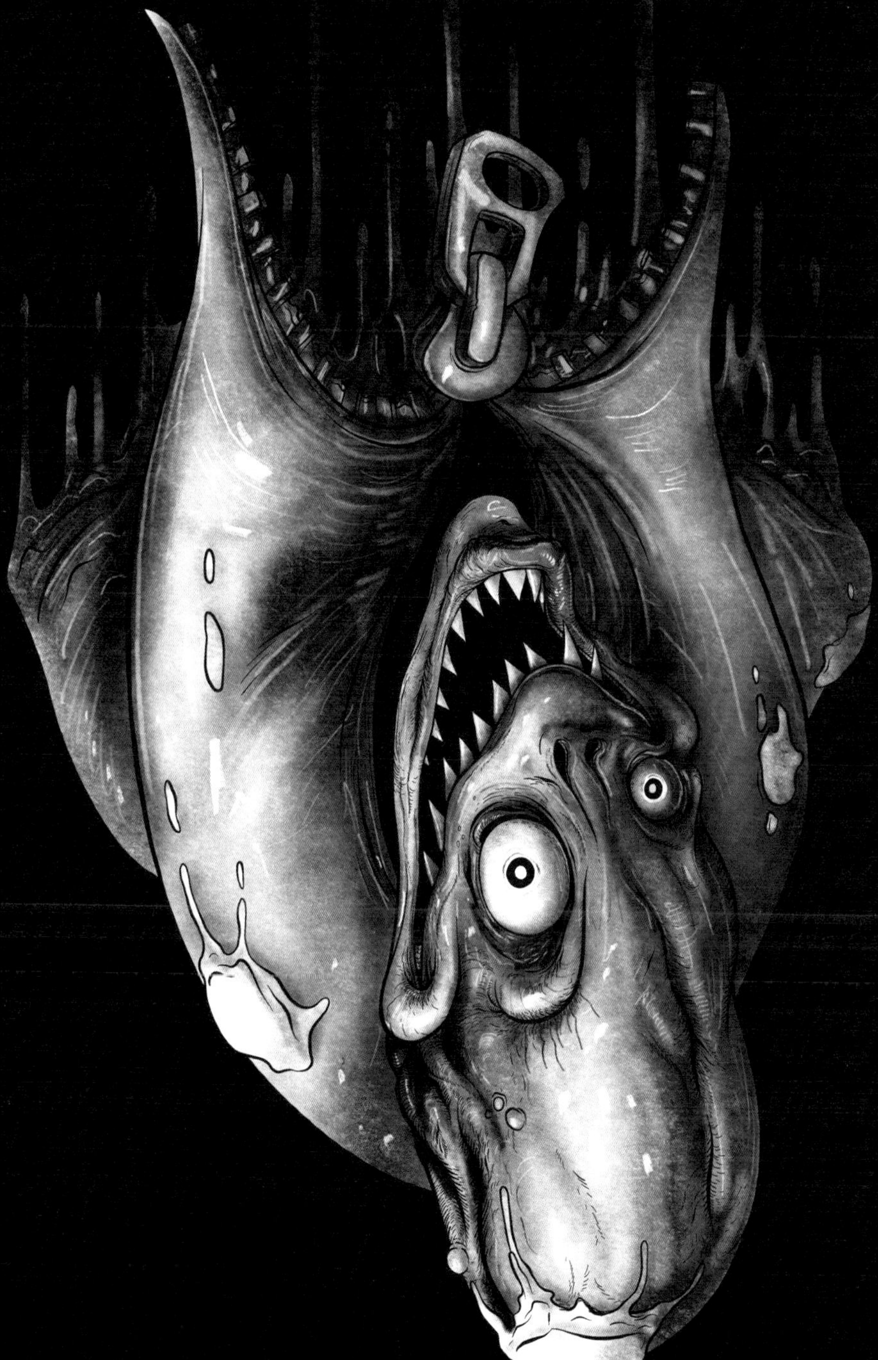

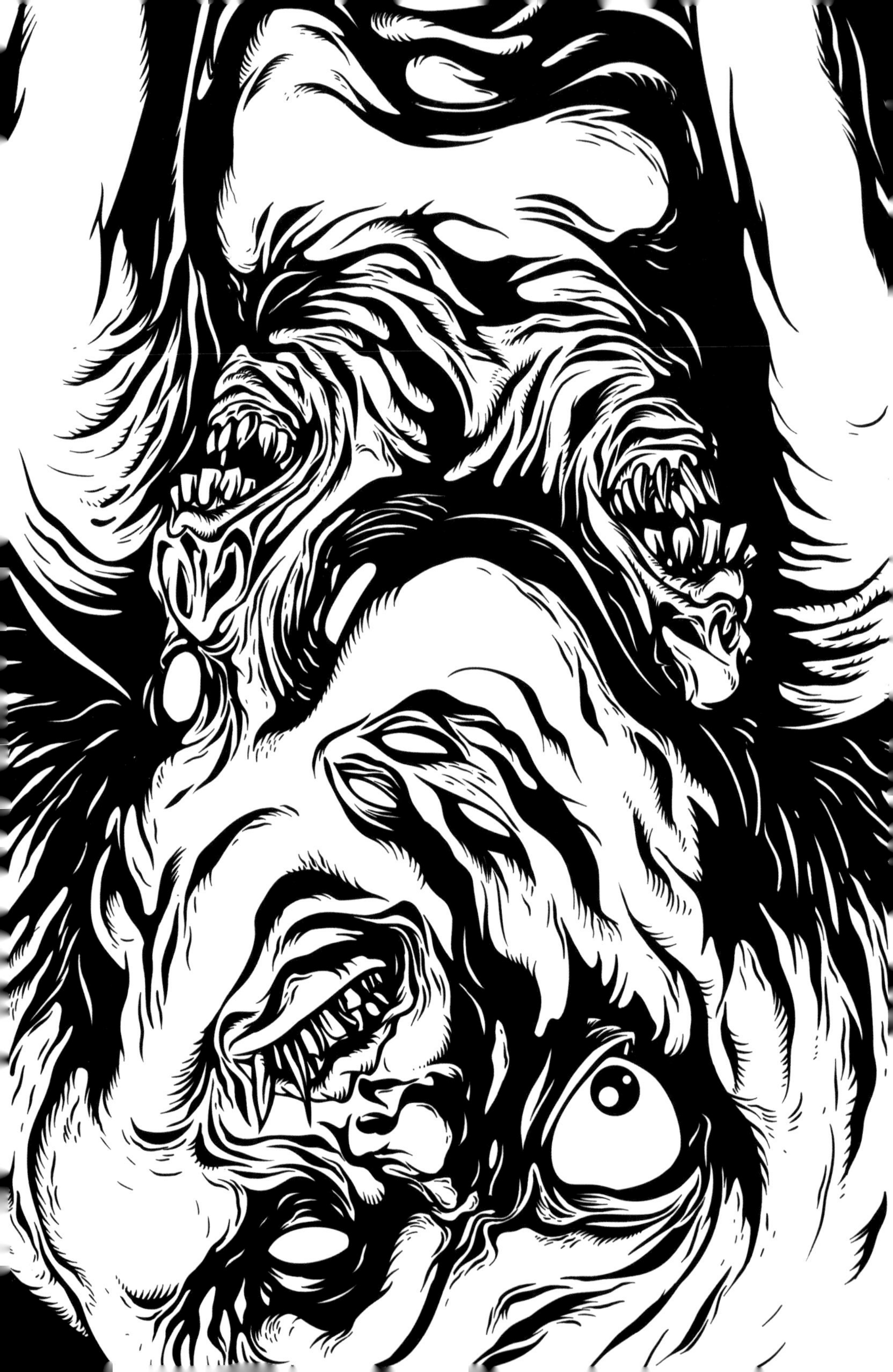

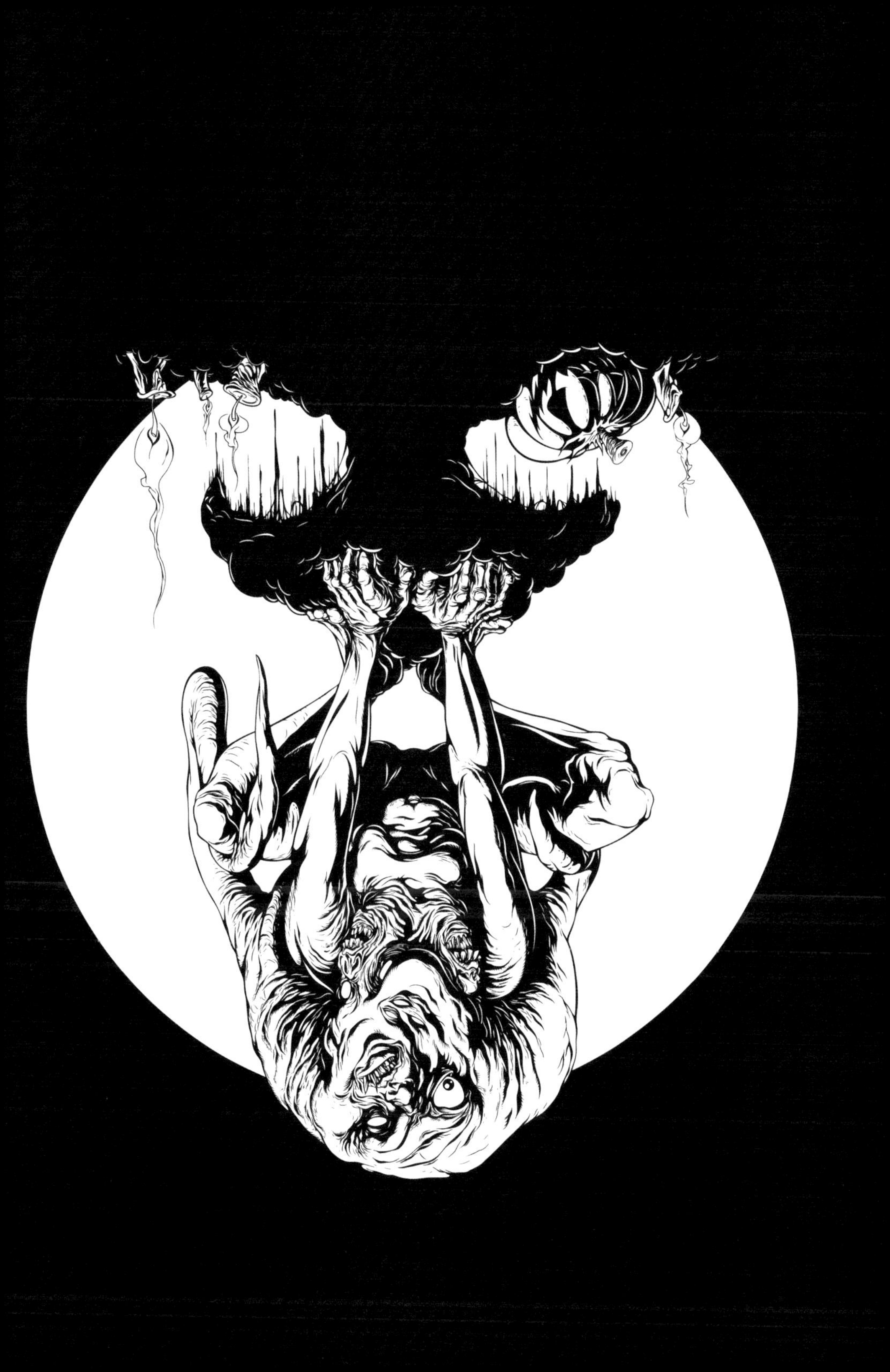

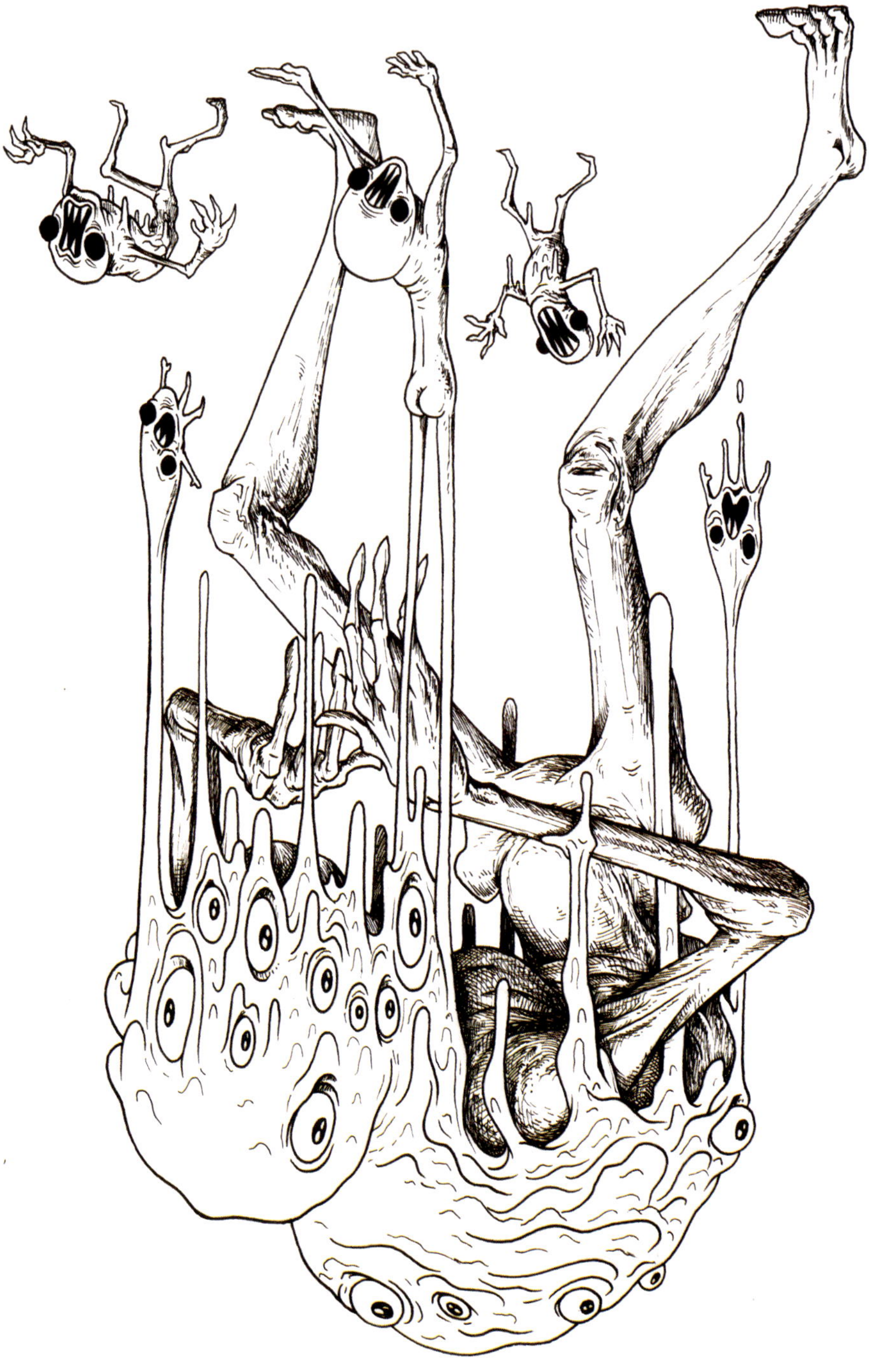

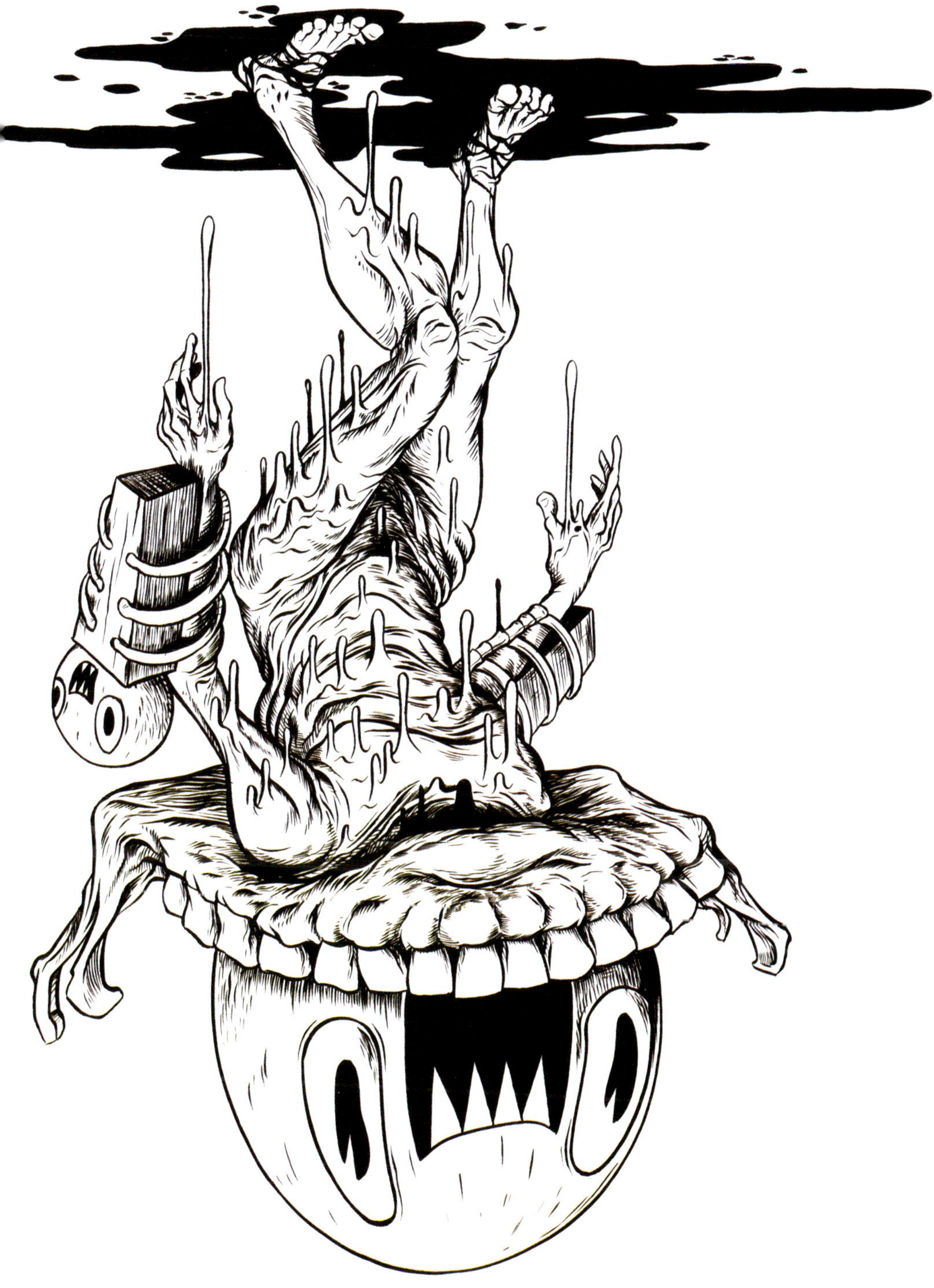

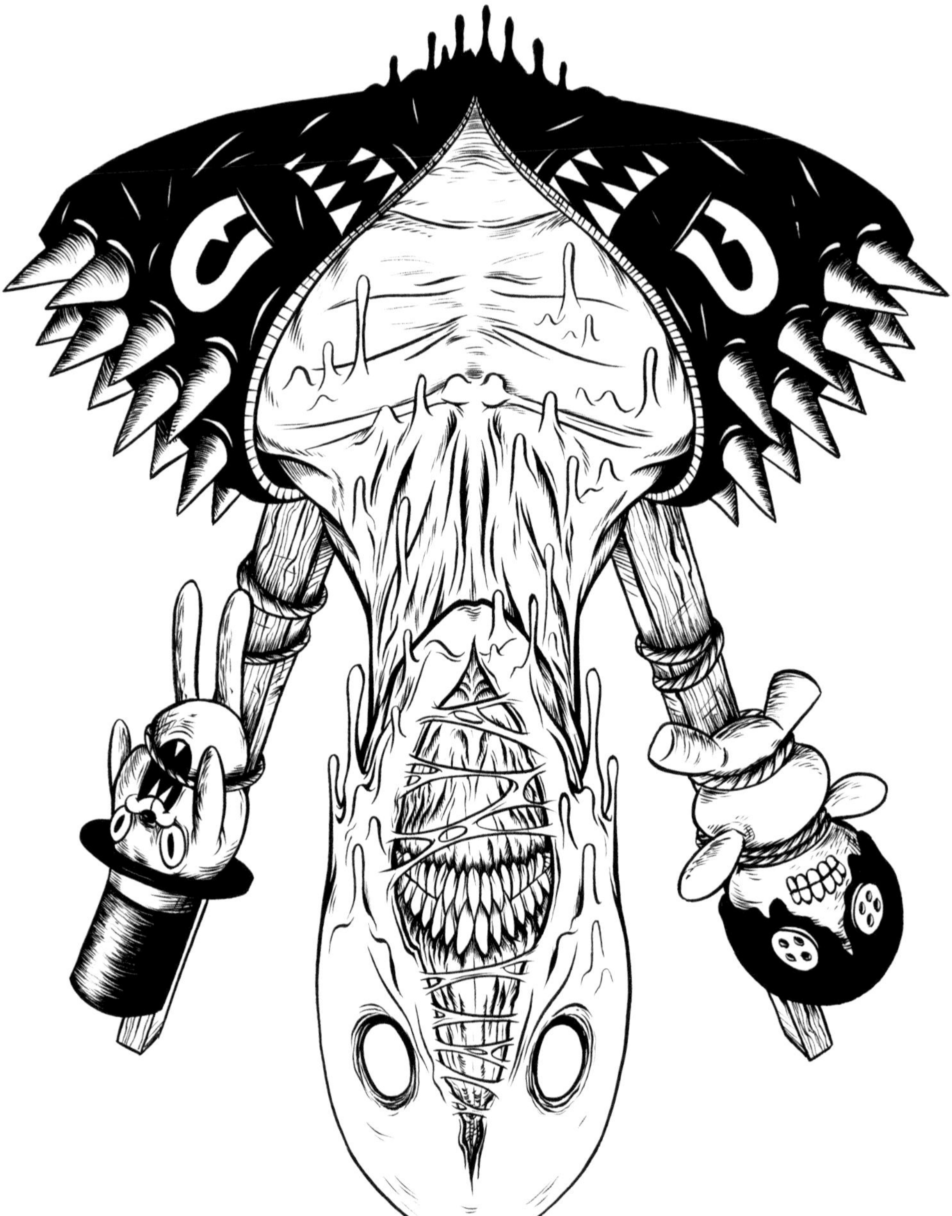

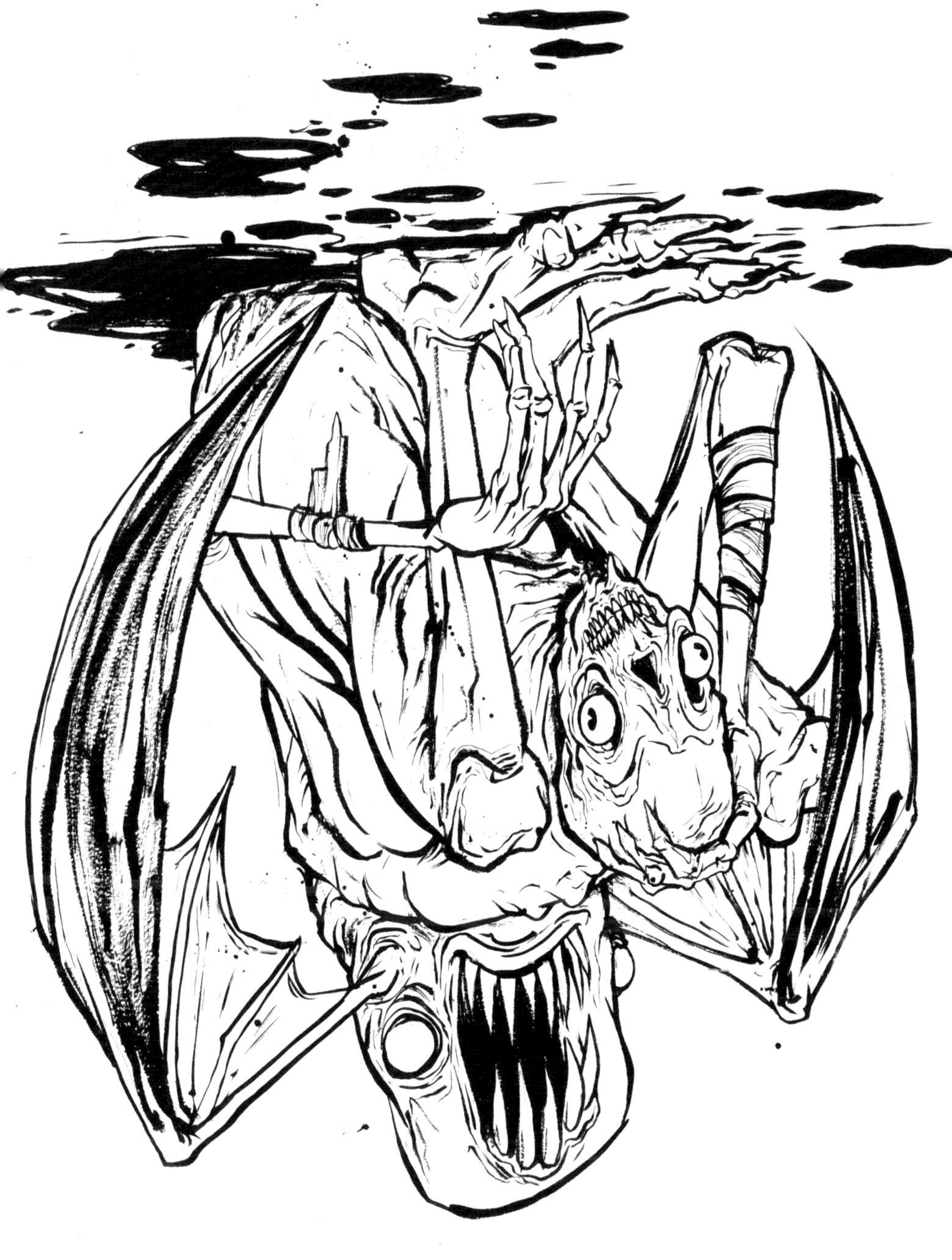

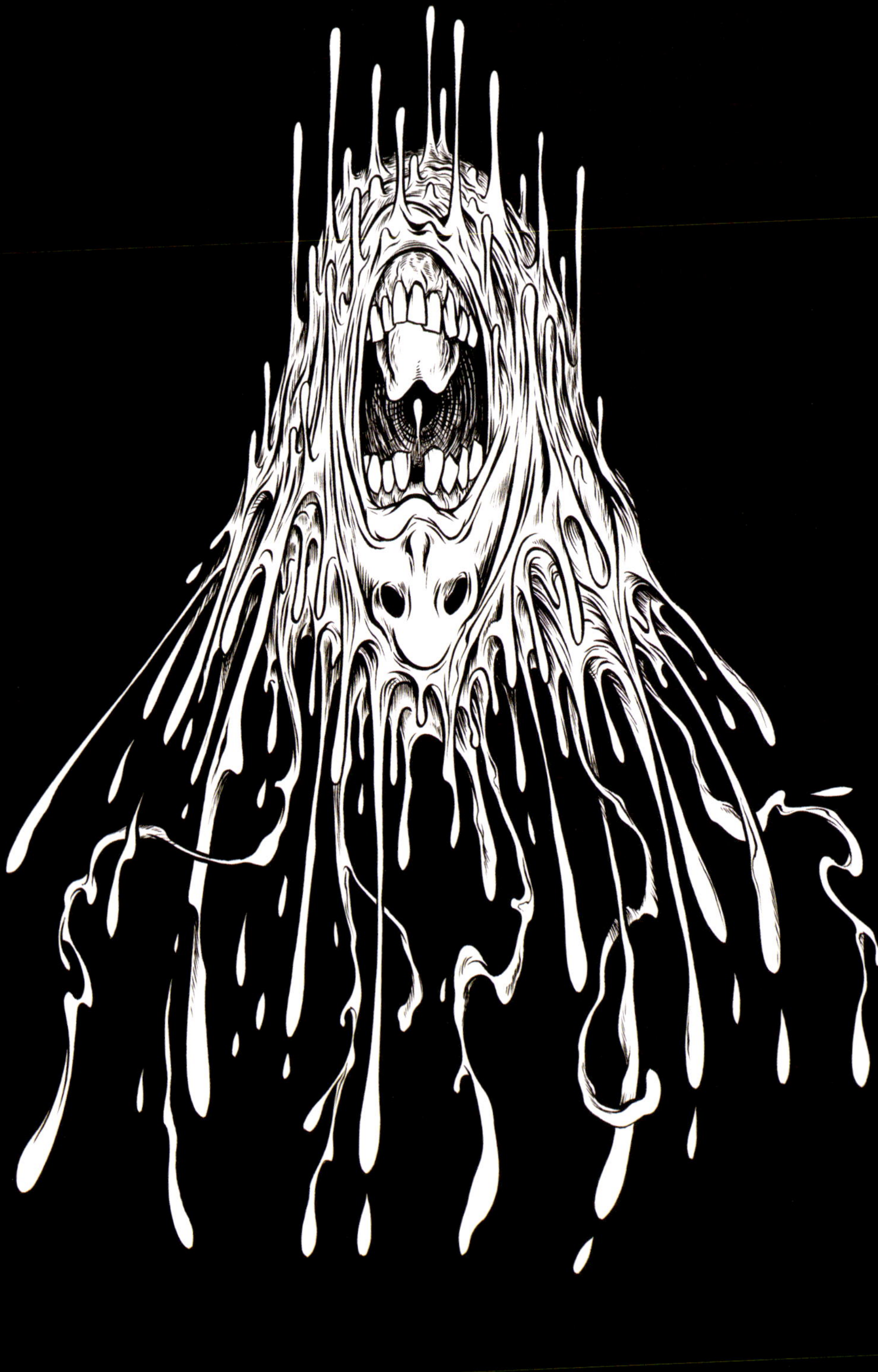

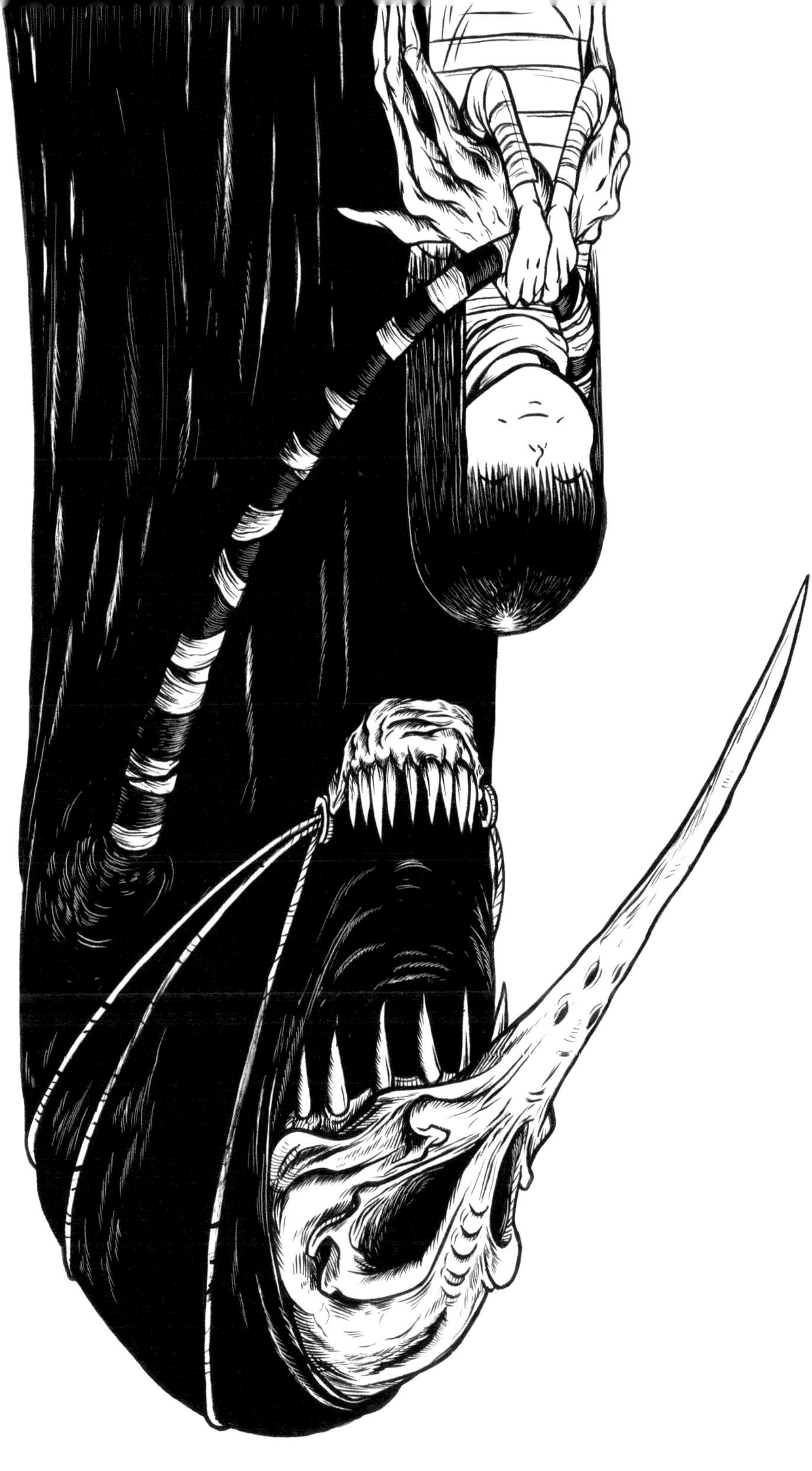

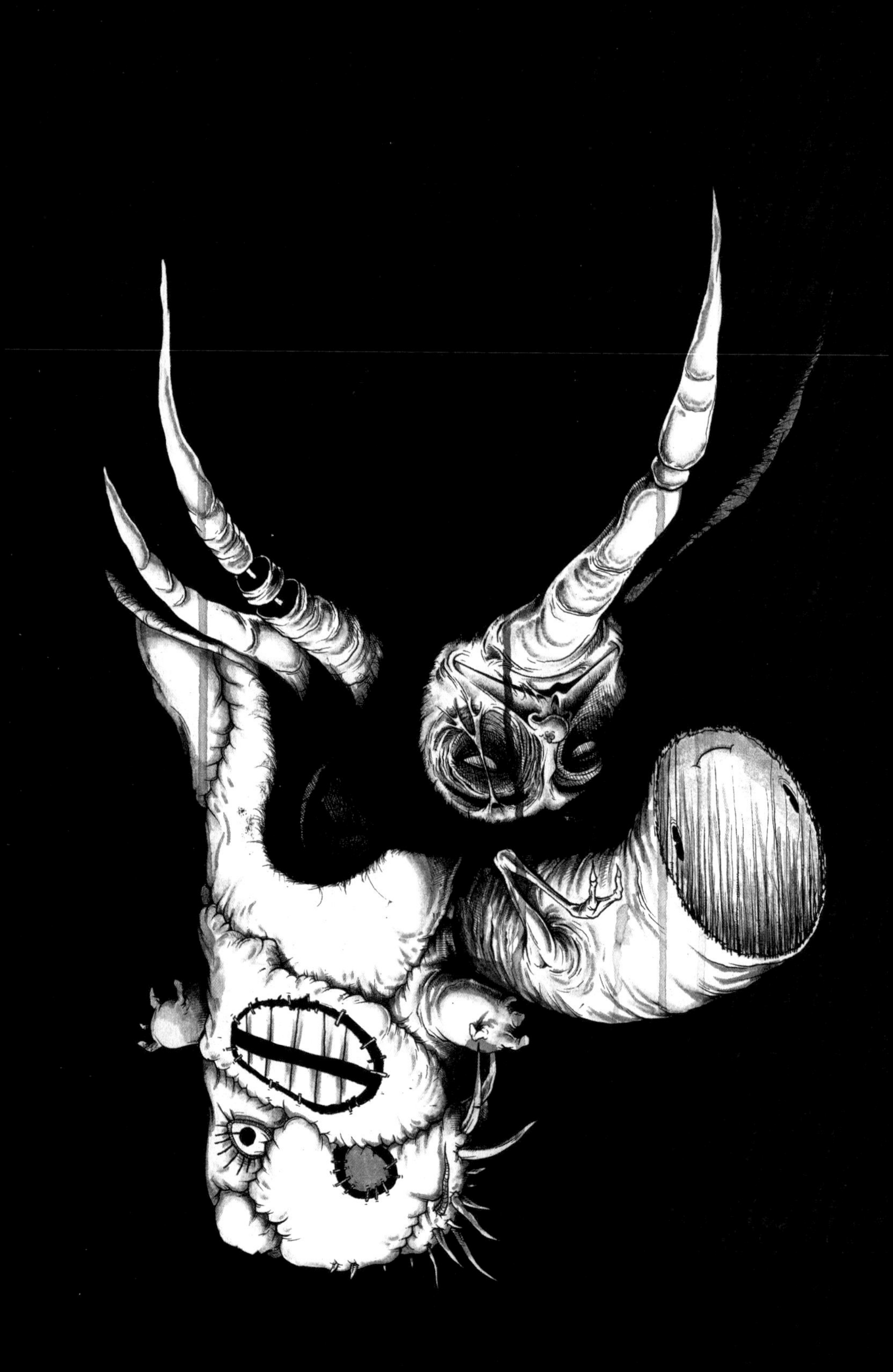

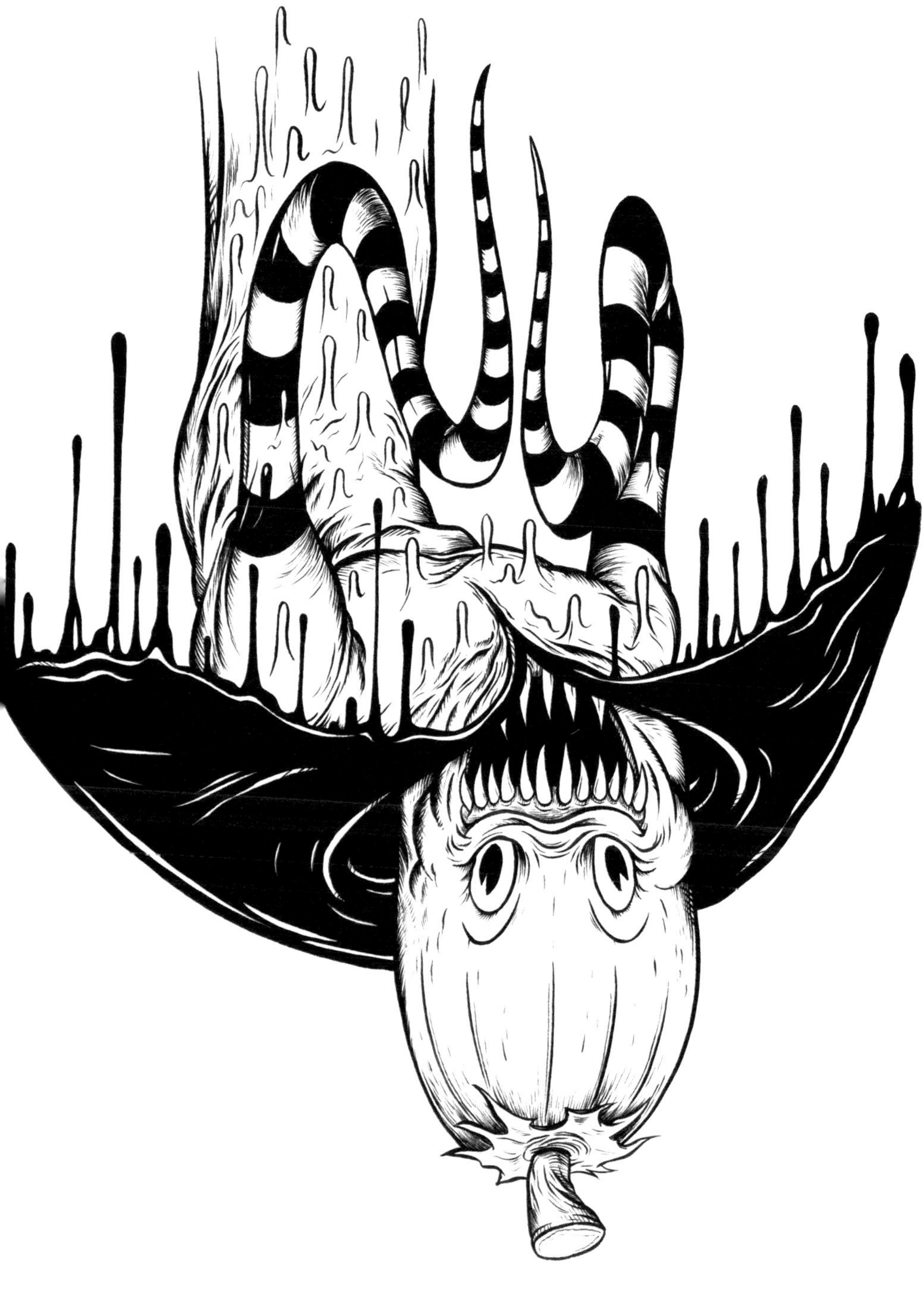

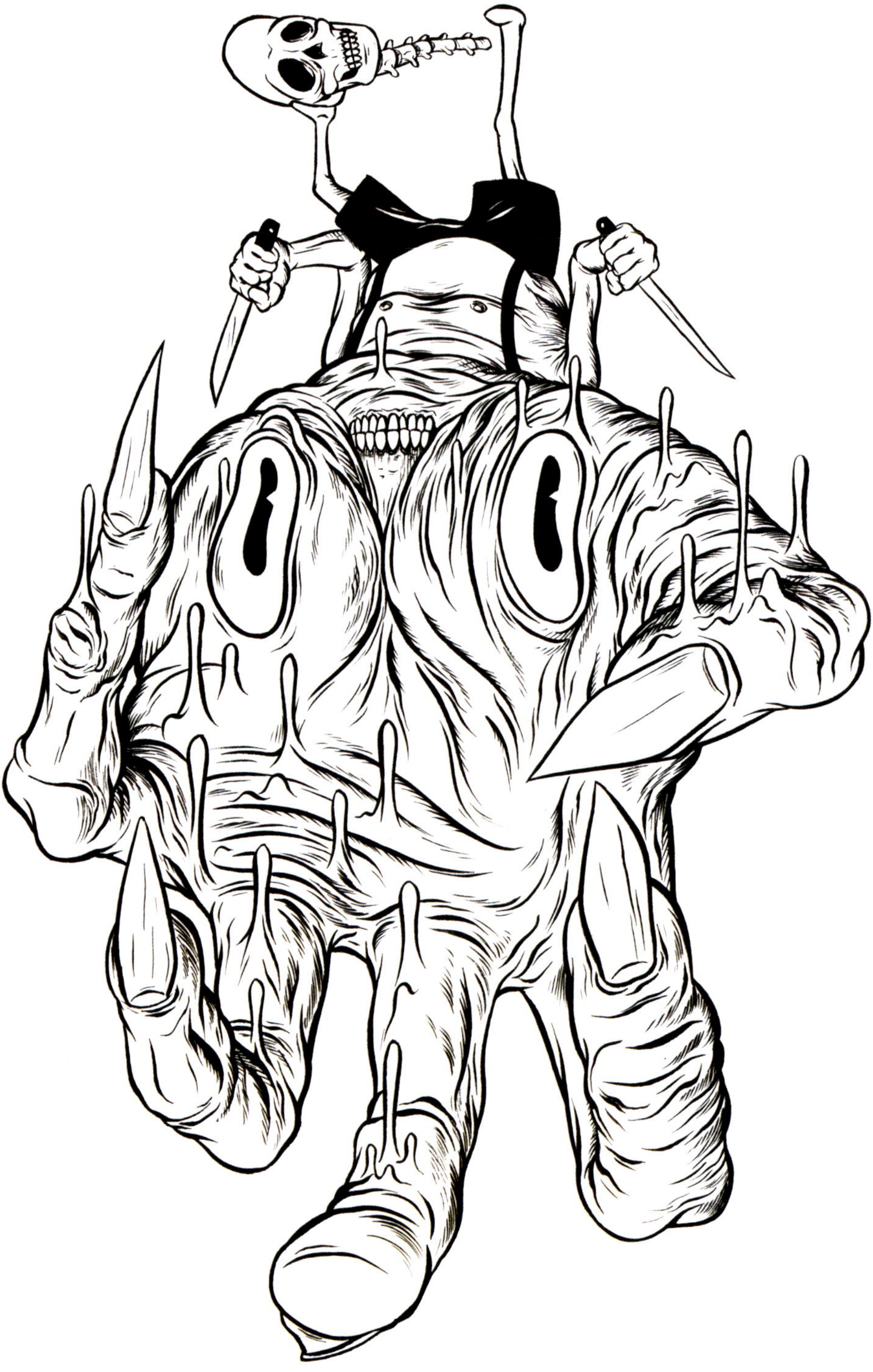

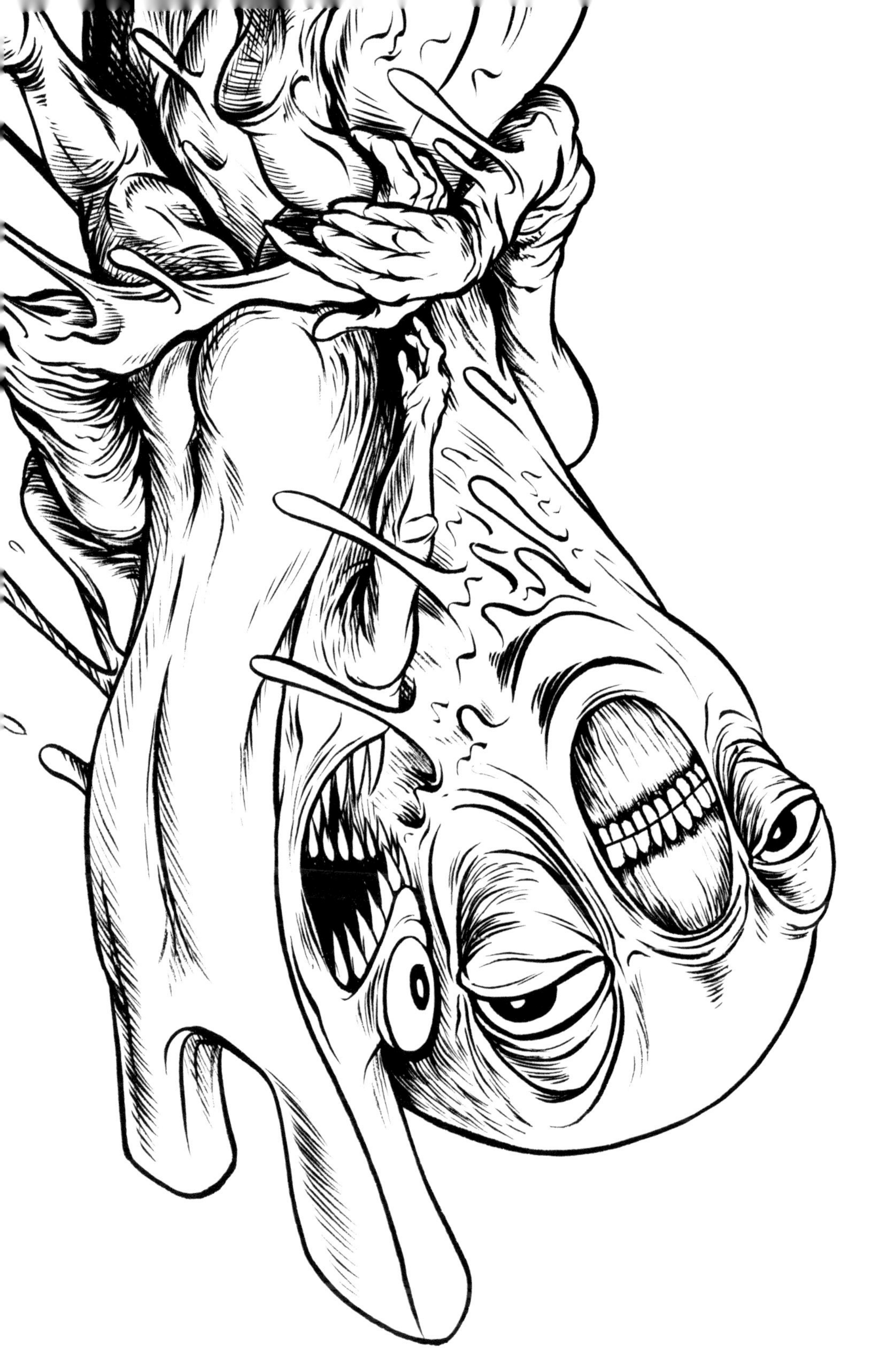

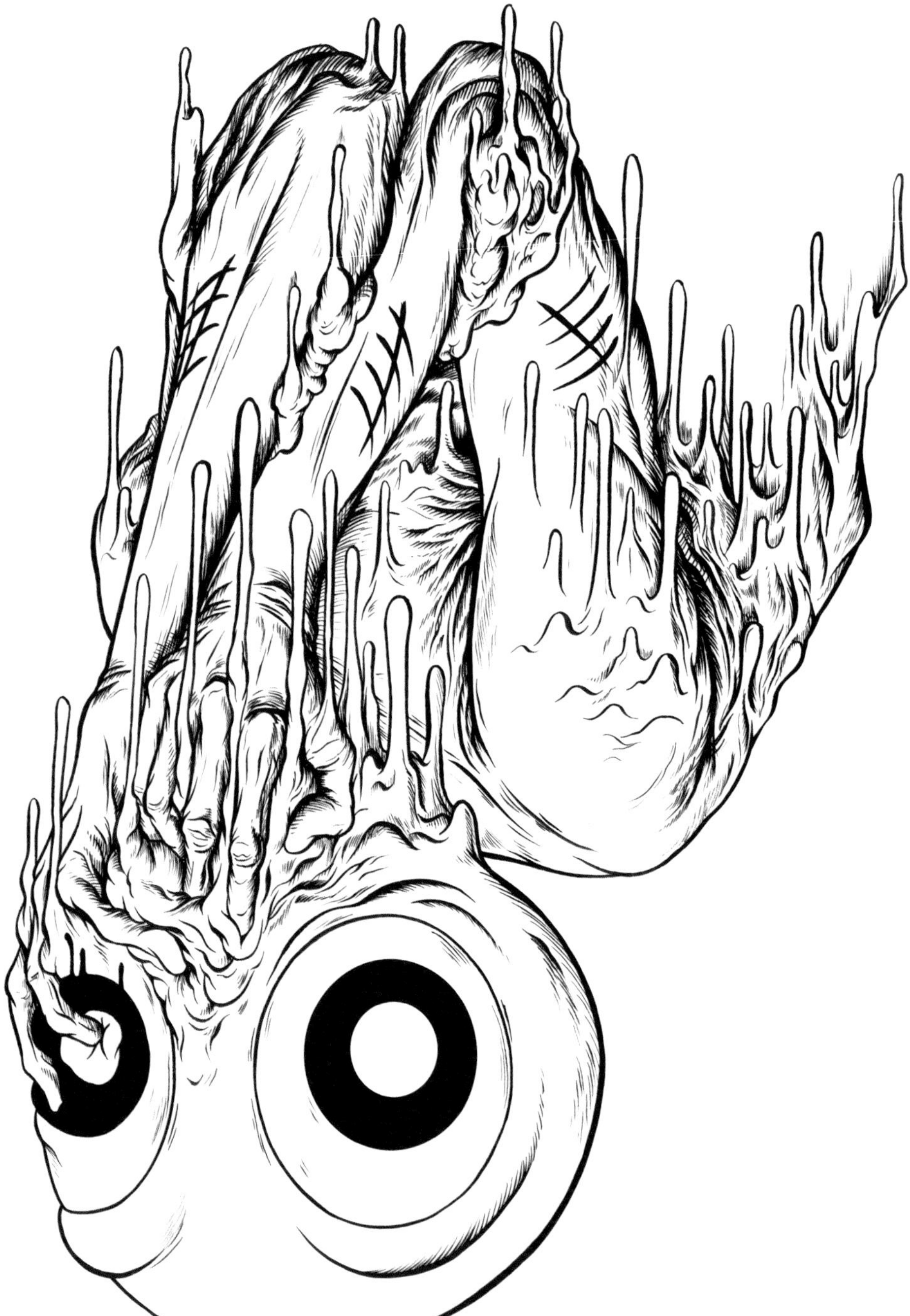

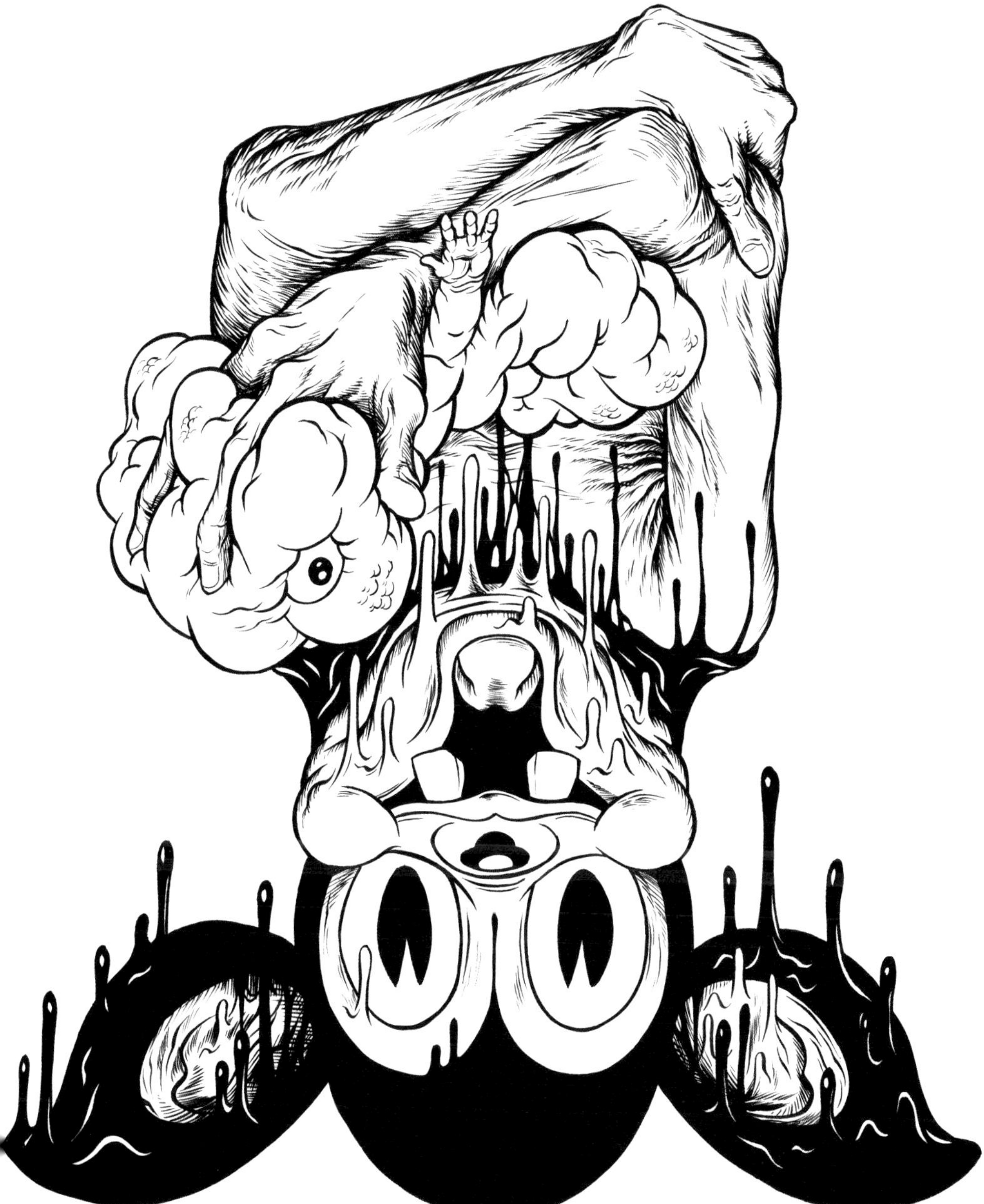

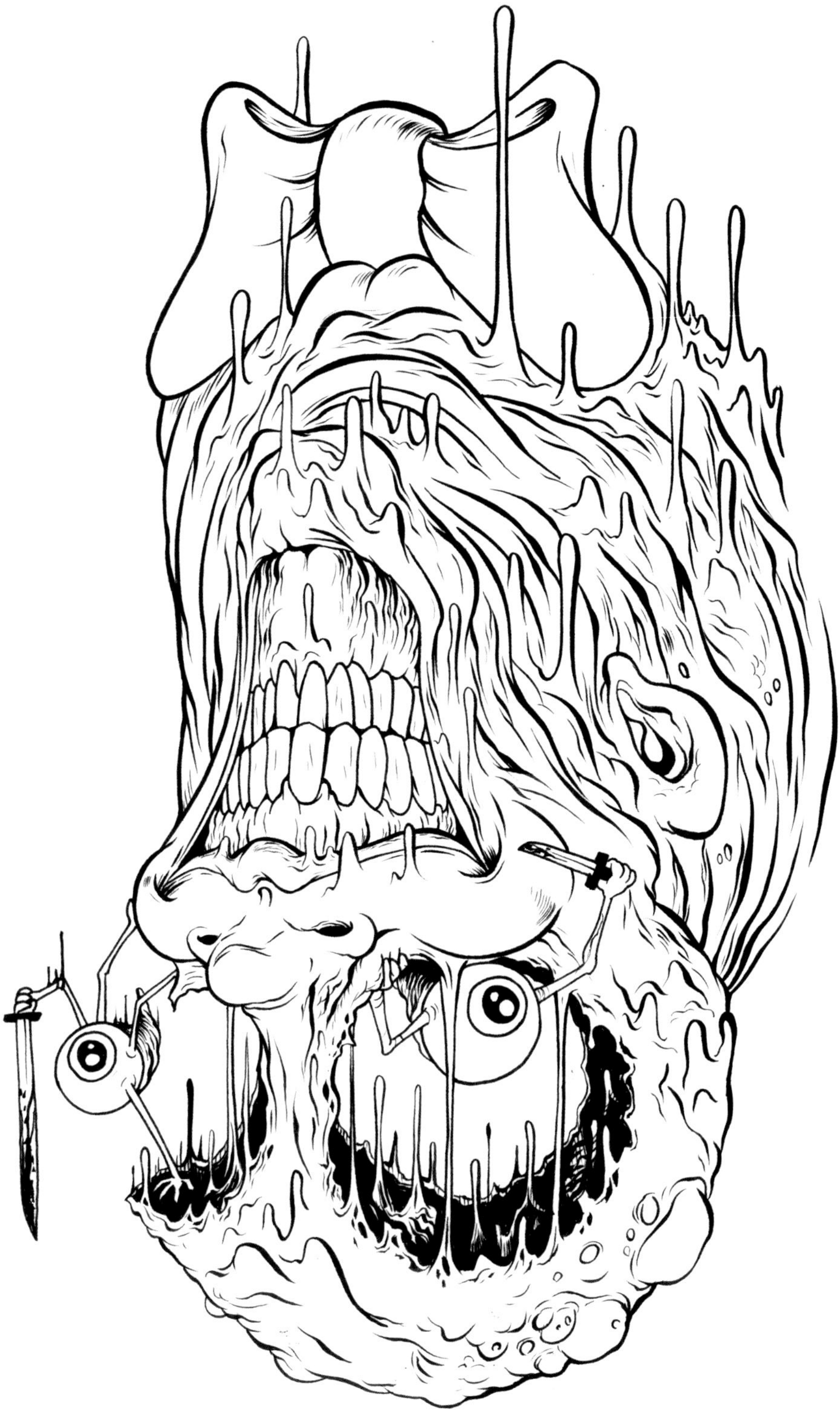

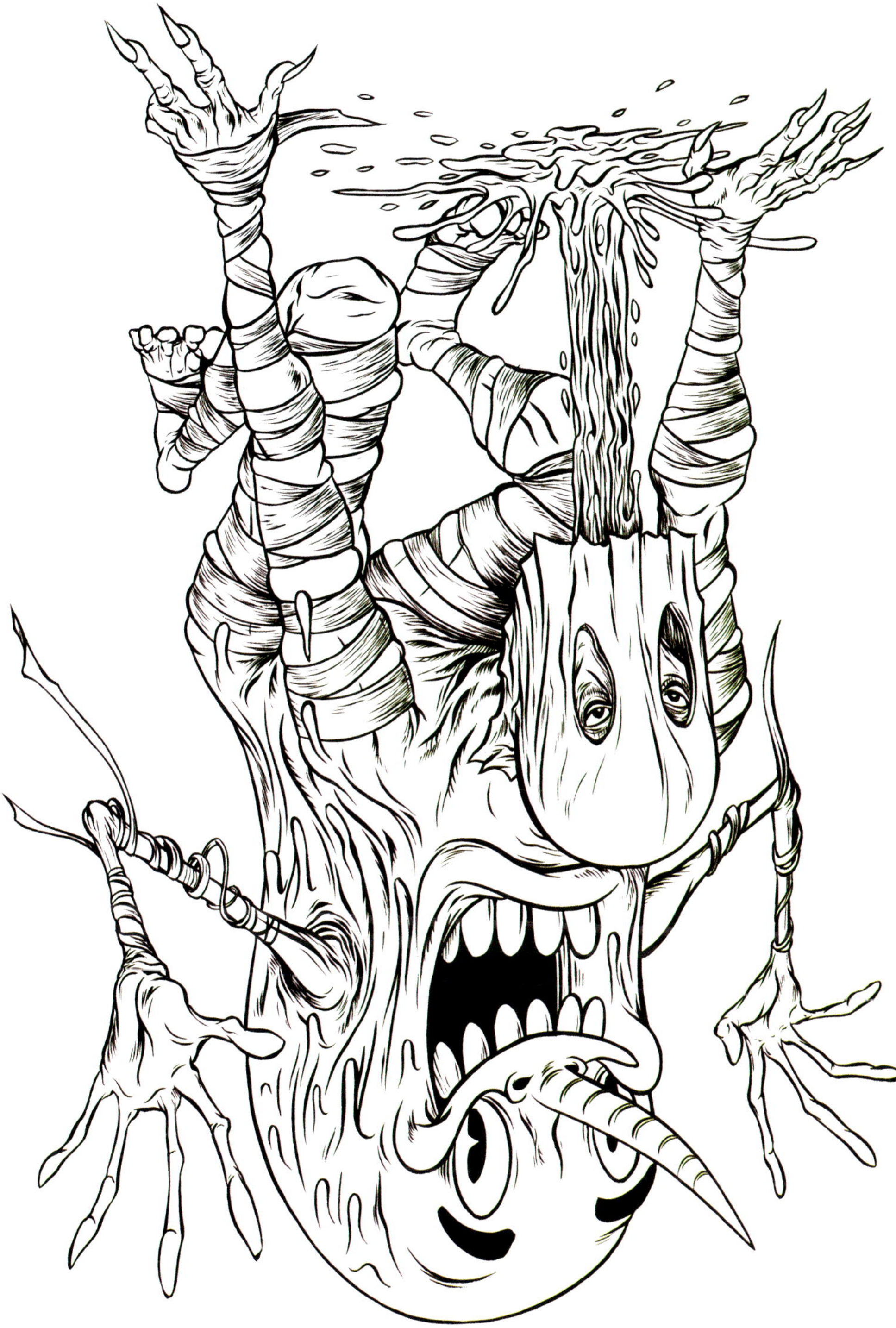

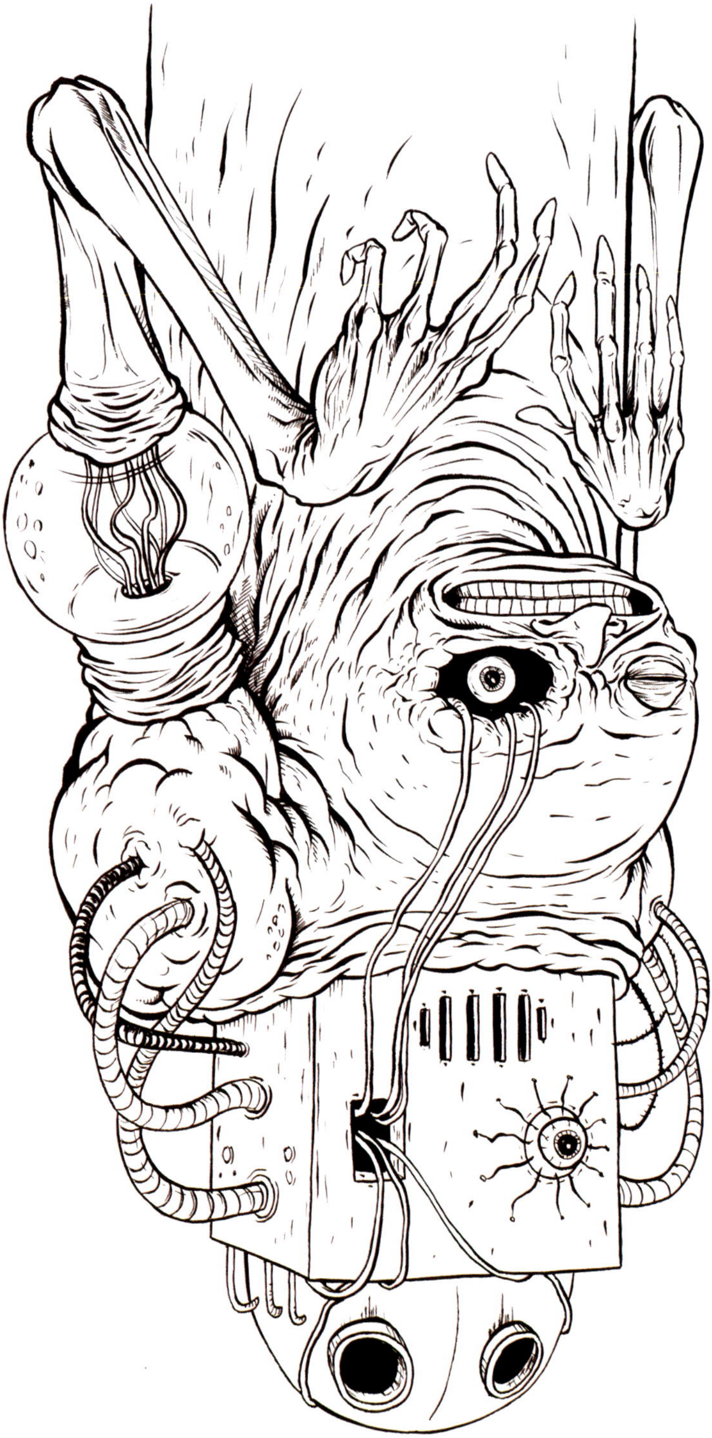

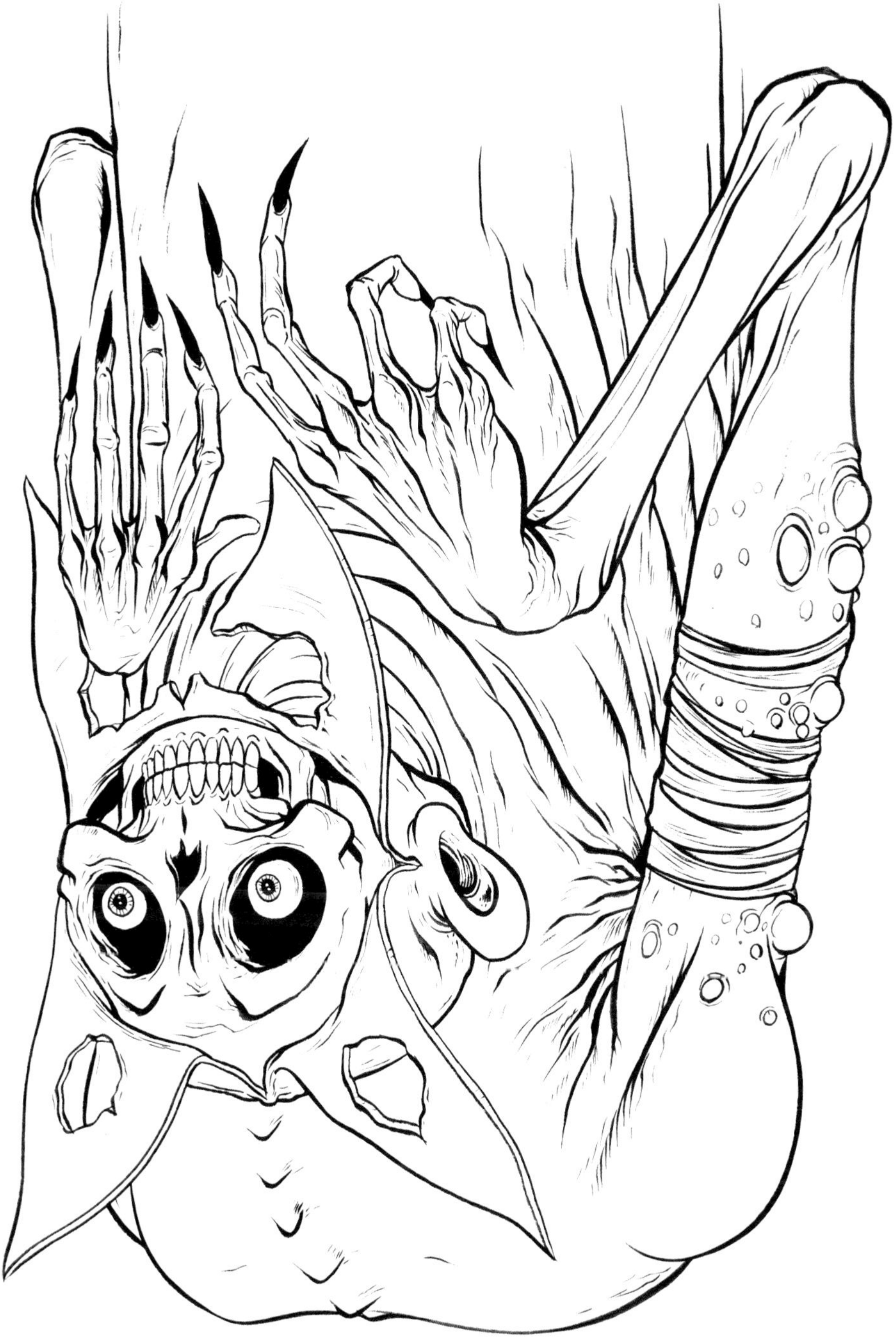

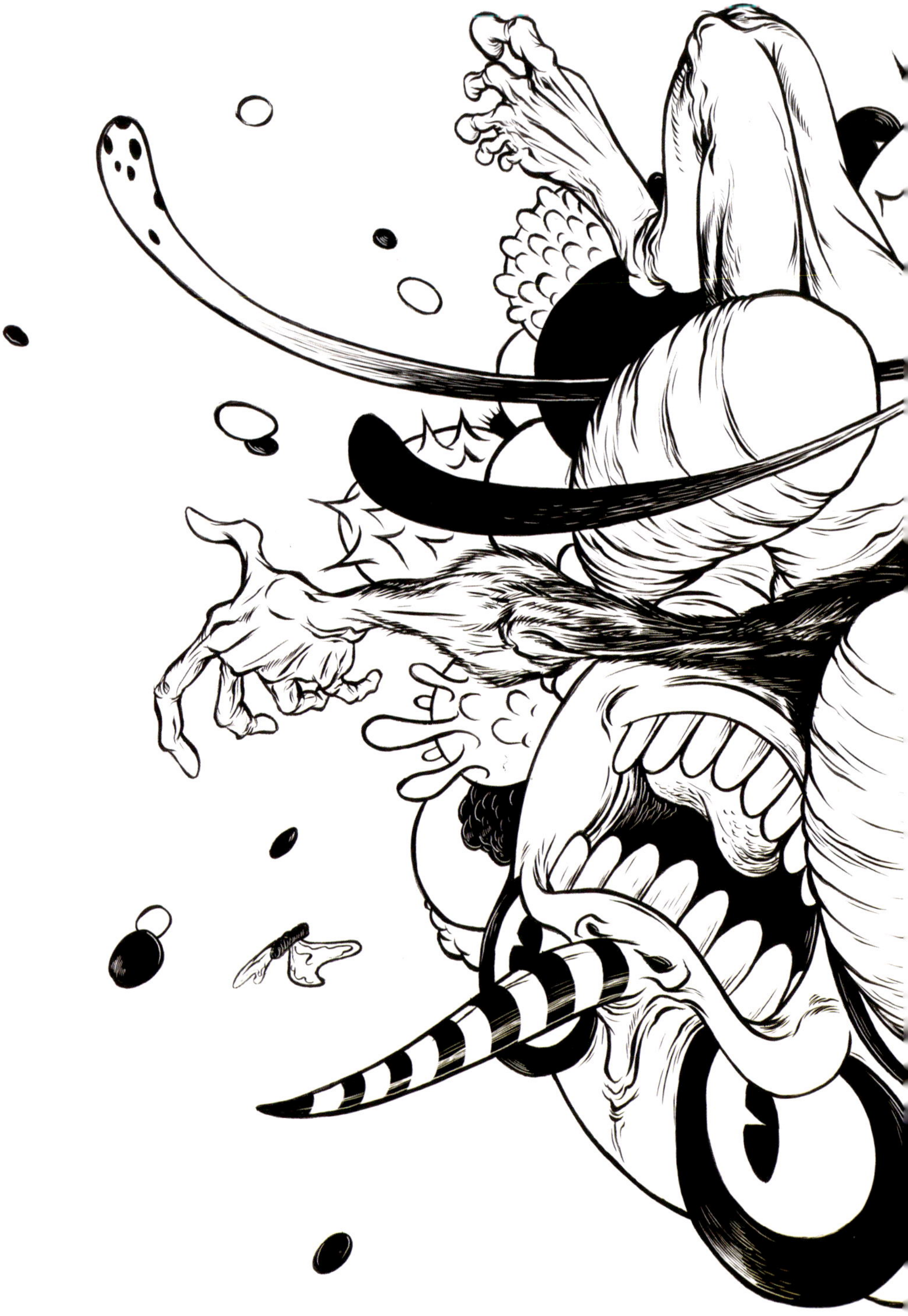

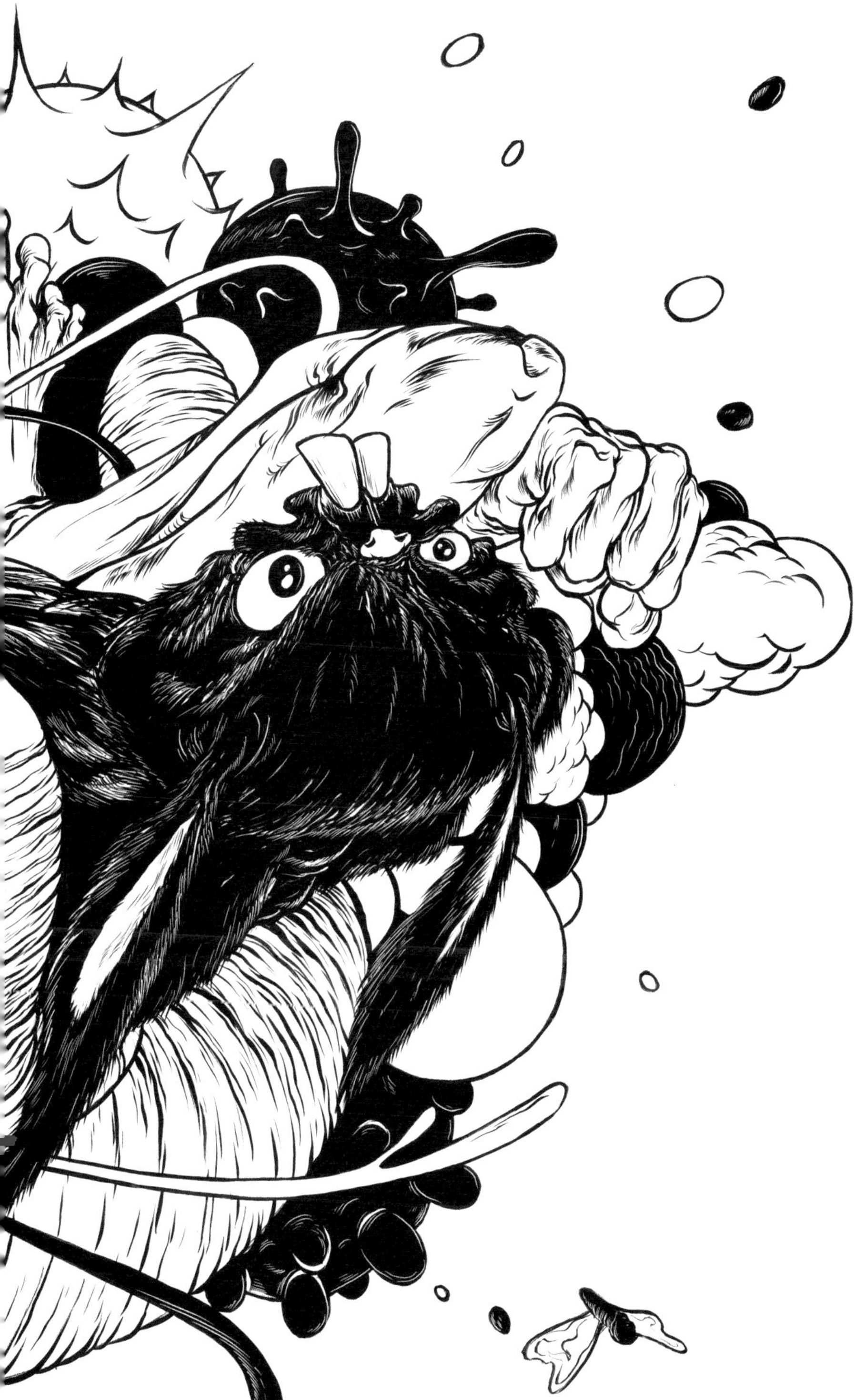

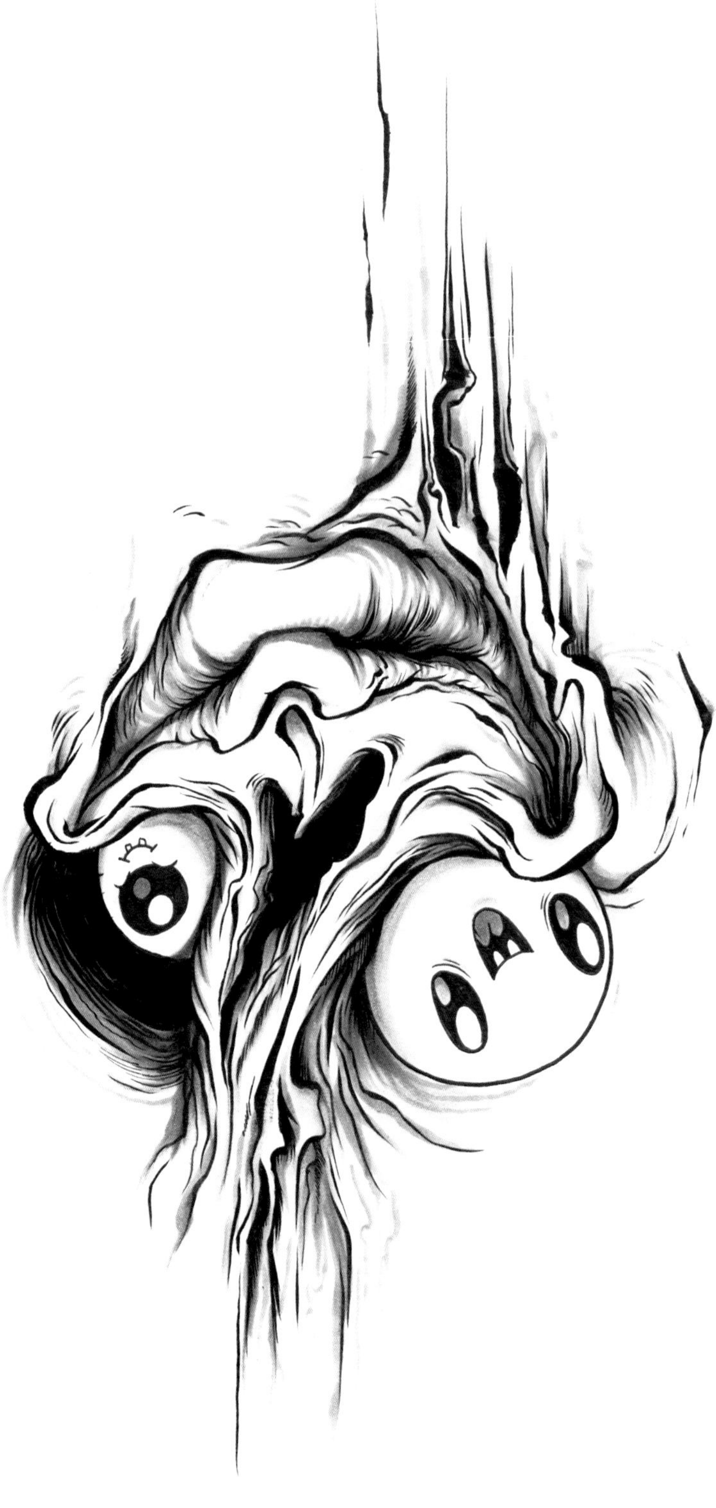

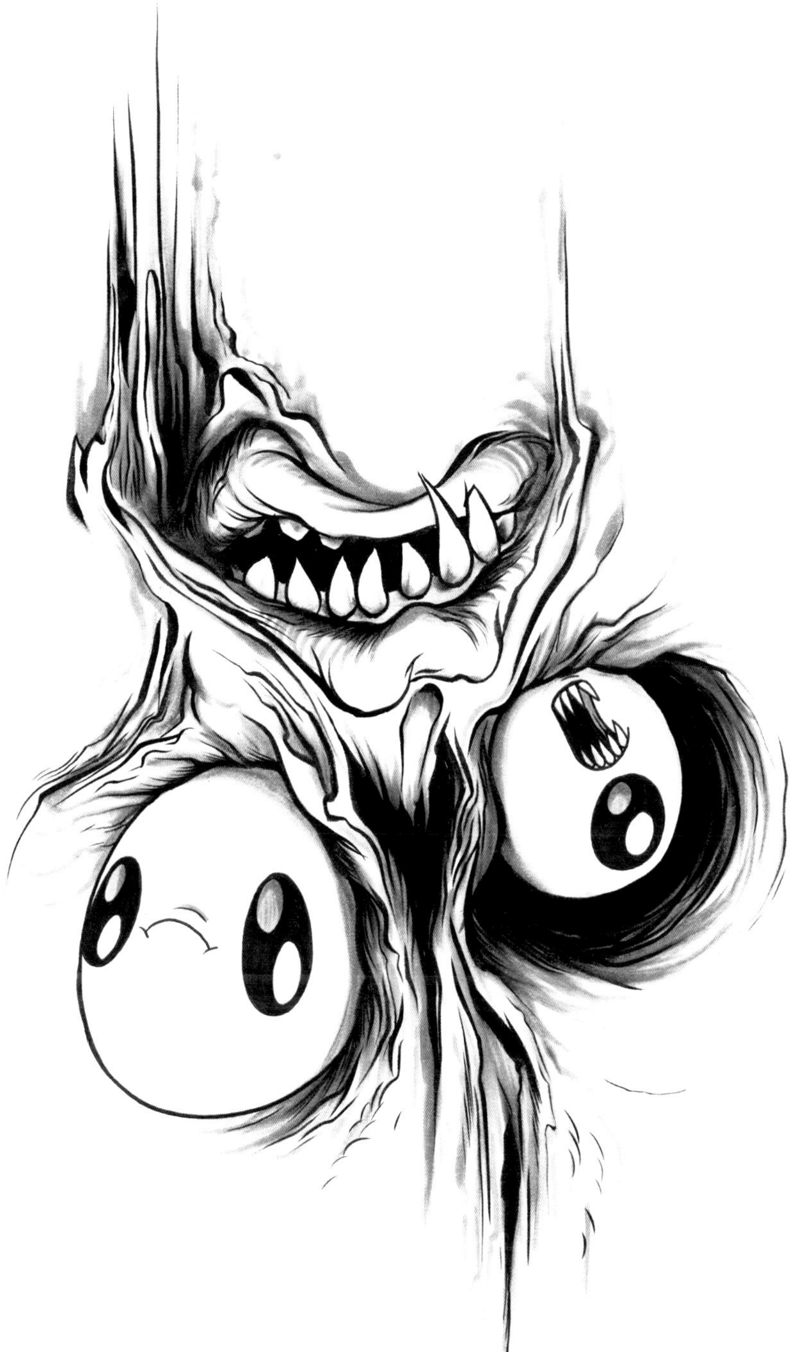

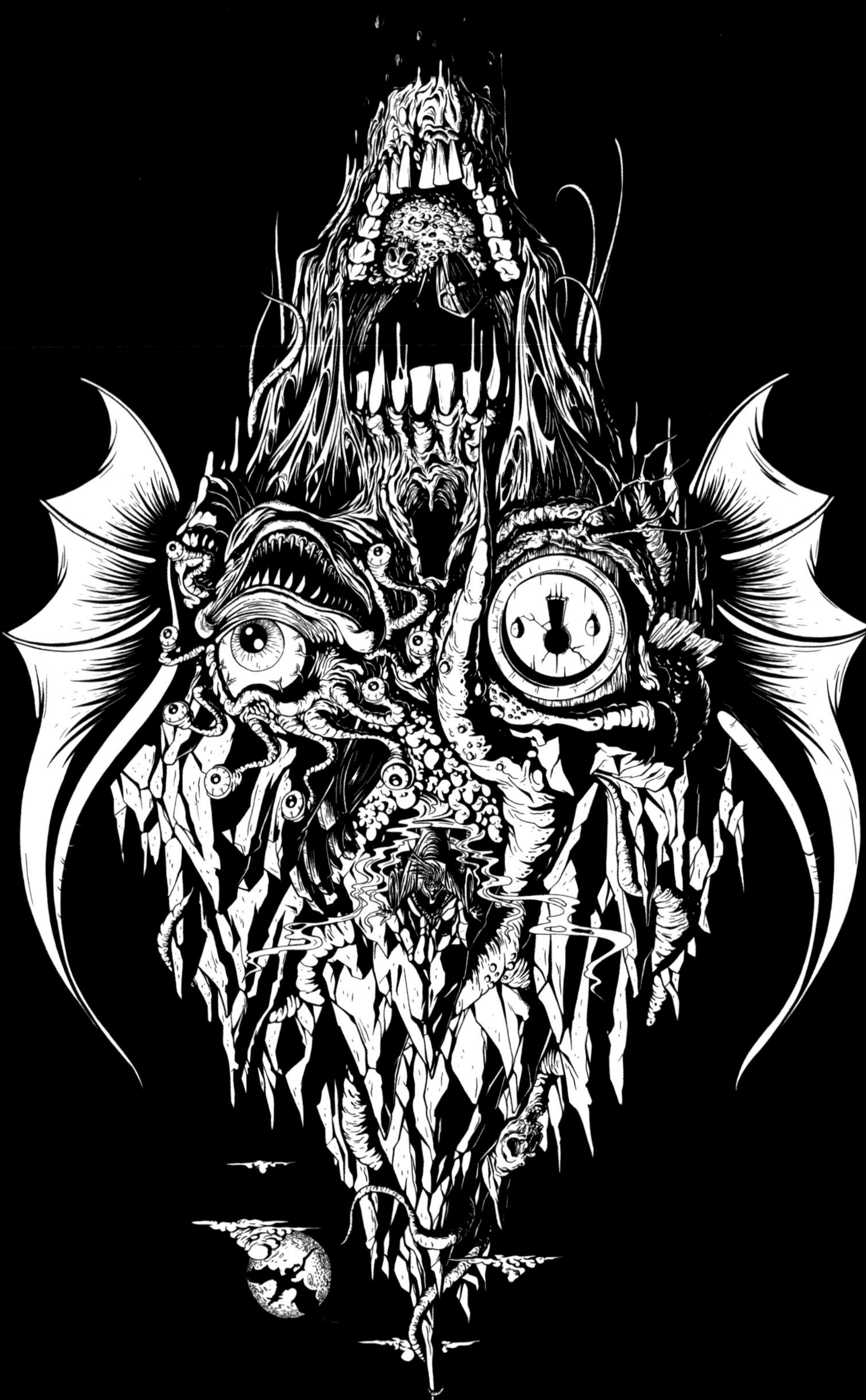

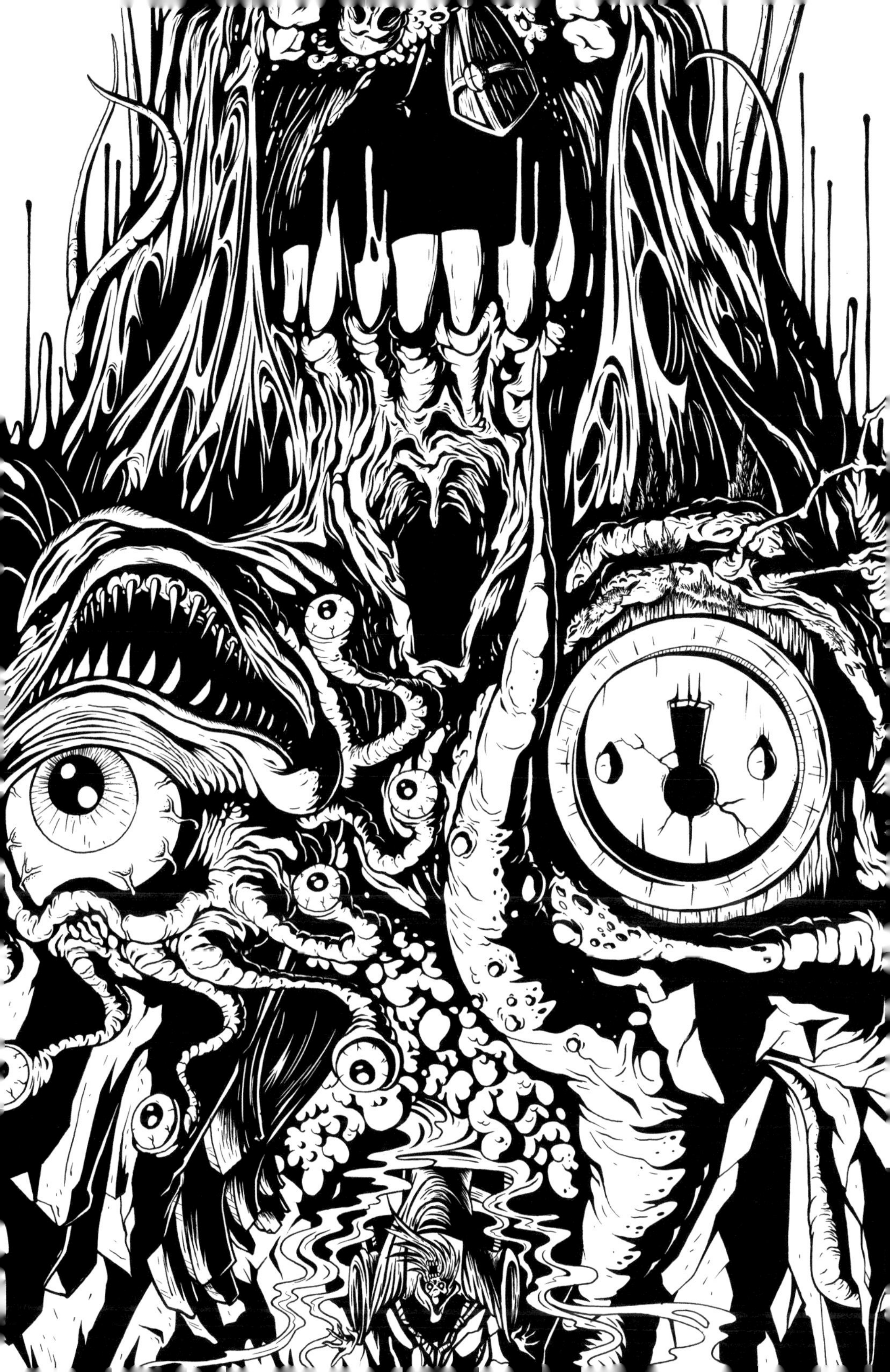

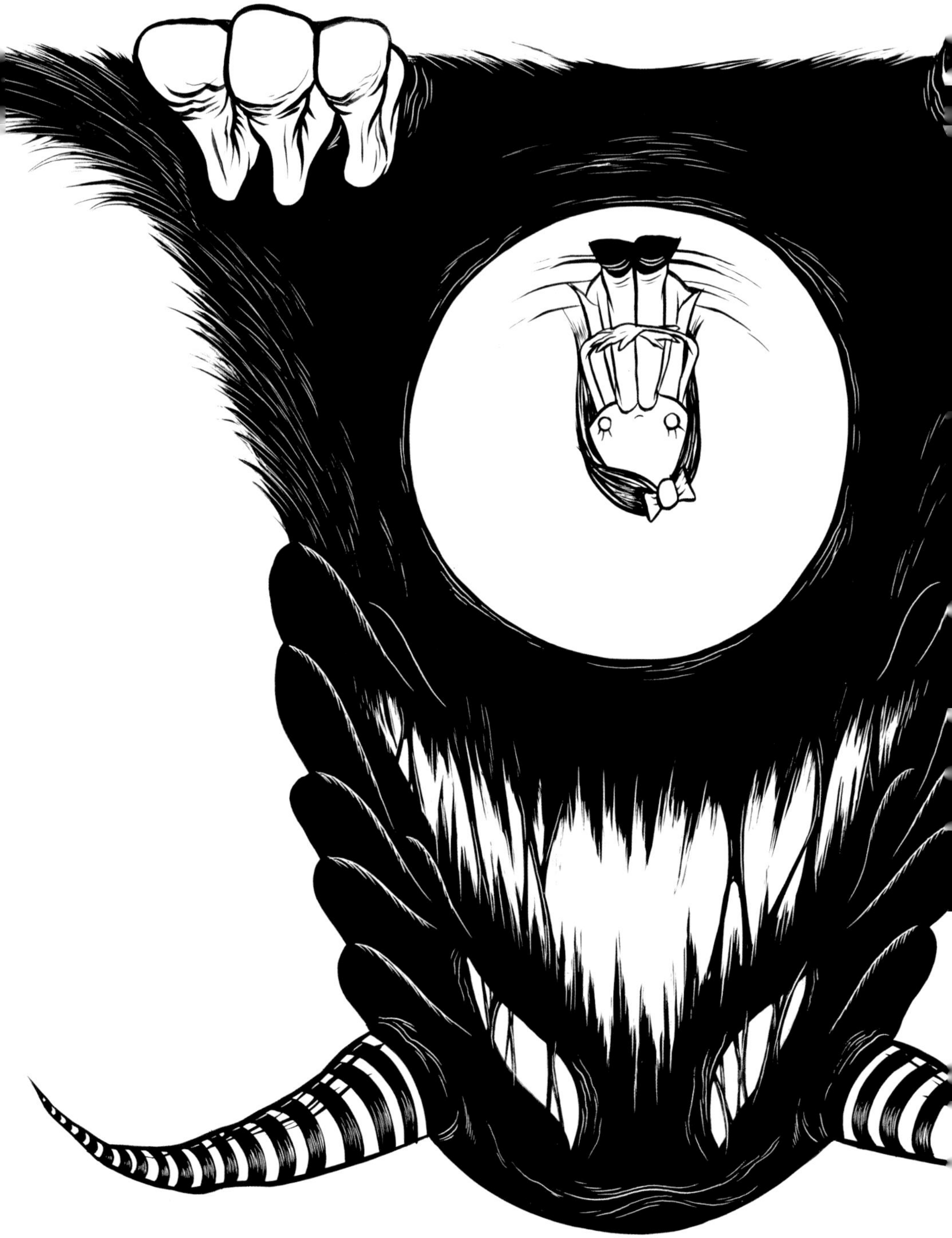

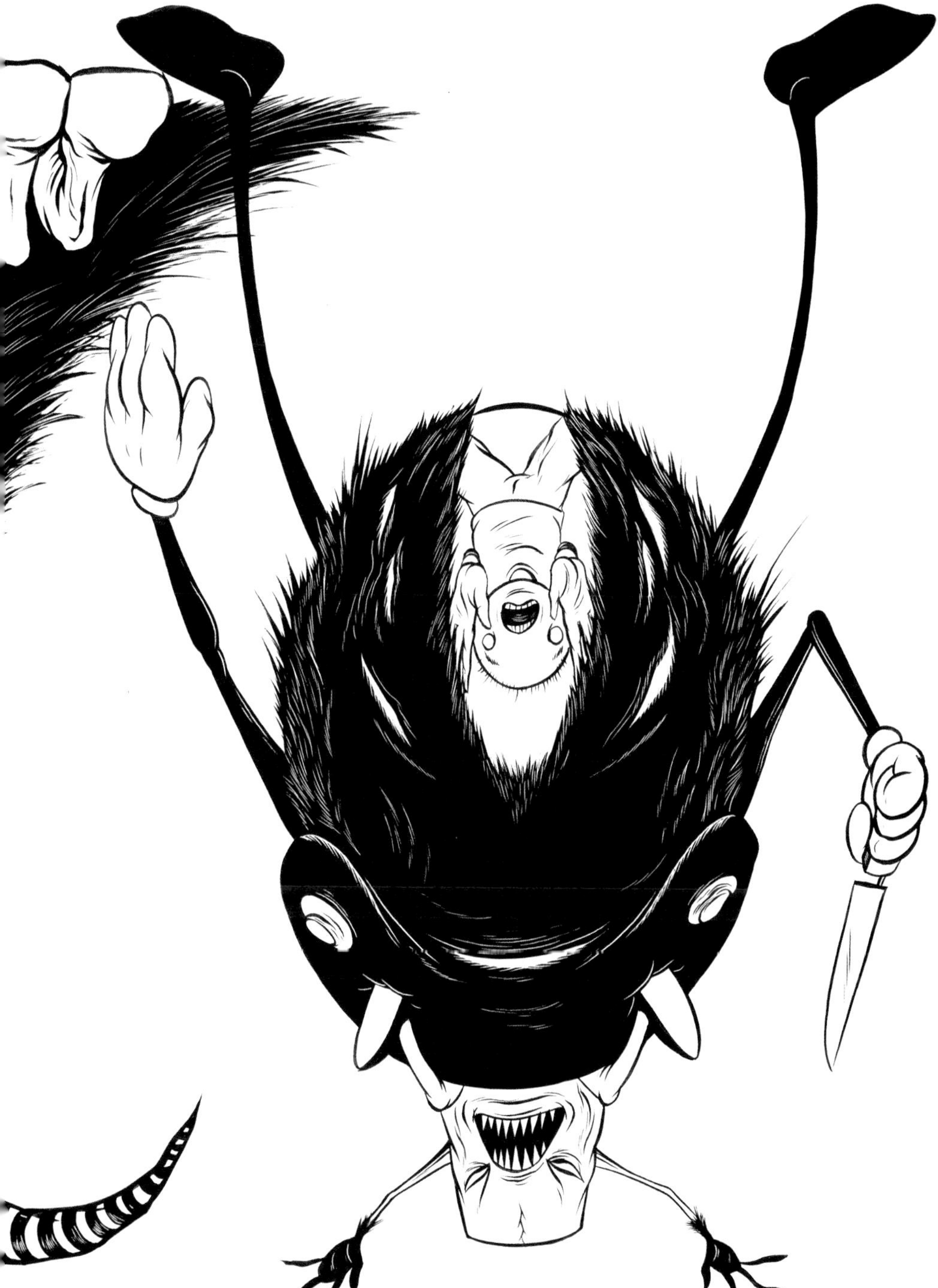

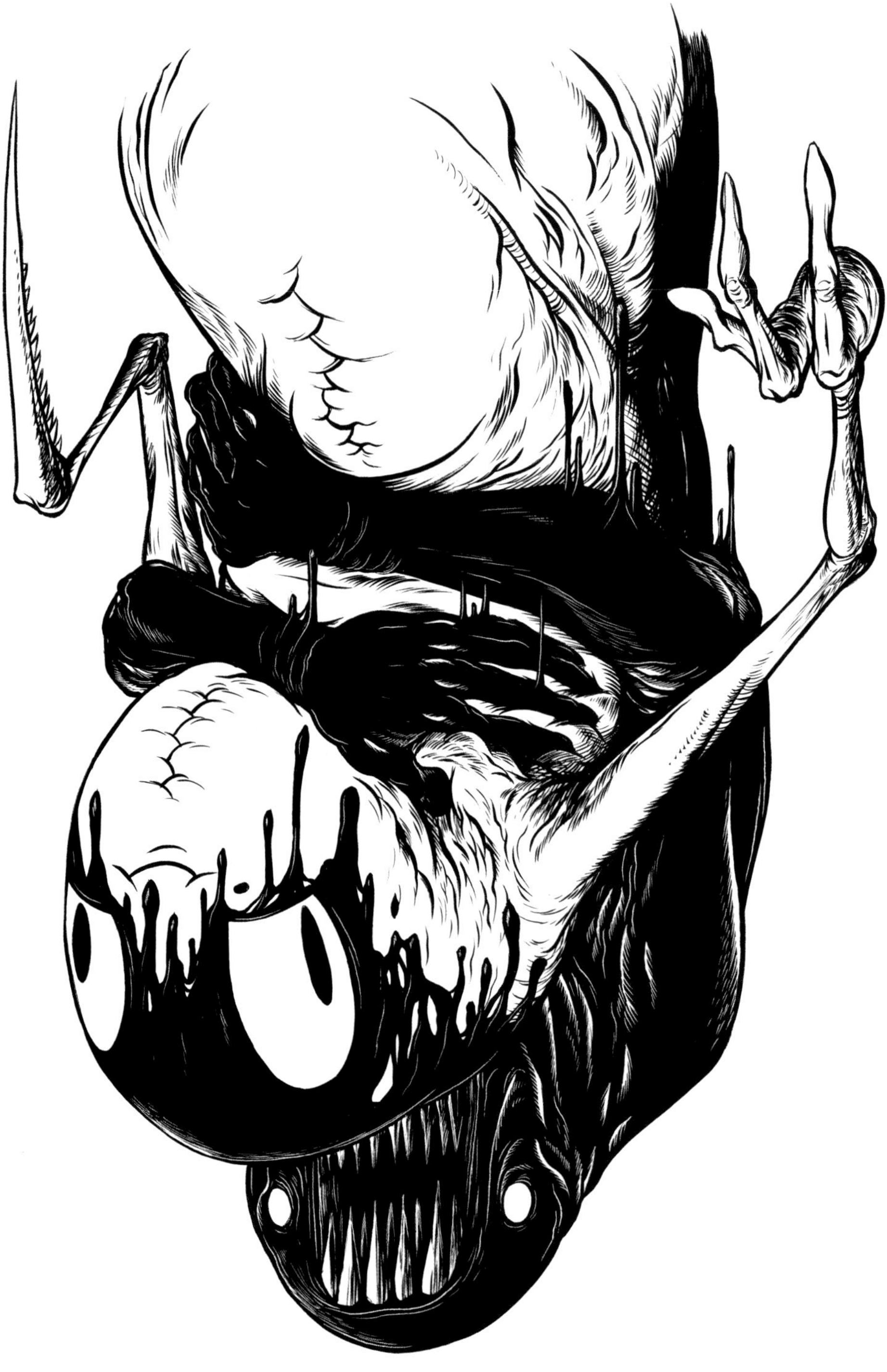

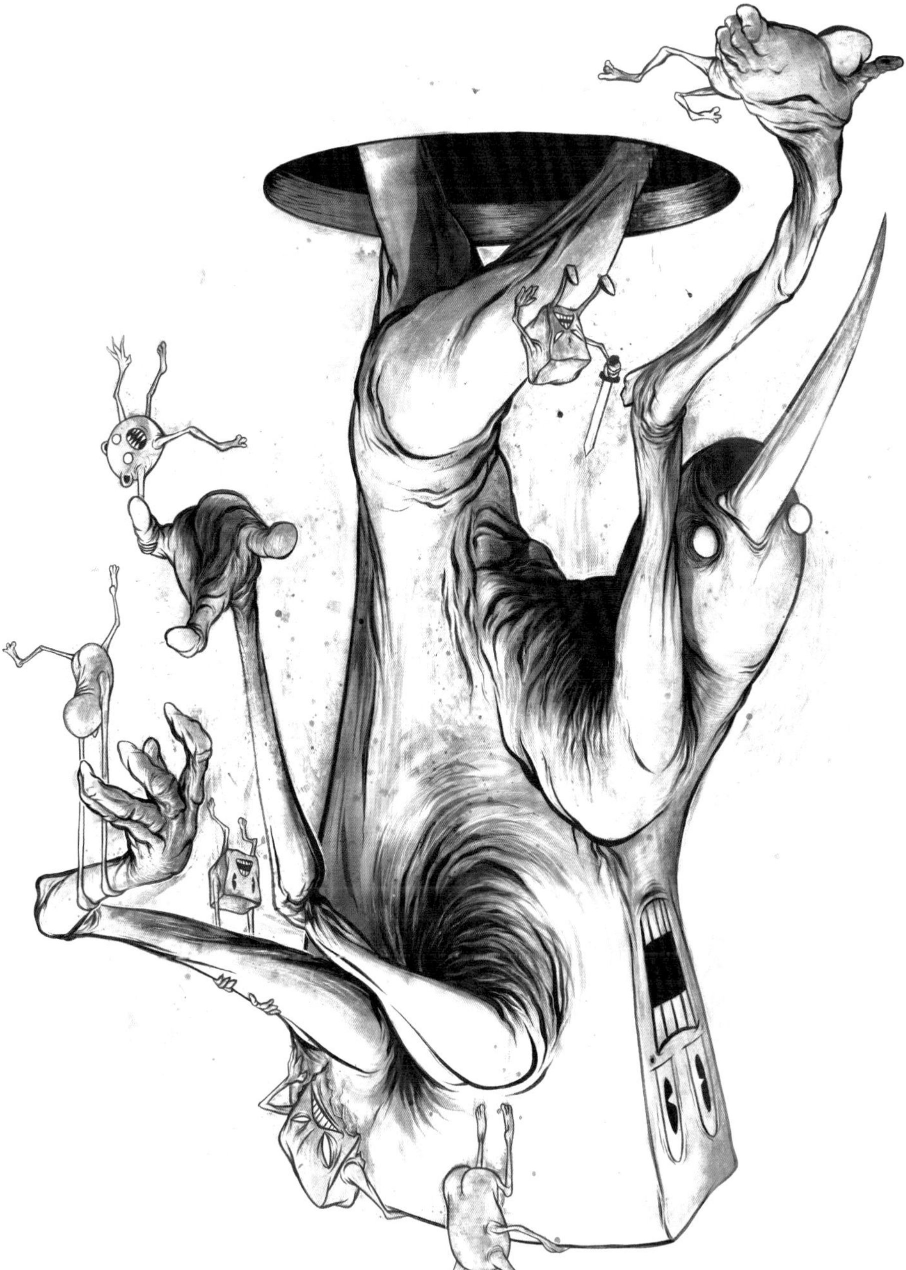

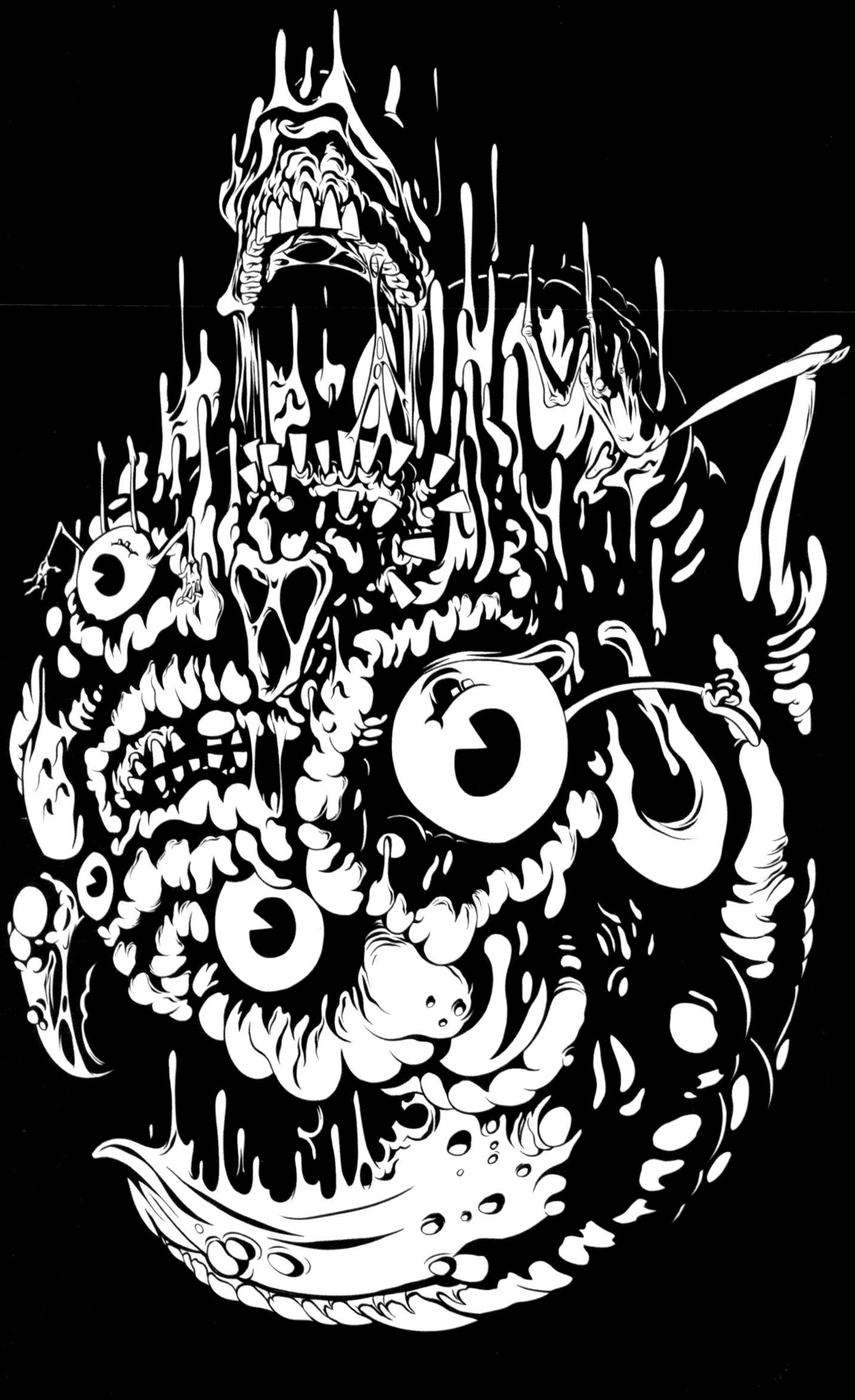

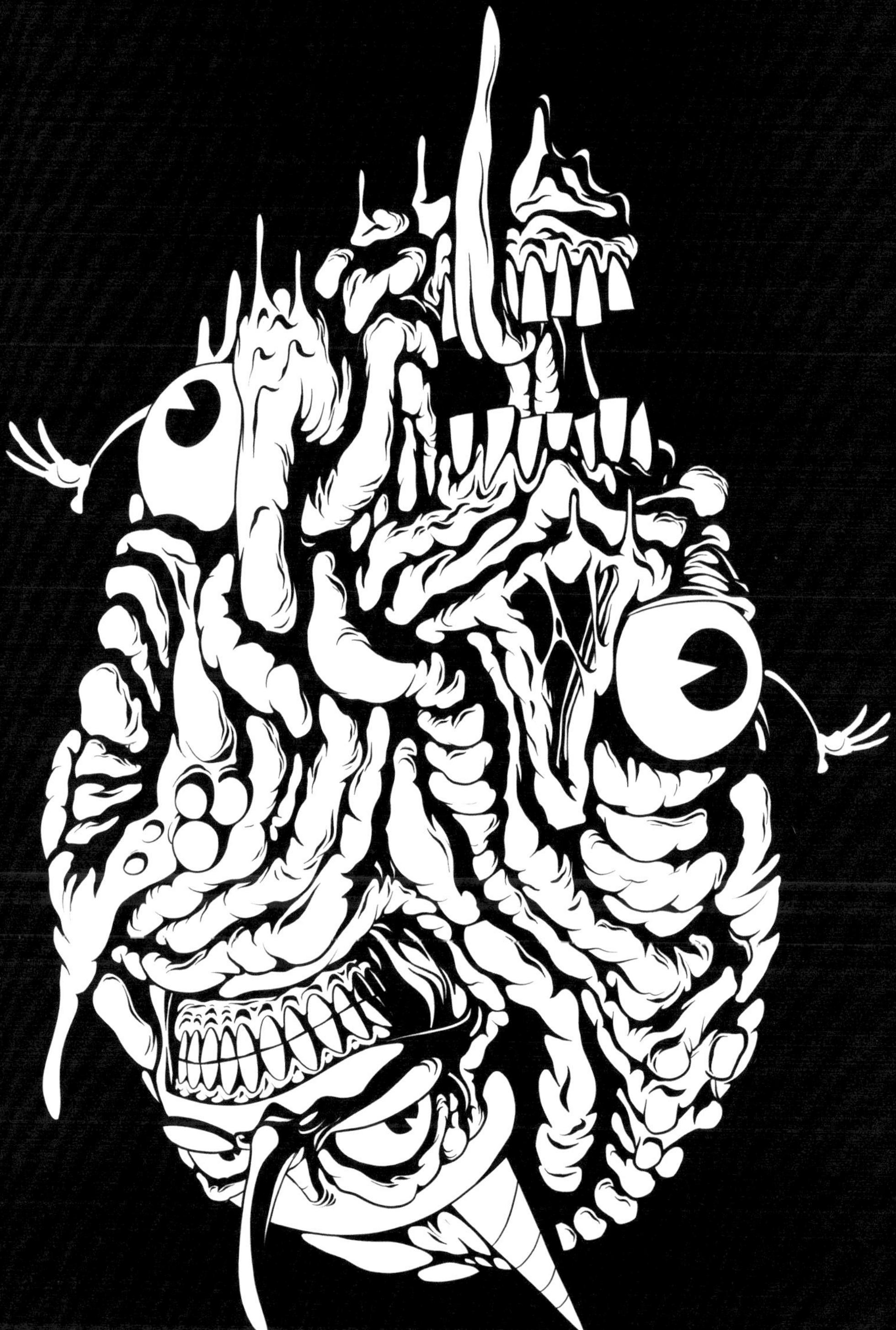

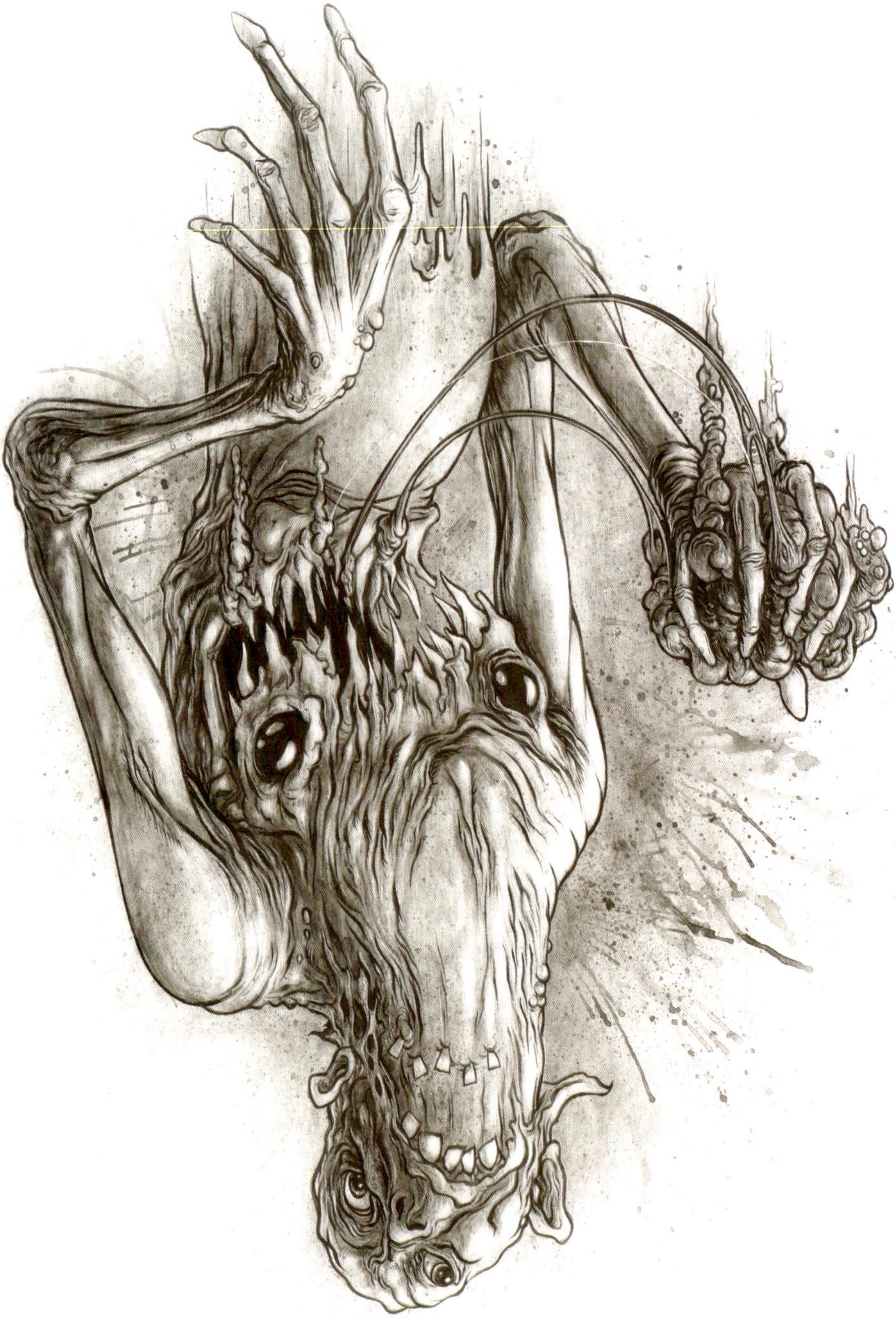

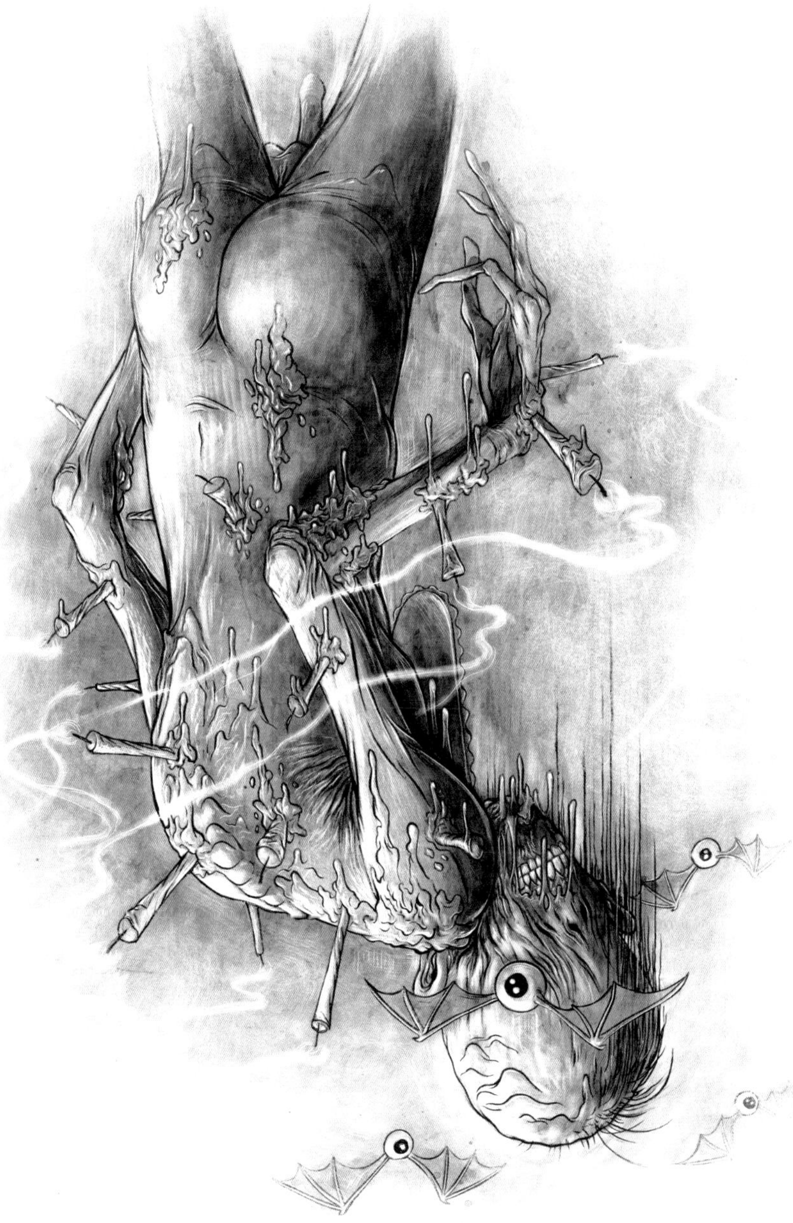

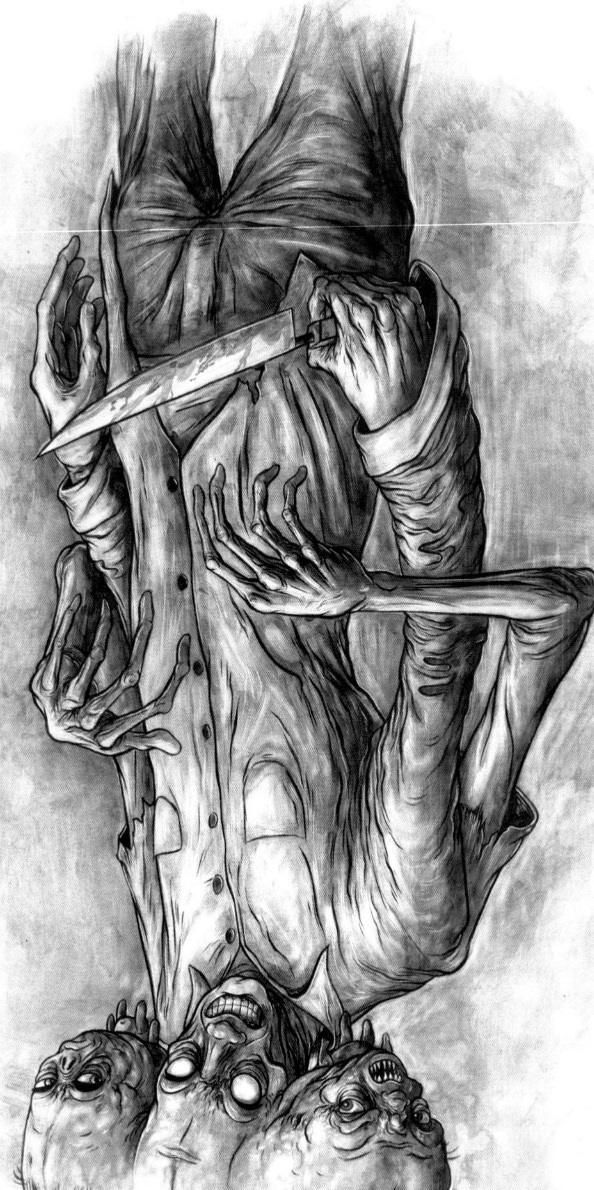

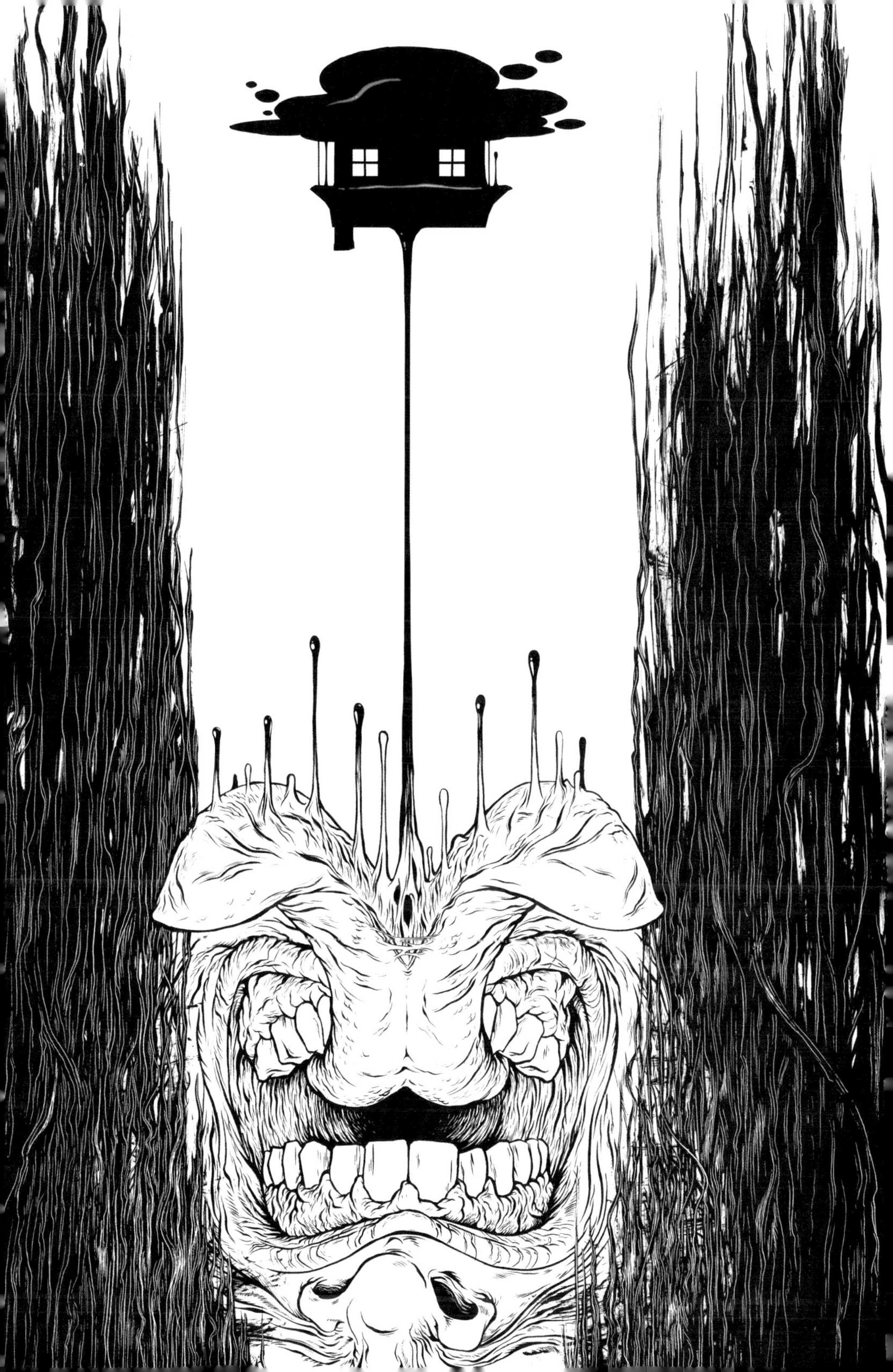

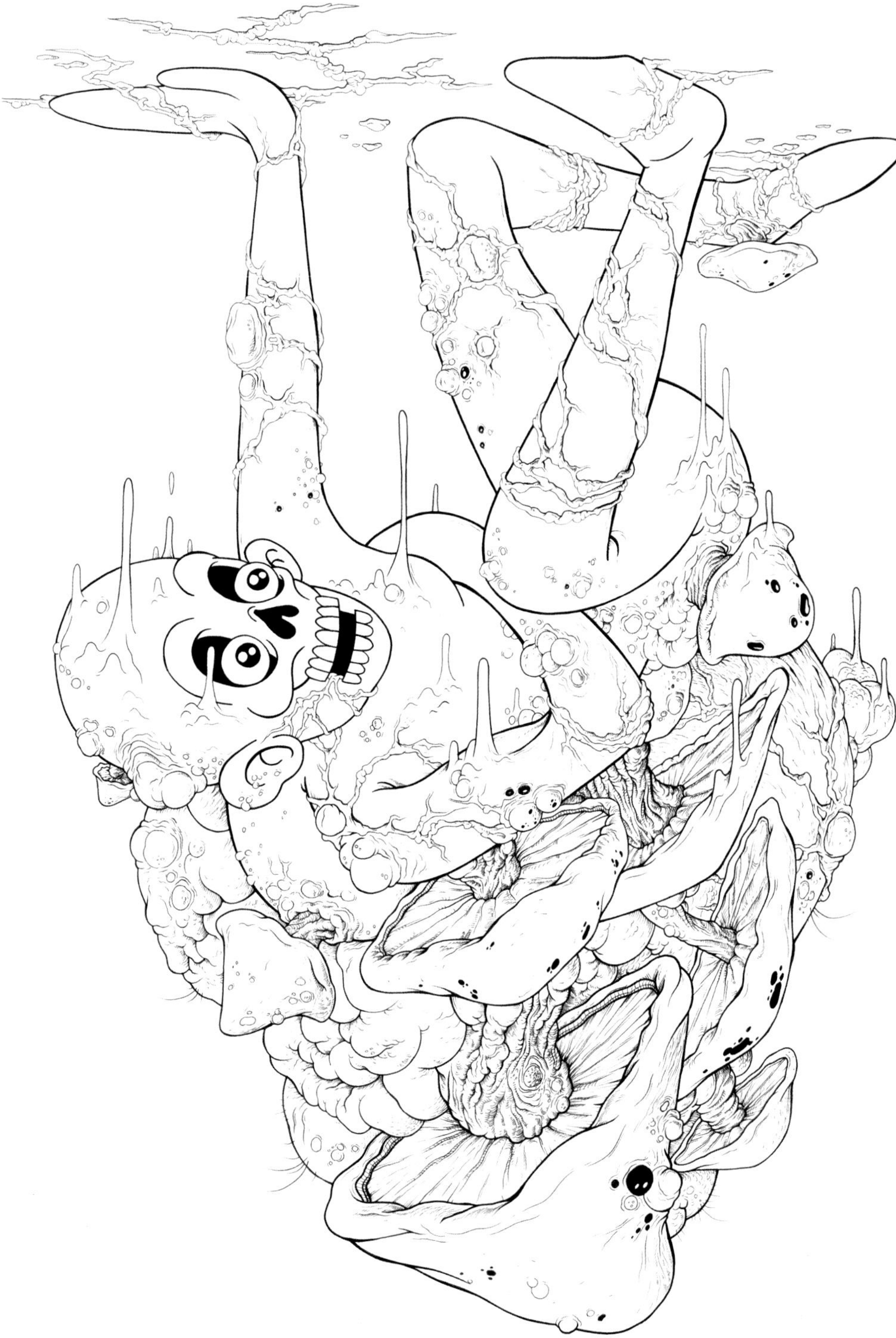

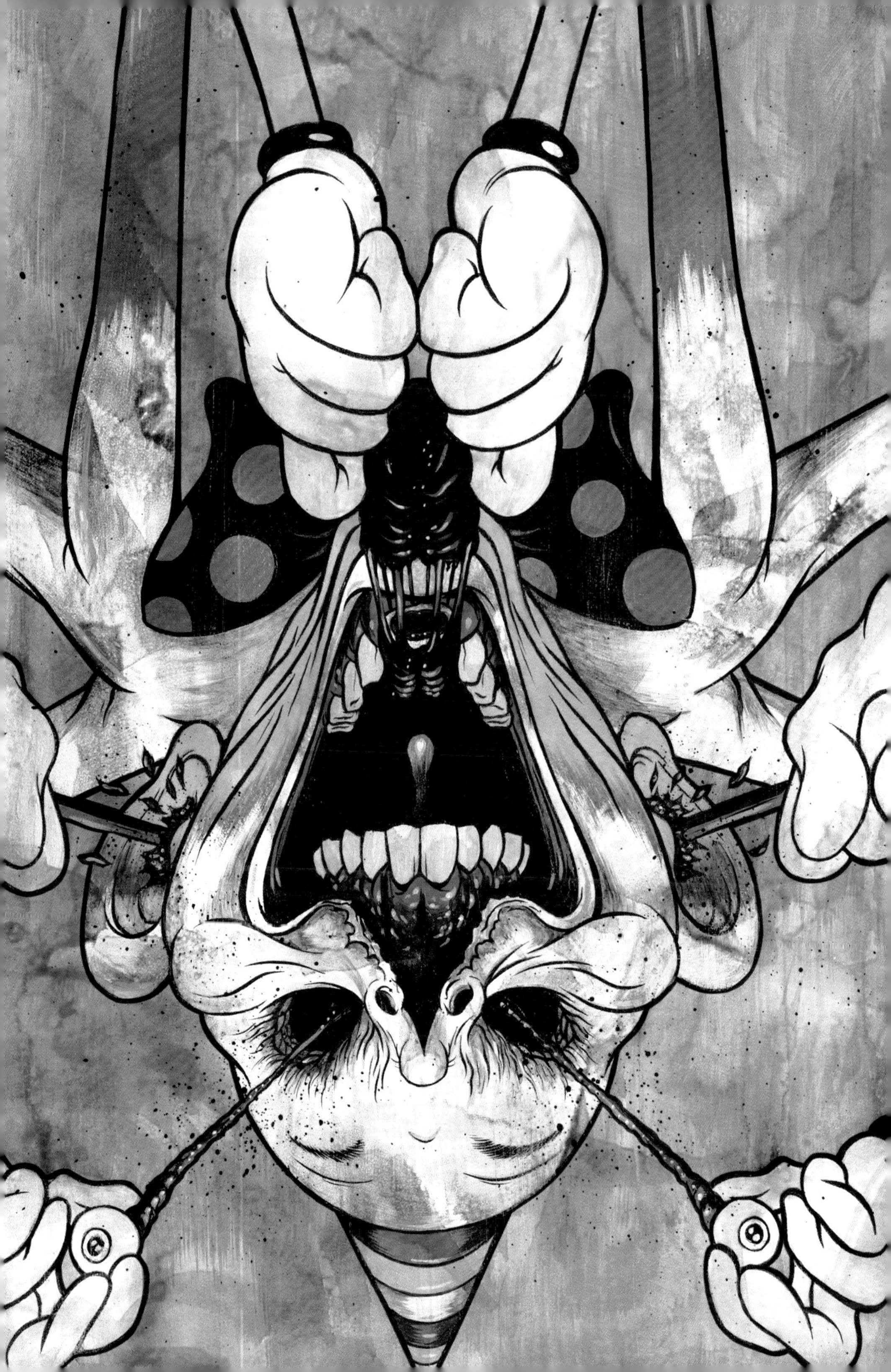

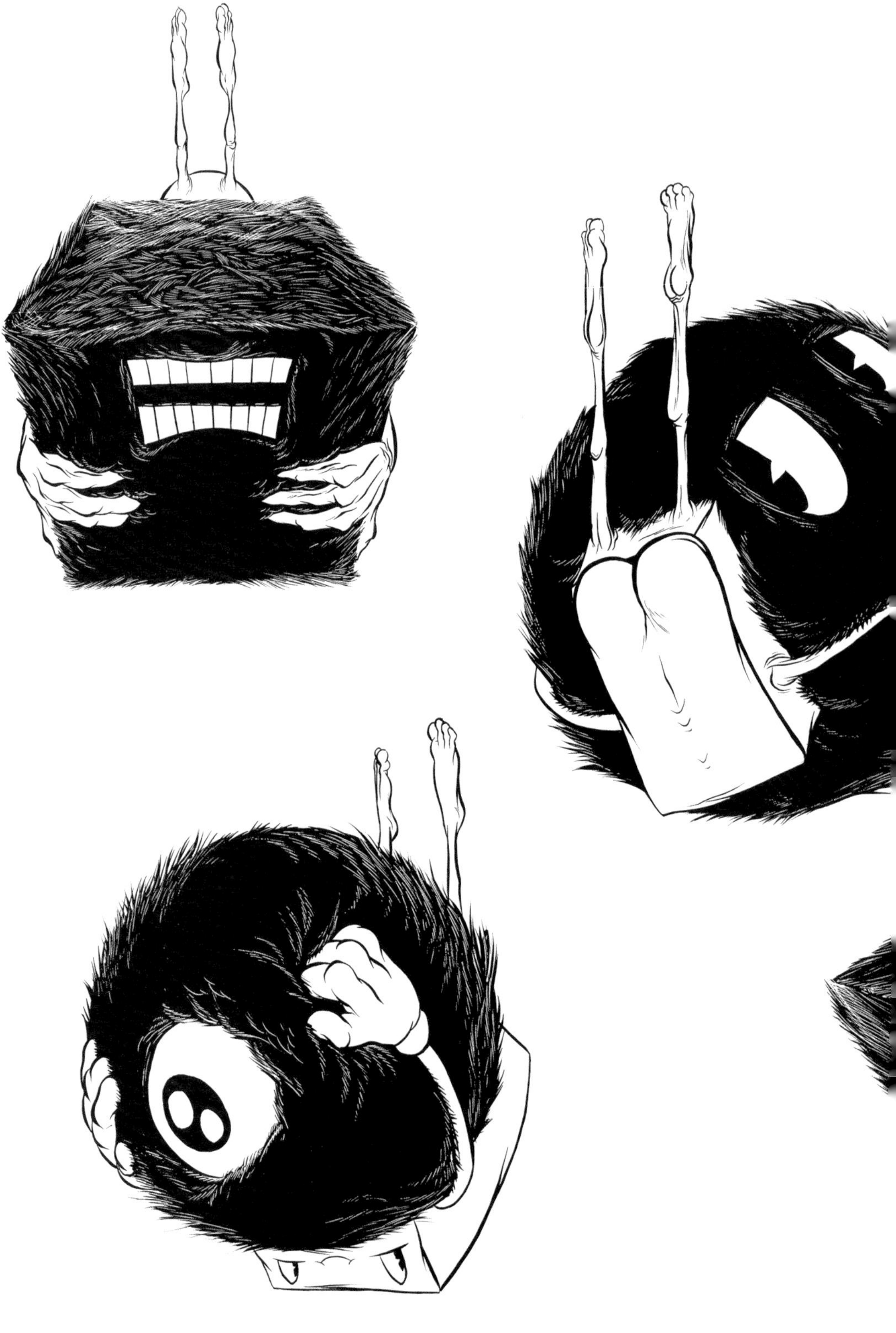

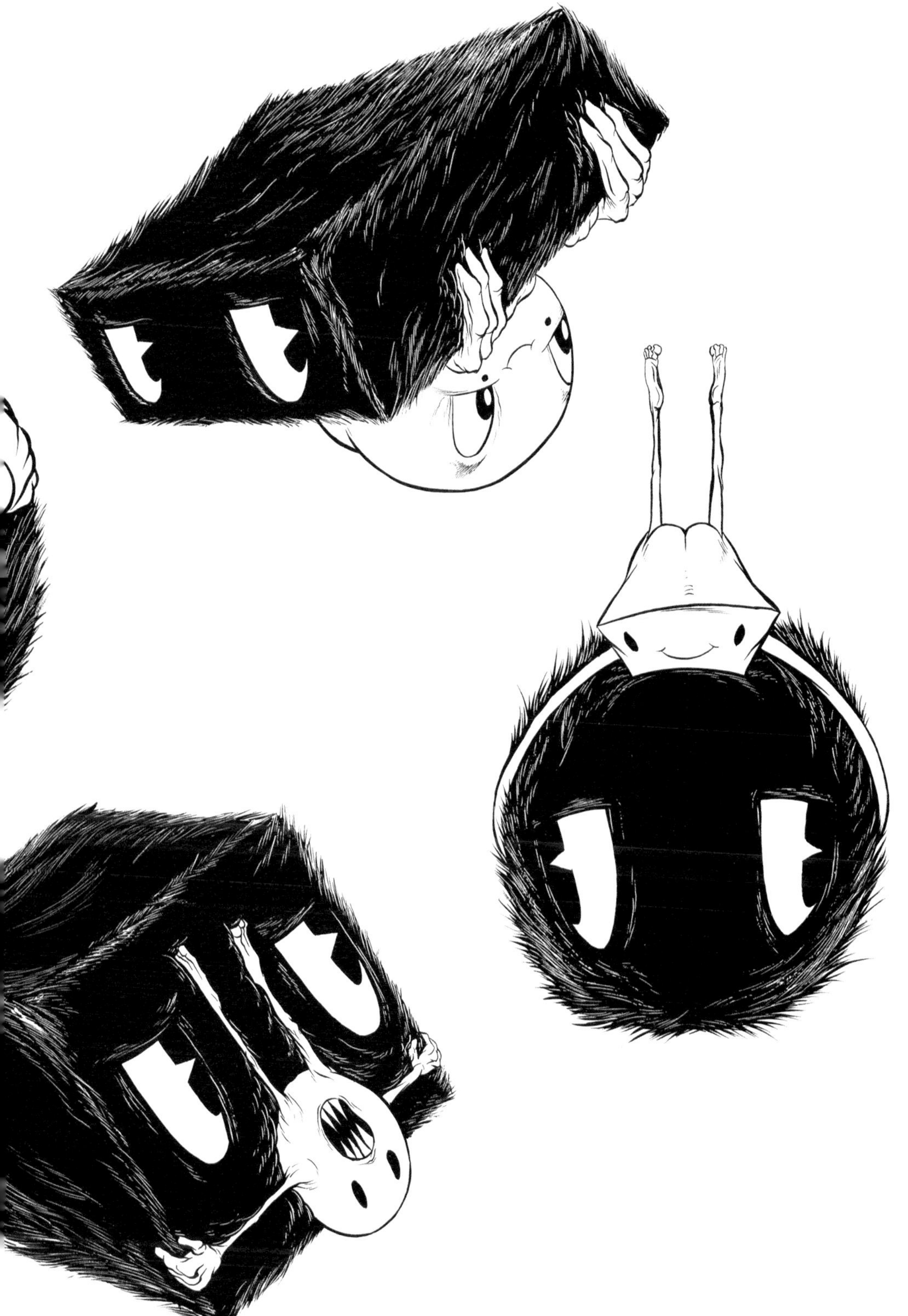

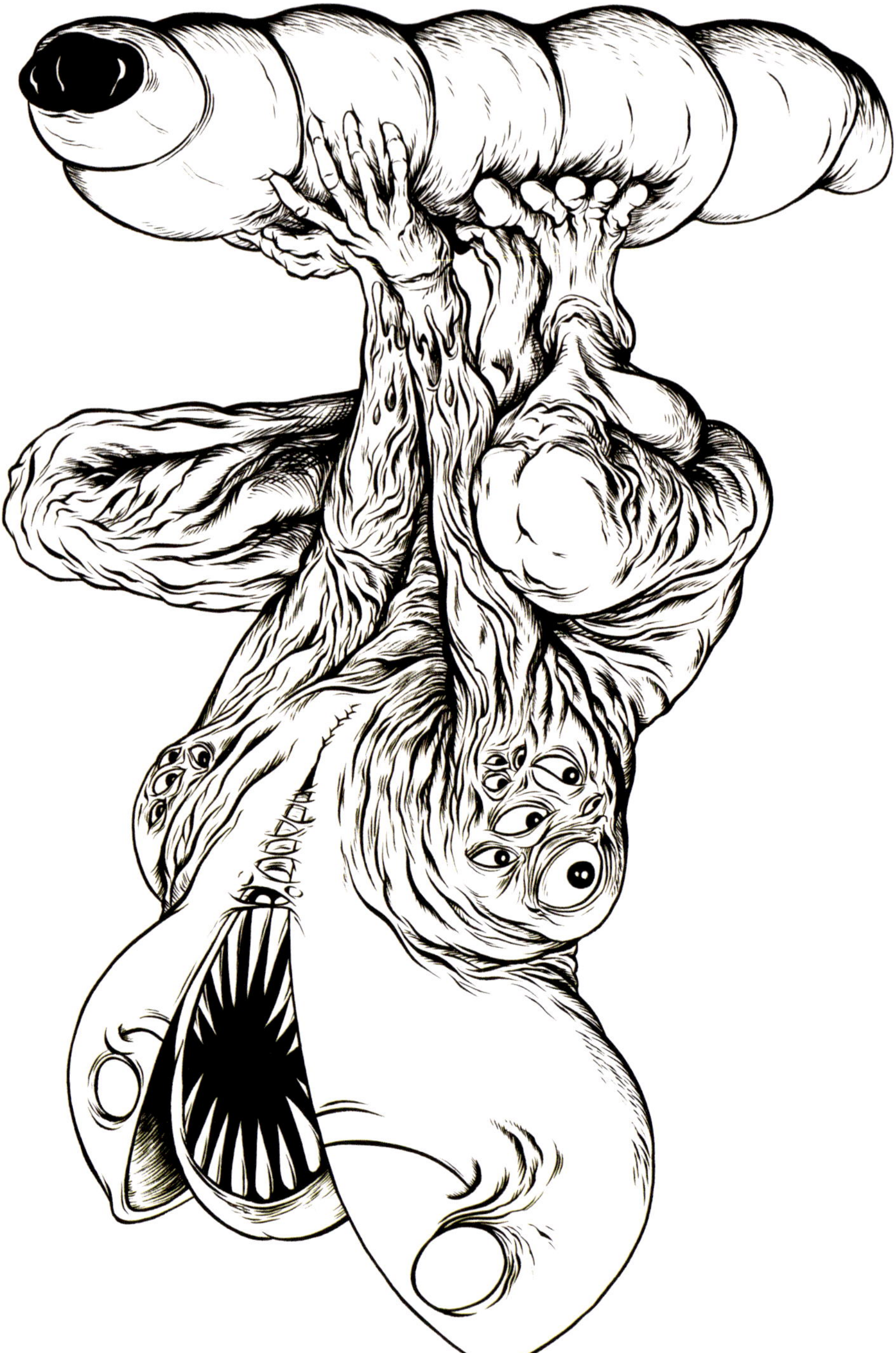

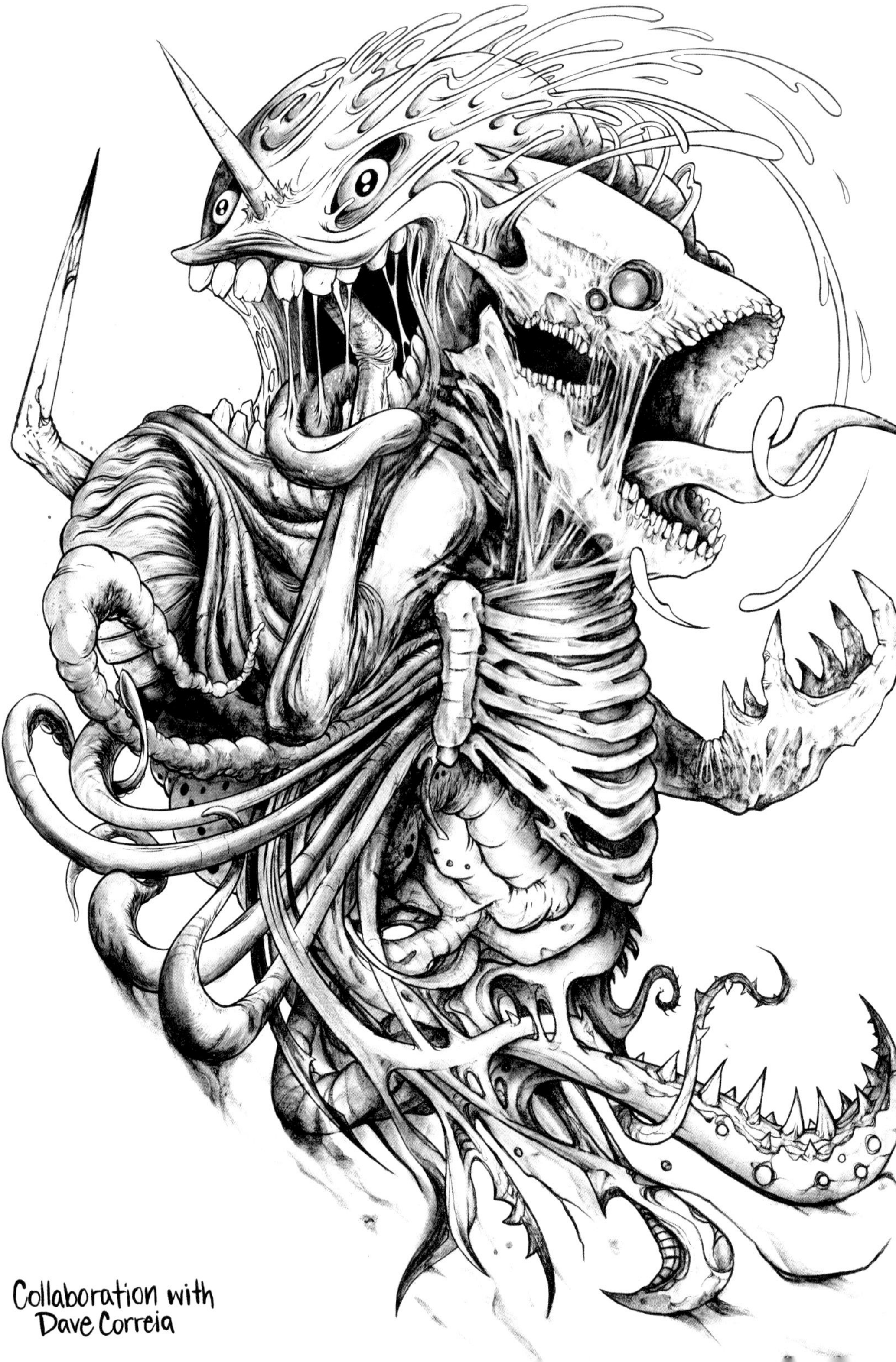

Collaboration with
Dave Correia

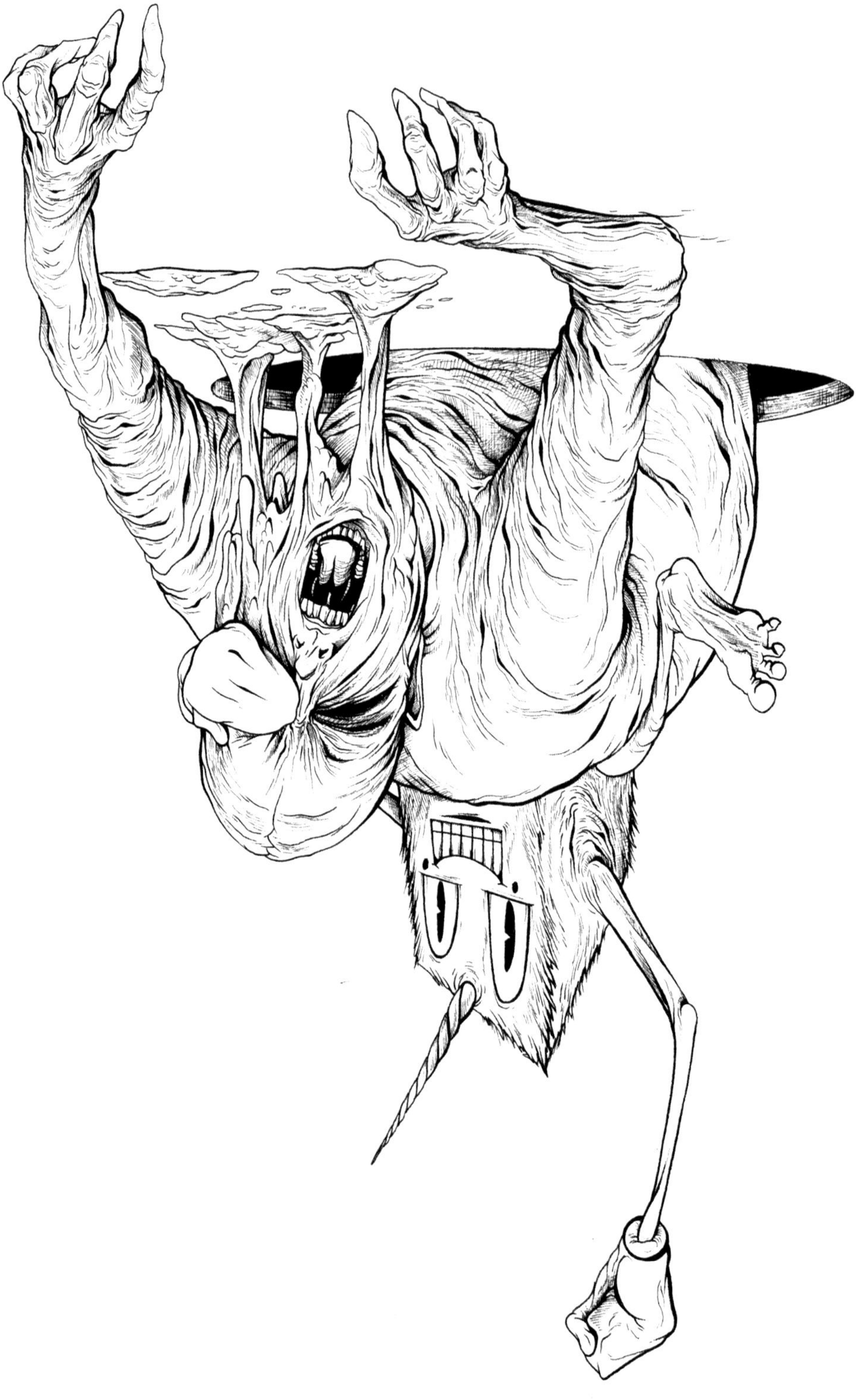

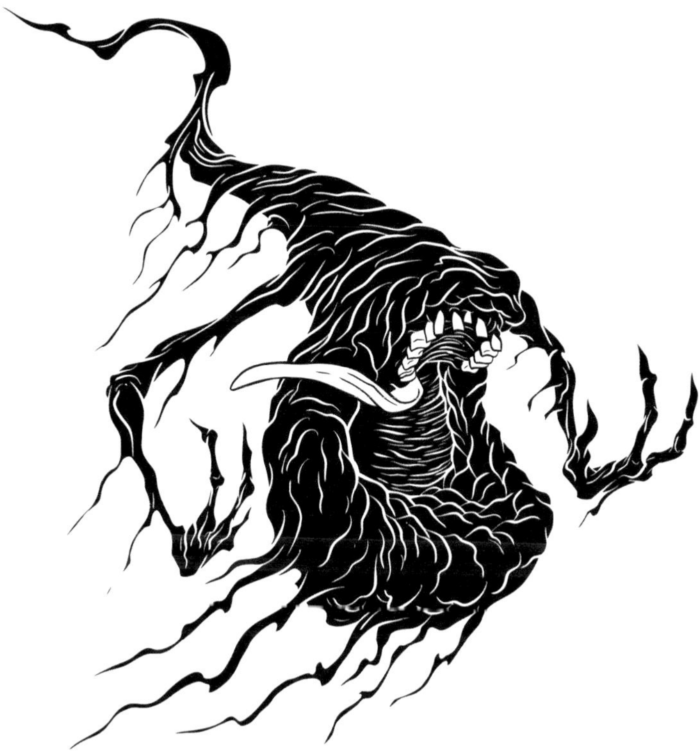

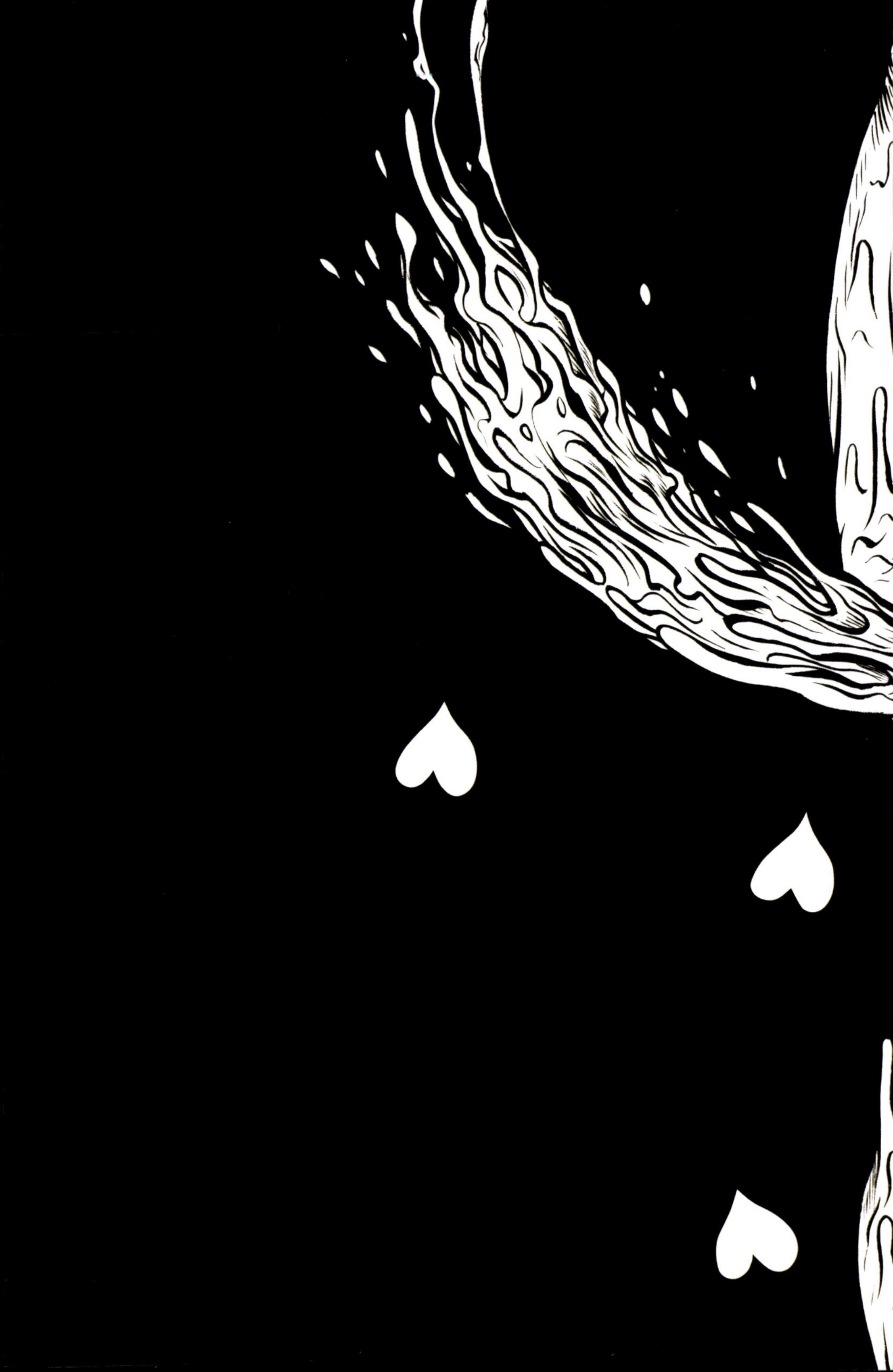

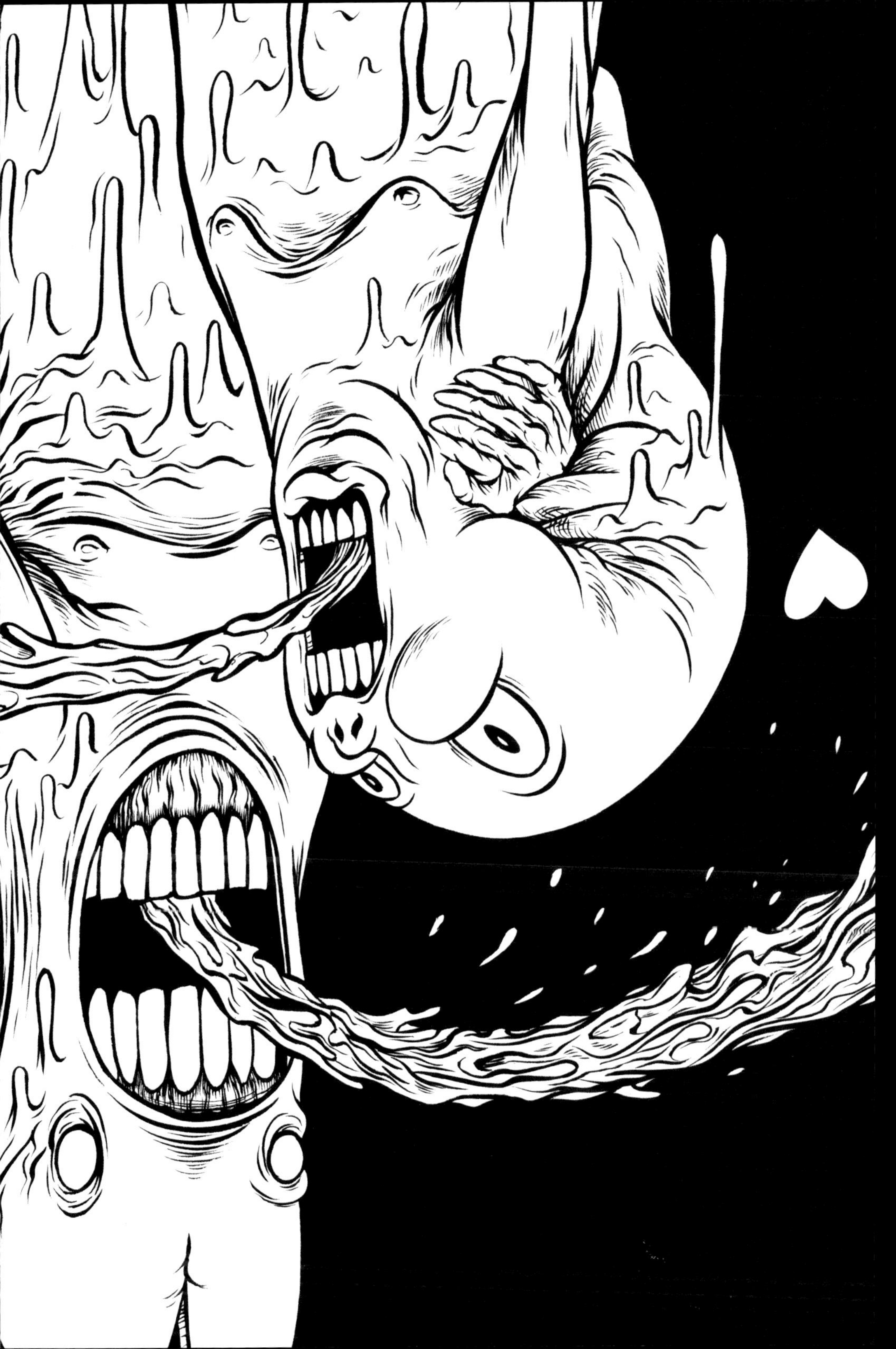

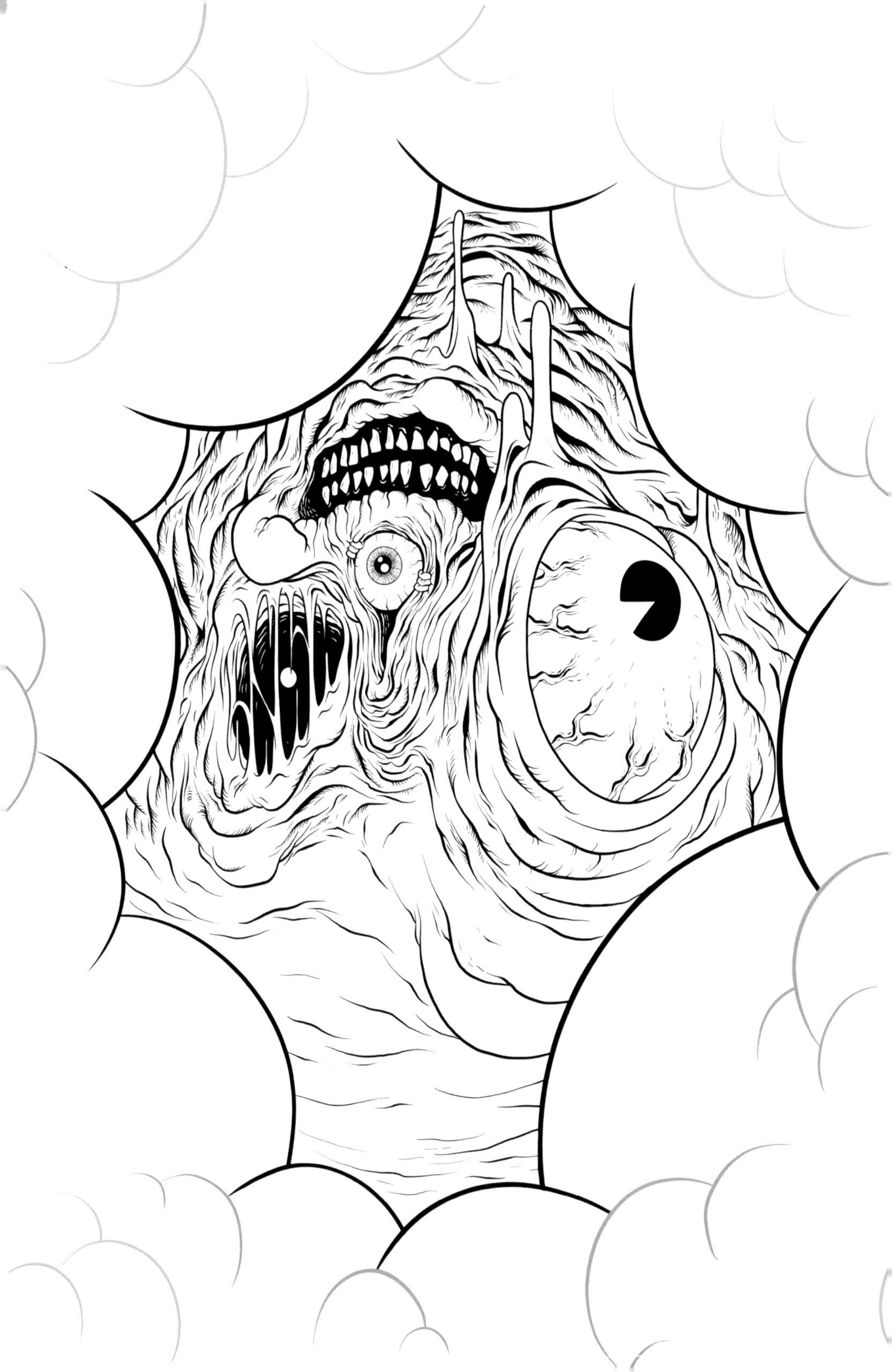

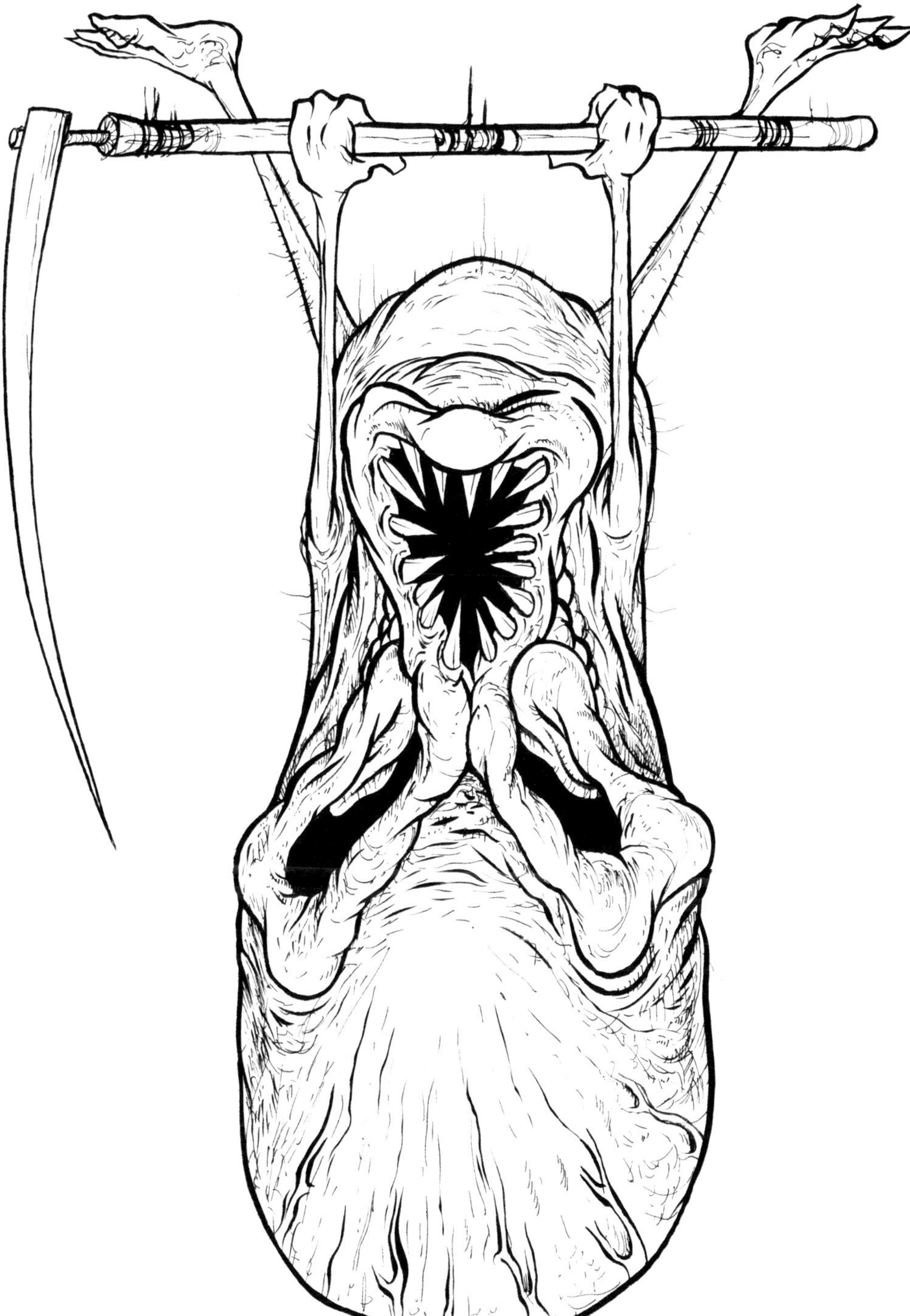

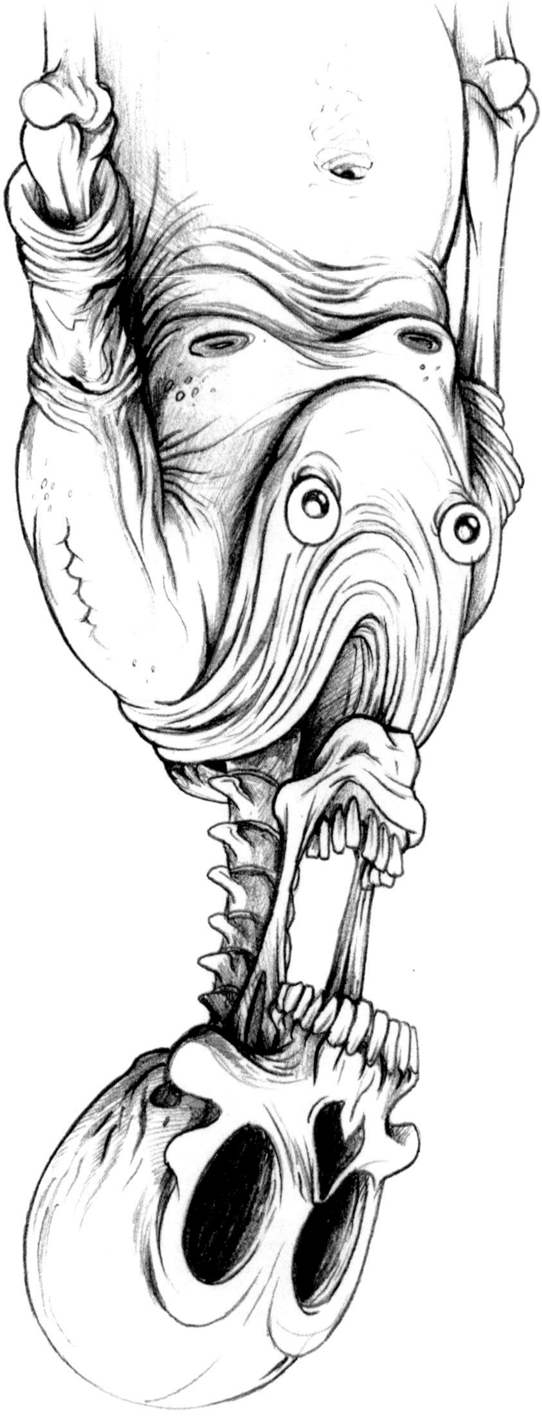

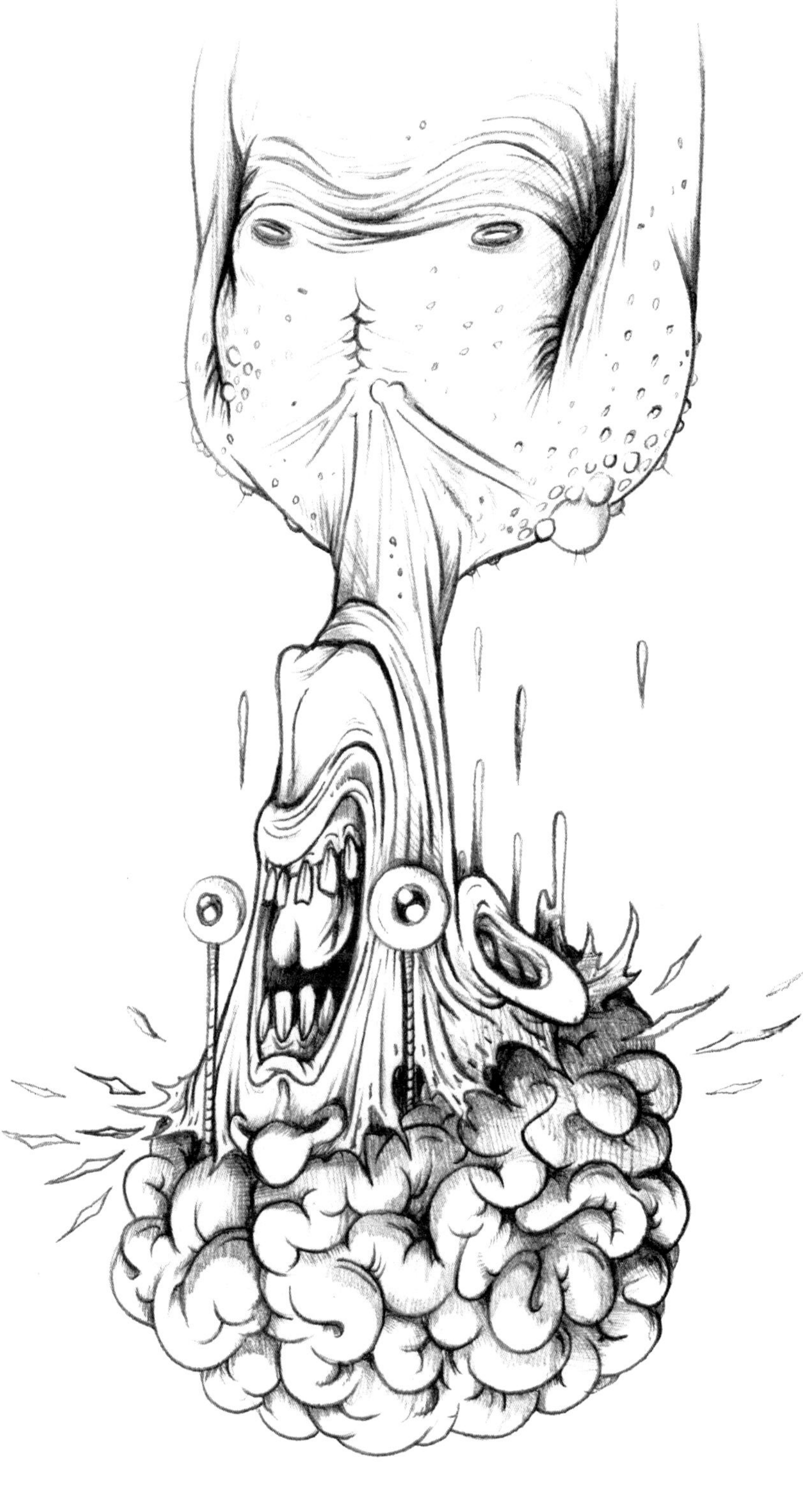

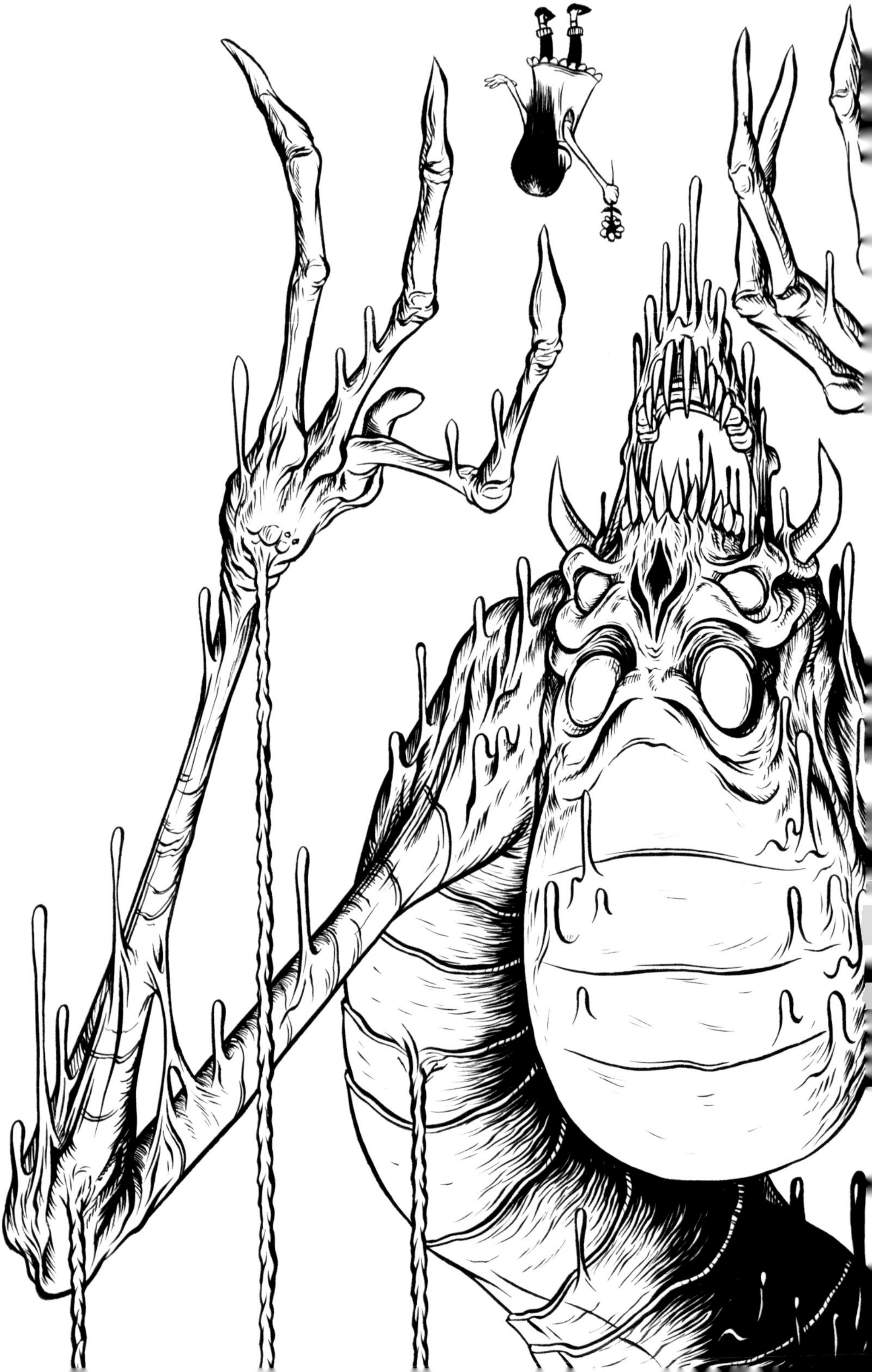

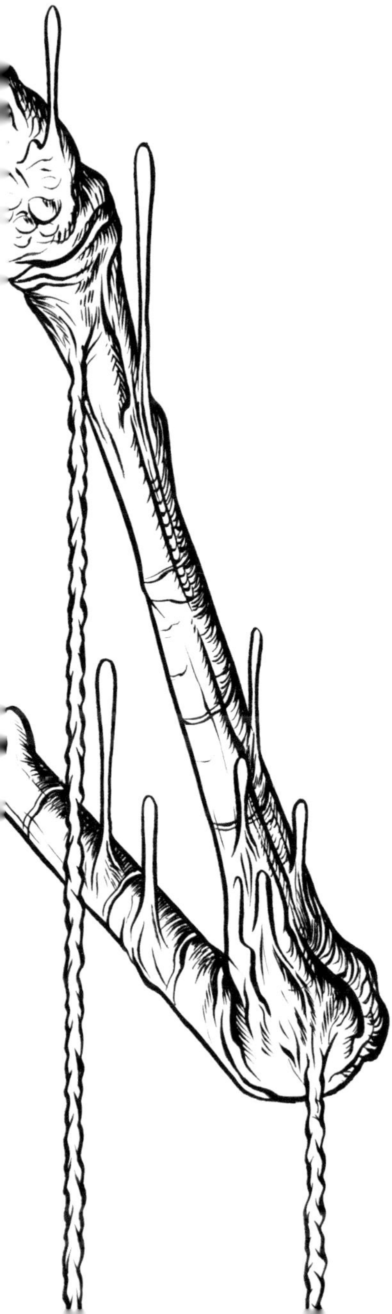

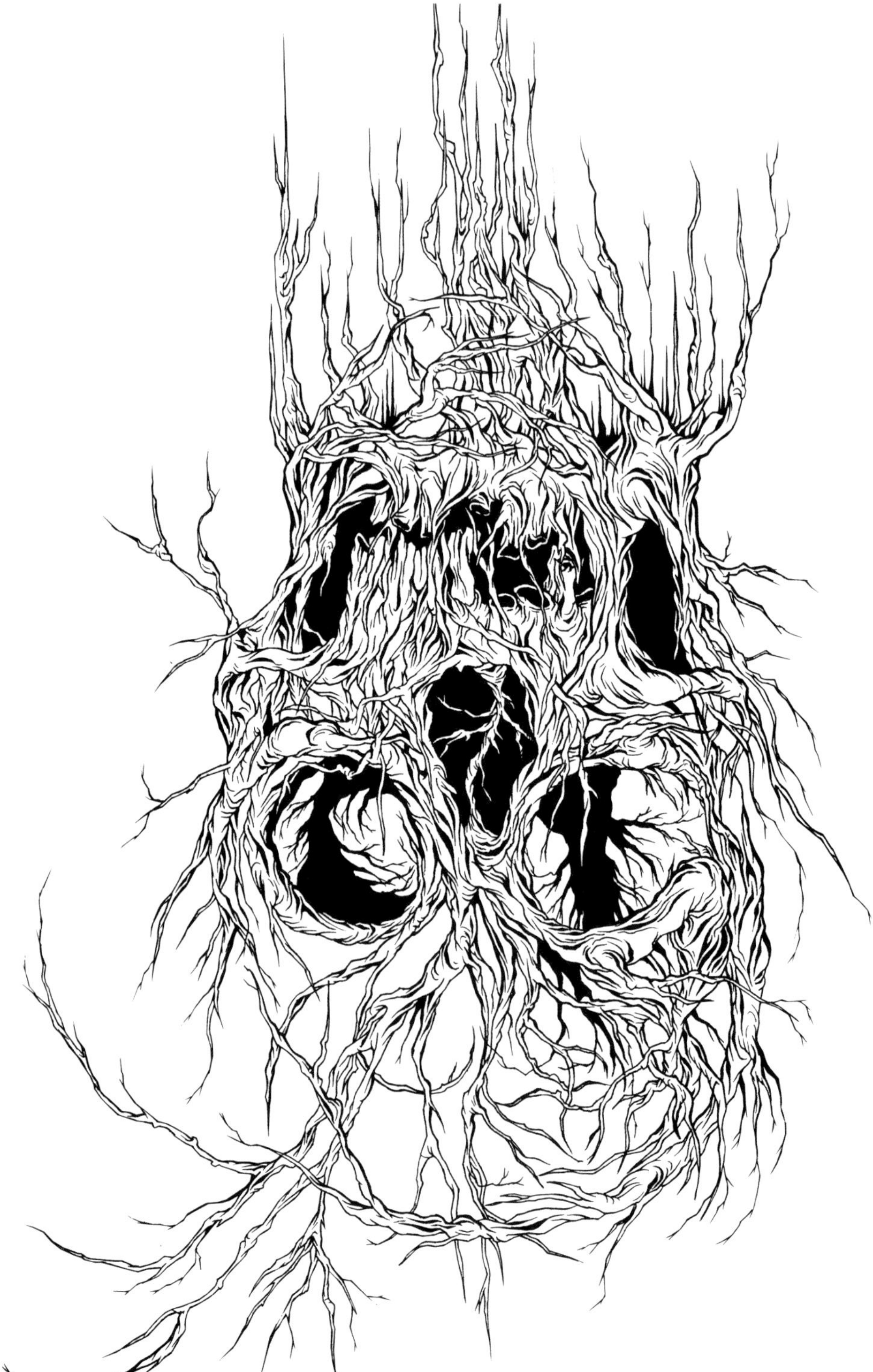

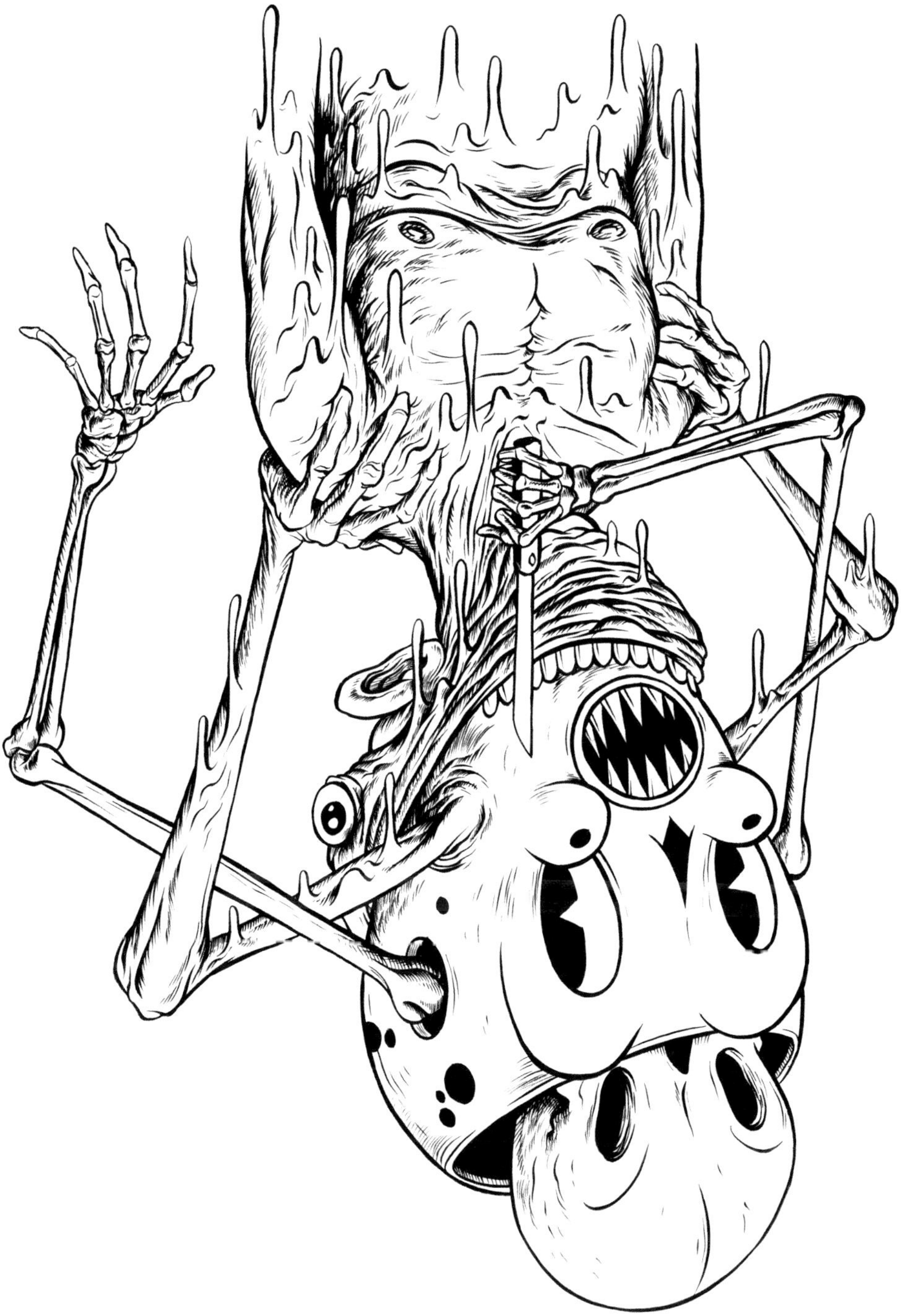

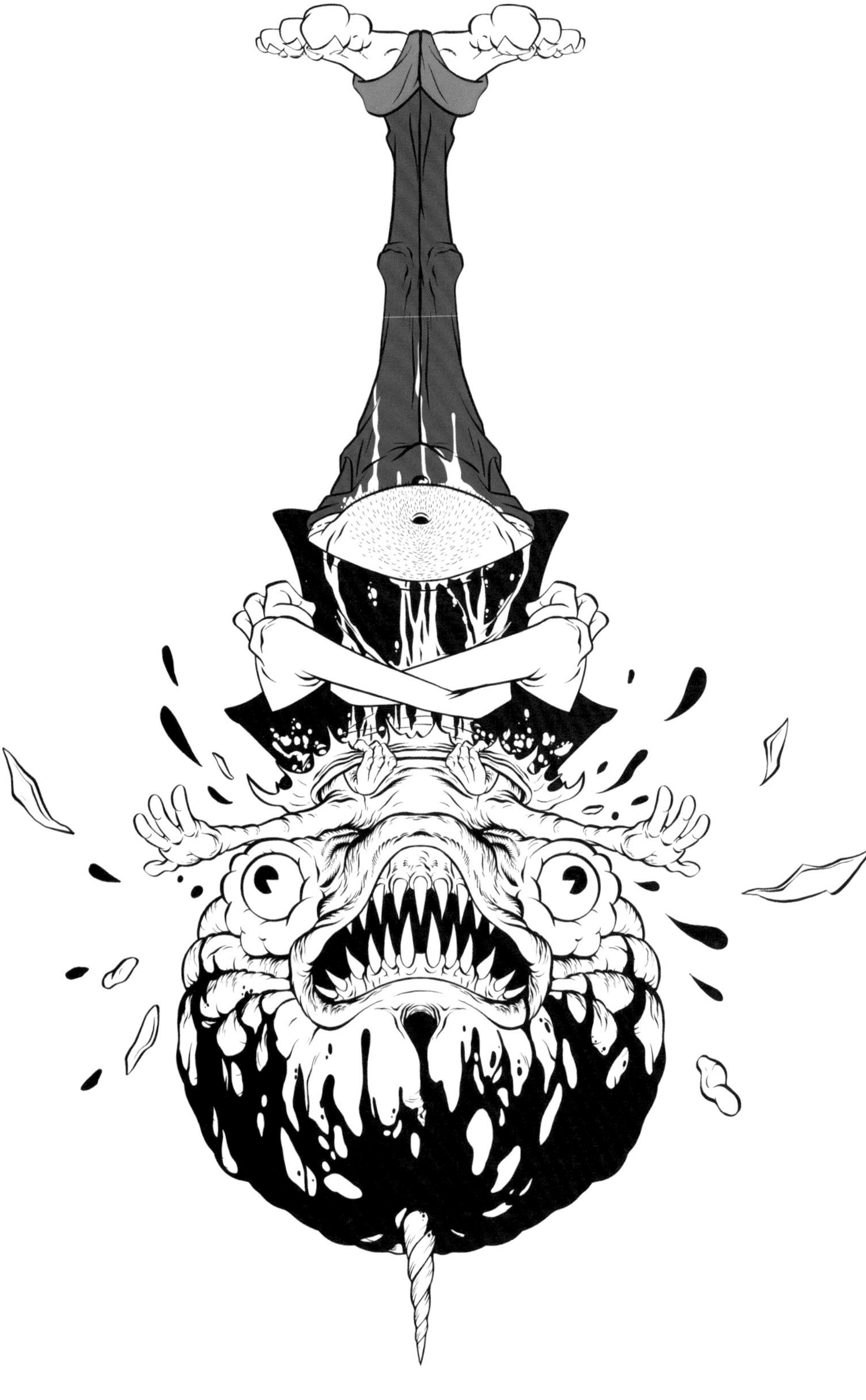

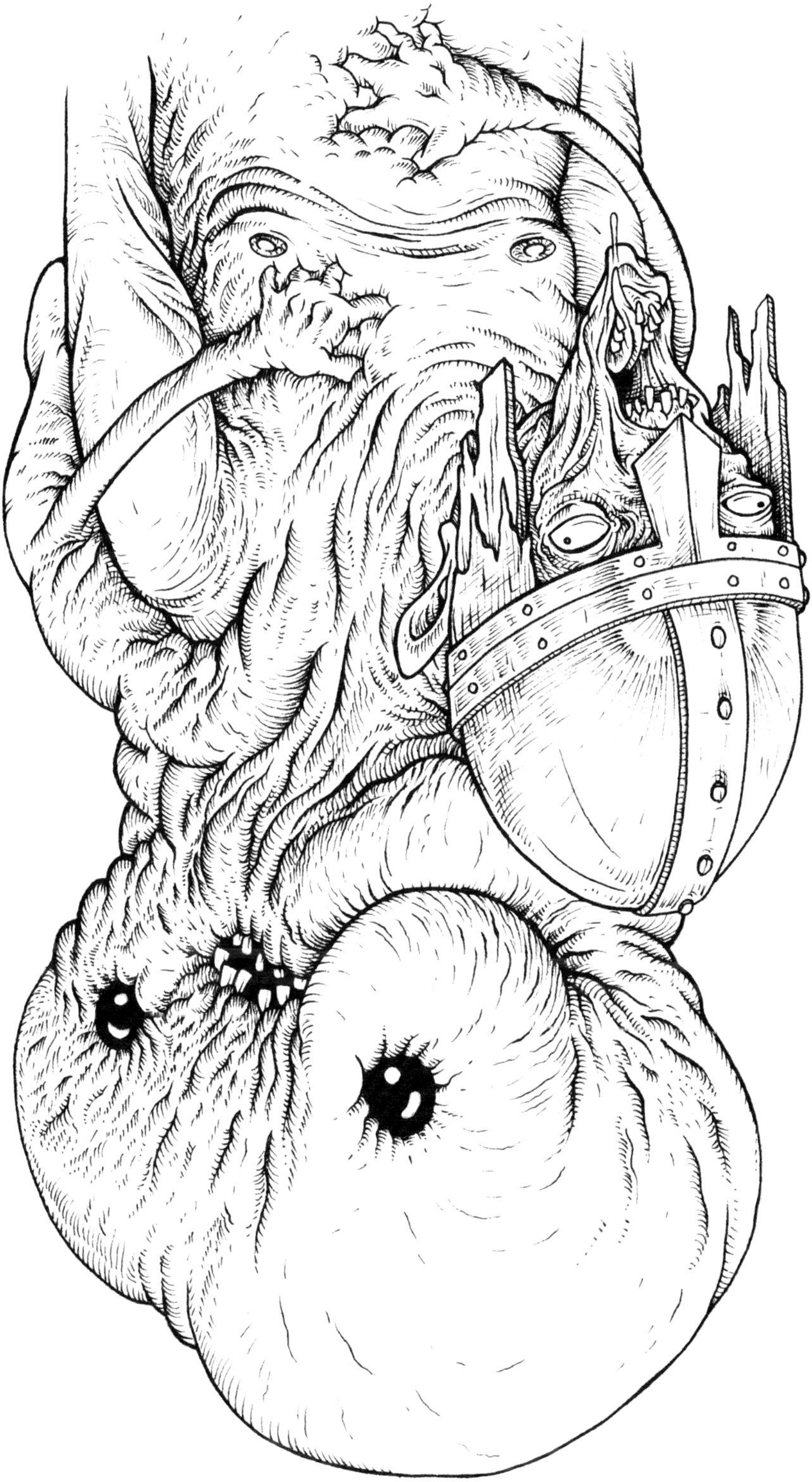

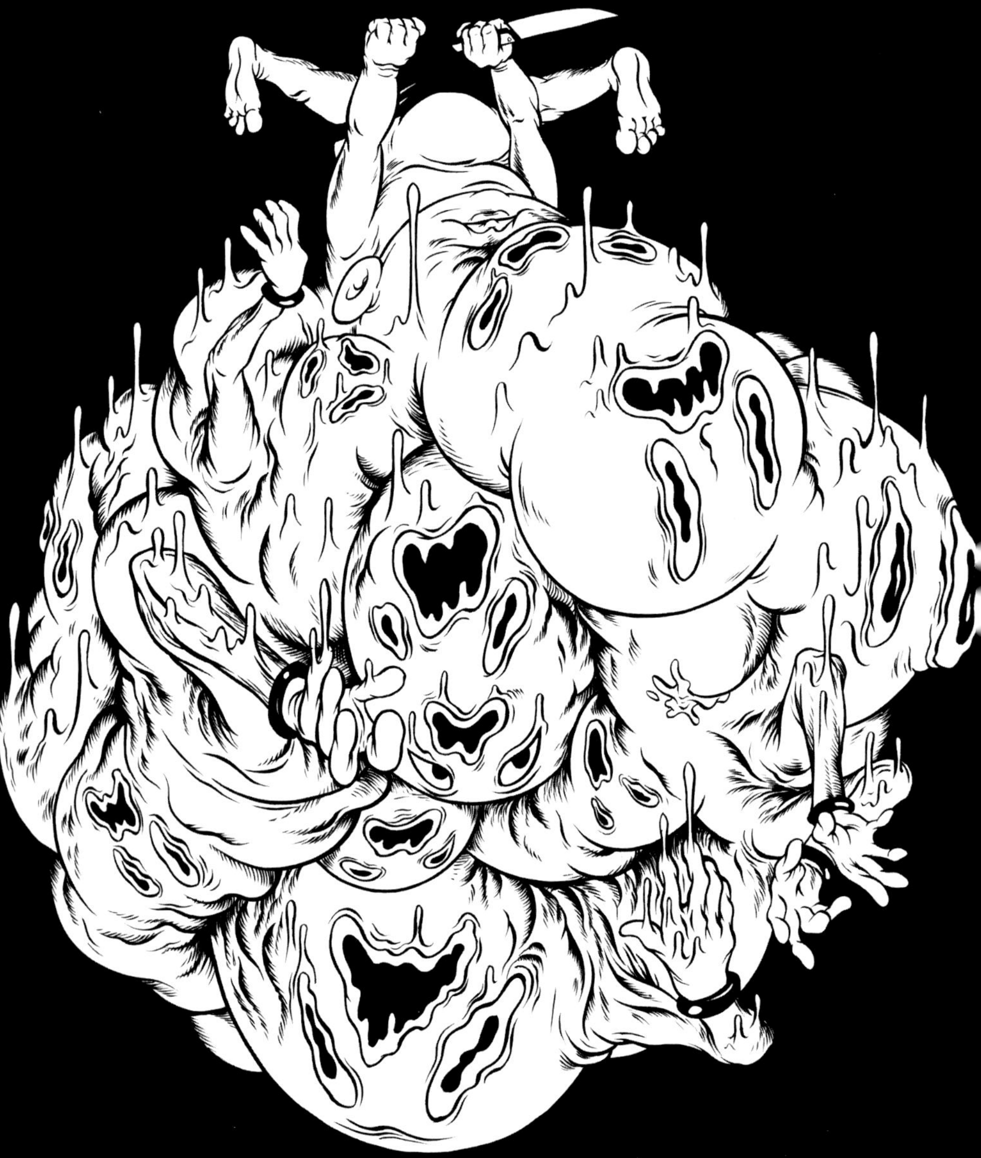

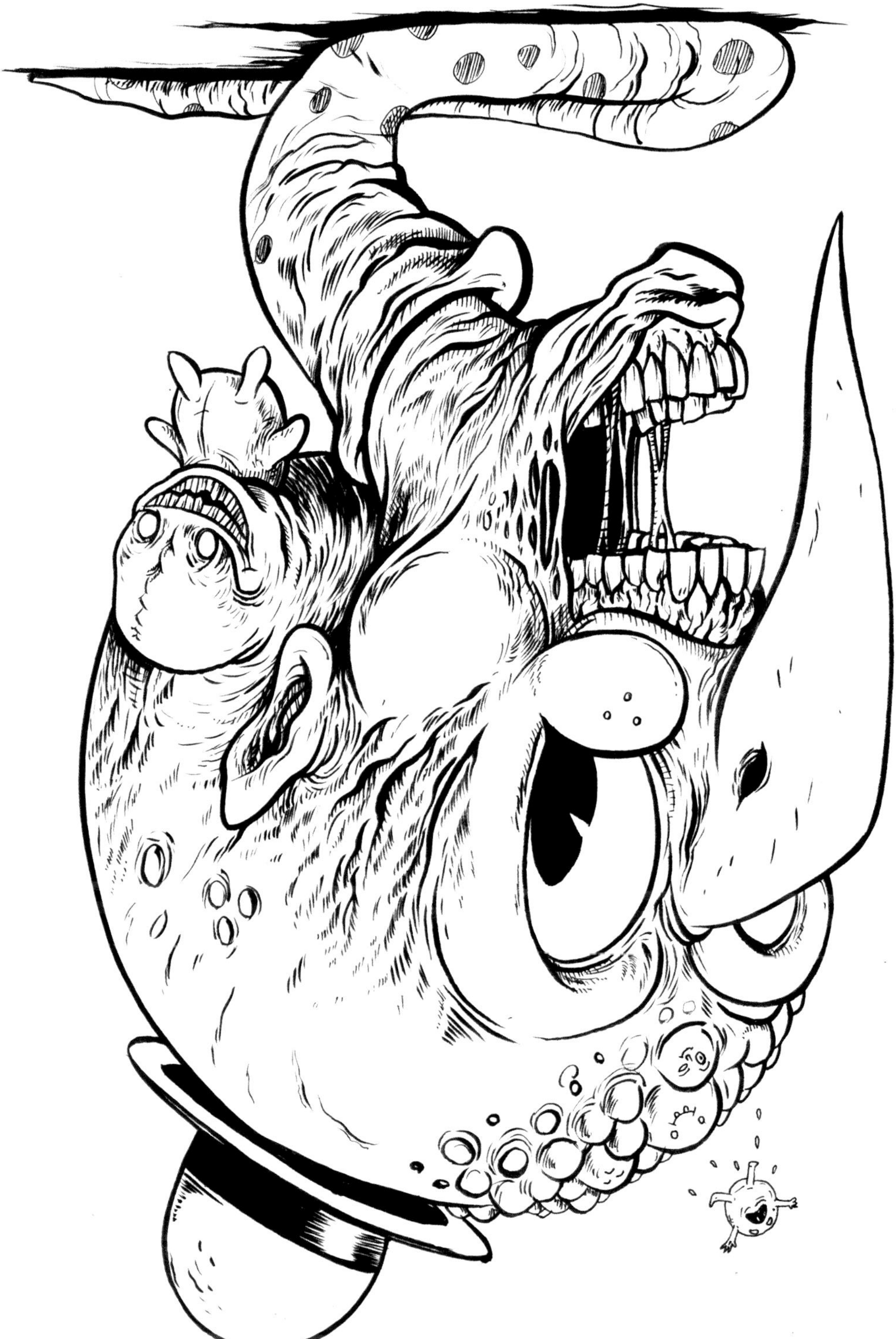

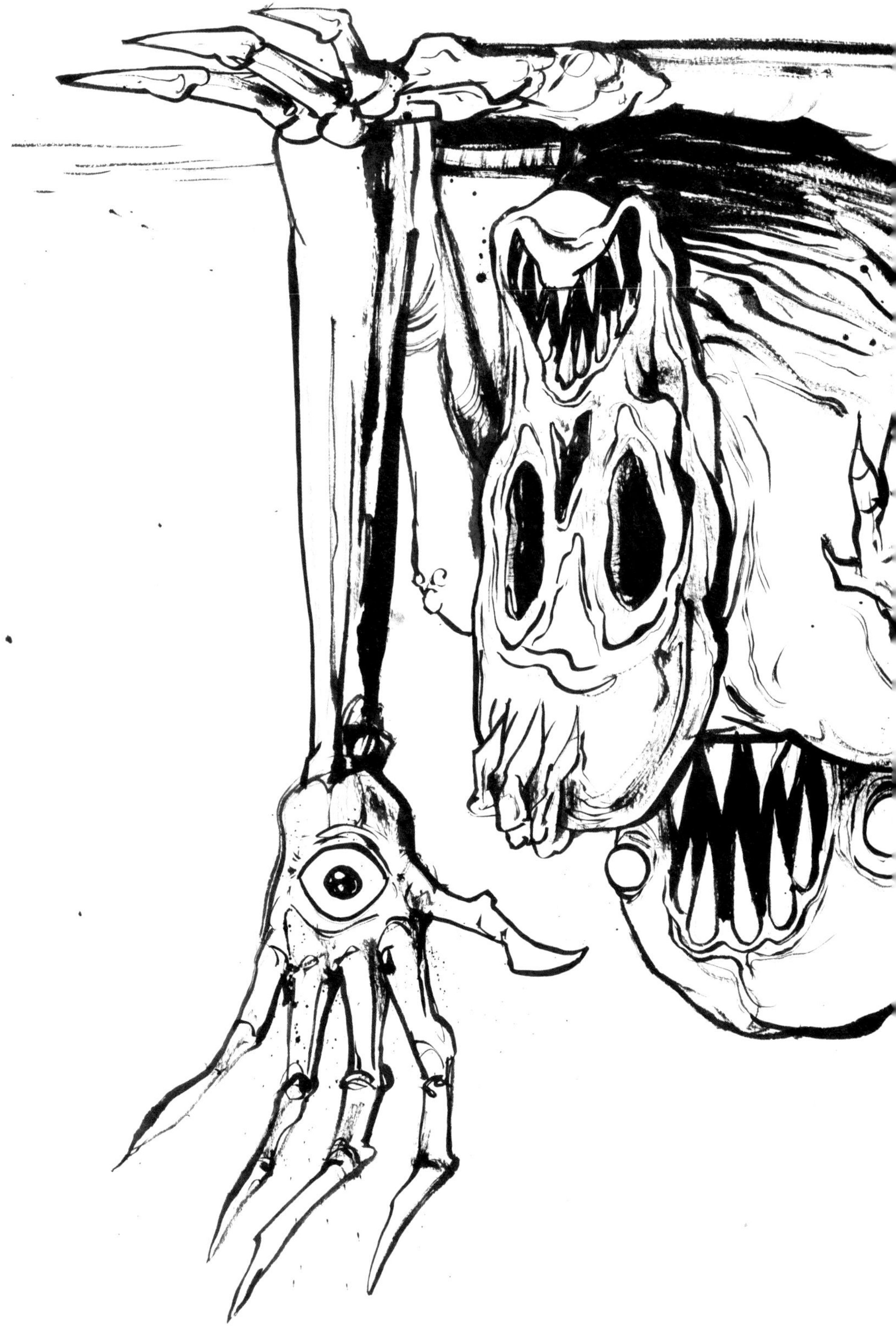

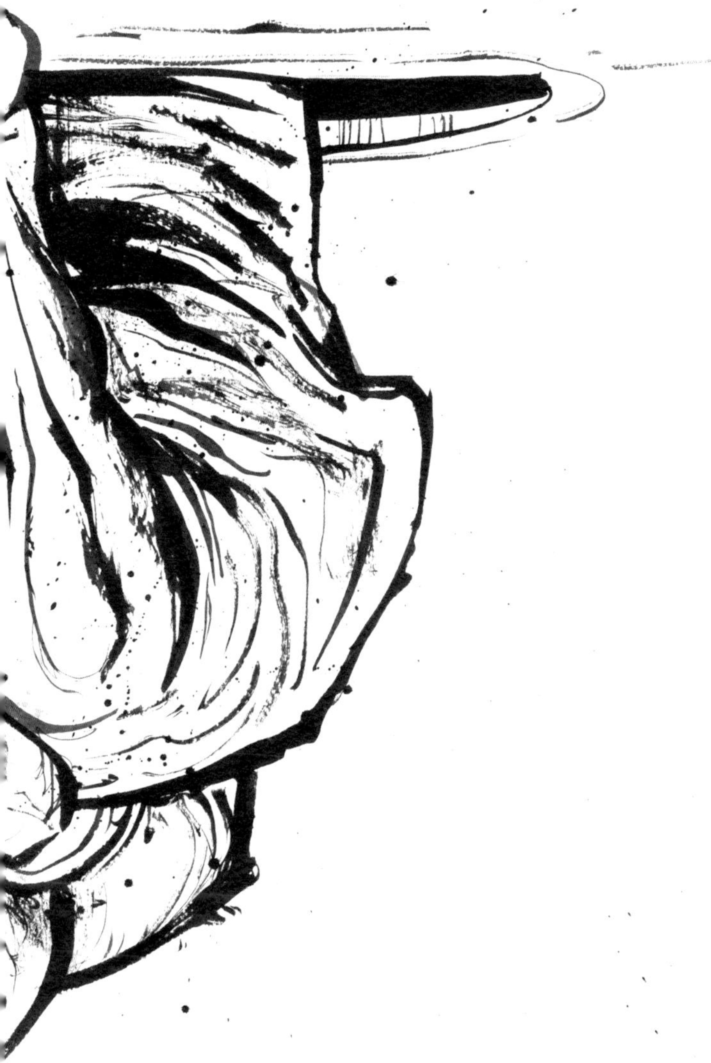

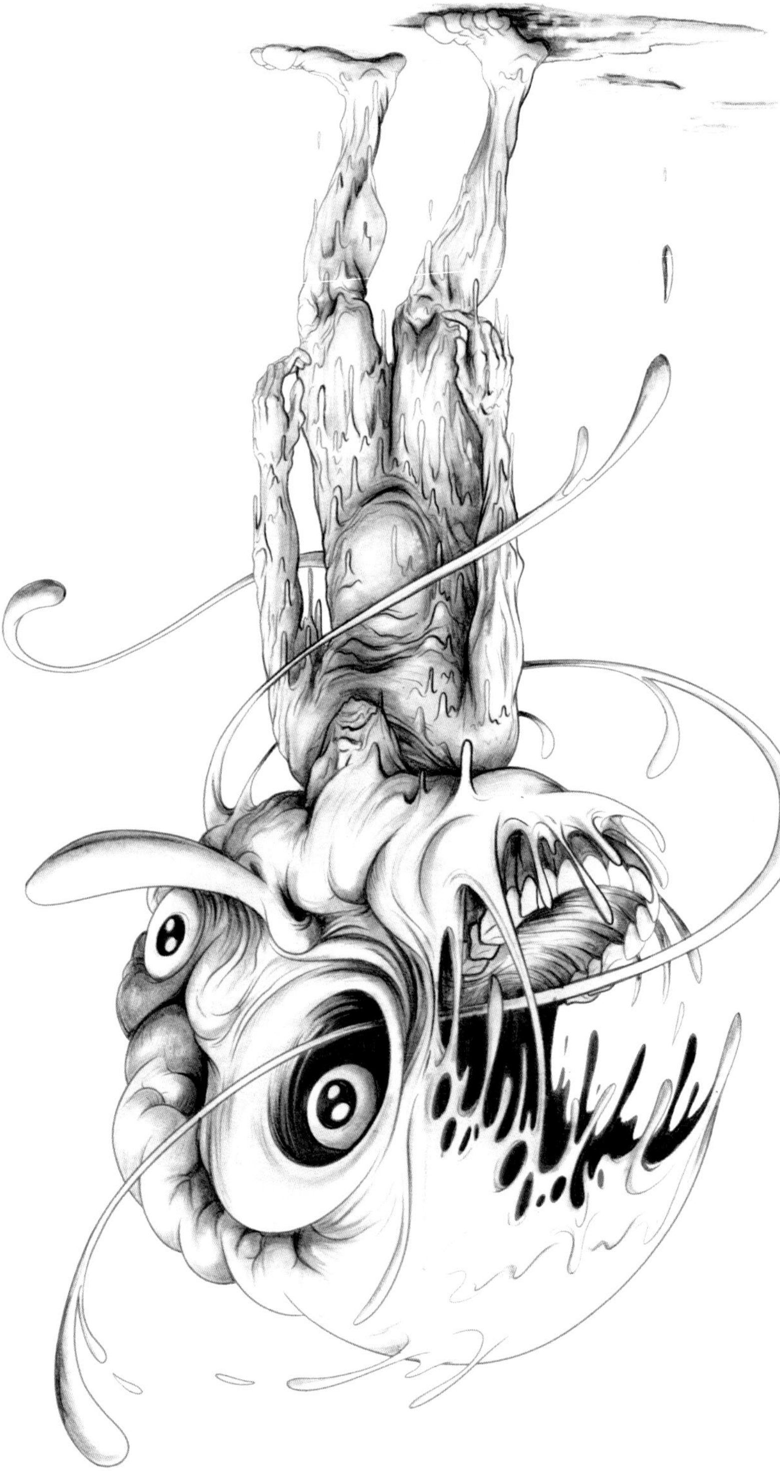

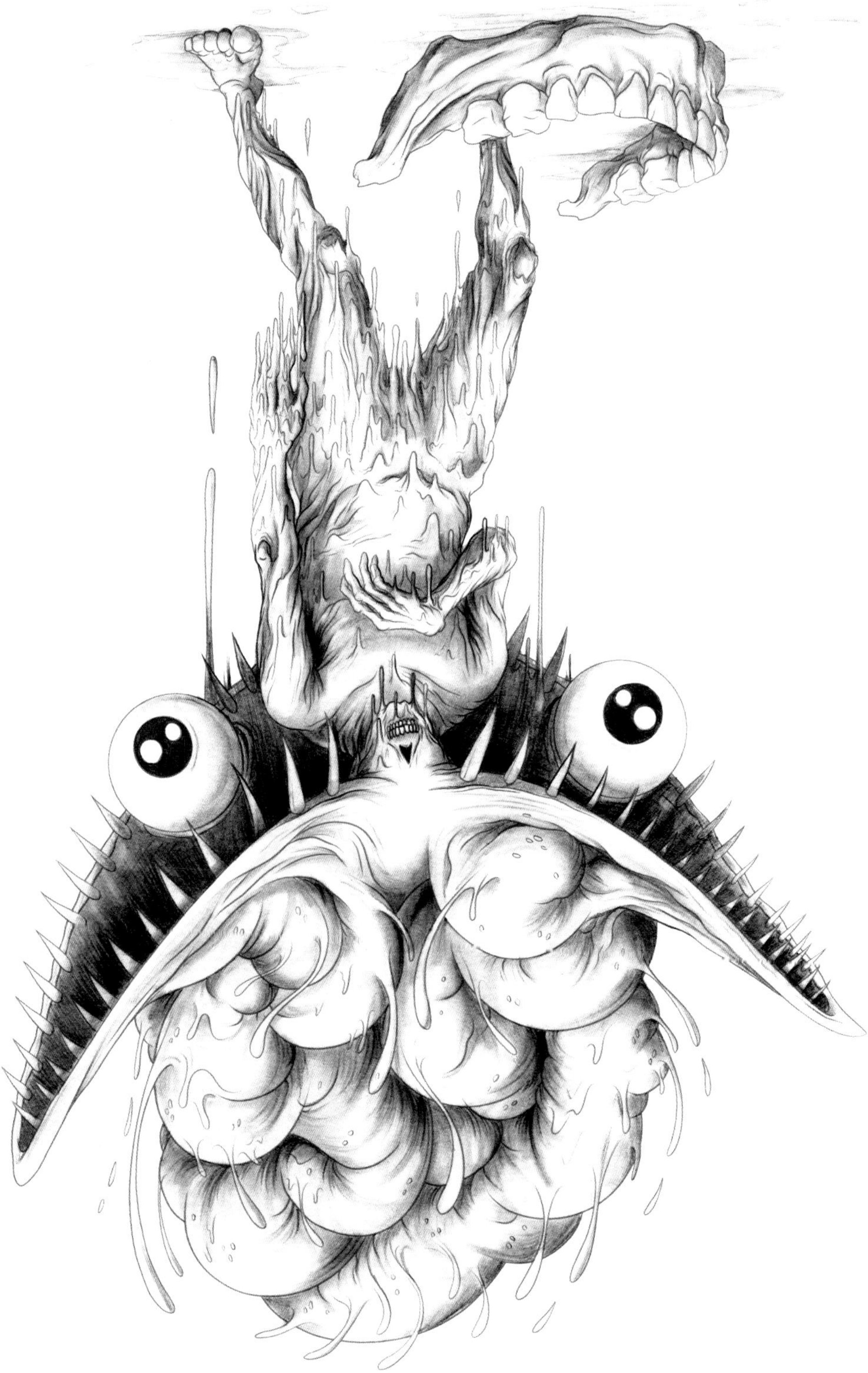

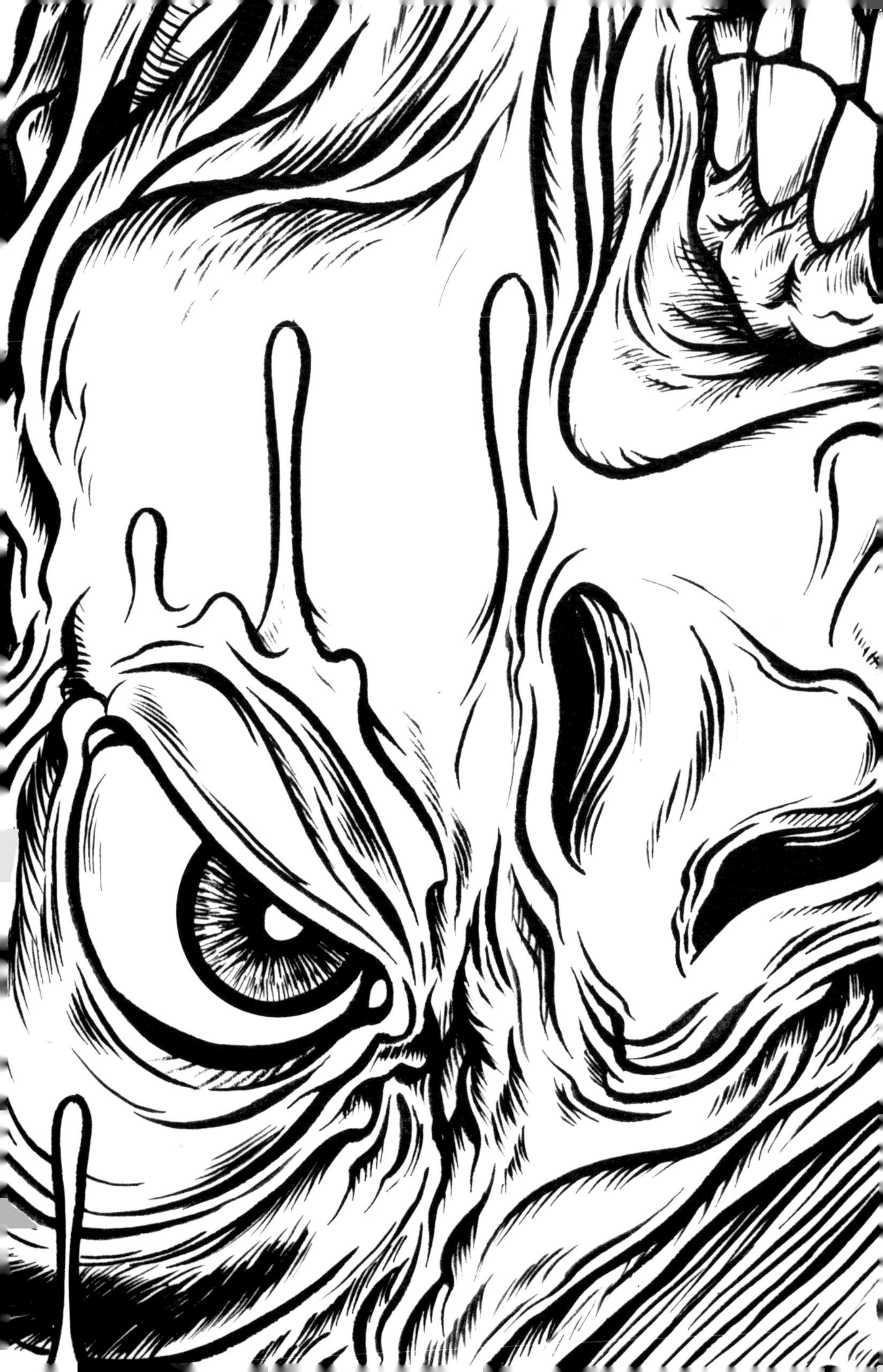

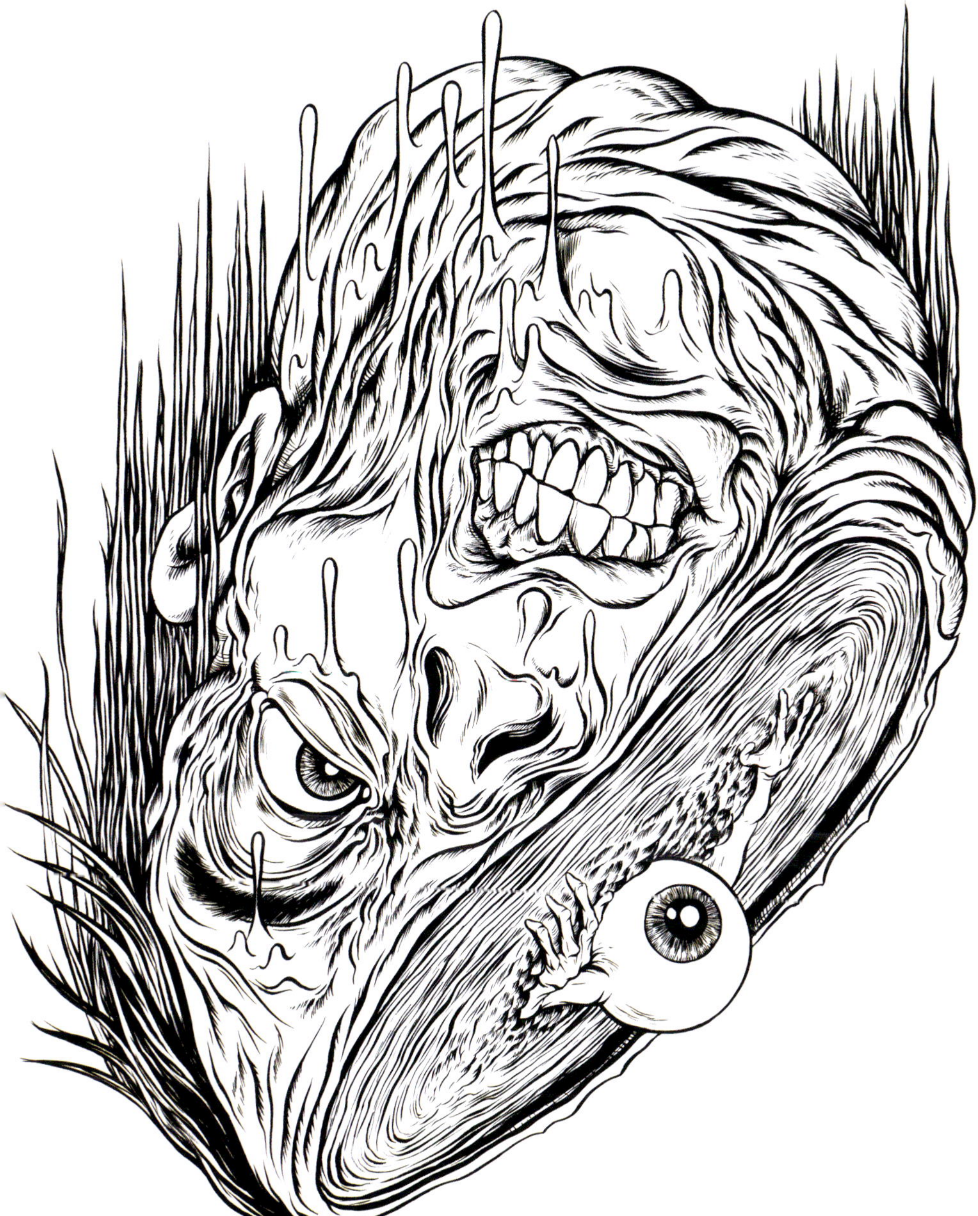

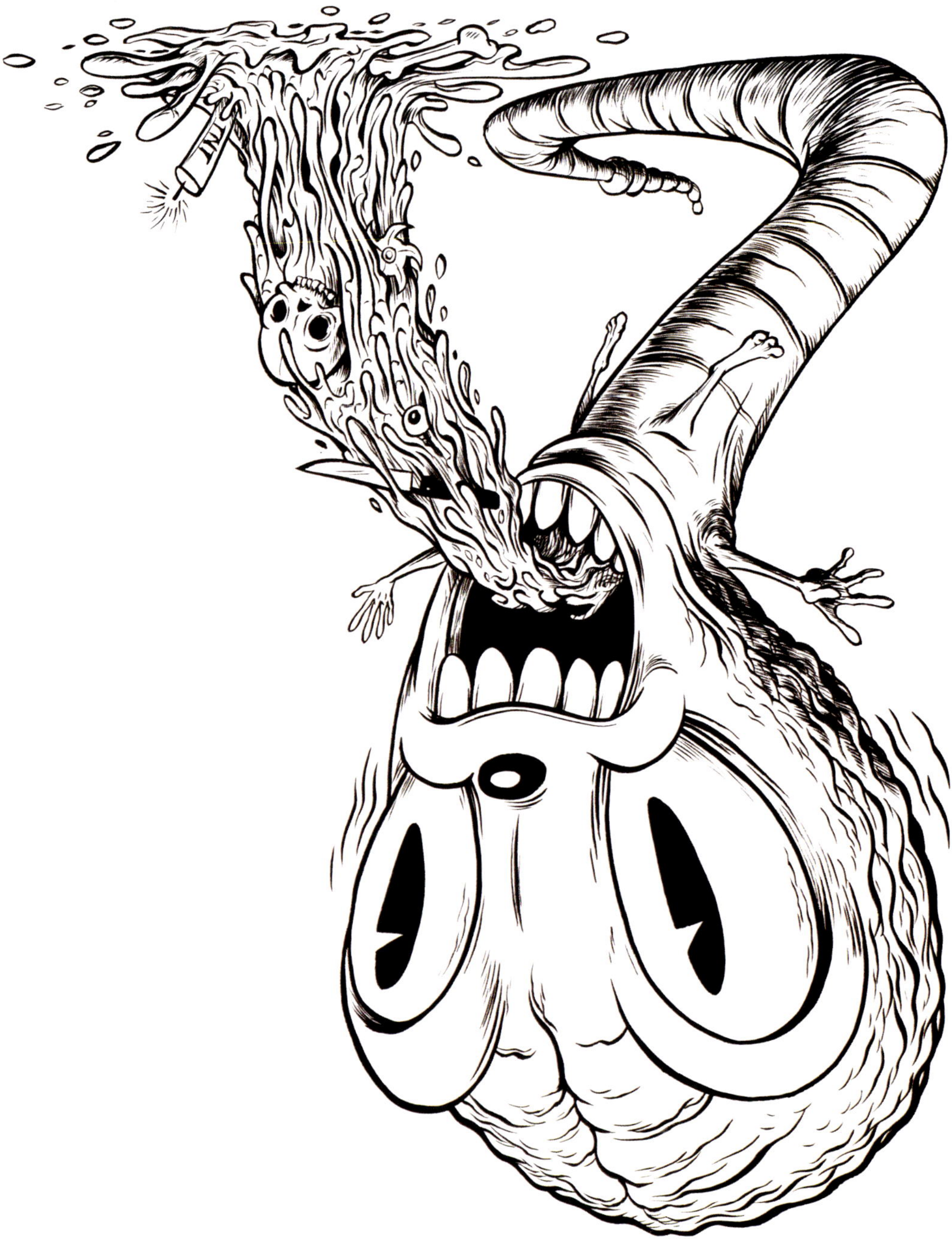
TNT

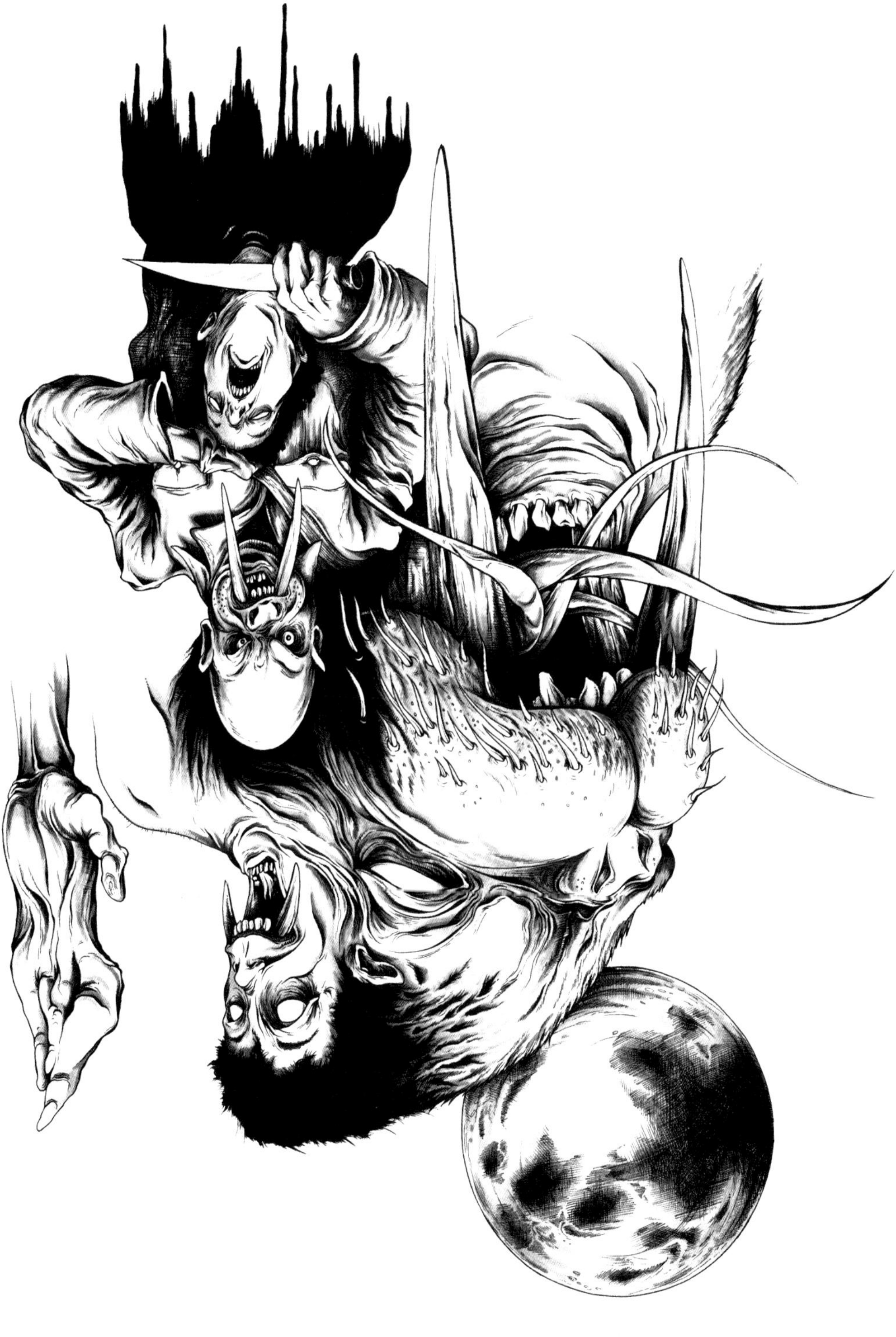

Anyone, including me, can throw a hundred different colors onto a piece of paper and trick someone into getting an emotional reaction from all of those colors. But the real test is trying to get that same reaction using only black and white. I'm gonna keep trying.

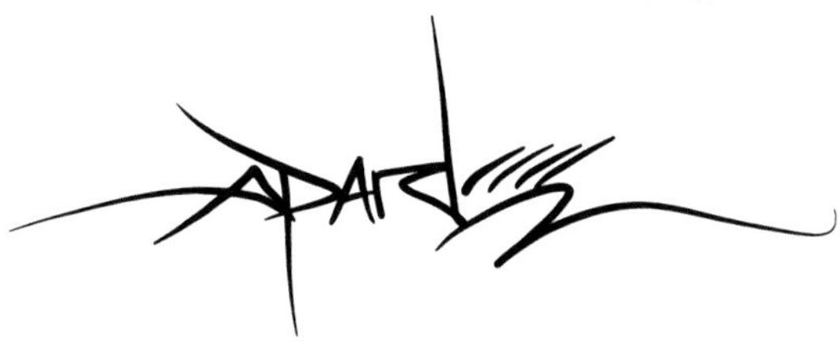

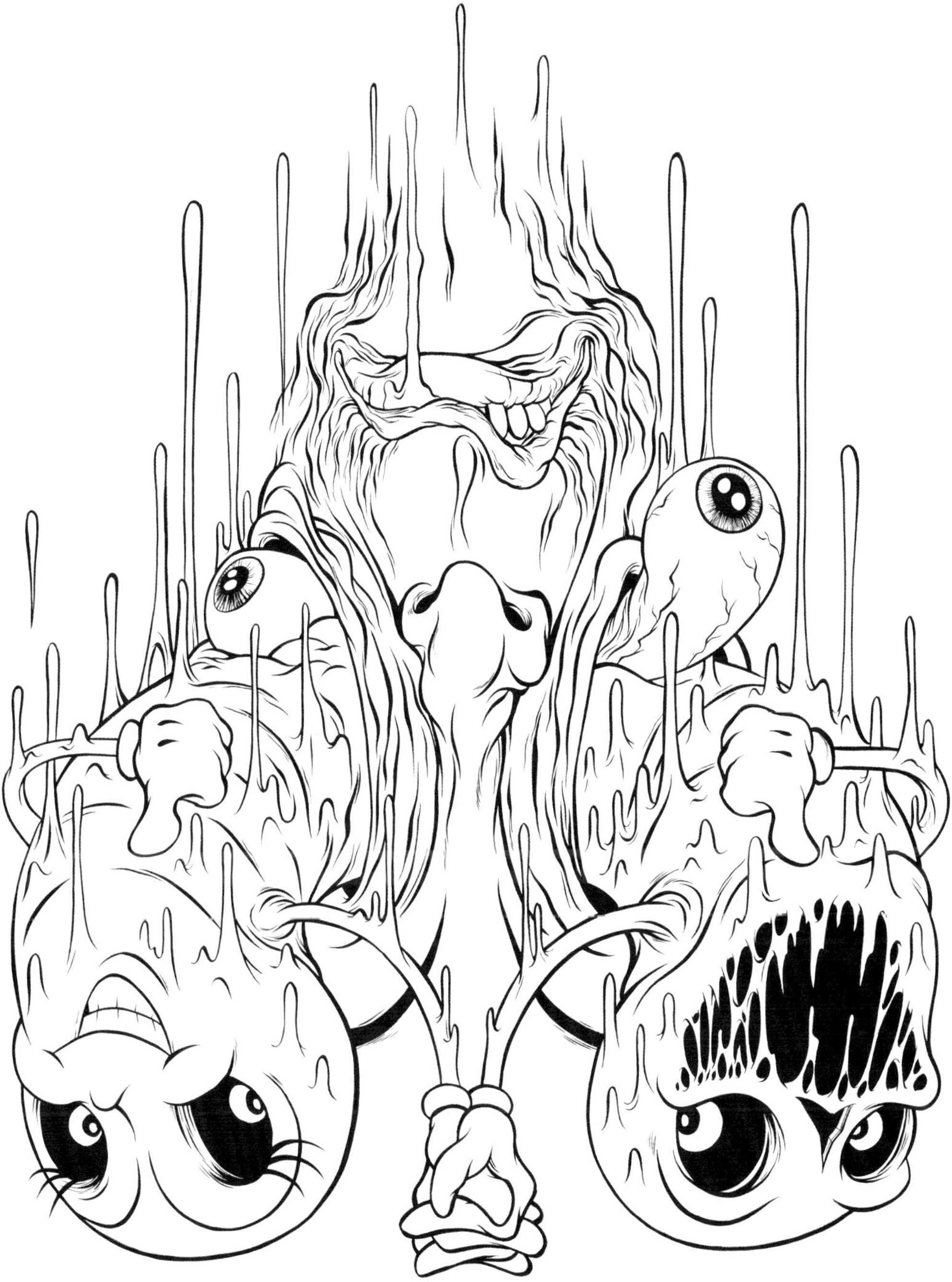

DEAD LINES

the Art of Alex Pardee

Printed in China.

All art, layout, design and years of confusion by ALEX PARDEE
@alexpardee
alexpardee.com

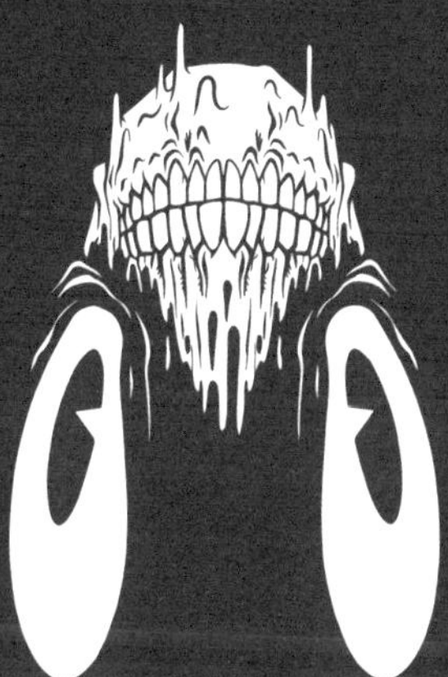

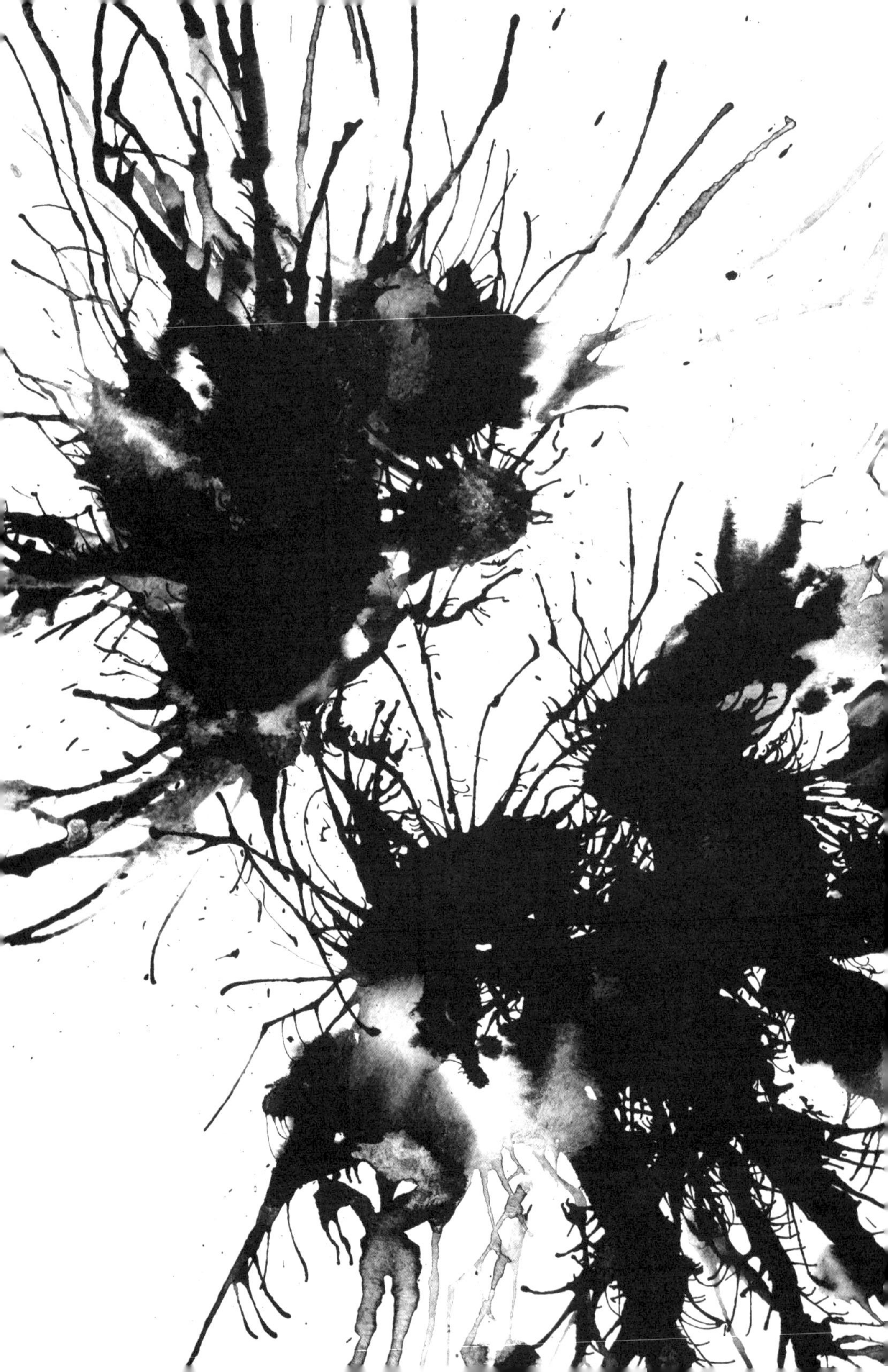